THE
TRAINER

THE TRAINER

BY

LAURA ANTONIOU

LUSTER EDITIONS

AN IMPRINT OF CIRCLET PRESS, INC.
CAMBRIDGE, MA

An earlier edition was published by Masquerade Books in 1995 and a second edition by Mystic Rose Books in 2001.

First Luster Editions print edition September 2011
ISBN 978-1-61390-025-3

Cover Art Credits:
Cover photography and art direction by Lochai Stine
http://lochaistine.com
Stylist: Janice Stine
Models: Through-a-Window, Bella, Green Eyed Devil, Emily (L to R)
With special thanks to Glenda Ryder of The Play House in Baltimore for use of her wonderful playroom.

Published by Luster Editions, an imprint of
Circlet Press, Inc.
39 Hurlbut Street
Cambridge, MA 02138

www.circlet.com

For Kate, Mike, Sky, Billy, Jack and the many who inspired, educated and provoked me over the years.

CONTENTS

INTRODUCTION

In the hierarchy of positions within the Marketplace, there is no role as vital as that of the responsible trainer.

The extraordinary trainer will at once be a pedagogue, a parent, an exacting employer, a model employee, and a drill sergeant. The skills needed to even approach a professional level of ability are rare.

We have found that there are certain types of individuals uniquely suited to the vocation, and may in fact feel a calling to it. Our challenge is in how to take that inspiration, that drive, and hone it to razor sharpness, in effect training the trainer, so that the results of their work will improve the stock of clientele.

By reading this document, you are being admitted to this circle. Do not take your training lightly; your success here will reflect on your professional life for the rest of your career with the Marketplace.

Be honest, and true. Never forget that you are the linchpin upon which the entire Marketplace swings; from bad trainers comes bad merchandise, which creates a chain of corruption and disruption which may influence the Market for years to come. Be ruthless in your drive for the unachievable, patient in your need for recognition, and loyal to the school in which you were taught.

And above all, seek personal control in all things. Your actions, emotions and very thoughts will be marking the merchandise whether you will it or not. You must be more disciplined than your clients, controlling anger, doubt, lust, humor, frustration, and love.

You will love them, probably all of them. That is part of your talent, and should be expected and cultivated.

But there is no figure more tragic than a trainer who falls in love with a client.

CHAPTER ONE

Brooklyn, New York—January

It was nearing the end of another mild winter. The skies were rippled gray silk, streaks of sunlight shining through only in the middle of the day, peeking out and then rushing to set again. No snow, and very little frost, but that particular kind of city climate that settles over the coast for a season and lifts so gradually that the spring seems to arrive almost by surprise.

The row of brownstones was lit with the scattered bands of light from street lamps shining through twisted, barren tree branches, a spooky but oddly pleasant effect. Michael stepped out of the cab and shivered slightly. He had checked his letter of instructions in the car as they drove down the Grand Central Parkway from the airport that bore his name. He had smiled when he received the ticket just a few weeks ago. Now, as he took a deep breath and checked the address again, his smile broadened.

He heard the cab driver hauling bags out of the trunk, but walked up the five steps to the glass-paneled front door and rang the bell. It took a few moments for him to hear responding footsteps inside, and he was half turning to the cabby to tell him to bring the bags closer to the door when the sound of a lock being undone interrupted him. He took a quick glance and snapped his fingers.

"Hey, took you long enough," he said. "I'm LaGuardia, Anderson is expecting me." Michael waved absently over one shoulder to indicate the tasks which awaited on the pavement and pushed past the undersized fellow who had opened the door.

At last! Stepping through a small hallway, he turned to the left and found a perfect urban oasis, a warm, comfortable sitting room with a large bay window and a heavy fireplace, now dark. Muted colors met his gaze, dark woods and shadowed burgundy, indirect light from other rooms flowing across an ancient, ornate carpet. Soft music was playing in the background—Vivaldi, also perfect—and the wide doorway through the sitting room led to a formal dining room. Very classy. Just like he imagined.

Like magic, as soon as he was in the room, another slave appeared; this one a charming little bundle, her russet hair drawn up into a bun, dressed in a formal maid's uniform with a pristine apron tied around her. She was round and plump, with heavy breasts and a rosy cheeked face; definitely not what he was used to, although she did have a beautiful smile. She curtsied at once, a very nice one indeed, understated yet satisfyingly obvious at the same time. He recalled that the twit on door duty didn't make a similar gesture, and reminded himself to make sure that Anderson found out.

"I'm Michael LaGuardia, is Ms. Anderson available?"

"Yes, Mr. LaGuardia, I'll fetch her at once. May I take your coat?" She was poised on the balls of her feet, ready to approach him or take off to fetch her mistress, yet displaying no hint of expectation. Her voice showed strong traces of a British accent. Michael sighed in pleasure; this was going to be fantastic! He started to shrug the raincoat off, and she caught it from his shoulders with a touch so light he thought it had grown wings and lifted of its own accord.

She swept it away, and left the room quietly, and Michael stretched out and looked around. From the door, he could hear the cabby thanking the doorman; at least he knew how to tip. Michael's luggage was poking inside the sitting room entranceway now, and as the doorman stepped back to close the door, Michael raised his voice.

"You can take those things to my room." There was no response, and Michael started to move forward to give the guy a good smack. Establish dominance and authority early, that was the key! But he stopped himself, and held still. Maybe the doorman was under instructions not to speak? It would probably be inappropriate to start off his training by hitting a slave who didn't really deserve it. Just as he decided to ignore him, the doorman stepped into view and casually leaned against the inside of the entranceway. He examined Michael with a look of studious curiosity.

This was not silence. It was sheer insolence.

"I don't know if you understood who I am," Michael said, rubbing his right knuckles. "I'm the new trainer here."

"Are you?" He adjusted the steel-rimmed glasses on his nose and examined Michael again. "Oh, I beg your pardon, sir." And he straightened his posture a little bit, smoothing down the suit jacket and tightening the tie.

Oh, he's itching for a beating, Michael thought, controlling a grin. Man, he's aching to be taken down.

"I'm not that easy to provoke—boy," Michael stated firmly. No sense in letting the squirt get an upper hand, no way.

"That's quite a relief, sir. Since that is the case, you may carry your own damn bags upstairs." One small hand pointed to the staircase, and the man actually started to walk into the room, intending to pass Michael on his right.

There was a second or three when Michael wondered if he had heard right—surely no one would speak to him that way in Anderson's house! But as his hand shot up instinctively, Michael got the second major surprise of his evening. The smaller man moved quickly—even as Michael's arm swung to deliver a classic disciplinary slap, he intercepted it. Michael felt his wrist hitting what seemed to be a steel post, followed by the disorienting sensation of being pushed back a step.

His mouth dropped open in astonishment even as he lost his balance and fell backward, awkwardly, into a large wingbacked chair.

"So, this is our new pupil," came a woman's voice from the direction of the dining room.

Michael turned his head and saw the mistress of the house and staggered to his feet. Blood rushed to and then from his face. He opened his mouth once to catch a breath and tried to gather himself. "Anderson—I'm—"

"Michael LaGuardia, I know. What I don't know is why you would possibly have the temerity to strike someone in my house without my permission."

She was tall, as oddly tall as her doorman was short. She was no longer a young woman, silver streaks running through her almost waist-length black hair, all bound behind her at the nape of her long neck. Standing in the doorway, she seemed all angles and lines, a hard, horsy woman who would have looked natural in the dusty plains of Kansas or in the hills of Arizona. Her voice was low and hoarse, her rhythm of words strong and direct, with the slightest of twangs.

She was everything he had imagined she was—except maybe a little bit older. Well, a lot older. She looked at least fifty-five. He swallowed and gave her a terse acknowledging nod with what he judged to be the proper deference.

"I beg your pardon, Ms. Anderson. I thought your boy here was challenging me."

"Really?" She turned slightly to look at the doorman, who was busy straightening the sleeve of his jacket. Michael didn't catch any meaning in the looks they traded, and started to feel very, very wary.

"Well." It was a statement, a verbal comma that came out as though she were summing up possible options of discourse. "This is not a very auspicious way to make an entrance, Mr. LaGuardia. Maybe I'd better make an introduction. Michael LaGuardia, trainer in training, please meet Mr. Chris Parker, my friend and house guest. And, in case you didn't know, a trainer who's been around the block a little longer than you. He definitely has seniority over you."

Michael looked at the man facing him, really looked this time, and felt a sudden need to sit down again. What an absolutely stunning way to make an entrance indeed.

"Ah, Mr. Parker," he searched for some kind of proper words to try to salvage this situation as best as he could. "I—I've made a terrible mistake. I'm so sorry if you took offense at what I did."

One glance at the hard look in Parker's eyes and the faint sound of a "tsk" coming from Anderson completed Michael's sensations of social vertigo. What did I do wrong now? he thought miserably.

"Maybe I'd better go out and come in again," he offered weakly.

"Only slaves get to do over mistakes in my house," Anderson said firmly. "You'll just have to work harder, that's all. And just so you know, no one raises a hand—or any other part of the body—to any one else in this house without permission from me. Is that understood?"

"Yes."

"Then take your bags upstairs. Joan will show you the way. Parker and I are about to go over your records. After you freshen up, you may join us in my office." With that, she turned and walked back through the doorway, and Parker followed her. The maid stood by his bags, waiting to show him upstairs. The slightest of drafts curled around his shoulders and he shivered way out of proportion to it. This was bad, very bad. He hadn't counted on there being two trainers in residence. He hadn't counted on there being other free people around, period. And he had never made such a spectacularly bad entrance in his entire life.

I'll just have to get better, he swore, gathering himself. He turned to Joan and picked up his bags to follow her.

&ve;

"Michael Xavier LaGuardia, born and raised in Los Angeles, California. BA in Communications from Berkeley, just twenty-six years old. Likely looking fellow, isn't he?"

"He's an arrogant, unobservant infant, straight out of kindergarten. How the hell did you get stuck with him?" Chris Parker was still brushing imaginary dust off of his jacket sleeve. He scowled and glanced at the folder on the table between them and pointed at another offending entry. "He's only been training for two years! You barely spoke to me when I was a two-year man!"

Anderson nodded. Her eyes danced slightly, and she kept her smile in the crinkles around them, not in her tightly drawn lips.

"You were different, bucko. I wanted to see where you'd go without me first. But now—have you seen the new crop of trainers in the past few years?"

"No, not especially. I tend to keep an eye on the older houses, and the formal apprentice relationships only. Why? Are all the new American trainers rude, ignorant twenty-somethings?"

The Trainer of Trainers sat down, her raven-black skirt fluttering down around her legs to settle around her like a silken lap robe. "No, not all of 'em. But in the past five years, I've only seen two American novices with the touch. The sight. And of that pair, only one will make a career out of it, if he actually gets out of the training whole."

"Are you saying I'm part of a dying breed?" He did smile, a crooked twist of one corner of his mouth. He sat down as well, and dropped one hand down to the side of his chair, where a blonde woman was kneeling, carefully assembling papers into assorted folders, hearing yet not listening to their conversation. When his hand brushed her shoulder, she turned slightly to kiss the flesh behind his thumb, but continued to work.

"Ah, the joys of a cliché. No, I didn't say that, although you might be. But whether you are or not, I do owe the Marketplace their new trainers—and this Mikey was the best looking out of the list they offered me."

"They were right about that. He's pretty as he can be. Those eyes! A potential distraction." He ran his fingers through the hair of the slave beside him, felt the slight tremor when he touched the back of her neck, and then stopped trying to distract her as he focused his attention back on the trainer.

"Is he?" Anderson looked up, and her flinty eyes caught Chris's across the table. "I hadn't noticed."

"Oh, of course not."

They stared at each other, calm and serious for all of a moment and then laughed, the sounds similar in tone and pitch.

"I can leave if you like," Chris offered, after the moment passed. He looked out the window as if the waving tree branches were suddenly captivating. "I do have other places to go."

"You'll stay until you finish," Anderson said.

"As you wish."

On the floor, Tara hid a slight smile of her own.

❧

Michael looked at himself in the mirror, and, as usual, liked what he saw. He ran his fingers through his hair, flipping it back so that the seemingly stray locks fell in an artful arc over his forehead. His face was cleanshaven and evenly tan, although not quite as dark as he would have preferred. He took all that skin cancer stuff seriously; no sense in spoiling this face.

His Italian father boasted that the good looks came from his side of the family, and Michael knew that it was at least half true. He had some mighty good-looking uncles and cousins in the LaGuardia clan. But it was his Irish mother's ancestry that gave him the naturally fair skin, and those magically blue eyes, so haunting under a mop of black hair. They were the ice blue of sapphires, ringed with black, always the first thing people noticed about him. Once, he had tried to darken them with contacts, thinking he'd look more natural, but found that it only made him look more ordinary.

Ordinary was hardly what he wanted to be.

Unlike a lot of his friends, he did not work out—and he didn't have a beautifully hard, cut body. But he was trim and in good health nonetheless, one of those lucky men with a good body and good hair—for now. Time enough to lift and push and investigate Rogaine when he was older.

His suitcase was on a rack near the bed, his garment bag hung on the closet door. Joan had shown him the room, given him directions to the bathroom, and left him alone. He had expected that his bags would have been unpacked, at least.

What a weird system, he thought, pulling his collar straight. Why have slaves in the house and not use them? Using people is the natural talent of a master, his Uncle Niall said.

If it hadn't been for Uncle Niall, I wouldn't be here.

There were no slaves and masters in the LaGuardia household, unless you counted a dysfunctional aspect or two in one or another family grouping. Nothing but a second and third generation, mixed heritage but all-American, hard-working family, based on the West Coast. Michael had gone to college because it was what everyone he knew did, and had a relatively normal sex life for an American boy, full of experimentation and discovery and the freedom that good looks, a car, and an easygoing personality will give you.

The family was politically divided on several issues, but generally liberal in many things. The question of whether Uncle Niall was gay wasn't really discussed as much as it was an unstated fact which had to be accepted. Invitations to him always included "and guest," and occasionally he did show up with a usually younger and very good looking man as his companion. Once, Michael heard his mother saying to her sister in law, "At least Niall doesn't flaunt it, dressing in women's clothing and dancing naked in the streets. You'd never know he was...that way."

Michael didn't think about it much—he had his past experiences with boys and preferred girls, and if Uncle Niall didn't, it was hardly any of Michael's business, was it? He just treated Niall like everyone else.

So when Uncle Niall invited Michael up the coast to his place for a weekend, Michael accepted more out of obligation than interest in spending a weekend with a relative. He packed his swim trunks and sunscreen, expecting to spend most of the time on the beach.

It was a nice place; small but classy, with huge bay windows that had a view of the ocean, and a long winding path that led to the dunes out back. Uncle Niall was a screenwriter; he did a lot of work for sitcoms and some commercials and a few straight-to-video movies, all of which he thought were outrageously funny. All in all, he was a great guy to hang out with, funny and full of industry gossip. When Michael got there, he was swiftly introduced to Ethan, his uncle's "companion," and Jerry, the older man who Niall said "runs the house." But as soon as hands were shaken, Michael was in his swim gear and heading down to the beach.

It was a great afternoon—he splashed alone for a while and then stretched out in the sun, loving the illusion that this entire area was his alone. He wondered if Uncle Niall and Ethan ever came down here and swam naked together. Michael had doffed his Speedo a couple of times at clothing optional beaches. He liked the feeling of the water against his genitals, the way his balls felt, tight because of the cold yet sensuously teased by the motion of the waves and the current. He also liked the looks he got when he walked along the beach, his cock swinging. He might not be some tremendous god of a bodybuilder, but hell, they were practically common in Los Angeles.

Just thinking about it made him pull the trunks off, that first caress of wind and sun enough to stir him tumescent. Yeah, that was better! He ran down to the surf and plunged in again, and laughed with the sheer exuberance of it. This was the life—out where no one could bother you, practically your own private beach—one day, he'd have this. How, he didn't know, not yet. But one day, somehow, he would.

He saw Ethan coming down the path just when he was ready to get back into the sun and dry off.

His first instinct was to blush, because man, to be caught skinny dipping by your uncle's boyfriend? How embarrassing. But there wasn't anything to do—the man was going to see Michael's abandoned trunks next to his sunscreen. Michael sighed and composed himself and began to make his way to shore. When he stepped free of the water, he shook his hair out and tried to act casual.

Ethan, whose apple-cheeked midwestern origins were betrayed by the slower, almost drawling way he had of speaking, was hardly casual. He gave Michael a long and measuring glance, and Michael found himself doing the same. Because Ethan was not in the jeans and sweater he'd been wearing at the door, but in a thong bikini, his cock a hard mass twisted to one side, clearly visible through the skimpy fabric. He had no hair on his chest or legs, like a competition swimmer, and his nipples were larger than any nipples Michael had ever seen on a man. And they were pierced, too— with heavy, silver-colored rings. Between his pierced nipples hung one of those little plastic cases that floated, someplace to put your change or Chapstick or car keys.

"Hi," Michael said lamely.

"Hi, Mike. Your uncle thought you might like some company." He flashed a friendly smile.

"Oh, yeah, sure."

"I see you've already gotten comfortable," Ethan continued, motioning to Michael's crotch. "Maybe I can help you out there."

"Huh?" The sunlight was definitely getting to him.

"You look like you could use a little release, Mike. Would you like a blowjob?" This was said in as casual a way as if Ethan was inviting him back up to the house for lunch. Michael stood silently for a moment, and tried to ignore the urgings of his cock, which definitely did want a blowjob. He struggled not to bring his hands together in front of the anxious organ, and covered his embarrassment verbally instead.

"Jesus, man, you're my uncle's boyfriend!"

"Sort of," Ethan admitted.

"Well, what is that, coming onto me? We're practically related! What if Uncle Niall found out?" Michael bit his lip; he hadn't wanted to ask that last question.

"Mike—he sent me here. It's no big deal. If you don't want to, that's all right, I won't be insulted. But it looks like you could use one—and I am good."

Michael looked up the hill toward the house. It was too far to see, covered by dunes and shrubs. He glanced down at his obviously eager cock, and then across to the man he thought was his uncle's lover. "Well—okay, sure."

"Great!" With that, Ethan led him up the beach, to an area where the sand was soft and warm, and settled him down comfortably. Michael leaned back, still amazed at the offer, but willing to believe that it was real.

And it was real—every minute of it. Ethan was right, too, he was really good. Excellent, in fact. Better than anyone, girl or guy, that Michael had ever had, even that hooker he picked up on Santa Monica Boulevard one night. He just slurped Michael's entire cock into his mouth and then settled down to work on it for a good long time.

This is heaven, Michael thought, throwing his head back. I'm never leaving.

He tried to hold on to his erection as long as possible, and Ethan helped by varying his speed and strength, and the motions of his head. But soon, the sun and the sand, the overall tightening of the skin on his body, and the wondrous, pulsating pressure on his cock made Michael's head begin to spin. Without even knowing it, he grabbed onto Ethan's hair and pulled him tighter into his own crotch, crying out when Ethan pulled back.

"Jesus! I'm ready to fucking explode!"

"I got you, Mike, I got you!" And suddenly, there was a cool touch on the head of Mike's cock, and then the reappearance of Ethan's sucking, swallowing mouth, only tighter this time, hotter, and Michael finally let it come, shooting so hard he couldn't even keep his head up. He arched his back and felt Ethan's lips smashing against his groin as he came, and groaned out loud.

"Oh man, oh man!" he said, when his cock stopped spurting and started that throbbing slide into softness. He felt Ethan's mouth gently surrounding his glans, licking, letting the cock fall slowly back against his thigh. Then he felt a condom being stripped off of him, and looked down.

"Shit, where did that come from?"

"My secret," grinned the other man. "I hope you didn't mind."

"Mind? I didn't even know it was there! Shit, that was fantastic!"

"I'm glad you enjoyed it," Ethan said. He wiped his mouth and scooped up a plastic wrapper from the sand, and then stood. "Dinner is at five, okay? You can stay here or come back and soak in the Jacuzzi, or whatever you want until then."

"Thanks—thanks, man."

"It was my pleasure to serve." And with that odd statement, Ethan walked away, heading back up to the house. Michael didn't know what to say to such a comment, so he didn't say anything. Besides, it was better to just lie back and relax in the afterglow of

22 LAURA ANTONIOU

that fabulous blowjob. Man, gay guys are really good, he noted. I'd
be gay, if I didn't like tits so much.

He let himself fall into a reverie of erotic images, and then,
when he was feeling more awake, went off to find his trunks and
went back to the house.

More surprises were in store for him that night.

"Did Ethan show you a good time on the beach?" was Uncle
Niall's first question when Michael came downstairs for dinner.
Michael had changed into pull-on pants and a T-shirt, and felt better than he'd felt in weeks, relaxed and rested. The question
stopped him in his tracks.

"It's okay, I know all about it," his uncle continued. "I sent
him."

"Um. Yeah, that's what he said." Michael looked around. Ethan
was nowhere in sight. "What can I say, Uncle Niall? He was great."

"Good. I thought you looked a little tense when you got here.
Let's sit down and eat, I have some things to tell you." The older
man waved at the table by the open doors that led to the deck. It
was set for two.

"Isn't Ethan eating with us?" Michael took a seat.

"No, he eats with Jerry, in the kitchen. That's part of what I'm
going to tell you about."

"Okay," Michael said. He glanced toward the kitchen, feeling
suddenly aware that it wasn't that far to the little room from where
he and his uncle were seated.

Uncle Niall dug into the grilled vegetables and sea scallops,
serving Michael and then pouring wine for both of them. "Here's
to the Marketplace," he said, raising his glass, "and to your introduction to it, nephew."

"The Marketplace?" Michael echoed, tapping his glass lightly
against Niall's. "You mean the stock market?"

"No, boyo, a slave market. Ethan isn't my lover, and Jerry isn't
my assistant or housekeeper. They're both my slaves; I bought them.
Eat, and I'll explain everything."

Michael didn't remember eating that night or drinking, or even
getting back to his room later on, after he and his uncle continued

their rather one-sided conversation out on the deck. He remembered asking lots of questions, and his uncle's long, complicated responses. But it was almost too much to believe all at once. A world—wide network of voluntary slaves? Secret auctions of human property? Actual money changing hands, and contracts signed, with training locations and special schools and entire houses filled with people who could be traded or gambled away on a whim?

And his Uncle Niall—his own mother's little brother—was a part of it?

He didn't remember saying that he had to think about all of it, but his uncle did usher him upstairs to the spare bedroom with gentle encouragement to do just that. Michael thought he was going to remain awake all night, but in due time he fell asleep, and when he awoke the next morning, Ethan was kneeling next to his bed, naked except for that little tube around his neck, swinging gently between the silver rings.

"Would you care for some more attention, sir?" he asked, his eyes bright. And as Michael turned back the sheets to reveal his morning erection, Ethan wordlessly moved his mouth over it and proved that yesterday's afternoon delight was no unique circumstance.

I could really get used to this, Michael reflected.

And I have gotten used to it, he thought, pushing the hair out of his eyes again. Used to people being deferential, slaves being eager to please, my luggage being carried and unpacked. It actually feels weird having to carry my own stuff. It should be no big deal—but it is. Maybe she does that with all her trainees. Surprises them; puts them off balance. Everyone knew that doing that was an essential part of training—you broke down expectations first, and then built new ones. Everyone knew that, because it was one of the methods she approved of.

There's nothing like an Anderson-trained slave. There were maybe ten trainers in her class in the whole world, and they could train only so many slaves at a time. But the trainers they taught were especially valued. Months—or even a year—with Anderson could guarantee him a prominent placement in a large household, or in a training facility. He knew that some trainers spent even more time with her—years even! But that wasn't necessary for his purposes. Just enough time to say that he had studied with her would be fine, and anyone would welcome him as a partner. Or, he could just go freelance and open a house of his own, or travel from job to job for a while. If he was properly trained. If Anderson approved of him when he left.

Anderson, the mystery trainer who saw no one except by appointment, who attended no auctions or parties or sporting events, visited none of the ranches or resorts where people of the Marketplace gathered. Her rare appearances at the trainer-only gatherings were spoken of like saintly visitations. Yet, her writings on the training of slaves and the responsibilities of owners were part of the canon of the field; her contracts and her method of structuring and ranking slaves were almost universally applied.

She had studied methods of teaching, indoctrination, and even brainwashing, and was rumored to have been an observer in military, medical, language, and penal instruction. Her writings certainly contained comparisons of every technique from toilet training in North America to captivity trauma training designed for the Mossad. And all of these methods were somehow entwined in her seemingly endless instructions about how to find, create, and maintain perfect servitors.

In a way, she was the ultimate master—for she taught not only slaves and trainers, but she taught the masters how to manage their slaves and trainers. Her structure of certifying owners for the North American markets was considered an international model for safety and security, and many of her former students spent their time flying all over the world to make sure that new owners would be ready for the valuable property they were about to take responsibility for. Hell, that wouldn't be such a bad way to make a living either!

Michael dropped his eyes from his reflection and gathered his dignity and confidence. It was time to make up for his embarrassing entrance into the world of the Trainer of Trainers. How on earth

had he misread the man at the front door as a slave? When
Anderson had introduced them formally, he looked into Chris
Parker's eyes and what he saw there made him almost gasp out
loud. Amusement, disdain and contempt, sure—but also a clear
and challenging look that read "I can take you down right now,
kid, just try me." It was hostility threaded through with such confidence that Michael had, for one split second, been actually afraid
of the man!

Impossible. And stupid. Michael put it down to jet lag and
nervousness. Of course he was a little off balance the first time he
entered the house of America's most famous trainer. It was only
natural to make a little mistake somewhere. There was no reason
for Parker to hold this against him, and certainly no reason to be
afraid of the little man. He was only a guest, after all. Perhaps he
would be gone soon.

If only he wasn't here at all! Michael allowed himself a moment of bitterness, and then buried it. He had work to do.
Anderson's guests were none of his concern. He had to focus on
her and his goals and make sure he handled this whole thing right
this time. There was no other alternative for him.

CHAPTER TWO

When Michael came back downstairs, he found that the house was larger than he had thought—it extended on both sides of the staircase, with two front rooms. He admired an art deco framed mirror in the hallway before he stepped into the room identified as the office. There was a wall of books, and another wall of shelves full of different colored binders with neat labels on the spines. There was a desk and a conference table, three file cabinets, and a computer set-up.

All work and no play, he thought ludicrously. But he gathered himself and approached the table where Anderson and Parker were sitting.

"Have a seat, Michael," she said, raising her eyes to him. "I want to get to know you a little before we begin."

"I thought my whole life was in my file." He took a seat and folded his hands on the tabletop. In an instant, he changed his mind and put them in his lap.

"Probably. But I can't be bothered to read all that. I was briefed on the important parts." She flipped it open and fingered a few pages.

Okay, it was lengthy. Geoff was a detail guy. Michael wondered who did the briefing. Probably Parker. Damn. The older man was just sitting there in his jacket and tie, his eyes neutral, quiet and patient, like a secretary. Well, at least he wasn't glaring at him any more.

"You're recommended by Mr. Geoff Negel, from Santa Cruz," Anderson remarked. "You've trained with him for two years. I'm familiar with his techniques, but I don't approve. Did you know that?"

"Yes." Oh boy, did he know! When she didn't say anything else, he took it as a request for more information. "Geoff—he was a good trainer. Is a good trainer. And I respect him, very much. But I can't say I approved of his methods and results either."

"Yet you still believe he's a good trainer?" Parker spoke up, leaning back in his chair. "It would seem that not liking his methods or results might indicate that his training left much to be desired."

"Well, it was okay for what it was," Michael said easily. Again, he was met by silence.

"Do go on," Anderson finally said.

"Geoff is kind of New Age, you know? He believes in a kinder, gentler Marketplace." Michael made a snorting sound of amusement, then ground his teeth as this was also met with silence. These two are about as fun as pallbearers, he thought. "Okay, here's the thing. Geoff has this idea that slaves and owners should be a 'working team of equal social importance.' So, he brought this into his training plan, which I think plays up to a slave's ego too much. I mean, I actually heard him tell them that their owners wouldn't exist without them! And that was just a little too much. It's one thing to talk about balance, the whole yin/yang thing. But he just went too far."

"I see." Anderson nodded. "And your personal philosophy?"

"The way I see it, slaves provide service to people who want it. They provide it in a specific way that's not really encouraged or even legally permitted in most of the world. They do it to get their needs met, but they sign on for the real thing, not just playing around on weekends." Michael leaned back himself, confident. "Our owners have a right to people who know what they want and are willing to pay a certain price to get it. They're entitled to well behaved property that fulfills their fantasies and makes their lives easier and more pleasurable. And a good trainer will produce just that—obedient, submissive slaves who are happy to be considered inferior to their masters. Not this 'co-partners in a social experiment' thing that Geoff is doing. I think that raises expectations too much."

Which was more or less what Anderson had said herself in a special brief she had appended to her notes and articles from the previous year. He untwined his fingers and watched her for reaction. Geoff always glowed when his students repeated his own words back to him.

She just nodded again. "We're not doing any social experiment here," she said. "I train slaves. I train trainers. I provide a service, and that's the extent of my role. You're not my usual type of student—you're new to the Marketplace, and you've been unconventionally schooled. So, I expect something extraordinary from you—I want to see a profound level of dedication to the craft and to the process of learning it. I want complete honesty in all things, and I want to hear about any problems or questions you have with my ideas or my methods. I probably won't give you answers, but you'll ask anyway. I also want you to keep a journal. I don't care what you put into it, as long as every day you have something to report about learning. I may not ask to look at it. But if I do ask, you're gonna turn it over to me immediately. Got that?"

"Yep."

Was that a tiny little sigh coming from Chris Parker? Michael shifted slightly to look at him, but the man had his eyes lowered to the tabletop, where he was examining one of the pages that Anderson had set aside. Michael felt the urge to reach over and grab it away, wondering how the hell this man got the right to read his file.

"Mr. Parker is my guest," Anderson said with a slight smile, "but he's also doing some work with the clients here. I strongly suggest that you listen to what he says about them—including the one you're training on. It should go without saying that you could learn from him as well—once you make up for your ill manners at the door." Parker smirked at that, and Michael controlled a sudden charge of both embarrassment and anger. Jeeze, weren't they going to let that go?

"We may have anywhere from two to four clients here at any time. You will be given the responsibility for one, under my supervision. I'll also have special training sessions with some of the others which you might be helping with. Eventually, you'll design your own training schedule, keeping in mind when I will want to see you, and making sure that your client is never idle or without guidance. But at first, I will tell you exactly what to do and when and with whom."

"Understood."

"Then we can begin the formal instruction tomorrow." She stood up, and the silver bracelets she wore on one wrist jangled slightly. "I suggest you take some reading material up to your room, and try to get a good night's sleep tonight. In the morning, I'll introduce you to your client, and to the rest of the house."

Michael nodded. "Okay, thanks." Then, suddenly, he felt that now familiar sensation of unease as she hit him with a stern, measuring gaze that was filled with expectation. He glanced over to Parker and saw that the man was standing. Michael stood up, slowly, and looked back at Anderson. Was this what he was supposed to do? She sighed and left the room, shaking her head.

As soon as the door closed behind her, Parker started to laugh.

"What's so funny?"

"Where did you learn your manners? Or, should I ask—how was it that you've failed to learn any manners?" Chris Parker walked over to the desk and picked up two brown leather binders and tossed them onto the table in front of Michael.

"What are you talking about?" Michael grabbed at them and glanced at the spines. They were two of Anderson's yearly briefs, from ten years ago.

"You're in the presence of the Trainer." And he said it like that, too. Michael could hear the capital letter, and for an instant, he shivered. He had never been sure how exactly one could make a word sound so different without being theatrical about it. But Parker was continuing, his hand gesturing as he spoke. "Anderson stands up, and you loll back in your chair like some kind of satrap, expecting her to make some gesture to you on the way out."

"I'm not a slave," Michael protested. "Where I come from, it's the slaves that jump up and down, not trainers. How the hell was I supposed to know what to do around here? It's not like she sent me a manual or anything. What kind of manners is that, anyway? From the '50s or something?"

"Where you came from doesn't matter anymore, Mr.

LaGuardia." The much shorter man leaned against the edge of the
desk and folded his arms. "And neither does where the protocol
comes from. You're here now. Is that what you're going to tell her
when she instructs you in anything else? That it's not the way you
used to do things? That you never heard of that way before?"

"I just said I didn't get any instructions," Michael repeated with
a scowl. "What's it to you anyway?"

Well, that did something. Parker's expression dropped from sarcastic and angry to almost gentle and amused in less than a second.

"Not a thing," he said lightly, as if he had been chastised. "Not
a single thing, Mr. LaGuardia." He dipped his head in an almost respectful nod and headed toward the door.

Michael watched him leave, a million questions mingling with
angry retorts in his mind. Don't make things worse, his caution-
ary side warned him. So, he waited until the door closed again and
then cursed out loud and headed for the open dictionary that was
on the stand across from the table. He looked up the word 'satrap,'
cursed again, and took his two binders to bed with him. It seemed
like they were going to be his only company that night.

He was correct in that, at least.

❧

"Good morning, sir, what would you like for breakfast?"

Well, finally, a smiling face at the house. Michael flipped back
that unruly strand of hair that endeared him to so many girls and
looked up into the eyes of a man who was actually taller than he
was—quite a feat, actually.

He must be 6'4" at least, he thought. He was also quite dark-
skinned, with tightly curly, ink-black hair. The white chef's jacket
he wore was a poetic contrast to his skin and his eyes, very classi-
cal.

"Um. What's fresh?" Michael asked, looking around the dining
room. There was little evidence that others had been here, except
for a stack of New York Times sections on one corner.

"I got some nice bagels, and there are two eggs left." The big man held up two fingers and grinned. "I also saved a glass of orange juice for you, since you come from the orange country." He had an accent Michael couldn't exactly place.

"Yeah, that's good. OJ, coffee, a bagel, that's just great."

"Okay, I get right on it." And he swept into the kitchen, where Michael caught the sight of someone else working.

Man, I don't know anyone, but it seems everyone knows me. He reached for the paper, and dropped it as he heard boot heels on the hallway floor.

Parker stepped in, a cup of coffee in one hand. He was neatly dressed, just like last night, in a suit and tie. He needed a shave, though.

"Good morning, Mr. LaGuardia."

"Morning."

"Have you met Vicente?"

"The cook?"

"Yes, among other things. Perhaps I should warn you that he is also not a slave." Parker said this evenly, without any hint of teasing, and Michael sighed.

"Thank you," he said. "I—wouldn't have realized that."

"I know." Again, there was no trace of smugness in Parker's manner, and Michael felt even more embarrassed about his behavior the night before.

"Listen," he said awkwardly. "I made a big mistake last night. I'm sorry. Can we start from a new beginning?"

"No, we can't. But that's a slightly better apology than the one you offered last night." Parker sat down and placed his cup on the table. Instantly, the door from the kitchen opened, and the unfamiliar woman came sailing out with a coffeepot, refilled Parker's cup, and then went back without a word. Michael admired her. She was not like Joan at all—taller, blonde, and with a slightly bookish air. She was also older, possibly in her forties. Michael had never met a slave in training who was so old. But she had class, and was even a little unconsciously sexy in the controlled way she moved.

"That's a nice piece of work," Michael said.

"Yes."

Michael tried again. "I mean, that was pretty good, the way she knew you needed coffee. How do you teach them to know when to come in?"

"Anderson instructs them in the art of seeing through walls."

"Seeing—through walls?"

"Yes." Parker added milk to the coffee and didn't say more.

Well, aren't we chatty this morning, Michael thought sourly. It was obvious that the seeing-through-walls thing wasn't going to go anywhere. He tried to think of something else to say, and was gratified when the blonde woman came back with his breakfast. The silence continued for a minute or two, broken only by the sounds of work being done in the kitchen.

"I thought you worked on Long Island," Michael finally said. "With Elliot and Selador."

"I did. I am... taking a break."

Well, that was interesting. That little hesitation brought Michael's curiosity up. "Huh. Some break! Going from an entry level house to this one?"

"I'm not exactly working here, Mr. LaGuardia. I am only a guest."

"Listen—Mr. LaGuardia is my dad. How about you call me Mike, like everyone else does?"

Parker sighed. "Very well. My name is Chris."

Michael sat back and laughed. "Jeeze, you're so formal around here! Standing when she leaves the room, using last names and titles—when do you relax?"

"I am relaxing." This was delivered with such deadpan ease that Michael didn't know how to react at first. Luckily, laughter rang from the hallway. This time, both men rose when she walked into the room.

"You certainly are, my dear," Anderson said as she passed him and pointed at Michael. "Time to work, Mike—it is Mike, isn't it? Let's introduce you to the bodies we have under this roof."

Michael crammed a piece of bagel in his mouth and gulped the rest of his juice and followed her.

It was not a large number of people to meet. The blonde woman at breakfast was Tara.

"Tara has been with me for four months," Anderson said. "She is currently serving a four-year contract, and is in her first year. Her owner sent her to brush up on anticipation skills, and she has improved dramatically."

"Thank you, Trainer." She was noticeably pleased, but didn't look like she was insufferably prideful. Michael took a quick inventory of her—definitely mid-forties, possibly very toned under the modern housemaid's uniform she was wearing. She had a silver chain around her throat that dipped below the neckline of the dress—probably her collar. Her sea-green eyes were unusually deep and dark, captivating in her somewhat sharp face.

"Tara will be helping Joan settle in," Anderson continued, "and then will be leaving us in a bit. Joan will be your project. We'll work on her together for two months, and then I'll leave part of Joan's training in your hands—if you're up to it."

"Oh, I will be!"

"Let's hope you are."

Joan was of course the pretty, plump girl from the previous night. He reappraised her as Geoff taught him, scanning her physically while looking for signs of emotional display. Next to the fair and experienced Tara, she seemed plain and chubby—dark-eyed and autumn- haired with that pale-skinned touch of color in her cheeks. Her stance was more stiff than Tara's, a sure sign of recent training, or perhaps tension. It was strange to examine fully dressed slaves; even Geoff hadn't allowed his clients to be dressed in normal clothing, preferring fetish wear of all kinds. And he would have never allowed a slave to carry so much weight. He wondered if Anderson had her on a strict diet.

"This is Michael LaGuardia, our new training student," Anderson said.

"How do you do, sir?" asked Joan. She smiled when she spoke, and her inflection indicated nothing but sincerity. Her maid's dress was an unrelieved black, and the apron she had been wearing the previous night was gone. He struggled with the sense that he should shake her hand—how absurd! He nodded briskly instead.

"Michael, this is Joan, our newest client. Joan is fresh from a year in Japan. This is her finishing up tour, before she enters into a ten-year contract with her owner."

"Wow!" Michael couldn't help it; the exclamation came out by itself. "Ten years?"

Anderson's face revealed neither surprise or dismay at his outburst. "Yes. As she will explain, she's following a tradition."

"I can't wait to hear this story." Michael smiled at her, and Joan smiled back, a slight, sweet little curve of her mouth that illuminated her entire face. He decided that although Tara was absolutely prettier, Joan looked like more fun. He instantly wondered what her ass was like, and whether she laughed in bed. Ten years! What a long service term! It was a little hard to snap back to the present and keep listening to Anderson.

"You'll be in charge of quite a bit regarding Joan. Eventually, I'll want you to keep detailed records, file daily reports to me about progress, and oversee use and discipline. However—" Anderson pinned him with one of those looks again. "However—for at least the first month, everything you want to do that is not on my schedule or at my direction must be cleared with me first. Is that understood?"

"Sure is." Michael nodded.

"Good. I will let you know when you have gotten to a point where you may take over her scheduling. Here is her file." She passed it over—it looked substantial. "You will interview her as a trainer this afternoon. Tape-record every interview session and keep the tapes labeled and available."

He kept nodding, itching to look in the file and get to work.

"If Vicente has extra duties, he'll come to me first. But if for any reason he comes to you, treat his chores as priorities. Everything else you'll learn as you go—and I do expect you to learn."

"That's what I'm here for!"

"Good. Tara, with me, Joan to your duties, and Mike off to study. I'll be busy the rest of the morning. Joan will be free for her first interview at two." With that, she swept out of the room, heels clicking and bangles shaking, her hair rising and falling behind her like a black and silver veil. Tara followed her gracefully and Joan dipped a curtsy to Michael before hurrying off upstairs.

Time to get to work.

CHAPTER THREE

By the time Michael finished going through Joan's paperwork, his first real inklings of inadequacy had started to take hold. There was little in there which seemed to agree with everything he had "known" about the Marketplace. And very little that had anything to do with everything he had spent so much time learning at Geoff's place.

She was not on some special weight-loss program; apparently no one gave two thoughts about her physical condition. Oh, she was healthy; her medical reports showed normal blood pressure and no weakness in her joints or muscles. But she was just—well—fat. Her required nude photographs were artfully done, but couldn't hide the excess flesh of her belly and thighs, and her big breasts were drawn down. But she was smiling nonetheless, just a little bashful, but not as glum or somber as he would have expected her to be in front of a camera and lights.

Also, she had not been recruited, or found, but had entered the system after years of knowing exactly what she was going to do, and how to go about doing it. Not only was his client far more experienced than he, but she had a history that his fellow students at Geoff's place probably wouldn't have even believed, let alone been able to deal with.

Joan was a family retainer. Included with her own documents was a list of other family members currently and formerly in service. The dates went back to the turn of the century, with a note at the bottom which read "Previous files upon permission of the family only."

"How far back do the records go?" Michael asked, after turning the tape recorder on.

Joan was kneeling on the floor opposite him, her hands behind her back. He had decided on that position before she came in, wondering if it would enhance her bosom. It did, nicely. He almost had her strip as well, but decided to save that for later. It wouldn't make her more interesting for him at this point, and it would be best used as a way to surprise her, since she seemed to go around clothed in this house. No sense in throwing everything into the first interview!

"The Marketplace records go back to 1856, sir," she answered promptly, her accent delightful. "But my family has been in service for nine generations."

"Nine?" Michael shook his head, amazed. "I didn't know that the Marketplace had people like that in it. And I thought all that feudal stuff went out with the end of the Dark Ages anyway. I mean, no one really has serfs in England anymore, do they?"

"Begging your pardon, sir, but we were not serfs. In fact, several of my ancestors were knights, and one was a baronet. Shall I explain?"

"You bet."

She composed herself and began. "In Great Britain, most of the familial ties have broken down because of the changes in the economy and the fall of many of the great old houses. But in the past, it was considered an honor to be associated with a great lord—one had to be in service to someone, after all. Some of these ties continued despite wars and similar upheavals. Such is the case with my family. We have served the Tillsdales and their various offshoots as military men, aides, butlers, footmen and nannies and housekeepers—and my uncles on my mother's side took over the keeping of the apple orchards when I was a child. My father was his Lordship's chauffeur for twenty years, and my mother served in the city house for ten years in her day; that was how they met."

"They were both slaves?"

"Oh, no sir. My father was, but my mother was a standard employee. However, she learned of my father's position, and decided to enter that level of service herself."

"Are they still slaves?"

"No, sir. They have retired to a cottage in the village. I have two uncles, one aunt, two cousins, and one sister who are currently in service. When I enter, my aunt will be finished with her contract and is expected to also retire."

"Uh-huh." Michael hardly knew what to say. Great—a slave who grew up surrounded by other slaves, exemplary slaves, if the records didn't lie. And she already had a place to go—what the hell was she doing here? "Anderson said you've been in Japan. I see you were in training there, too. What were you learning?"

"Japanese, sir. I also learned the rudiments of their way of making and serving tea, and acquired some basic kitchen skills, plus some instruction in how to dress a lady in a kimono and similar tasks. Mostly, I was there to learn about the culture."

"And did you? Learn Japanese, in one year?"

"Not enough to carry on a conversation, sir. But I do know enough to understand basic requests for service, and how to be polite when I don't understand. I am continuing my studies, and am expected to be fluent in two years."

"Good, good." Getting better, he thought sarcastically. I took Spanish for three years in high school and still can't remember how to ask where the bathroom is.

"And you're here for—?"

"Polishing work, sir." She smiled, raising a pair of cute dimples. "I'm to learn about American culture, and finish up my training in basic service requirements so that I may take up my position in the great house upon returning to England."

"Position—yes." Michael glanced down at the papers. "You're going to be—"

"Second upstairs maid, sir."

"Right." There were books on staffing and household management in Geoff's library, and Michael had glanced at a few. God, what it used to take to staff one of those old English castles, or manors, or whatever. You had butlers and housekeepers with an army of maids, footmen, and assorted gardeners, groundskeepers, and various specialists like wine stewards. It had been funny to imagine twenty people taking care of a family of four or five— what on earth did these people do all day? How many times can you dust and sweep—how many people did it really take to cook three meals a day?

And then, he and a few other trainees accompanied Geoff to a weekend-long trainers event at a British manor house, and damn if every single one of the servants wasn't busy every time you saw one. He had also tried to learn a little there—but the less he thought about that, the better. Still—it must be nice to have all the servants in a house also be slaves, he thought. So classy! Pull 'em off to one side and whack 'em a little and screw 'em. Watch them put their uniforms back on, flip the skirts down, pull up the pants, get that just-fucked look off their faces and get back to work a minute later.

Not surprisingly, he felt an erection growing. He glanced down at the papers again. "Okay. So, you know I'm Anderson's apprentice." (He thought that sounded better than student.) "But don't think that because I'm learning here I won't be a tough trainer."

"Oh, no sir."

"Because all this means is that you have two trainers instead of one—twice the potential to screw up."

"Yes, sir." She looked so damn earnest.

On Anderson's schedule was nothing but chores, training sessions in skills such as speech and movement, and two times a day when she had blocked in "use." Michael hadn't asked what that meant—it seemed obvious.

"How are you at sex?" he asked, trying to shake her.

"Please sir, I haven't been rated in sexual activities." Oh, but look at that nice pink glow on her cheeks, and that gentle rise of her chest as she lowered her eyes!

"Why not?"

"His Lordship will have certain people who are trained in that area, sir. He would not wish me to spend time learning what he has experts for." She blushed a little more.

"But you will be used," Michael said confidently. "Every slave is used eventually."

"As you say, sir."

"So come over here and let's see how you do in some other

tests, shall we?" He gestured with one finger, twisting it down in a kind of reverse beckoning and she immediately dropped forward onto her hands and knees.

Carefully, she crawled to him, the maid gone, the slave at once appearing.

Nice. He watched the curve of her body, the sway in her hips as she crossed the floor, and when she rose up again in front of him, she was close enough to touch, but not even brushing the fabric of his trousers. He leaned over her to unfasten the dress behind her neck, and then he pushed it down her shoulders.

Her breasts were cupped by a pristine white lace bra which lifted them for his visual enjoyment. They were round and invited touch, and he didn't waste any time admiring them. Oh yes, soft and heavy, and just right. The bra helped to keep them up, make them attractive. He slipped his fingers inside the bra and lightly pressed them against her warm flesh, and she shivered appropriately.

"I like this," he murmured, brushing his thumbs against her nipples. They tightened under his pressure, and became erect. "I like the bra. But your nipples aren't sore enough."

For a moment, he felt rather than heard confusion and momentary indecision rising from her. Perhaps it was the drawing of a breath too sharply, a sudden jolt in the gentle rise of her chest. But she didn't say a word, and Michael almost froze himself.

Shit, she's just a slave, he thought angrily. If I surprise her, that's part of the training, remember? Keep 'em off balance. He twisted her nipples sharply and smiled when she gasped.

"Yeah," he said, continuing to fondle her. "These need to be sore, as much as possible. Don't tell me you can't take a little bit of pain like this?" He twisted them again, and pulled them out of the lacy cups, tugging sharply.

"Yes, sir, if it pleases you, sir!" The words came out in a rush, but didn't sound too panicked. He dropped her tits and grabbed a handful of her hair and pulled it back, tilting her head up.

"It does please me." Michael found her lips to be as warm and full as her breasts—soft, inviting and welcoming. No complaints there, even when he pressed her to him so hard that he could feel her teeth almost scraping his. When he let her go, she rocked back, gasping. A good kiss always shook a slave—they were rarely kissed like that. In fact, he had gotten quite a reputation for that, back at Geoff's. Slaves worked harder to please him, thinking of that un-expected intimacy which might serve as a reward. And Geoff had approved of it, saying that individual trainers should have their own marks of rewarding attention to keep the slaves guessing and on their toes.

But she recovered quickly, her dress sliding down her arms, her breasts falling out of the bra cups, her light lipstick smudged. It was charming, that lovely moment of disturbed dignity, when her flesh was touched by color and her poise shaken and not quite up to restoration. But it was only a moment—and then it was gone, and she was waiting for more instruction or another action from him, her eyes open and ready.

There was a fleeting second where Michael thought that this was enough, but the stirring between his legs was insistent. And why the hell not? Get her used to one of her new duties. Smiling, he indicated his fly. He had missed his usual morning blowjob—now was a good enough time to catch up. He didn't have a con-dom, so he wouldn't finish in her—but a splash of jism was just what those big tits needed.

"I know your Japanese isn't conversational. Let's try your French." He leaned back, stretching his arms out, and felt again that split second of hesitation from her. He glanced down even as she was moving her hands toward his belt buckle, but couldn't find a single thing to criticize. Biting back an unsaid reprimand, he looked stern and she continued with her task.

Her fingers were sure and nimble, even at the awkward part where the belt had to be tightened to unfasten it. Her breath was a warm wind across his crotch as she maneuvered the zipper down, and the cool touch of her fingers teased him deliciously. His cock was so hard it hurt, and he wanted very much to batter her throat the way he learned to use his uncle's boys. But he waited, sighed as she lowered her full lips to kiss the head of his cock, very gently. It seemed to be a ritual; he liked it. But there wasn't a lot of patience left for such subtlety. He pressed her head down further and she engulfed him, not as smoothly as he was used to, but adequately enough for a first try. It felt marvelous, that familiar warmth flooding his body, the rise in heat that tingled his skin all the way from his forehead to the soles of his feet.

Her bowed back was very pretty as she worked on him. Okay, maybe she was heavier than he liked, but she was still a nice piece of work. He relaxed as she began to suck him, and then tried to pay attention to her technique. That was one of the hardest jobs a trainer had, he reflected. Trying to keep your mind working while someone's doing their best to make you happy. Everyone should have these kinds of problems with their work.

She wasn't nearly as good as most of the slaves he was accustomed to. Although she was eager, and did seem to approach the task with enthusiasm, there was a guardedness behind every motion which seemed jarring. Michael flashed back to one of his earliest girlfriends, trying to go down on him in the front seat of his car, her motives questionable and her technique not worth bragging about.

But no, it wasn't that Joan was bad—she kept her lips over her teeth and drew in warm breaths and didn't just play with it like girls do. It was just—something was missing. Gritting his teeth, he pulled her away from him. "You have no idea how to do this," he snapped.

Immediately, she cast her eyes down. "No sir," she responded. "Please sir, forgive my failing, and teach me to please you."

"Oh, you'll learn, sweetie. We'll be doing this a lot. No slave leaves my training without knowing how to really suck cock."

"As you say, sir."

"Right—the first thing to do is realize that you need to take it all smoothly—and you have to keep your lips firm. Show me how much you love my cock—don't just suck it, make love to it. Worship it. I want to see enthusiasm, energy, devotion. You are going to make yourself a slut for me, ready to take it all. When you get to do this, you're pleasing a man the best way possible, you got that?"

"Yes, sir." She nodded slightly, and licked her lips to moisten them. She did look slightly dismayed at the word "slut," and stabbing through his pleasure at shaking her up again was just a bit of confusion. What the hell was wrong with "slut?" All slaves loved to be sluts, that's what they were there for. Well, he'd teach her to love the word. Maybe he could ask Anderson if that was the way he could refer to her from now on. Yeah, that would be hot. He grinned and gripped his cock, angling it toward her face again. "Let's start at the beginning, slut. Take the head of the cock in your mouth, and swirl your tongue around it—"

The door did not squeak, but the floorboards did. Michael's head shot up when he heard the sound, and he caught Chris Parker's eyes instantly. His mouth dropped open and confusion mingled with anger at the intrusion.

"I'm busy—" he started to say, but Parker cut him off.

"That will be all, Joan," he said, snapping his fingers. "Fix yourself and attend the Trainer upstairs."

"Yes, Chris," she said quickly. And with a lightning-quick glance at Michael, she rose, drawing her dress up over her shoulders. Quickly, her fingers did up the closures, and she dropped a neat little exit curtsy as she passed Parker in the doorway. She was blushing furiously.

Michael bit back his initial retort and shoved his still-hard cock back into his pants. He waited until the door closed behind Joan to explode. "What the fuck was that about? I was interviewing her, for crissakes! You just blew my authority with her, thank you very fucking much!"

"You had no authority with her, Mike," Chris snapped back, his emphasis sharp on the name. "And what you were doing was not an acceptable part of an initial interview—or didn't you notice that sexual conduct was not recommended for first contacts?"

Michael fastened his belt. "It wasn't her first interview! She's been here for almost a month!"

"It was her first interview with you." Parker smiled tightly, and tilted his head in amusement.

"And my methods are obviously different than yours! You had

no right to interrupt like that!" Michael slammed his fist down on the table. "What the fuck am I supposed to do now? She's not going to respect me as much as she should." He stood up and started shoving his shirt down into his waistband. "I don't believe you did that."

"Then we have something in common, Mike. It's hard for me to believe how spectacularly you are making a fool out of yourself." Parker walked past him and opened Joan's file and shifted through the papers. "Look. She has been rated novice level in sexual performance—does that suggest anything to you?"

Michael looked down, fuming. Sure, the pages of her ratings were familiar, he had looked through them before the interview. "Yeah, so? What the fuck are you talking about?"

"Doesn't it strike you as rather odd that someone who has been in training for so long would be a novice at sexual pleasure?" Chris looked over the top rim of his glasses and then back down to the page. "And here—do you see any suggestion that her training has included sexual skills? No—domestic skills, language skills, and social skills—and that's it."

"What are you saying? That she doesn't have to screw? That's bullshit! All slaves have to be good in bed, that's the whole fucking point!"

Chris sighed and closed the file. "It was a... pleasure to meet you, Mr. LaGuardia. Good luck in your future employment." He turned to leave.

Michael grabbed for his arm angrily. "And what the fuck does that mean?"

Parker looked at the hand locked around his bicep and then up into Michael's face, and Michael opened his fingers. Michael was astonished at the muscle density he had felt, but he wasn't afraid. They stared at each other for heartbeats, and Michael felt about ready to snap when the Trainer's low voice cut through the tension.

"Profanity is so unoriginal," Anderson said, stepping through the doorway. "I try not to use it—it provides such a bad example for the clients. Particularly that word—fuck. It has to be the ugliest word in the English language."

"Trainer," Chris said. Michael shut his mouth and watched the moves the smaller man made. Parker took a slight step back, just enough to make the dipping of his shoulders look gracefully natural. Then, he straightened back up—just the sort of move that an Anderson-trained slave might make—smooth, unobtrusive, yet absolutely clear. For a moment, he lost himself in the study of it— how do you show someone that move? Step back, dip, but not too low, keep that eye contact except for a brief second... where had he seen this before?

"I'm ever so fascinated to hear all about how you botched up your first assignment, Mike," Anderson was saying, interrupting his train of thought. "Chris, will you please attend to Joan? We had planned to continue with organizing skills today."

"Of course." Chris exited without another glance at Michael.

"Well—doesn't follow instructions, doesn't play well with others—you're not on the way to making up for your initial entrance, Mike." Anderson shuffled the scattered pages of Joan's file back into a neat stack.

"Look, I'm sorry—Jeez, how many times am I going to have to say I'm sorry about making a simple mistake at the door?"

"Until you get it right, kiddo. Sit down." Anderson turned quickly and pointed. Her eyes were hard and cold, and Michael felt the first genuine moment of dread. He collapsed back down into his chair, compressing his lips in an effort to keep himself from saying more. He felt like he needed to explode! Anderson waited as he blew out a stream of exasperated breath, and then pulled out a chair for herself.

"Mike, has it occurred to you to ask why we haven't fully forgiven you for last night?"

"Not as much as it's occurred to me that you're blowing the entire fucking thing out of proportion!" The words were out before he even had a chance to consider them. He grimaced as a look of displeasure crossed the Trainer's face.

"How about we try this," she said gently. "You lose that word, and I'll try to forget that you just had that little slip."

"Yeah, yeah, I'm sorry."

"For what?"

"For saying...the word you don't like!" What was this, some kind of absurd, childish drama here? He fought the impulse to say "the f-word."

"And?"

"What is there to add?" He could barely keep his voice from scaling up, but at least he was controlling the volume. Michael looked away to avoid those dark, analytical eyes.

Anderson brushed a few strands of hair away from her throat and sat back. "You're sorry that you offended me by using language you knew I find distasteful. You would make up for this lapse if you could, but you can at least assure me that you won't ever use such language in my presence again."

"Fine. I mean, yeah. Is that what you wanted me to say?"

"Michael—let me clue you in on something which I usually don't reveal this early in someone's training. My clients don't always learn because I sit and teach them by explaining how something is done. They sometimes learn because I set an example for them. Therefore, you must set an example for them."

He stared back at her in amazement. "You mean I have to act like a slave?"

"I mean that you have to know how to do everything that I teach, so that you can teach it yourself. You must at the very least make an effort, understanding that in most things you will probably never achieve the skill level of one of my clients. And I mean that you have to lose this hypocrisy."

"I am not a hypocrite!"

"Perhaps not. I've been known to make judgment errors. But what you are is a student—an apprentice trainer without professional ranking. As far as I'm concerned, senior slaves are far superior to you. Maybe you should keep this in mind, and try to be a little less impatient and a little more open to learning new things. That is what you're here for, isn't it? To learn?"

Just a little bit chagrined, Michael nodded. "Yeah. I'm sorry. It's just that nothing in your writing prepared me for this. Everyone else—I mean—where I was trained before—we all used the slaves. And there wasn't this... formality between us. It would have been helpful if you explained this all to me last night, instead of waiting until it got this far."

"Mike, it's not my job to make this easy for you," Anderson said as she rose from her seat. She gazed down at him for a second, and then turned to the table as she continued to speak. "And it is certainly not my job to teach you basic etiquette. Since you have belatedly discovered that you need to learn it, I suggest you come up with a plan to do so. Now, let's review what you did in your first assignment. You were sloppy, you did not follow my instructions—let's hear the tape and see how else you made a fool out of me."

"Out of you?"

She turned to level her eyes at him as she hit the rewind button on the tape recorder. "Of course me, Mike. I chose you."

As the machine whirred, Michael's gut joined it. This was turning out even worse than he had ever imagined. Nothing was happening as he had planned! He sighed and eased back in his chair, and then bit his lip as he realized that maybe he should have made some acknowledgment when she rose. Maybe he should have gone to the tape recorder first.

Shit, he fumed, knotting his fingers around the chair arms. This is nothing like California!

Chapter Four

It hadn't taken him too long to realize that he would never be able to afford a slave—let alone two—with whatever his degree could fetch him on the job market. Niall was sympathetic, but didn't offer to buy him one or even float him a loan.

"If you want to come out and live here for a few months and try your hand at writing, you're always welcome," he had offered. And Michael, even in his deepest funks, couldn't deny that it was a generous offer. But whatever writers had, Michael lacked. He tried going the rounds of acting and modeling agencies, but his pretty face and body were just more meat on the market—nothing ever came of it. He was still unemployed and sort of living with Niall when the visitors came and offered him an interesting opportunity.

"And this is my nephew Michael," Niall had said, introducing him to a tall, bronzed man with stylishly graying hair and dancing eyes. "Mike, this is Geoff Negel, the man who trained Ethan."

"Great job!" Michael laughed, shaking the older man's hand. They all smiled, and across the room, Ethan blushed, even as he scurried with a tray in his chained hands.

"Thank you, Michael. Yeah, Ethan's a good boy. I'm glad you're getting some use out of him."

"Mike here wants to be an owner one of these days," Niall added, patting Michael on the shoulder. "A regular chip off the old block, huh? And he's just waiting for the day when some prime girl comes his way, aren't you, kid? This one swings both ways, Geoff. I don't know about this younger generation!"

"Oh, I'd say that it's an improvement on the old, Niall. After all, there's always a handy plaything if you don't limit yourself to one gender!" Geoff flashed a very white smile at Mike. "Good for you,

Mike, you follow those ambitions. The Marketplace always needs
new, young owners, blazing new territory and expanding our understanding of what slaves are, and what we're all doing."

"Yeah, well, unless I win the lottery, it doesn't look like I'll be
in the market anytime soon," Mike said mournfully.

"Oh, don't you worry, Mike. You can always come by and use
my boys," Niall said cheerfully. "I'll be getting on with the rest of
my guests then!"

When he left, Mike shifted nervously for a moment, but Geoff
showed no similar impatience to get on with the socializing. Behind him, Mike heard a sharp slapping sound, but didn't turn to
see what was happening. There would always be something else
to see later.

"It's always a pity when someone who wants to be a part of the
Marketplace can't afford it," Geoff said, also ignoring the fun or
discipline going on. "I've been trying to find a way to lower the
prices of novice slaves, but when you factor in the time and costs
which go into their pre-sale training, it's still more than I'd like.
And if a spotter brought them in, the price starts edging up even
more."

"What's a spotter?" Michael asked, suddenly interested.

"That's someone who spends their time scouting for potential
Marketplace material. It's a time-consuming job—they go to all
these SM clubs and they answer ads, read and write books—all
their time is spent looking for someone who could make the
grade. And for this, they get a cut of the first purchase price, and
sometimes even a percentage of future prices as well."

"No kidding! I could do that!"

"Well, no, Michael, you probably couldn't. It takes a certain
amount of training and a lot of natural intuition—you just can't
run out, grab a hot trick, and start teaching them about us." Geoff
smiled as Michael's face fell. "But there's no reason why you
couldn't be trained to do it, and maybe see if you have the gift."

"That would be cool!"

And that was all it took. Before long, he was living in Geoff's
spacious designer house in Santa Cruz, with a never-ending bevy

of willing men and women to play with, and all under the aus-
pices of teaching him a business! Life would never get better than
this, Michael was sure.

Every morning, after some sort of sexual frolic with a slave of
either gender, he would head off to where Geoff and at least two
junior trainers conducted rounds of interviews and intense classes
of instruction, using the house slaves as examples. It was a huge
operation—Geoff proudly mentioned that his "house," as the
training centers were usually called, had produced more slaves than
any other on the entire West Coast. He himself had garnered a good
share of notoriety for his avant garde methods and his recom-
mendations for ownership guidelines.

For months, it was nothing less than paradise. Michael fell easily into the routine, and found that he did in fact have a gift. It
wasn't for spotting, though. It was for handling.

"That's what we call the people who manage slaves," Geoff had
told him one evening, over dinner. "There was once a rigid hierarchy of titles and job descriptions in the Marketplace, you know.
Most of it is fairly obscure these days, but years ago, a handler was
the type of person you'd engage to manage an entire household
full of slaves."

"You mean, like an overseer?" Michael had asked.

Geoff's dining room was a huge, tiled solarium-style room
with a southwestern exposure, great for sunset watching. Barefoot
slaves padded from the kitchen to the long, glass-topped table in
abbreviated serving uniforms, taking time to individually serve
each diner, their bodies available for caressing and teasing even as
they fetched and carried.

"Well, you could use that model, yes," Geoff said easily. "But
a handler is more than a slave manager—a good handler is also a
trainer, a motivational coach, a therapist when necessary. Handling
slaves is a skill and a calling to some of us, Michael. You have to
have that certain touch, a way about you that slaves respect, something that they can be drawn to." He smiled and beckoned, and a
young, lithe man in a steel collar and matching cuffs swept over to
kneel at the side of Geoff's chair. Geoff broke off a piece of bread

and dipped it in the rich, spicy mole sauce that had been part of dinner, and fed it to the slave from his hands as Michael watched.

The slave shivered as he bent his head back to receive this treat and this honor of being fed from the master's hand. His eyes closed in near ecstasy. Geoff allowed the slave to lick his fingers clean, and then stroked his throat gently. The slave shuddered even harder, and arched himself taller, as if offering his body for any use Geoff might consider, not an inch of his skin hidden or protected. Geoff smiled indulgently and pinched a nipple, and then waved the slave off with a laugh.

"When you can do that to any slave, you are a true handler," he said to Michael, leaning forward. "A worthy goal, don't you think?"

Michael thought so very, very much. And slaves did respond well to his touch, and worked hard to please him. He developed the basic emotional control that Geoff said was the mark of a good trainer, and worked on figuring out new exercises for slaves to use in order to mold their behavior. That was very hard—why come up with new things when there were whole books full of older things he hadn't run through yet? But he tried anyway, and was encouraged every step of the way, both by his trainer and by the reactions of the many slaves he got to practice with.

He read quite a bit, or so he thought. Geoff kept records of every slave that passed through his hands, and encouraged the trainers under him to make use of them, examining how different training methods worked on different people. He often spoke of how vital the interviews were, and how methods should be continually revised and refined. For a while, it was pornographically thrilling— the erotic histories of dozens of people from all walks of life, spread out for Mike to examine, pictures, video tapes and all.

And Geoff himself was fascinating—charismatic, friendly, and always ready to play, teach, or talk. He was rarely without someone hanging onto his every word, and often dictated into a recorder he carried, so that transcriptions of his new ideas and thoughts were showing up every week or so. Owners and slaves loved him—he created a happy, open atmosphere with a casual kind of ambient sensuality, the ultimate New Age school for slaves. He was always concerned with how people felt—and if anything started to chip away at Michael's happiness, it was that little, gently nagging question.

"How do you feel about being on your belly, Tina?" Geoff would ask, his voice captivating and soothing all at once. "Does it make you ashamed? Does it get you wet? Are you bored?"

And they would answer him in partial sentences and full ones, in detail, or with "I don't know"—and whatever they said he would record, nodding and reassuring them that their thoughts and feelings were important to him. And then he would talk to them about their feelings, tell them it was okay to have them, coach them on new ways to express them.

He would question the owners. "How did it make you feel when Paul failed to please your guest? Did it make you feel betrayed? Embarrassed? Did you want to hurt him outside the limits of the contract?" And he'd listen, patiently, sometimes as owners ranted and raved, nodding and looking at them until they calmed down, eager to hear his affirming words of support for them, whether he was about to agree completely or correct them for some minor way they'd hurt their slaves' feelings. And all the while, he'd be validating their own, too. Tricky. But it seemed to work, no matter how strange it was. Disappointed owners would come out of Geoff's study ready to take their property back home—or leave them there for a few days or weeks for touch-up training—and either way, they'd go home praising the trainer like a guru who'd just shown them the way to nirvana.

Geoff conducted—in fact, he pioneered—discussion groups of slave clients, part consciousness raising, part therapy, all designed to keep them in touch with their thoughts, desires, and of course, their feelings. "The client needs a safe place to vent, to express their fears and doubts without the threat of punishment," he had written, "or else they become neurotic, moody, and easily prone to passive-aggressive behavior. Safe space fosters an inner sense of self-awareness and identity which makes them stronger individuals, better suited to the service they desire."

What he didn't write about was the fact that he videotaped these sessions of "safe space." They were never shown to the owners of those slaves, or course, but to his apprentice trainers, as part of their training. They would listen to the complaints and the joking and the bitter tears, and Geoff would provide countless suggestions on what they could do to make the lives of the slaves a bit easier, or perhaps properly challenging. There were never tapes of the slaves currently in training or back for refresher work—only last year's group, or older ones. All of it was very ethical.

He also wrote: "It's impossible to maintain the perfect balance of mastery and compassion, unless the owner is always aware of the true self worth and vital personality of their chosen clients. Every order must come with the understanding that the client is willing to undertake anything reasonable—and therefore the owner must practice the art of reason."

During special events designed for owners and potential owners, Geoff would conduct extensive workshops on slave management and psychology, providing his buyers with guidebooks for behavior and household rules. Each time, he would give a carefully encouraging speech, telling them that of course, they would determine their own ways and styles with time, but that slaves did best under familiar circumstances. And they listened, eagerly, the same way they watched hungrily as the newly trained slaves were brought out for beautifully choreographed sex and SM shows, and doled out to these workshop attendees by orientation and gender preference. And then, eventually, they bought a slave. Or two. Or more. And came back when those contracts ended for a new one. Or two. Or more.

Geoff's cadre of owners was a vital part of his business and social life. He partied with them as well as trained them, socialized at their homes all over the world, sometimes taking with him favored students or exceptionally talented client slaves. (He was most likely to take a slave in training if he thought the owner might find them interesting. On many of those trips, Geoff laughingly tossed out the return half of a round trip ticket as he headed for home.)

Michael was often in favor, and got to visit some homes of the rich and famous and the rich and unknown alike. At first, he was a little uneasy, but his good looks and natural charm won him a sure place at the table anywhere they went, and his ability to play with any handsome slave who was placed in his care was clearly an asset. So over and over again, he watched Geoff enter these mansions and exquisite condominiums, these luxury yachts and sprawling estates, and just take over.

That's what it was like. Geoff Negel would waltz in through the door and slaves would perk up. Paid staff, if present, would start to shine, as if they were in a sharp competition. Even owners would fawn on him, pleased to be spoken to as a personal friend, to be flattered on the care of their property, joked with, teased.

He never hesitated at control, never seemed to doubt himself. None of his former trainees were free from his influence, and he handled them with a dominant sense of propriety the moment they were in his domain—wherever he happened to be. "Take control early and often," he had cautioned Mike on several occasions. "Otherwise, they might be tempted to think that you are beyond them now, that your mastery of them was something they can forget about. They should never forget, never think that you could possibly be ignored. There's an old phrase among we old trainers," he would laugh. "They used to call it 'taking them in hand,' like taking the leash of a trained animal. That's what you need to do, especially for old clients with some experience. And they'll be glad for it, believe me. Because sometimes, their own owners will let them slip, and forgive them. But we, as trainers, must never do that. Don't hesitate to correct, even if it's in front of their owner. It just might spur that owner to better management skills; remind them that they, too, should have the upper hand. When they see how well their slave improves when a trainer is around, they will be sure to clean up their act."

And somehow, even when Geoff did exactly that—disciplined a sloppy or lazy or downright insolent slave in front of their owner—the owners forgave him. In fact, they frequently apologized for the misbehavior themselves. But by the end of the visit, Geoff would console them, and then encourage them to take control again, even giving them hints or actually conducting a punishment session with them. And they loved him for it.

Geoff was a master at reading people—he listened with such intensity and openness that sometimes you left his presence thinking that he was perhaps the only man who really understood you. It was easy to trust him. He had an easygoing, friendly manner and a very illustrious past, both inside and outside of the Marketplace. He came from California real estate money, and had contacts ranging up and down the coast in all the right industries, from citrus groves to Hollywood to silicon chip manufacturing. But he'd also spent a lot of time traveling, and modestly noted that he had connections with one of the finest slave training houses in Great Britain. Naturally, he had not chosen to set up shop there, not when North America was positively brimming with excellent potential for slaves and their masters.

Besides, he had his own ways now. New ways, possibly revolutionary ways. His theories, carefully bound into neat books, many of them illustrated, were sent to training houses all over the world. He had his own newsletter, which he circulated to owners who had purchased from him or taken one of his training courses. He believed, passionately, that the way to expand and nurture the Marketplace was to create a new breed of slave matched with a new breed of owner. Partners, in a new way of relationship building.

After a while, it all began to sound suspiciously like new-age pop psychology for SMers. The talking cure for whatever ailed you, whether it was a nagging feeling of dissatisfaction or a lower-than-required level of commitment. Matchmaking instead of auction sales. Time out instead of physical discipline, listening instead of just relying on a slave to do as they are told without complaint. It seemed an odd way to manage slave training—after all, Michael thought, it wasn't as if these people were getting married. Contracts were for short amounts of time, leading to either more contracts or new ones. Either everyone got what they wanted, or they started again with someone new. No need to get all involved with personal problems or actually do relationship counseling with someone you could literally give away to someone else, was there?

According to Geoff, there was exactly such a need.

"In a lot of ways, the classic style of slave ownership is just a model based on real life exploitation," he explained. "Romans and Greeks owned slaves, one nation conquered another and took slaves, colonists spent years making sure that they'd have some underclass to buy and sell—but why should we just copy what they did?"

"Geoff, no one fought to get into slavery in those times," Michael pointed out. "You have people backed up on a waiting list for months. It's totally different now! Yeah, we have to use some rules based on old stuff, but so is everything else in life! You take what works and toss the rest. So, we're not killing people or kidnapping them or separating families and all that shit—isn't that enough of a difference?"

"No! If we had found some way to strip a person of their humanity as well, it might be. But you can't ever forget that these slaves are people first, people with needs." He indicated his back files with pride. "Needs that were met, because I took the time to find out who they were and what they wanted. To make sure that their qualifications were perfect for the market, and that the buyers knew what kind of training they had. To find just the right sort of buyers, who could be counted on to take care of these precious people, make sure they have the right environment to grow in. And how many complaints have I had, Mike? None! So trust me, this is the way of the future. You stick with me, and you'll have that beach house and the matched set of slaves you're dreaming about."

And he would wink, give Mike something to do, and then get back to that amazing way he had of making everyone think he had given them his total attention.

It was easy to believe Geoff, in so many things. He had it all— the lifestyle, the panache—and the house full of slaves and trainers ready to bolster his claims. And so much of it did make sense from a compassionate point of view—even from a logical one. It was so simple to just run someone through the exercises, ask the questions and keep right on going—so simple, in fact, that it became boring far sooner than Michael ever dreamed it could.

CHAPTER FIVE

Michael stirred under the covers and stretched. God, was it morning already? He rolled over to check the digital reading on the clock. Yep—fifteen more minutes until wake-up. Not enough time to go back to sleep. Just enough time for a quickie, though—but no one to sheet-wrestle with.

He threw himself onto his back in frustration. Damn, a man gets used to things when he has them every day. *I have to stop thinking about it,* he counseled himself. *It's only sex.*

Yeah, right.

Well, enough self-pity. Out of bed, and into the shower, it's another wacky day at the Anderson home.

Dressing also made him pause. His usual clothing consisted of pull-over shirts and light sweaters and jeans—leather pants when weather permitted. Boots, unless he was wearing the latest designer running shoes.

But Parker wore a damn shirt and tie every fucking day, as far as he could tell. Maybe he should, too? Except that he only had two dress shirts and two ties with him. It could get pretty boring.

Boring being the operative word. Three days had gone by, and he had gotten little or no access to his training slave. Instead, Anderson had him reading and taking notes, making outlines and studying the household schedule. He had thought that the lengthy lecture he received on interview techniques and following instructions had been punishment enough for messing up Joan's interview. That, and the shame of having her stop the tape and grill him on why he asked the few questions he did. But no, his real punishment was having his client taken away from him until he learned what to do with her. Not that it was exactly spelled out that way, but it was clear what was going on.

He was never invited to sit in with Anderson when she took one of the girls into her office, and found himself incensed when he realized that Parker had his little sessions with them as well. He found Chris drilling Joan one day, Joan seated at the dining room table blindfolded. At once, Michael's heart beat wildly—a blindfold was the kinkiest thing he had seen used since he had arrived, and he stopped as he was passing by the door to gaze at the scene, half-thrilled and half-scared at the prospect of being shooed away like a curious toddler who found his parents necking.

But Chris didn't even seem to notice him. He was leaning forward and holding something toward Joan's face, and Michael slid further along the doorway to see what it was.

It was a cup. Joan sniffed the contents and said, confidently, "Oh, that one's Lapsang Souchong!"

Michael blinked as Chris took the cup away and jotted something down on his clipboard. "Excellent, Joan, perfect marks. You may remove the blindfold."

The slave did so, saying, "Thank you, Chris."

"You're very welcome. Clear all of this up, and why not brew some of the Lapsang for the Trainer? She'll take it in the office."

"Yes, Chris, of course." As she rose from her chair, Michael almost ran from the doorway, but he held himself still as Chris's eyes turned up toward him. The senior trainer said nothing, though. What was there to say?

Oh yes, and Michael also had the distinct pleasure of watching Parker handle a little disciplinary problem with a heavy leather strap, how exciting. Tara was a sight to see, though, her skirts hiked up, her pretty ass bared, her face streaked with tears. Parker had a steady, unerring hand, and that brutal strap colored her up nicely—and yet there was no sexiness about it, no overlaying miasma of sex-to-come, that weight of SM sensuality. Michael had ached to take those red cheeks in his hands and knead them, the way all trainers were encouraged to at Geoff's, to stroke the inflamed flesh, and take pleasure in the how the slave reacted with whimpers and small gasps of pleasure and pain. To hear their breathless thanks, the shame-filled pleas for

forgiveness. To pull on a condom and have them spread open—
It was only sex. Uh-huh.

But Parker didn't screw the dickens out of Tara when he was
through. He simply accepted a brief kiss on his boot, and then sent
her away, looking as though nothing particularly special had occurred.

"Isn't that kind of cold?" Michael had asked Anderson later on.

"Punishment is not supposed to be fun," she had replied.

"Yes, I know—but what about for the trainer? For the owner?
Shouldn't we get something out of this?"

"The satisfaction of a job well done?" She looked a little over
his shoulder for a moment and then sighed. "Tomorrow, I want
you to work with Vicente for a little while—he needs an extra pair
of hands."

With Vicente—the non-slave cook/housekeeper/whatever.
There was no understanding what was going on around here! And
no one to ask. Michael had reported to Vicente, expecting to get a
run-down on household time schedules or something like that,
but instead wound up going shopping. Yep—the dark skinned man
handed him a list, a set of car keys, and directions to a local supermarket. There was also some dry cleaning to pick up.

Michael steamed at a steady rate as he ran through the list,
crashing his cart more than once against innocent corner displays
in the market. Some training this was! He cursed out loud as he
loaded the car, and all the way to the dry cleaners. But he was composed by the time he came back—cheerful, even.

It was just helping out, that was all! He had decided that there
had been nothing intentionally insulting in Anderson's request—
after all, he was an extra hand in the house, why shouldn't he pitch
in? He was taking it all wrong—and being unfair to the Trainer. I'm
on the fucking edge, he thought, chastising himself and glad that
no one saw his temper tantrums. I gotta calm down, chill out.
Being asked to chip in was part of being made you a member of
the household instead of being treated like a guest. Now, perhaps,
there would be some attention paid to making him more of a
trainer.

But when he got back, Vicente only directed him to start putting things away—and Tara "helped" him. She was too busy actually cooking to do anything but directed him to where things went. After the last bag was empty, Vicente thanked him, and told him that he was free for the rest of the day.

"Great! Glad to help. Where's the Trainer?"

"Oh, she is not to be disturbed," the big man said. "There are no duties—you may do what you like until tomorrow."

"Until tomorrow?" Michael's voice started to scale up, and he fought it down to a more proper, controlled level. "That was it for me today? Shopping?"

Vicente looked around as though searching for another task. Tara kept her eyes down as she diced carrots for soup. "There is nothing, Mr. Michael," Vicente smiled. "Not until dinner, when you will be wanted to eat, hm?"

"Thanks," Michael muttered, leaving the kitchen. Great. Alone in a strange town, no wheels, no place to go, and he was free for the rest of the day. Shit, there wasn't even a TV in the whole house! Well, that wasn't true, there was a small one in a cabinet in the office, which was mainly for watching videos of other trainers and occasional sale catalogs. Anderson did not get cable.

He kept running into Joan, which made it even more annoying that he wasn't continuing the interview process and overseeing her training the way he was supposed to. She always curtsied when she saw him, and faint blushes touched her cheeks. He wondered if she had laughed at his predicament. It made him want to slap her just out of principle. And make her suck him again, this time to completion, and to hell with Parker's opinion on whether she'd be used like that! Another trainer, one of the European ones, had once written: "A slave having witnessed the humiliation of a master is a tarnished servant and must be reminded of their place before they can regain any luster."

Michael was positive that Anderson did not agree with that assessment, but he certainly did. At least he did now. Topping Joan in a lengthy scene, with nipple clamps and whips and paddles and tight bondage would be just the right thing. Tie those big tits up tight, make her wince with pain, and get all red from the shame of having them stuck out for everyone to see and fondle. He'd work her hard, make her cry and beg his forgiveness, beg to suck him or anything else he wanted. If he were back in California, he'd make a fucking example of her. Get another trainer to help, maybe. Or, two. Fill all three holes, how would you like that for sexual use, huh? Then he'd feel better. And there'd be a little less doubt that she respected him, too.

These thoughts did not console him long. In fact, he found that dwelling on the matter made him feel even more frustrated, and at one point, he thought, oh, what's the use? I need to live under these new rules. I have to learn what the hell it is about this style that makes it so special. I can always go back to the things that worked at Geoff's later on. When I have my own place, maybe, or when I join some more relaxed house somewhere.

One day at chores became two, and then three. In fact, the third day was the most interesting; he got his first exposure to the New York City Subway system, taking the train into Manhattan to pick up some CDs Anderson had ordered from Tower Records. Again, Vicente gave him the errand, and this time advised him to take as long as he liked doing it. "Enjoy yourself," he said cheerfully. "Go and look in the stores." His accent continued to be a mystery—it seemed faintly Hispanic, but nothing like the Mexican rhythms Michael had known back in LA. Mike wanted to ask about it, but never felt that the time was right to ask. Besides, you never knew how sensitive people were going to be about an innocent question.

But meanwhile, he was being sent off to shop like some nitwit valley girl. Well, he did need some new shirts anyway—and maybe a few ties. Spending most of the day in Soho and the East Village lightened his mood for a while, but as he studied the subway map to find his way back to Brooklyn during the rush hour, he began to feel a nervousness in the pit of his stomach that was vaguely nauseating.

I'm not being given a chance, he complained inwardly, steeling himself to the rocking motion of the train and idly looking at the skyline. How can I do anything right if she won't let me do anything at all? I have to ask her what's wrong, that's all, and insist that I be given a proper opportunity to prove myself.

Resolved to do that, he sprang up the steps to the house with an energy he hadn't felt since the first day he arrived. He deposited the CDs with Vicente and ran upstairs to change for dinner. He even showered first, shaving and combing his hair before slipping into one of his crisp new shirts. It was powder blue with a spread collar, and he had gotten a brightly colored, stylish tie. Yes, very sharp. He hummed as he came down the stairs, and nearly ran into Anderson as she was coming out of her office.

"Good evening, Mike," she said, shifting a sheaf of papers in her arms. "How nice you look."

He beamed. "Thanks, Trainer. Listen, could we talk for a moment before dinner?"

She nodded and pushed the office door open again. He held it for her and then followed her in. "I got your music today," he said.

"Thank you. And yet, why don't I think that's what you wanted to chat about?"

"I'll come to the point," Michael said quickly, wishing he'd dropped the small talk. "What's on my mind is—well, I've been thinking—"

"The point, Mike?"

He charged ahead. "It's not fair what you're doing to me. You're not giving me a chance to work, and I want to know why."

Anderson's eyes opened a little wider at the tone of his voice, but she didn't even bother to lay her papers down. She just shook her head and leaned one hip against the edge of her desk. "I believe I told you that I'm not going to be telling you why I do anything, Mike. I'm the Trainer and you're the student—you figure it out."

"But—if I'm the student, shouldn't I be learning things? I mean, shouldn't you be teaching me something? I'm glad to help, don't get me wrong, but what does running errands have to do with slave training?"

"Why, that's another good question, Mike," Anderson said with a slight, slight smile. Her eyes were rigidly cold, though. "Apply yourself to it, why don't you?"

Michael stopped himself from saying that he didn't know, but no new answers came to him. He stared at her, eye to eye, and felt a weird, prickling sensation, like he had said something wrong again, or that she was asking something of him in some secret language he couldn't understand. What have I done now? he thought wildly. Or, what should I be doing? There was an air of expectation around her, something she was waiting for, and the anger at not knowing what to say burst through him.

"How the hell am I supposed to figure it out if you don't say anything to me?" he snapped. "You don't even give me a clue! It's not fair!"

"Maybe it is, and maybe it isn't—but we're not on a playground here, buckaroo. Complaining that something's not fair ain't gonna get you nothin'. You either keep up, or you fail. There's a reason why you're all alone here. Think about it." She indicated that he open the door, and when he did, passed him on her way upstairs. Over her shoulder, she said casually, "Please tell Mr. Parker that I'll be down later on to work with Tara. I won't be eating dinner with you boys tonight."

How could things go from bad to worse so quickly? Michael waited until he was calm again before he left the room. It took a few minutes. He struggled with the urge to head upstairs, toss his suitcase on the bed, and call the fucking airport for the first flight home. But there's no turning back, he reminded himself. Back home is nothing.

Well, here is pretty nothing too, his other inner voice snapped.

He headed for the dining room, where Parker was already seated, looking sharp except for that new beard growing in. It would probably look nice when it was finished, Michael thought charitably. I guess when you're that short, you go for anything that ups your masculinity. That petty observation helped a little—he was even able to smile as he took his seat.

"Anderson's not coming to dinner," he said lightly, tossing his napkin in his lap. "She says she'll see you later to work with Tara."

"Thank you," Chris said pleasantly.

Tara entered almost immediately, and started to serve. Vicente poked his head in for compliments, as usual, and the silence that reigned was almost as effective an appetite suppressant as that vague feeling of nausea which had returned after he had been so casually dismissed by the Trainer. Michael poked at the food, knowing that the soup was excellent and the bread was probably as good as bread got—but that he was also in no mood to enjoy them. Tara was her usual well behaved self, earning nothing more interesting than one quick stern look from Chris when she touched the rim of a glass with the water pitcher.

God! How could he not compare this austere setting with dinner at home (why was he thinking of Geoff's place as home?), with everyone serving or kneeling on the floor waiting for choice tidbits and lewd caresses. The clatter of the silver and china was always drowned out by happy chatter and gossip, plus the various reports of who had gotten into trouble today, and what had been done about it. Noisy and friendly and just a little bit chaotic. Where the figure of authority was more like a really cool dad than a cold, distant... Don't even think that word, Michael cautioned himself.

But here was nothing but dark gloominess. Michael knew he was being sulky and didn't care. It was Parker who broke the silence first.

"Did you enjoy the city today?"

"Yeah." Michael leaned back, giving up the pretense of eating. "Yeah, it was nice to get out. I'd like to see some of the sights, I guess. You born here?"

"A New Yorker by the breed."

"Great. Maybe you can tell me where the scene is around here."

"The scene? Do you mean the local sado-dabblers?"

Michael smirked in spite of himself. "Cute, I like that. Yeah, the clubs and stuff. I'd like to touch base with the community out here."

"Perhaps we're crossing lines, then. Do you mean the leather clubs? The bars for men, the organizations for D-and-S'ers? Or the local Marketplace people?"

"The amateurs," Michael acknowledged. "Like Gates of Pleasure. Or the International SM Activist Organization. They got a local Chapter?"

Parker looked a little amused. "I suppose they do," he admitted. "In the office, you'll find a few local sex papers—at least one of them will have a listing of the various organizations. There is a community of sorts, in the broader, non-political definition of the term. Some clubs, public and not so. Do you like to slum?"

"Hell, yeah!" Michael brightened a little. This was the most he'd gotten from Chris in days.

"Really? Even after what happened?"

Michael sat back, a little surprised. "Oh. You heard."

"Anderson has shared all of your history with me."

The weight of that settled in, and Michael bit his lip. "Well, you know, everyone makes mistakes. That doesn't mean I should deny myself the pleasure of playing in the uncultivated fields." That had been a favorite phrase of Geoff's.

"I suppose not. I do a little leather bar hopping myself." Chris tossed his napkin on the table, and within seconds, Tara was at his side, clearing the dishes away. "I think Mike is finished, Tara, you may clear his as well. And we'll take coffee in the front room."

"Yes, Chris," she said brightly, dropping a smile toward Mike as she gathered up his plate and utensils. Well, well, Michael thought, watching the woman work. Leather bars, huh? The little guy's a fag—and that explains why he's so cool about not slipping the old sausage to the girls. What a fucking waste, man—to be surrounded by pussy and want only dick. He turned to follow Tara with his eyes, and then switched back to Chris when she left the room.

"God, she's good."

"Yes, she's a good girl. She'll do very well." Chris stood up and headed toward the front room, and Michael followed him. This was also a first—usually, they had a cup of coffee at the table, and Vicente kept more on hand if they wanted dessert later.

It was a cold evening—you could hear the wind whistle around the bay window, and watch the tree branches sway back and forth. And it was so very dark, so early in the day. Michael fought back a shiver and dropped into a wingbacked chair, grateful that it didn't face the window. One benefit of the cold, though—you could light a fire and enjoy the benefits of the heat. He watched as Chris laid kindling and positioned a few thicker branches around a log.

"Why doesn't she call you 'sir?'" Michael asked.

"I don't like it," Chris answered, never taking an eye away from what he was doing. "It also becomes a form of discipline for the clients—they must remember to call me by my name. I find it a useful exercise."

"I'm not doing anything wrong by having them call me 'sir,' am I?"

"No. It's a good thing for clients to have differing expectations during training. They will certainly have them while in service." Chris struck a long match and lit the twisted paper at the bottom and sides of his neat stack of wood. He tossed the match into the fireplace and stood, closing the metal grate. Then, he took the seat opposite Michael, just in time to receive a cup from Tara. "After serving, you may have a half hour of free time, Tara."

"Thank you, Chris."

She handed a cup to Michael with another smile, and he felt as warmed by her as he did by the steadily curling flames. Yes, you could tell she was an Anderson slave. Never a moment of hesitation, always a pleasant expression, and that indefinable aura of... confidence?

As he watched her place a silver coffee pot on the sideboard, Michael pondered the sudden revelation. Was it confidence that he was watching? Yes—a certain sureness of step, as though she knew that what she was doing was proper, a kind of well practiced dance, subtle and deliberate at the same time.

When she was gone, he slumped into his chair, reassuming his morose mood as quickly as he had lost it. How the hell am I ever going to learn that? he asked himself. How the hell can you teach it?

"You have to let go of the past," said Chris, almost making Michael spill his coffee.

"What?"

"You're wondering what is going on—and how you're going to get over your current difficulties—or am I incorrect?" He

looked so cool, calmly sitting there, his legs crossed and his tie so
straight. He spoke gently, and looked Michael directly in the eyes
waiting for an answer.

"Jesus, does Anderson teach you how to read minds as well as
see through walls?"

Chris smiled. "As a matter of fact, yes, she does. Or, you pick
it up after years of working with people who must reveal all of
their secrets to you."

"But how am I supposed to learn if she doesn't give me a
chance?" Michael stood up and began to pace. "I've been here for
days, and it seems like I've done nothing! Yeah, I fucked up my
first interview, but people make mistakes—how else can you learn?
Isn't it wasting her time if she's not going to bother to actually
teach me?"

"It might be, if that was what she was doing."

"What do you mean by that?"

"Perhaps you are being taught something."

"What? Where the supermarket is? What music she likes?"

"The modern equivalent, perhaps, of chopping wood and carrying water."

Michael looked back at Chris, who now avoided eye contact.
He stared out of the window and gathered his thoughts. Chopping wood and carrying water? Wasn't that a line in a Van Morri-
son song, something about enlightenment...

Oh yeah! Michael remembered seeing a movie once, about
some kind of samurai. He had rented it by accident with a load of
chop-socky films, something to waste a Saturday afternoon with.
Late at night, he had popped the tape in, and found himself fascinated by the tale, despite it not being dubbed and not containing
too many fight scenes until the end of the movie.

It was the story of a young man who went to learn from an old
guy living alone in the forest, a guy who was supposed to be this
great warrior. The young guy thought he was going to learn all
about swordplay, but for months, all he did was chop and gather
wood, hunt small animals, and carry endless buckets of water. The
old guy beat on him a lot, too—smacking him with sticks, hitting

him when he least expected it—until the kid finally wised up and began to defend himself. Slowly, he was being trained—but very slowly. By the end of the movie, he was invincible, wiping out huge armored bad guys left and right.

Michael turned back to Chris and sighed. "When does she start smacking me with a big stick?"

Something that might have been a snicker escaped Chris's lips. "Perhaps when you ask nicely."

Michael sank back down into the chair. "Man, I've been an idiot."

"Yes."

Michael shot Chris a glare. "Gee, thanks." The snotty little bastard.

"I only agreed with your honest assessment. The question now is: what are you going to do about it?"

"I don't know!"

"Then you have a problem."

"You're a lot of help!"

"Yes, I know." Again, that little smirk. "Perhaps we should continue with a safer topic? You were asking about the local scene—you know, Ken Mandarin lives in Manhattan at least part of the year, and she is very familiar with it. Perhaps you should pay her a courtesy call. I'm sure she'd love to show you around. You're young, healthy—just her type."

Mandarin—oh yeah, the very successful Asian spotter. She didn't send clients to Geoff, but she was known in the West Coast circles. Michael smiled. "She's hot! I saw her in LA with these two slaves—they looked like a married couple, you know the type. They were the hit of a party I went to. Everyone wanted a piece of them. I thought she handled them well... and let me tell you, I wouldn't have minded a piece of the slaves or the owner."

"She claims those two are siblings, actually. Yes, they were a good buy for her." Chris nodded, a momentary look of pleasure crossing his face. "One of my favorite projects. They responded very well to training."

"Brother and sister? Now that's kinky. You trained them?"

"Well, they were trained at my... my former house." Michael looked up at that little hesitation and opened his mouth, a question all ready to go. But Chris was deliberately looking away again, and he held it back.

So, you've got some difficulties of your own, you cocky shit, he thought, sipping his now lukewarm coffee. I wonder what happened that you're not there any more. Fired? Left on your own? Why haven't you gone someplace else yet? How come you haven't opened a house of your own? Bigshot-pal-of-Anderson-who's-not-really-on-vacation, what the hell are you doing here?

"So, what are you guys doing with Tara tonight?" Michael asked casually, breaking the momentary silence.

"Tonight, we're going over some of the very skills you mentioned earlier. Tara has shaped up considerably in the time she's been here, finding ways to anticipate the wishes and expectations of her service. Tonight we're going to do a little testing. She's almost ready to leave, you know."

"Yeah, I heard." And meanwhile, Joan's not getting the benefit of my training, he thought. He kept his face composed, trying not to show his annoyance. "Do you think—could I watch you guys while you do Tara? Test her, I mean?"

"No." Chris topped off his own coffee and raised his eyebrow to ask Mike if he wanted more. Mike, feeling a flush of humiliation and anger growing, compressed his lips and shook his head.

"Why not?" he demanded.

"Because you're not ready."

"Well, how the hell can I ever be ready if I can't do my fucking job!"

Chris carefully put the coffee pot back down and settled into his chair. "Perhaps you can begin by listening carefully to what you're told and obeying Anderson's instructions to the letter. For example, you could clean up your language." He smiled slightly and curiously began to rise back out of his chair.

"Yeah? Well, fuck you, asshole! How the fuck do you like that fucking language!"

"Oh, I'm sure he likes it just fine," came the Trainer's voice from the doorway. "Why, Chris is a big fan of trash talk, aren't you, Chris?"

"Occasionally, Trainer. In small amounts, when appropriate."

Oh Jesus, Michael thought. How did I know that was going to happen? I even saw Chris starting to get up, but I didn't think about why! He wearily got to his feet and turned to see Anderson leaning against the door jamb, her arms folded. The light from the fire caught the silver bracelets on one arm and shot beams of reflected light across the room.

"I'm sorry, Anderson, I shouldn't have said all that," Michael sighed.

"Uh-huh."

"And—and I won't do it again."

"Uh-huh."

"And, well, I'm really sorry."

Anderson sighed and nodded. "Okay, Mike. I think you've had enough time with that particular shovel. Let's switch to another one—tell me why you're here."

He didn't understand the shovel remark, but ignored it. "To learn how to train slaves."

"And what have you been doing?"

"Nothing!"

"Now, whose fault is that?" She walked into the room and Parker moved out of the way so she could take the chair he had just vacated. She sat down without even a nod of acknowledgment, and Mike ached with stronger curiosity about their relationship. But he remained standing, and focused on her, trying to find words to answer her question.

"Well—I came here to learn. I told you that—"

"The question, Mike, the question! Who's fault it is that you think you're not learning?"

"What do you mean I think I'm not learning? What have I learned so far? How not to piss you off?"

"Apparently not," she snapped.

Michael groaned and hit the back of his chair with a tightly clenched fist.

"If you're frustrated, that's too bad, Mike. No one does anything in this house until I know that they're ready—and you've done everything in your power to make me wonder why you're here. Chris is right—if you want to impress me, cursing only behind my back won't help. Whining about fairness and lost opportunity won't help."

"But I've made myself available to you! I'm up on time, I cleaned up my act, I even went shopping for you! What else do I have to do? Sleep at the foot of your bed and kiss your feet in the morning?"

"Let's try something less drastic. Show me your journal."

He stared at her, that cold nausea returning. "There's nothing in it," he said.

"Is that so?"

"Anderson—Trainer—what was I supposed to put in it? 'Today I went to a record store?'" He threw himself down into his chair and ran a hand through his hair. "It's supposed to be a record of my training, isn't it? So what could I say about the last three days that wasn't 'I did nothing today?'"

"You read nothing? Your hours with my papers and the books—they were nothing? You have a library in there—a priceless library full of more than a hundred years of slave records, the training methods of a hundred trainers, and you didn't even pull a single book off the shelf. Parker had to hand them to you. And you observed nothing? The rhythm of the house, the way the work is scheduled, the way the clients act and react—all this is nothing? Your own frustration and questions about what is happening to you—nothing?" Anderson smiled and shook her head. "You've got a lot of nothin' in your life, young man."

Michael felt like exploding again, but remained quiet. What was the point? She had her own little points to make, and he was going to be wrong no matter what he said. He tugged at the tie that felt like it was strangling him. "So, when do you want me to leave?" he asked.

"When I'm finished with you," Anderson replied. "Now, why don't you go upstairs and get some rest before you start that journal? Chris and I have a little work to do tonight, and you're going to have a busy day tomorrow."

Michael looked into her dark eyes for a hint as to what the hell was going on, but saw nothing but faint amusement. Chris's eyes were also a little hooded by that aura of patient irony—sly and piercing at the same time. He stood up and walked toward the hallway, turning before he left to make that shoulder incline gesture that Chris used before he left a room. Anderson wasn't looking— but Chris was. And he was obviously amused.

Upstairs, Michael flipped his book open, smoothed out the page, and began to write. His pen cut through the first two pages and he cursed loudly when he ripped them out to begin again.

❧

"You are the very personage of patience, O Trainer," Chris said when he returned from the kitchen. He presented Anderson with a cup of coffee and placed the small plate of Vicente's ginger cookies on the table by her right hand.

"And you are one of the smoothest bullshitters I know, Mr. Parker." She laughed at her own profanity and looked up at him with an almost vulpine expression. "Now, why do you hate that boy so much?"

"I don't hate him at all. I envy him. He's beautiful and has access to the life of his dreams. I wish I had what he had. Yet, despite some rather interesting past failures, you still pick him out—taking him before at least six other candidates I could now name for you off the top of my head. And, he hasn't got the faintest idea why you're not in love with him. His arrogance is so monumental that it's poetic." Chris cleared his throat as he stood before her, arms folded over his chest.

"My, my. We've been doing a little homework."

"It's all part of my research, which you've been encouraging me to continue, I might point out."

Anderson acknowledged that with a nod and dunked a cookie into her cup. "These are good," she said, eyes bright in the firelight. "You should have some."

"Thank you, no. Are you sure you still want me here? He sees me as interference, a rival for your attention. And in this case, with all respect, I do not believe it will be helpful."

"Why not?"

"He is not a striver. When faced with competition, he fights only so much, and then gives up in frustration. He probably swears he will try harder every time you rebuke him, but then he dwells on his insecurities and lays blame instead of honestly working toward understanding." Chris delivered this assessment coldly, his arms coming down to join behind his back. Anderson watched him with pleasure.

"Perhaps he has not been given enough of an opportunity for honest competition," she suggested.

"Then by all means, give him one. Deva Graham, from Bloom in Chicago, is an excellently trained novice. She's done a year as an apprentice, and although Bloom is a bit over-generous in some of his assessments for my tastes, he's a good judge of character. She's exactly the same age as Michael, with about the same amount of time in the system. She'd be an appropriate co-trainee for him, proper competition. But for him to imagine—to even imagine!— that he's competing with me? It is indeed not fair, although not for the reasons he might suspect."

"Then he should learn when he's not in competition," Anderson said with a slight shrug. "Or, how to choose his contests. Both are good lessons. If it's that unbearable for you, then you are free to come and go whenever you want." She brushed some crumbs off her lap. "I know you'll continue to work on your project. But—I could actually use more of your help. I'm going to change tactics with him, so I'll need you to work Joan for a while."

Chris smirked. "Oh, that will please the golden boy."

"We are a bit sensitive about him, aren't we? Is it love already?"

He looked offended at her teasing. "There's not a brain in his pretty little head. I'd like to think I set my standards a little higher."

"Hm. You've played a broad field. Speaking of which, Rachel called again today. You know I think it's rude not to return phone calls."

They stared at each other in silence, and Chris's shoulders slumped a little. "Yes, of course," he said finally. "I'll see to it as soon as possible."

"That's m'boy. Now let's make sure Tara is ready to use her X-Ray vision for more than coffee fetching."

CHAPTER SIX

The priceless library was more than priceless; it was downright intimidating.

Michael started at one end and examined every shelf. He had been impressed by the sheer number of books and binders there to begin with, never having been a big reader himself. But once he actually looked at what these collections actually were, he was hit by two truths.

He had been foolish to not pop in here and look the collection over, let alone ask Anderson (or even Parker) if they could recommend something to start with. Hell, Parker had given him two of Anderson's own collected works, and he'd barely cracked them. He thought that maybe he would be given actual reading assignments, page this to page that, something clear-cut.

But the second truth was he didn't want to read any of it.

Okay, maybe that was an exaggeration. Of course he wanted to know what was in these books, from the handwritten pages carefully preserved in archive boxes to the bound books on subjects relating to slave training but in more mundane fields, like business management and housekeeping and military history and philosophy.

But it was so much! Too much. And, he felt stupid now, trying to figure out how to ask for help. Would it have been that hard to say something like, "These books will be first on your reading list—we'll discuss them on Friday," or something like that? Some indication that this was the right thing to do? How was he supposed to have known that she wasn't one of those people who get upset when you touch their books or something?

I could have asked Parker, he thought.

I'd rather eat worms, was his immediate rejoinder. I'll be fucked before I go to him for help, the arrogant bastard. It had been a shock to find that Parker had his own binders on the shelves here, too. Would he be expected to read them? Do reports on them?

It was enough to make a man queasy.

Why did so many Marketplace big shots seem to delight in making it so hard on trainees? he asked himself, pulling a binder labeled First Interview Techniques from the shelf and tucking it under one arm. Anderson's collection had things in other languages in it—none of which he could read. But she also collected works from other trainers, and Michael found a few names he recognized and groaned out loud. They were other high level trainers, from all over the world, famous in the slave training circles. He'd even met one or two.

Geoff knew them all, of course. He went to their gatherings all the time, came back with stories of hobnobbing with all the movers and shakers, what was in, what was out. And he'd taken Michael with him once, and Michael had been thrilled at the opportunity to learn from the world's greatest trainers.

But it had been another waste of time—a bunch of snobs who didn't like Americans, or didn't like Geoff in particular, and just loved to lord it over novices, making it impossible for a guy to just get a simple answer.

No wonder Geoff was so popular! He didn't go out of his way to make it difficult for someone to learn! He laid it out on the table for you, told you what he planned to teach, went through it step by step, and when he was done, he told you what you had just learned. And he encouraged—hell, he required questions!

But some of these people—man, it was like they were guarding the secrets of the universe or something. Or, they just wanted you to jump through hoops and sit up and beg until they felt like throwing you a crumb.

Michael had been in training for over a year when Geoff brought him into his office and invited him to come along for one of these all-trainer weekends. It was an honor—he always took his best students, the ones ready for exposure in the highly politicized world of the Marketplace Trainers and Handlers.

And it was expensive. Not terribly so—the Marketplace always partially subsidized such gatherings, making accommodations more affordable and airfares lower, and some trainers were simply sent there by their countries or local regions to represent everyone back home. But instead of taking just one student or slave attendant, Geoff traveled with an entourage whenever possible. Two students, or perhaps three, and lots of slaves so no one felt left without a playmate. His travel was subsidized by his owner circle—especially the ones who fancied themselves trainers as well.

For this particular trip, Geoff had chosen Mike and a fellow trainee named Crystal, and an owner/trainee named Bradley Cofflin. Brad was okay, as far as Michael was concerned—eager for new things, his mantra upon entering Geoff's house was always "what's hot?"—as though his own fantasies weren't enough. He wasn't a serious, fulltime trainer, or even a real student trainer. But he came to classes and workshops from time to time, and liked socializing with the trainers. He also kept four or five slaves at a time, never for longer than a one-year contract, and he agreed to bring three of them with him.

The conference was in England, at an honest-to-God manor house, rolling hills, formal gardens and all. It was relatively small—Geoff explained that the trainers present were all of one "line," a training link that could be traced back like a family genealogy. The chief trainer of this line was a man named Howard Ward, who trained the woman whom Geoff was trained by. Even though she was no longer an active trainer, Geoff was nonetheless of this line. It seemed all very old fashioned, and kind of impressive. Geoff was careful to note that being of a trainer-line meant nothing as far as techniques were concerned. "Every generation invents its own realities," he would say. "We honor the past by all means. But that doesn't mean we have to live in it."

The manor house, Rothmere, did have many guest rooms, but Geoff had arranged for the rental of a vacation cottage in a village a few miles away, for privacy, space, and a sense of atmosphere. "When you visit a new country," he'd said to Mike on the flight over, "It's best to get a feel for it away from the main reason you're there. This way, we have our own space to come home to, with our own people attending us. You'll be glad for the break from high protocol, I think."

And it was nice—the low, three-bedroom cottage was charming and comfortable, and with Geoff in one room, Brad in another, and Mike and Crystal taking the room with the twin beds, there was more than enough space. The three slaves (two girls and a boy) would sleep where their masters put them, of course, and Geoff had been thoughtful enough to request extra pillows and blankets so they could be comfortable on the floor if desired.

It was all very exciting and cozy, but nothing prepared Michael for walking through the massive front entry into Rothmere and seeing, for the first time, a world in which there were no people who were not Marketplace—and one in which this was so natural, no one seemed to pay it any mind at all.

They came in out of a pounding rain, and were met by slaves in house livery who removed coats and hats and umbrellas as though they were magicked away. Towels and dry socks appeared swiftly and without fuss, and Michael's own shoes were lifted away for a minute and returned brushed off and dried before he even finished running a comb through his hair. As suddenly as they descended, they were gone again, and the American visitors were left in the hands of an elegant man in a formal coat with tails, who escorted them to Howard Ward, who was in the magnificent drawing room with some of the other attendees, surrounded by ancient family portraits and coats of arms.

And then Michael began to notice something odd.

Whenever Geoff traveled in the US, he was met with great pleasure and excitement—his coming anticipated and his arrival a reason to be celebratory. But at Rothmere, Howard Ward only rose and only shook Geoff's hand briefly with an air of polite distance. Michael could feel it immediately, even though Geoff seemed to act as though nothing was wrong at all. Ward doesn't like him, Michael thought, watching how the man idly nodded to what Geoff was saying, and how his eyes darted occasionally to find someone else to move on to. Other people in the room watched as Geoff introduced his little party, and Michael could feel slight amusement, curiosity, and even a touch of confusion coming from the people whose hands he shook, but not even a second of warmth in their welcomes. Uh-oh.

It seemed to get worse, too, although sometimes Michael doubted his sanity, because he seemed to be the only one disturbed by these things. Brad was his typical, glad-handing self, heartily greeting strangers as though they were long-lost friends, slipping his card into their hands before they even had a chance to say hello back. And Crystal was very impressed by both the opulence of the Georgian manor house and the various British accents she heard, falling in love and lust with one speaker after another, grabbing Michael and sighing from time to time as she pointed out the latest object of her attention.

But while his companions were getting along in a fairly oblivious way, it didn't take Michael too long to realize that Geoff was the only trainer who had brought more than one student with him. During that first evening, when they all wandered from room to room, Michael never met an apprentice who didn't seem to be identified as "my pupil," or "my junior," or once, "my best student."

To be one of three—with two others still at home!—seemed suddenly odd. And what was odder was that they were the only Americans there, too! Almost everyone else was British—or, as he was corrected more than once, they were English, or they were Scots, or Welsh, or Irish. There were two Germans there, but they were not of the training line; they were presenters. There was also a married couple from South Africa.

But Geoff was the only American. At first, it was easy to believe that it had been a singular honor.

Yet, even arriving back at their rented cottage was another moment that shook Michael up and left him lying awake in confusion. Because, when the four of them piled out of the car and ran to the door through the rain, there was no light on. Brad searched for the key while Geoff knocked, and the door was finally opened by a sleepy-eyed slave, pleasantly naked, whose eyes widened as she let the travelers in.

The other two slaves had to be awakened, too. And they had to

be told what to do—even basic things like get robes from the bedrooms. Oh, they were very solicitous—one of the girls even wound
a leg around Mike's own thigh as she dried his hair, and whispered
a sexy suggestion into his ear.

But all Michael really wanted was to get into bed and sleep off
the jet lag in peace and dry warmth. He was grateful, as usual, that
Geoff took control and sent the slaves running to fetch things and
get them all settled, but when it came time to get into bed, the last
thing Michael wanted was company. He listened to Crystal whim-
pering and panting for a while as her chosen slave went down on
her, but stayed awake long after the breathing calmed and the room
was in complete silence. His only consolation, as he finally drifted
off to sleep, was that compared to the slaves who had helped them
so well at Rothmere—including the ones who served drinks and
passed canapés—the three here were much better looking. Probably more fun in bed, too, since the Rothmere slaves seemed so
damn serious. But he hadn't needed a pretty girl in bed. He needed
one at the door with a cup of tea and his warmed bathrobe and a
pair of slippers.

Obviously, Brad wasn't keeping his slaves in line the way he
should, Michael had decided. It was a good thing they would have
this time with Geoff, to set things right.

The next day was even worse. They entered into the more formal style of the weekend, with set roundtable discussions and seminars. On that day, Michael found out just how small a pond Geoff
was the big fish in.

The Rothmere gathering wasn't just a chance to get these trainers of Ward's line together to reminisce and chat—it was a chance
for Ward to report on what had been learned at the larger, international gatherings, and for more experienced trainers to present
work they had written themselves, or the work of colleagues. That
morning, when the American contingent showed up, they found
a long table set up in the vast entry way, containing bound collections from the annual meeting called the Academy, as well as folders and binders of reports and papers done by individual trainers
of merit all over the world.

Geoff had brought his own collections, which Crystal and Michael made room for and displayed with their printed summary cards. But Geoff didn't stop to pick up any literature—he gathered his troupe and gave them their instructions and then set them "free" to explore. As usual, he didn't require anything specific of them, only that they didn't clump all into one discussion together, so they could each share something new when they got home later that night. And with a smile and a warm pat on the back for each, he took only Brad to accompany him as he went to the first meeting Howard Ward was running.

Michael waited until Crystal chose a topic of interest to her, and then spent about an hour studying the table and taking mental notes. He'd never heard of many of these names—but he had heard of some of them.

The German, Walther Kurgan, for example. Geoff didn't like him, and there was no mystery there. Kurgan was a military man, who looked for former military personnel as slaves. His methods came right out of boot camp, or whatever boot camp was called in Germany, and he produced top-notch bodyguards and drivers, the types of slaves who would serve and protect your family. Or, simply the well-disciplined type who could run your house or business or your life with aplomb. Or even personal trainers! One of the presenters at Rothmere was one of Kurgan's former trainees, now a trainer on his own.

There were many more—Arturo Massimiliano, who trained slaves to be exquisite tops, becoming the dream mistresses and masters for their demanding, masochist owners. Geoff did that sort of training too, and was always reminding his trainers that there was no shame in being a bottom, and that the only shame was in being afraid to be who you were whenever you wanted to be. And the trainers would hide their snickers and grin with tolerant understanding, and Geoff would smile back at them with the slightest of winks.

And more! Did the Frenchwoman Corinne really only take slaves with a talent for six languages or more? Were there that many slaves, and was there a need for them that was so regular?

Everywhere you turned, there was an expert in a particular method or a type of slave—a couple whose work was primarily in novices, a man who would not even think of considering a slave without ten years in service. There were trainers who used their own spotters, trainers who did their own spotting, and trainers who only took slaves who were referred by owners.

Michael found himself overwhelmed by the variety and the scope of topics. He looked for American houses and was gratified to find a few, especially glad when he saw that some of them were heavily sought after by other attendees. But Geoff's were ignored. Sometimes, they were idly picked up and examined, but then put back down. One American trainer's work got snatched up, though.

Anderson. No first name. People whispered the name to each other and passed the folder on to friends. Before they were all gone, Michael slipped one of them into his briefcase and examined the schedule for the next round of seminars, so he could get a better feel for what was "out there."

By the end of the day, what seemed like a nice and kinky, mostly Californian way to handle matchmaking between sex-hungry bottoms and wealthy tops just vanished. It was much bigger, much older, and much more complicated than he could have ever imagined. And his place in it—favored student of Geoff Negel—was tinier than he had ever really wanted to know.

It was hard to even get into the swing of things—he would introduce himself and his accent would give him away. Someone nearby might whisper "Negel," or even worse, he'd see a spark in the eyes of the person he was speaking to suddenly fade, and then he'd be brushed off with polite civility.

He did try to attend a seminar and see if he could learn something new. But when Geoff or one of his trainers taught, they used slides, movies and live slaves to demonstrate things, the slaves always naked or in thongs or something, and they used humor and charts to liven things up.

Instead of all that, Michael found himself seated in the library with six other people, listening to an old man gently discuss—of all things—servants. Not slaves, but servants. Butlers, maids, and that sort of thing. It took a while for Michael to realize that the man was talking about slaves, and just using different language. He was explaining what it took to staff a full-sized manor house, back in older days and now, and how the hierarchy worked, and who reported to whom, and what their duties were... and Michael almost fell asleep. It was so damn dull he had to blink and shake his head over and over again to stay alert. Yet around him, the men and women were either nodding or taking notes. Notes? On what? Michael thought.

When the old guy finally got around to talking about training, Michael perked up a bit. They didn't do a lot of domestic service training at Geoff's, although all the slaves were expected to know the basic housekeeping chores, like making beds, loading dishwashers, laundry, that sort of thing. Why train all-purpose household cleaners if most of the owners would use their slaves for sex and light work anyway? But maybe domestic service might be a good sideline to go into.

Well, if it had been, Michael couldn't say by the end of that long day. Because instead of handing out lists and moving on to showing off some pretty girl in a French Maid's uniform and making her serve drinks or something, the guy just kept talking! And some of what he said just didn't make any sense at all. Training done by other slaves?

Michael fell asleep at last, and awoke as people were politely applauding. He sheepishly gathered up his stuff and tried to slip out, but the man who had run the seminar was near the door, where people were shaking his hand and chatting with him. Michael tried to look interested in the ornate, free standing model of the solar system in one corner of the room, waiting for people to clear out.

Finally it seemed that they were all gone, so he dashed to the door. But as he tried to work his way through the long corridor leading back to the central hallway, he stopped as he heard voices around the corner ahead of him.

"I've always thought of you as an evil queen, Dalton, but never a wicked witch," someone was saying softly, to masculine chuckles. "You certainly put that sleeping beauty down, now, didn't you?"

"You are incorrect, Evander; that was indeed an evil queen who cast a spell on Sleeping Beauty. And, I must note that had I some magical power over such lads, it would have been to my advantage to use it for more nefarious adventures, rather than to send them into slumber! In any event, I hardly think the topic was of interest to the poor boy." The second speaker, Dalton, seemed more amused than insulted, but Michael shrank away from the corner in horror. It was the man who had just presented on servants. There was no doubt who they were talking about. Michael knew he should just back away down the corridor and leave them to their private conversation, but his face burned and he stayed where he was.

"I agree," said the first man with another chuckle. "I think it might have been the first time he ever heard that actual labor might be associated with service. Such a shame for old Ward, isn't it? To have that American chap in his line. Bad enough to have him there—worse to have him here! Him and his nest of goslings, following him about. Three juniors, can you imagine? I would have bloody well liked to bring three, if I had them."

"The one you have introduced me to is quite sufficient," Dalton laughed. "Although I shudder to consider how many pages of notes you will have to examine later on."

"Her notes are quite remarkable, actually. I shall send you some of her writing, I think you will approve. I need to discuss her finishing with you anyway. Finishing!" The speaker laughed. "Oh, if only we could do a little finishing on some of Negel's lot! It would spare us some embarrassment later on, what? Damn shame. Listen, old man, we're all off to the pantry tonight for a brandy, shall we see you there?"

"At my age, I shall be astounded to find myself still breathing after hours, dear boy. But if life remains in me, I shall. Bring your remarkable girl. Save the comfortable seat by the fire for me, and tell Mr. Glin that I have requested it."

"Ta, then!"

Michael waited, head down, until he heard retreating footsteps. So, they didn't think much of Geoff, huh? He started to move for-

ward, his temper up. Bunch of snobs, all of them, with their high-
class accents and their fancy phrasing and their... Piercing light
blue eyes, wavy like the reflection of light over a shallow lake, and
staring into his own as he almost ran into the man named Dalton.

"Oh! I—I'm sorry," Michael stammered.

"No, please forgive me, I was clearly in your pathway," the
older man said, with a nod of his head. "My sincere apologies."

"No—no, it was my fault," Michael said, feeling another blush
coming up. Of all times for it! But it didn't help knowing that this
man had just been referring to him as "Sleeping Beauty." Being an
object of admiration was one thing—by a man old enough to be
his grandfather was something else! He swallowed and wondered
if he should apologize for falling asleep, make some excuse. But it
seemed to awkward to bring up, so instead, he said, "Um—nice
workshop. I enjoyed it. Really."

"Thank you, young man. I am gratified to hear that." The man
nodded gently again, and Michael could just feel that he was being
dismissed. This only served to get him angrier.

"You know," he said, before he even thought it through,
"we're not as bad as you think. We Americans. Geoff is a pretty
major trainer out in California." For a second, Michael wondered
whether he should have referred to Geoff as Mr. Negel—but Geoff
said that he hated that, so why put on airs to impress the natives?

"Undoubtedly he is," Dalton said easily. "But I assure you, no
one here has or shall cast aspersions upon all American trainers. We
are very pleased to have such strong ties with many of our American friends and fellow professionals."

"Well—good," Michael said. But he heard the careful phrasing.
This lecturer was not saying that they liked or respected Geoff—
only that there were some American trainers they did get along
with. He still felt angry—but how could he really show it to this
patient old man? Hell, with his deep eyes and high cheekbones,
pale skin over a high, domed and nearly hairless forehead, he
looked like some movie version of a butler or the headmaster of a
school for boys. And even though his tone of voice suggested dismissal, he didn't turn away, and Michael felt as though this was a

perfect chance to move beyond his gaffe—and to perhaps make a bigger move than he even imagined before flying to England.

"I'm actually interested in making some new connections," Michael said suddenly, trying to be cool about it. "I—I am really impressed with everything here. Like, you guys have been around forever. You must know—everything! And I could use some more, um, experience myself. With different methods, you know? Different traditions. So—er—who in the States do you think is—someone you'd have strong ties with?"

Dalton blinked for a moment, and Michael wondered what he did wrong. Betrayed Geoff? he asked himself. But I'm not doing anything! he argued back. I'm just asking!

"Perhaps Mr. Negel would be of greater assistance to you in this matter," the older man said gently. "I cannot seem to recall any particular names right now."

"What about Anderson?"

Dalton looked down and smiled for a moment, and then back up into Michael's eyes. "Oh, indeed," he said slowly. "I would say Master Trainer Anderson is quite a worthy individual. A splendid trainer. But young man—if I might be so bold—she is slightly out of your league at this time."

"She?" Michael echoed.

Dalton nodded, as though that answered everything. "Yes, my dear boy. I am afraid I must be going. Best of luck to you, and... perhaps you might consider getting a better rest tonight."

Well, forget about that! All through the formal dinner that night and all the way back into the village, Michael was stricken with dark thoughts about his future. When Brad woke the slaves up again and made them dash into his luggage for sex toys, Michael almost groaned out loud. He was in no mood to play! But desperate to keep from showing Geoff how disturbed he was, he did pick up a whip and really did a number on the male slave for Brad's enjoyment, while the master had one girl suck his cock and the other girl spread her legs for Crystal to fist. Geoff watched it all, happily proud of the tableau, and took one of the girls into his room with him when he was ready to turn in. Brad offered a choice of boy or girl for Mike and Crystal to share, but this time, Crystal admitted that she, too, was tired, and Brad went happily off with one of each sex, the way he liked it best.

And Michael stared at the ceiling, wishing that he could forget the look of pity that he'd seen in Dalton's water-blue eyes before the old man excused himself. The folder with Anderson's name on it was in his briefcase.

In the middle of the night, he crept out of his bed and into the kitchen to read from it. He thought, even as he forced his tired mind to make sense of the paragraphs, how come I never heard of her? How come I didn't even know she was a woman, for crying out loud? What is a Master Trainer?

What are you hiding from us, Geoff?

And, he felt guilty as hell.

Chapter Seven

If Michael had any single question about what exactly Anderson did with her clients, it would have been, "What can you do to improve perfection?" Because Anderson never took on a client who was inexperienced or untrained—in fact, her guidelines specified somewhat extensive training or years of experience in the collar before she would even agree to read a file. And slaves weren't static—every day in the collar made them better, sharper. Geoff always said, "Anything a trainer misses, time will provide." Of course, that wasn't always the case. A bad owner could easily ruin a good slave by not utilizing them, or by being capricious in their control. Brad's slaves were perfect examples of that. So, okay, maybe they weren't the polished personal slaves at Rothmere when they left Geoff's training house. But Brad did nothing to keep them sharp or improve them, so naturally they got lazy! That's what slaves were like!

But if attention was paid to the structure of a slave's life, and they were kept suitably busy, they would achieve a higher level of response in all things. Their service would sharpen, their sexual abilities would strengthen, and boom, you'd have one piece of prime material on your hands. It was conventional wisdom.

But how do you make them even better?

Simple, according to Anderson. Step one was to teach them how to learn.

The morning after Michael belatedly began his journal, Anderson finally took him in hand, introducing him to a session with Tara. At first, Michael thought it was going to be strictly observation—he had never interviewed Tara, and she was already almost finished with her training. But Anderson put him to work right away—and not next to her, either. Next to Tara.

The situation was sketched out for them both.

"You're assigned to clip all articles containing references to Italy," Anderson instructed, pointing to a pile of old newspapers and magazines. "They have to be attached to file cards and filed according to the topics in the folders. In the meantime, your owner is going to be wanting your services elsewhere. The exercise is to pass from task to task seamlessly, and to complete the assignment. To complicate matters, here is a new person who you have to instruct in filing." She pointed to Michael. "He is not a slave, so you must treat him with respect due your owner's paid staff."

"Yes, Trainer." Tara smiled at Michael and he nodded, somewhat confused about what exactly he had to do. Anderson had not given him separate instructions at all, only said to play along and fulfill his part.

"Okay—begin working." Anderson watched for a few seconds, and the left the room.

Tara carried the papers over to the table and began sorting. Michael took a few off the top and began scanning.

"Have you done this work before, sir?"

"Well, no not exactly." He sat down and waved a hand over the stacks of papers. "Why don't you show me how?" How absurd, to learn training by having a slave teach you something. But if that's what Anderson wants...

"First, we lay out the papers according to type, and then we go through them looking for articles," Tara said, continuing to work. "Anything having to do with the topic gets marked, and then laid aside. Everything else is immediately thrown away. The recycle bin is over there."

Michael nodded.

"Then, we cut out the articles and fill out the reference card for them. We can separate them first, or just file as we finish them. Both ways seem to take the same amount of time, at least in my experience. Is there anything else I can tell you, sir?"

Well, that was a better way of asking if he understood. "I don't think so," he replied. "You just show me how you're splitting the papers up, and I'll follow your lead."

"Thank you, sir." And she did—quickly and without any confusing directions. She would make a good manager, Michael reflected. She could organize a job and explain it well.

"What exactly will you be doing?" he asked after a few minutes of working in silence. "When you get home I mean."

"I will be the Judge's personal assistant and his accountant," she said.

"Oh yeah? I didn't realize you belonged to a Judge."

"Yes, sir." She smiled again, and he felt a slight jump of erotic pleasure that surprised him. This had been the first morning he hadn't thought of sex before anything else—it was a delayed reaction, no doubt.

"He is my third owner, sir," Tara continued. "His former assistant was Anderson-trained as well."

"So he's gotten used to having slaves with X-ray vision, I guess."

She blushed, that oh-so-charming reaction that made so many slaves a delight to play with. "As you say, sir."

They would have to start reading soon, which would cut down on Michael's opportunity to chat and flirt a little more. He leaned over the table, ignoring the papers. "Will you be his only slave?"

"No sir, he also has a security manager and chauffeur."

"A lucky man. Will he use you sexually?"

Another blush. "Yes sir, I believe he will. He has already."

"Oh yeah?" He looked her over, trying to see past the simple black dress. "When was the last time you were fucked?"

"Er—"

Well, finally! Something to trip her up. Michael grinned and hooked one leg over the table edge.

"That would be about six days ago, sir." She busied herself with finishing up the separations, and then turning away to get a pair of pens and two scissors.

"Six days!" Michael wondered who it was. Surely not Parker—but Anderson? He tried to imagine the cool, laid-back woman actually getting worked up and fucking. It was difficult.

"Who—"

The door banged open, and Anderson appeared again. "Find out who the fourth signatory was on the Declaration of Independence, and change the towels in the blue bathroom."

"Yes, Trainer," Tara said instantly. And with a nod to Michael, she headed out the door.

Michael waited until he could hear her footsteps on the stairs before speaking. "Listen, Trainer—is there anything I should know about what my part is here? It's okay for me to talk to her, isn't it?"

"Absolutely, Mike. I want you to talk to her. You can also make use of her in practical ways—you are an employee of her owner, and she is his slave. Flirt with her, touch her—she will be expected to tell you if you are requesting something she may not give. Also, remember that you're both responsible for finishing the task. I want you to study the way she manages her time and how she manages you."

"You got it." Well, that was understandable at least. He shuffled through a few papers and decided to wait until Tara got back to pick up the work again.

Tara returned in about three minutes and picked up the phone, dialing a long number.

"Who are you calling?"

"The New York Public Library, sir," she said, covering the mouthpiece. She listened for a while, and punched another number. While she was on hold, she picked up a scissors and began to cut articles out. Most industrious. After a while, she got to ask her question, wait some more, and then she picked up one of the pens and jotted a name down onto an index card.

"I didn't know you could do that," Michael commented.

"Oh, yes sir. Most central branches have a line to connect to researchers. Even the Library of Congress has one. Excuse me please, while I deliver this." She bounded out, and Michael whistled through his teeth. Well, how the hell else could you find out something like that, he wondered. If you had a big library, and it had a history section, how would you know where to look? You could waste time looking through several books before you found one that listed the signers in order.

A very important thing to know—how to find out what you don't know.

"Did you know about that service before you got here?" he asked her when she returned.

"There is a similar service in St. Louis, sir. I called the first week I was here to make sure I had the proper telephone numbers. It will be part of my job to do simple research, in order to save the paralegal for more important tasks."

"Now, how did you know I wanted to know that?"

She looked at him through demurely lowered eyelashes. "Forgive my presumption, sir—I thought you had intended to ask me about my service."

"I did. That's what's so amazing." He watched her trim the edges of the last article she cut out, and write a summary of the topic on the file card. Her handwriting was very neat. "I guess I'll get back to work here."

The next interruption came about a half hour later, with a request for two glasses of water to be taken upstairs to water a plant at the end of the hallway, and then returned to the kitchen. When Tara returned from that little errand, she was naked and barefoot. Another blush, this one a little more obvious than the first. Michael smiled, and knew why it seemed a little warmer in the house that morning.

"What's this about?" he asked teasingly.

"It is an order, sir," she said. "Do you—do you find it distracting?"

"Yeah, very. But not enough to change it. Come over here and show yourself—this is the first time I've seen you looking like a slave."

"Yes, sir!" Carefully, she made her way around the table to his side.

She showed her body to him. Raising her arms up behind her head showed off her small breasts and lifted their tight, pointy nipples up. What a delicious contrast to Joan's heavy, round globes! Her back straight, her legs parted, she was like a pale statue, not so much toned as she flowed like silk poured over a mannequin. And bent over—oh, yes, that perfect, heart-shaped ass. Her flesh showed some light bruising, especially right across the middle.

Michael whistled again and drew a finger across the bruises. Her flesh rippled where he touched, like waves of shivers—a nice effect. And she did the show postures very well, too. But that was to be expected. Not only were they the first moves taught to a Marketplace slave, but the procedure was originally choreographed by Anderson.

Geoff preferred a different set of movements—damn, he was doing it again! I have to stop comparing her to Geoff, Michael promised himself. I have to stop thinking about what used to be.

He straightened up and cupped Tara's rear in his hands. By touching her, he interrupted the smooth movements of the series of display postures. She stayed still, betraying her surprise with a little murmuring sound.

"Six days is a long time between screws, isn't it, Tara?"

"As you say, sir," she replied. Her voice sounded strange at that angle, muffled by her bent over posture, tense with the unfamiliarity of the situation. Michael grinned and smacked her on the left cheek, lightly.

"That's a good stock answer; it'll work with most guests and one-time users. Now, pretend I'm the Judge. Tell me the truth."

"Please sir, I am very satisfied with my use, sir!"

"So once every six days is good for you?"

"Yes, sir!"

He tapped her thighs a little more apart and slid one hand between her legs. Under a short layer of pubic hair—another change from what he was used to—she was soft, and a little wet, opening easily to his touch. He pinched one fold of her labia, kneading it in his fingers, and listened to the soft moans she made.

"Tell me who screwed you six days ago," he said, continuing to work her flesh.

"Please, sir, I'm forbidden to."

Damn! Well, there was no need to try and go further on that topic. If she was forbidden, then that was it—

But on the other hand, would an employee of her master know

that? He grinned and pulled her up by a fistful of hair. She gasped as her body came up next to his. He pressed his erection against her ass, letting her know what he was feeling, perhaps what he was thinking. With the hand that used to be on her sex, he reached around her to take hold of a nipple.

"You can tell me," he crooned, falling easily into a cajoling, seductive tone. He pulled her head back onto his shoulder, and looked down at her body, now taut against his. Her ass felt good against his groin, and he shifted her comfortably. "Come on, who took you to bed? Was is Parker? Does he have a great big dick?" He pinched the nipple, hard, and she arched her back just a little, not exactly fighting him, but reacting strongly just the same.

Oh, that was nice.

"Please, sir, I am not permitted to tell!"

Firm, but with respect. Also damn good. And what was that? Just a little wiggle in the butt, scraping against him, so distracting, so appeasing! Damn, she was good!

"Was it Anderson?" he whispered into her ear, stopping to nibble on the earlobe. He never let her go, only shifted her body against his. "Did you go down on her like a good girl? Did she finger you open, like I will?"

"I—I beg your pardon, sir—I may not answer those—those questions! Ah!"

That nipple turned out to be perfect for eliciting response. Just one sharp twist, and she stumbled over words. Good, something can shake up that Anderson-trained perfection. He turned her toward the table and bent her over the edge.

"Maybe you're right," he said drawing both hands across her ass again. "Maybe I shouldn't be asking. Maybe I should be doing." If she had been told not to do anything sexual with him, now would be the time to hear about it. Or, maybe he could just do an extended teasing thing. Spank her a little, maybe finger her. Get her hot. But leave the dick in the pants. Until he was absolutely sure he could take that liberty. That would be the safe way, he decided. "You're just a slave," he said out loud, caressing her boldly. "I can do this whenever I want to, can't I?

"Yes, sir, as you wish!" She gave a little moan as his fingers reached up between her legs again and casually invaded her. So, he could screw her! Fantastic! Damn—if only he had his training kit, with the stiff paddles and slender riding crops, the clamps and clips, the heavy gags and the body-filling plugs! But his instructions were to bring no fetish gear with him—and now, all he had on hand were his hands and maybe some binder clips in one of the desk drawers. No time for that. Not when there was this enticing butt right in front of him, with a cute cunt right underneath!

He swung his hands together and impacted on her flesh with a heavy smack that made her body inch up on the table. Her breath left her body all at once, and she cradled her head in her arms, little whimpers escaping.

"Come on, push that sweet butt out to me, that's it," Michael said, taking another swat. "This is what you're here for, isn't it?"

"Yes, sir!" She did as he instructed, rising up on her toes in order to push her rear toward him and his punishing hands. Watching as she tensed for another hard spank, Michael smiled and trailed his fingers across her flesh instead, curving down her buttocks to her thighs, where once again he prodded until she adjusted her position to spread them wider.

Well, this was a nice change from the coolly efficient bookkeeper image she normally presented! This was a slave—a nicely turned out, eager-for-pleasure-or-pain slave.

The trick was to keep her on the edge until just before Anderson returned, and then watch her as she collected herself and got back to work. Yeah, he thought, as he continued to fondle her. I can fuck her later. When I'm really, really sure I can. But maybe, in this role as an employee, I'd just try to get away with this light stuff.

He gasped as he realized the truth of that. Of course, as an employee, he wouldn't try to fuck his boss's girl! Especially if I knew that the boss fucked her! "This is a test for you, too," was more or less what Anderson had said. So even if Tara didn't tell him he couldn't... would he? As part of this role playing exercise? Snatching a glance at the wall clock, he stroked her again, trailing his fingers through her soft pubic hair, snaking his index finger gently along the slit. She moaned and pressed softly back.

"Okay!" he said loudly, pulling away. He smacked her ass hard and walked back to his place at the table. "Guess we should be getting back to work here!"

She gasped and the color deepened in her face. She waited until she rose to face him to say, softly, "Yes, sir. Thank you for calling my attention to duty, sir." Then, she carefully went back to her own spot and picked up her papers. She trembled slightly—but she didn't collapse into a chair or take great big gulping breaths. Instead, she marshaled her composure—took measured breaths and looked studiously attentive until she started to calm down. Then, she ran her fingers through her mussed hair to smooth it down.

Anderson arrived a minute later. Perfect timing. Michael congratulated himself on making the right choice.

The exercise ran most of the day, and it was a sweet torment for them both. By mid-afternoon, Michael was so horny he felt ready to explode, but the excitement, the sheer tension of concentrating on the mundane task, teasing Tara and playing time games with Anderson was so exhilarating that he didn't much care. The Trainer caught him several times, walking in while he had Tara bent over backward across the table, one hand at her cleft, the fingers of his other hand easing in and out of her pursed mouth. He coughed and let her go, but Anderson didn't make any comment. She just delivered her new task and left, Tara following her. And when Tara did return, there were warm, pink marks on her ass and shoulders. But still, she didn't make any official protest when Michael guided her onto his lap so he could play with her nipples.

Well, this was more like it! When Anderson came in at about 3:30, a clipboard in one hand, Michael was feeling pretty damn pleased with himself. He had played his role very well, and the opportunity to watch Tara at work was invaluable. He had been very good about holding himself back. Surely, this had marked the start of his real training.

"Time's up," Anderson announced as she entered. "Mike, you'd be fired, but Tara did fairly well."

He laughed. "I sure as hell wouldn't want me working for me!"

"Easily distracted," Anderson agreed. "Tara, get yourself cleaned up for the kitchen. Mike, you start working on your impressions of the exercise. I'll want to read them after dinner."

"After dinner, right." Belatedly he stood, cursing to himself after she left. Damn, how was he going to remember to do that? Well, he had bigger problems to deal with. His first homework assignment. Geoff hadn't been real big on written reports, but he audio and video taped everything.

Shit, there I go again, he thought, pushing the leftovers from the day's task to one side. I can't help but think of how we used to do things. It would be easier to be able to switch the camera on and talk about what he'd seen, describe Tara's actions and responses with his hands and body moving, to communicate with grins and raised eyebrows and all that body language that was so important to Geoff. Body language—it was another central idea about training, another key toward control and behavior. It could reveal so much more than words could—but it could mislead, too.

He picked up a yellow legal pad and wrote the date and time at the top of the first page. The last time he had filed a report on a slave had been the worst; it was hard to get it out of his mind.

And Parker knew about it. Fuck and double fuck.

CHAPTER EIGHT

Two years with Geoff, living, thinking and breathing slavery. But it wasn't his entire life—the Marketplace, that is. There was still what he liked to call the secular SM world out there, the places where people who didn't live it all the time went to hang out and share experiences and good times. On a planned weekend away from work he had gone to Leather Forever, a three-day conference put on by the International SM Activist Organization, the group people called "Is-Mao," like a bad old Communist joke. God, what fun it was, to go and wander among all the people who were inches away from folks who were actually living a lifestyle that most of them dared not dream of.

Not that many of them would want it, he had found out. Hell, kinky sex was easy enough to manage! You found out what you were into, found a group of local people into the same thing, and dated around until you found the partner who best suited your fetish or paraphilia. You did the couple thing, sleeping together, living together, getting married if you were het, maybe doing the domestic partnership thing if you weren't. You had the box of toys under your bed or in the closet or the chiffonier, or maybe you set up the second bedroom or the basement with over-designed wooden crosses and frames. You bought the jacket, the keychain, the deerskin whips, and the Japanese nipple clamps, and you purchased white plumbers candles and lengths of rope and chain.

But in the meantime, you still had that job to go to, and that family that needed attention. You still watered the lawn or went to the shareholders meeting, paid the bills, played softball or pool, or watched Monday Night Football. No matter who was on the bottom when you pulled out the toys and played, you still watched TV, had your favorite shows, went to movies, or to do some bowling, or ballroom dancing. You had fights over family, money, the kids or lack of kids. You kissed and made up. You had nice, gentle sex on Saturday mornings. You planned vacations. You lived a real life— and had a secret pastime your neighbors didn't need to know about. If you were really an exhibitionist, you went on television talk shows.

Who would want to screw something up like that? It was better than what a lot of people had. At least you had a context for those feelings of control or lack thereof. You could get away from the boss by tying up the spouse. Forget the economy while you're tickling your lover's ribs with a silky whip. Lose yourself in a cocoon of Saran Wrap; much better than the bubble bath women's magazines were always suggesting as the cure-all for stress.

And, if you were devoted enough, you'd buy more clothes and toys and take off every once in a while for one of these weekend events, where you could mingle with a few hundred other perverts in leather, show off your play style or learn new ones and go home, secure in the knowledge that you were not alone. Hell, you were in the forefront of the sexual outlaw movement—if there could honestly be such a thing.

Marketplace people either loathed or loved such affairs; there was rarely a middle ground. Some had come out of that very world, pushing their love and lifestyle faster and harder until someone spotted them and tested them and brought them into the fold when the time was right. Some had never known that world, raised in the ultra-rarefied world of those born to the Marketplace, raised in households that had owned slaves, or, like Joan, raised by slaves themselves, always aware of the opportunity to serve or be served. But regardless of their background, Marketplace people knew one major caveat about what was sometimes called the Soft World—it could be highly dangerous.

Not to one's physical safety, but to the Marketplace itself. Lose your sense of caution with the wrong people, and you could have an explosive situation on your hands. It was absolutely necessary that the Marketplace be considered mythical for it to survive. People who carried over-romanticized ideals about the potential quality of outsiders were always warned away from trying to act as spotters. Leave that to the professionals, was the constant advice. Spotters spend years sifting, they know what to ask, what to do, what reactions to look for. So don't ever invite a stranger to partake, don't volunteer information unless you've had years of experience, seen, heard and met many Marketplace folk and can know the feel of one.

This seemed reasonable, and Michael had followed the generally accepted rules about confidentiality. To gain access to the soft world, he joined some local SM and leather organizations, presenting himself as a mostly heterosexual topman, a master. It was so tempting to play with the women he met, to romance them, knowing that he could take them home and make them really know what a master was like—but he didn't. Geoff was proud of his self-restraint.

"A trainer has to be aware of their temptations and be able to know when to indulge and when to resist," he would say, patting Michael reassuringly on the back. "It's great that you can have a good time at these events—and they'll help you a lot, especially when we're dealing with clients who come out of that tradition."

That was Geoff, all the way—he could always find something encouraging to say.

So, there he was, resplendent in his leather jeans, his black shirt and the leather vest, little colorful cloisonné pins showing off where he'd been and who had given him a token of their esteem. He was looking forward to the panel discussions, the demonstrations, and especially the dealer's room, where he was bound to find some new toy to bring back and show off. Geoff had recently presented him with the designer leather bag he gave all of his trainers when they reached a certain level of ability, and Michael was eager to fill it with fancy toys of all sorts. He'd already gotten some real beauties in terms of whips, but felt he could use a nice wooden paddle, a riding crop or two, a big, fat, ball gag, and maybe one of those bullwhips, too. One as long as he was tall, perhaps, in gleaming black. He already knew where to learn how to use one—Geoff had an expert come by once in a while to teach all the trainers.

As he scanned the hotel lobby, there was a sense of almost juvenile excitement in the air, a camaraderie of souls, if not lifestyles. Leathermen swaggered by, denim-covered asses and crotches squeezed into erotic packages by skin-tight leather chaps. Dykes in vaguely imitation mode swung their hips and jangled with dangling keys and spiky haircuts. Heterosexual couples walked in arm in arm only to show up later with one half wearing a collar and the other half holding a leash. Furtive single men and searching women dotted the fringes, casting lingering gazes over each other, gauging orientation, tastes, expertise.

A playground for perverts. Michael wanted to hug himself with delight. He could spot the Marketplace people he knew instantly, but never even suggested that he recognized them, nor did they acknowledge him. It was no loss—he could socialize with them anytime! This was a weekend for strange faces and a few laughs.

"What do you think?" he asked the vendor, twisting to catch his reflection in the angled mirror.

"Oh, it's you," exclaimed the heavyset, bearded man, his voice strangely gentle and soft. "Really sets off those amazing eyes."

And it did, too. The chrome band on the brim of the cap settled neatly over the bridge of his nose, and the triangular segments of blue were even more arresting than usual. Yeah, black everywhere, down to that heavy ring around the blue, and then these bright orbs, staring right back at you...

"I'll take it."

"Great! That'll be eighty dollars."

Michael snorted. Eighty dollars for a fucking hat! Oh well. Training didn't pay much, but it did include room and board, so he could splurge once in a while. If he didn't get any new toys this time around, he'd come out under budget. And maybe Uncle Niall might be counted on for a bullwhip at Christmas. He paid the money and turned back to the room, now confident that he would turn every head there or die trying.

"That's a great cover, sir," came another astonishingly high and sweet-sounding voice from next to him. He turned, prepared to flirt, and found himself looking down into a pair of eyes as eager as his own, surrounded by masses of light brown curls. She was almost a full head shorter than he was, and round-bodied, a full, sensuous chest that spoke of delightfully pillowy breasts, and a bottom that was made for spanking. His heart leapt in time with his dick—here was tonight's entertainment for sure!

"That was very bold of you," he said with a smile.

She smiled back and sweetly lowered her eyes. Nope, no chain or bulky leather collar around her neck. He glanced down toward her hands, but couldn't spot the flash of a ring, either. "I'm Mike."

"Karen," she said, extending her hand. He kept the smile in place, amused at the gesture, but shook her hand firmly.

"Pleased to meet you, Karen, and I'm glad you like the hat. Would you be looking for company by any chance?"

Her smile broadened. "You read my mind!"

It was easy to read Karen's mind. It was even easier to get her entire life story from her, accomplished in less than two hours of casual shopping. It was a simple tale—native Californian, middle class, bright kid, college, steady job, old boyfriend not into kinky sex, and a small local SM organization where she volunteered her time as a secretary and the publisher of a newsletter called The Flogger. She wrote sexy stories too, for a local computer bulletin board. This was her vacation money—last year, she had gone to Aruba for a week with the old boyfriend. This year, she was having a good time with her kinky friends, hoping to find a new boyfriend.

It was also absurdly easy to get her to bed. Hell, it was easy to do everything with her—she was fun and cute and direct and open—just the kind of girl Michael liked in and out of the leather-set. And what's more, she was kind of bold—not only in her way of introducing herself to him, but in the way she responded to his sex play.

Michael took her to the dungeon party that night, after having her describe all the clothing she had brought with her and telling her what to wear. He spent another few bucks on a black lace thong in the dealer's room, holding it up against her body and chatting with the saleswoman behind the table as Karen blushed and looked embarrassed. But she didn't walk away, or protest. And when he tucked the new purchase into the front of her jeans—"to keep it warm"—she put her hands behind her back and didn't try to stop him from so publicly groping her.

It was a very promising beginning.

She looked sweet in the thong, her high-heeled boots, a bra, and her little leather club vest with all the pins on it. He wanted to put a collar on her, too. All slaves, even brand new trainees, were collared the minute they entered training or stepped into Geoff's house. But even though he knew that she wasn't a trainee and wouldn't know what the collar meant to him... it would somehow be wrong.

Still, he couldn't ignore the nagging feeling that a collar would look natural on her. The ten minutes they spent as she outlined the things she was not willing or interested in doing hammered home a strange sense of near guilt. There's nothing wrong with what I'm doing, he told himself. I'm playing! I'm allowed to play! But he had to struggle to keep from grabbing her by the hair and forcing her to her knees and telling her what he was going to do and giving her a nice slap if she tried to talk back to him. He just knew she'd love it.

But he was only there to play.

He taught her how to follow him, one step behind on his left, and walked slowly around the converted warehouse that was the playspace for Leather Forever. It had been divided into rough sections with hung tarps and strategically placed pieces of equipment like standing crosses and stocks and spanking benches and cages. He avoided the curtained-off corner for medical play and piercings—not only wasn't she ready for anything like that, but he had no idea what he would do once they got in. No, he had everything he needed in his training kit.

When he sensed that she was getting bored, he reached casually over to her and pulled her breasts free of the bra, exposing her. Her face colored, but she didn't object and he turned away and kept walking, trying to hide his grin of satisfaction. He hoped that someone would ask if they could touch her—it would be great to be able to say "sure" and keep walking! But no one did, although more than one man looked up and grinned as they passed.

He watched a few scenes, controlling his impatience to get his hands on her body. He needed to know how she would behave. Once, during an especially hot girl-on-girl waxing scene, he pulled Karen over to him and fondled her nipples. As the wax piled up and the girl receiving it moaned and arched her back, he pinched Karen's nipples harder and harder, until her moans rivaled the moans coming from the other girl. It was nice. He watched as colored wax dribbled down the girl's breasts and across her full, round belly and thighs, and wished that she were prettier. But then, he grinned and glanced at Karen. What did it matter if the waxed lady wasn't hot? He had a hot little babe of his own. He clamped her tender nipples and dragged her through the dungeon by the connecting chain, a slight smile remaining on his face.

Finally, he found the place he'd been looking for, a nice, sturdy X-shaped cross with chain attachments for bondage. He had his own cuffs, of course, heavy duty leather cuffs lined with sheepskin. He put them on her, checking them for security, stretching her arms over her body until she stood on her toes for him. She whimpered as he laid out his array of handsome floggers—the big, black leather one, the long and skinny one of narrow suede tresses, the braided deerskin in bright red. Before he secured her to the cross, naked except for the cuffs and that little thong, he removed the nipple clamps and made her thank him.

When she did, her voice a whisper, he felt his cock stiffen in the way it almost never did in these situations. She's worth it, he thought. She's close to what we play with every day! Maybe I can be a spotter after all! I picked the best one here!

But the proof would be in the playing. He teased her first, draping the tresses over her shoulders and down her back, letting them slide down her hips and thighs. She moaned and twisted her body to meet the gentle rushes of leather, even wiggling her ass a little when he slapped it lightly with the deerskin.

"Show me what a good girl you can be," he said, drawing it

back. The first strike landed squarely on one shoulder blade, and he loved the sound of it, snapping and sharp. She gasped and her head flew back. "Oh, yes!" she cried out, and he grinned. Geoff believed that slaves should be as verbal as possible.

It was easy to fall into a natural rhythm beating her—and he did for a while. He covered her back until it was pink, and then switched to the narrower whip to actually make some stripes. She didn't disappoint him—in fact, she seemed to like this even better. She writhed and threw herself back into the falling tresses, her body twisting to catch them, as if she were eager to be striped. When he started to really sweat, he stopped long enough to take off his shirt and put just his vest back on. The smooth leather felt good against his naked back. He came up behind her and pressed his body into hers, feeling the warmth of her skin against his chest and stomach. His erection pressed into her ass, and she moaned and pushed back.

"Oh, God, sir, please, please, yes, touch me, kiss me, hold me, please!" she panted. He leaned around her, covering her body with his, wrapping his hands around her breasts as she ground her ass against him. She was ready for it, even if her pre-play negotiation said that she would want to be asked before he fucked her. Oh, she was more than ready, he thought, biting her neck as he rubbed himself against her even harder. I bet you regret thinking that you might say no to anything, he thought with savage amusement.

Time to make her regret it even more! He pulled out the nipple clamps again and re-attached them. She groaned and whimpered, but didn't try to stop him. Then he picked up his heaviest whip and started really working her over.

When he had started all of this, it was hard for him to really hit the girls. A little spanking, sure. But use a heavy whip on one? Even canes seemed too harsh for their delicate bodies and skin.

But Geoff had laughed at him and his concerns. "Oh, don't be so sexist," he said, clapping Michael on the back. "Women have proven over and over again that they far surpass we mere males in pain tolerance, Mike! And these women want you to hit them. You're not bullying them, Mike, you're giving them what they crave. Hell, they could take more than most of the boys we'll ever see! You'll find out."

And boy, did he! There was always a guy or two who liked a good thumping, liked an array of bruises or stripes to carry for a few days. But some of the slave girls he'd played with truly defined the term "pain slut."

So now, he wasn't afraid to pull his arm way back and let fly with this fat bundle of black tresses, even when her body hit the cross and she lost a bit of breath. He laughed as he gave her a few seconds to gather and brace herself. "Remember—be a good girl!" he warned. He hoped that wanting to impress him might keep her from using the "safe word" which would make him stop the scene. Nothing made him lose interest more than some bottom whining out a code word to make him stop playing, walk over to ask what's wrong, et cetera.

But he didn't have to worry on that account. Far from fighting him or starting to whine or cry, Karen braced herself eagerly for it, twisting her body from side to side as he thumped her over and over again. She sighed and groaned and whimpered sometimes, but she loved it, every second of it, as his arm grew sore and sweat dripped down his chest and back.

He paused to take a drink himself, wiping his mouth with the back of his hand, and took an extra long draft and pulled her head back by the hair. Covering her mouth with his, he fed her water, a hot move much favored in Geoff's training house. What was more primal than feeding and watering a slave in this intimate way? He let her go with a grin and walked back to his whips to change to the narrow-tressed one again, and as he did, he caught sight of one of Geoff's regular spotters, who was in the small group of spectators who had ringed this little corner of the dungeon. The man's eyes flew open wider, and he grinned back at Mike with a "thumbs up" gesture, and Mike felt like there was nothing he could do wrong.

It was turning out to be a better weekend than he expected.

Back in his hotel room, he did grab her by the hair as he pulled her into the middle of the floor. "I bet you want to be fucked," he said, popping the button of his leather jeans.

"Oh, God, yes, yes, sir, please!" she begged, from her knees. Her eyes were wide, her back and legs all red and striped, and he knew her nipples were so sore that a gentle touch would make her flinch.

"But you didn't think you would," he said teasingly. "You wanted to make me ask for it, didn't you? Wanted to make me beg to fuck your hot sweaty body, hmmm?"

"I—I was just trying to go slow," she insisted, with the slightest of whimpers. "It's only common sense... I don't usually... I mean, I never..."

"Don't usually fuck on the first date?" he asked, taking a seat. "Well, that's okay. You can go now."

Her mouth dropped open in shock, and she blushed. "But—but—I want to with you!"

"Then apologize for thinking that you wouldn't," Michael said, feeling his cock swelling at the sight of her despair. "Tell me how sorry you are for not saying I could fuck you any way I wanted to."

"But that's what they say you should do," she said with a look of confusion. "Hardly anyone I know has sex the first time they play with someone. I mean, we never even discussed safe sex!"

Michael reached into his bag and pulled out the silver box that held his safe sex supplies. He tossed a condom and a little tube of lube onto the floor between them. "Next question?" he said. "I'm still waiting for that apology."

Karen looked up at him, and then her eyes scanned down to his crotch and lingered, and then flitted to the condom on the floor in front of her. She looked back up, and her lips parted. Her face was still red, and she closed her eyes as she whispered, "I'm sorry, sir."

"Tell me how much you want it," Michael sneered. "And call me master, slut."

"Yes! Yes, master! Please... oh, God, I need to get fucked so bad," she whimpered. "Please, master, fuck me!"

His cock grew harder. "Tell me how much you want my cock," he said, unfastening the fly of his jeans. The chilled air of the room touched his cock as it jutted from the fly, but that did nothing to lessen the erection.

"Oh! Yes, yes, I want that cock in me, please," she murmured, moving forward on her knees. She picked up the condom and offered it to him like a sacrifice. "Oh, please, master, fuck me, I want it so bad!"

"Kiss my boots like a good little slave bitch," he said, taking the condom from her hands. "Lick them and make me believe you'll take my cock wherever I want to put it!"

He could feel her mouth as she pressed frantic kisses to his boots, and he took his cock in one hand as she abased herself. Oh, yes, that was more like it! No longer was she the independent, negotiating bottom who could tell him what to do, but his own personal cock-slave, begging for a taste, begging to be used.

He made her lie on her back and spread her legs wide, opening her pussy lips for him. Then he changed his mind and had her present to him doggy style, her ass up in the air, head down to the floor. Finally, he had her lie on her back on the table, holding her own ankles as she displayed herself in the lewdest position he could come up with, and he stood between her legs and thrust in with one hard slam.

By the time he had eased the condom down over his cock, he was far too aroused to have a nice, long fuck. He used her quickly and roughly, and wasn't surprised when she came as fast as he did. She was sweet and dripping wet, and when he called her his slut, she responded by bucking up against him and drawing him in so tight that there was nothing else to do but shoot.

He didn't put her on the floor, as he would have done with a proper slave, but cuddled with her in bed, an interesting change of pace for him. In the morning, she jumped out of bed when the room service came, and served him without being told to, even waiting for him to invite her before perching on the edge of the bed to devour some toast and coffee.

"So where did you learn your manners?" he asked over orange juice.

"Self taught," she boasted, tossing her hair back. "That's all I could do, since I haven't found a man who can really master me."

"Oh?" He laughed and stretched. "That's news to me!"

"Does that mean you want to be my real master?" she asked. Suddenly, there was a serious note in her voice, and Michael paused and bit back the quick agreement that was on his lips. It was almost funny how she said "real" like that. How little she knew how real it could be!

But she was soft world! He couldn't—shouldn't—say anything.

"Well—" he started to say.

She brought one finger up to her lips and made a "shushing" sound. "It's okay," she said, her smile just touched by sadness. "I know, it's too early to make any decision about that, we hardly know each other, you're married, or gay, or both, and besides, you couldn't possibly give up training for the Olympic rowing team or something."

"And you overcompensate," he drawled.

She sighed. "Yes, I guess I do. I'm sorry. But I also know that this is a weekend conference, and not the time to do anything but have fun. Wanna stay with me today, or play the field?"

He marveled at her composure. Damn, he thought, reaching out to caress those shining curls. She's Marketplace material, or I'll eat my brand new eighty-buck cap. Even the spotter last night had been watching them play, surely that was a positive sign that she was something special! "Let's see what's on the schedule for today," he said.

She made it easy for him. She gave him a very nice blow job in the shower, while the hot water ran down his back, and didn't even look humiliated when he deliberately came in her face and then shoved her under the water. No, she loved it! A natural slave, for sure!

His eyes wandered during the day, as they always did. But as they sat together in the back rows of the conference rooms set up for discussions about how to use medical devices as torment producers and how people used a family metaphor in order to structure their sex and power issues, he found it pleasant to wrap an arm around her, to play with her hair or tease her during moments of great seriousness and get her to laugh. It was also enjoyable to watch her use these self-taught skills on him—fading gently into the background when his attention was on something or someone else, jumping up before he did and waiting until he was seated to sit down herself, opening doors—for such a supposed novice, she had all the right instincts. Yeah, her timing was off, and she didn't catch all the nuances, but she was pretty damn good. Hell, Geoff had accepted trainees who had less of a feel for the art than she did.

He fucked her again at lunch time, this time in the ass. He made her hold her cheeks open for him, the hotel television tuned to the pay-for-porn channel, and he fucked her a good long time while watching better-looking women cavort on the screen. Again, she didn't turn on him and look uncomfortable or hateful at this sort of use, only profoundly humiliated—and massively turned on.

More and more perfect!

He took her to dinner in the hotel restaurant that night, and ordered for her. She finally looked a little put out, but bit her lip and smiled anyway.

"Well, that's very dominant," she said after the waiter had gone. "But what if I had dietary restrictions? What if I was a vegetarian?"

"Then you would have said, 'I'm sorry, sir, but I'm allergic to radishes, or my religion forbids me to eat shellfish,'" Michael responded. It was the standard way slaves were coached to respond to situations like that. It was out of his mouth before he realized it, and he felt a flash of doubt. Should he have said that? Hell, what did it matter? It was only one thing, and not that important anyway.

"Why would I be sorry?" she asked.

"Because you neglected to tell me that important part of your life, taking away from me the opportunity to do the right thing by you."

She nodded. "You mean, it's part of the negotiation."

"No! I mean it's part of the contract. You reveal everything, so that I can always know what to do."

"Isn't it a little too early for a contract?" She giggled and drank some ice water—he hadn't ordered her any wine. He snickered a little too—one of the seminars that day had been on slave contracts. The central part of the presentation had a one page contract which involved signing over one's soul, with the proviso that emotional harm to the slave may sever the contract at any time. "But does the master get to keep the soul?" Michael had whispered to Karen.

"Oh, definitely too early for the kinds of contracts we heard today," he said. "What I mean was the contract that takes place between the—the dominant and the submissive." He had been about to say "owner and owned" but decided that it sounded too Marketplace. It was no big deal to use the popular vernacular, though. It was pretty common in Geoff's place. "It's not so much a written contract, but a social one. But it's always conditional—the dominant can't be depended on to make the right decisions without all the information on hand. That's why the submissive has to be honest, and tell their dominant everything."

"You sound like you've been doing this for a while," she said softly.

"Oh yeah!" He leaned back in the chair, throwing one arm across the back. "You can say it's my life."

"That's great. I wish it could be my life." The waiter brought over the appetizer and Michael didn't follow up on that obvious invitation. He heard the inner voice cautioning him—you never discuss Marketplace business with strangers, and never in an open area where you might be overheard. You do not approach soft-world people and tell them about the Marketplace, not without a lengthy spotting process. But he was already planning to pack his training kit with everything he'd brought with him and take Karen to the play party that night, to tie her up somewhere very visible and make her scream for pleasure. Maybe share her with someone, if he could find someone he could trust—that was always a good test. And, if she still responded well, to take her back to his room and this time, use her for a good long time and put her on the floor, where real slaves belonged.

He also began to wonder what Geoff would think of her.

Chapter Nine

The days began to pass with some sense of order, at last. Every day now, Michael woke up to hours of work with Anderson and Tara, observing and helping the Trainer out, doing everything from basic role-playing to actually acting as her assistant. This was more like it—in the hands of the Trainer of Trainers, he was finally getting some instruction.

Not that it was formal or anything. She never really talked to him about "this is the way to do things." Instead, she merely did whatever she was doing with Tara, and gave him the briefest of instructions concerning what he was supposed to do. But she insisted that he keep exhaustive notes, very occasionally asking for the journal and scanning a page at random. Then, she would return his handwritten pages to him with a request for more commentary and more details, always more details.

But he was working with her at last. And what was more, he had plenty of chances to interact with Tara, the best trained and best looking slave in the house.

Tara was there to brush up on her anticipatory skills—the priceless ability of a slave to know what an owner would want and when, and deliver it on time and with as little fuss as possible. Sometimes, it was as obvious as knowing how long it took before someone's coffee cup would need to be refilled. Michael found himself counting drinks on different days, noting that Chris took coffee more or less all day long as his preferred beverage, and damn if there wasn't always a pot on. Cups seemed to follow him around the house, too, replaced—usually—when he wasn't looking. But when Tara served at the table, she learned that Mike rarely drank more than one cup himself, and he never found that he had to shake his head at her to refuse a refill.

It was how she knew when to give him more that was a real puzzlement.

Anderson gave him a look at a typed-up report on eating and drinking behaviors, and he found himself reading it with his mouth open in astonishment. It included descriptions of an assortment of dining styles ranging from fast food to formal dinners, and the amount of time people spent in each environment. It compared dinners in restaurants to private clubs to homes. Then, it continued to detail things like how patrons caught waiters' attention in different countries, which verbal and hand motion cues were used for things like simply summoning someone, and how to ask for something in sign language.

"All this?" he'd said, flipping through the hundred and forty pages. "To figure out that people spend more time at the table at home than at McDonalds?"

"No—all that to show the difference between laying your napkin on the chair and laying it on the side of the plate. Or, between tasting something and never returning to it and eating delicately of all the things offered. Between putting your mug back close at hand, or further away from the table edge. Pay attention, Michael. These are the things Tara has studied—and Joan too, in case she is given the task of serving at the table one day. Somewhere in here are the clues to why they will know that you didn't like the jerked chicken we had last night." She raised an eyebrow at him and he grinned.

"I thought I hid that pretty well," he admitted. "I mean, I'm sure it was great. But too spicy for me."

"Didn't think it had much zip myself," the Trainer said with a shrug. "Vicente barely used the real hot stuff I keep on hand. But Tara noticed you. Your reaction to it was right out of this. Read it and summarize, please."

Oh, well. But then, he reminded himself, it was what he had wished for when he got there—clear instructions on what to read and what to do. But it wasn't exciting to read reports on people's eating habits. Why not just say, "If you don't keep an eye on things and bring stuff at the right time, you'll be punished!" At least then, you got to smack them around if they didn't get the fucking slippers to you or whatever. You needed excuses to play with slaves, right? Otherwise, they'd get sloppy.

But—apparently not. Tara didn't seem to like it when Chris was asked to punish her physically—and it was always Chris who did it as far as Michael could tell. Sometimes, it was over something small—a second of hesitation, a mislaid item like a pen or a comb. Ten swats with that heavy leather strap of his, and then back to work, not a thing said except for "thank you and I won't do it again," all recited to some neat formula that Michael hadn't uncovered in his reading yet but was piecing together from hearing the slaves say it.

But that was when Chris noticed something wrong. Most of the time when Anderson noted an imperfection, she'd just have the slaves do it again. And again. And again. She wasn't kidding when she'd said that only slaves got do-overs in her house! No matter how silly it looked or how much time it took, she would back the slave up and start them all over, whether it was in something like carrying a tray or polishing a piece of silver or kneeling a certain way or even answering an imaginary caller—a role Michael played several times. A raised eyebrow or a disappointed look or even that rare sharp gaze that Michael felt more often than he suspected the slaves did—and both girls would look about ready to throw themselves on the nearest sword in shame.

And if the Trainer sighed and called for Chris—that was when the slaves would drop to their knees and beg for forgiveness or mercy, even if it was just the same kind of strapping they'd get from the man for doing the same mistake.

It was confusing to no end! What made it different when Anderson made that move to call in her surrogate? Was it the degree of the error? And why was that the trigger for permission to beg for mercy? And what element made Anderson choose to grant it or refuse it? Because she did actually seem to consider it a genuine request—her responses were never an automatic yes or no. Michael had always thought of begging for mercy as just some of the more organized ways that slaves could make noise while you were using or punishing them. But Anderson actually considered it—looked at the client and thought about it, and delivered her verdict, freeing them from the approaching short man with his strap, or sending them off to take their medicine.

It was all just plain weird! As far as he could tell, the Trainer only touched the clients to correct a posture or in praise. She certainly didn't grope them or stroke them to arousal, or casually tweak delicate or sensitive parts of their bodies. Parker did, occasionally—but always in a quiet and subtle way, looking into their eyes until they blushed or squirmed, or even touching them while his attention was elsewhere.

But neither Anderson nor Parker ever seemed to take the girls to bed, as far as he could tell. Yes, Tara did tell him that she had been fucked. But since that day, he had realized that from time to time, Anderson received callers and saw them privately. Then, she would either summon a client into her office while her visitor was there, or allow the visitor to go off in private with a slave for a period of time.

Some of these people were other trainers, he was sure. He was rarely, if ever, introduced to them with more than a name and a handshake. But if they were taking the girls off to the slave bedroom at the back of the house and beating and screwing them, there sure wasn't any evidence of it. No one ever explained what it was all about, and he never gathered up the courage to ask. Somehow, he thought that someone should just tell him.

And of course all this wondering and speculating did nothing to keep his horniness in check. If they thought that a good trainer had to be celibate, man, did they have the wrong guy! He couldn't figure out why the hell Anderson would not be using her own trainees—how else could you know how good they were? What they needed to learn? Even if Joan wasn't always going to be used purely like a sex slave in her new position, it's possible she might be sometimes! What if some chubby-chaser guest of her master wanted to lift her skirts and asked to borrow her? Wouldn't it make sense to make sure she knew how to show a guy a good time?

And they knew that Tara would be sexually used by her master, so why keep her from pleasuring at least one of the two men here? Hell, whether Chris was gay or not, surely he wouldn't object to getting a blowjob every now and then. And as much as the prospect of sharing her with Chris made him itchy, sharing would be better than getting nothing. But if Chris really was fucking her on the side, it certainly wasn't for long periods of time or showy extended erotic torture sessions; the man was too damn busy! When he wasn't writing or researching, he was out running errands, or working with one or both of the girls, or even helping Vicente in the kitchen from time to time. Anderson occasionally curled up in her big chair with a book and a slice of cake and hot tea, but if Parker did anything close to relaxing and having a good time, it sure wasn't in view of any of the people in this house.

In fact, Michael himself had little time to establish a social life outside the house, not with all this reading and summarization. He jerked off more than he did when he was a kid, before he discovered that girls would lie down for him and guys would kneel. And he felt about as displeased with the situation as he had been then.

But finally, Anderson began to use him as more than the persistent caller who wanted to know why the master hadn't returned his calls, or the annoying employee or staff member who harassed the hard-working slave. He got to do things like follow Tara as she moved through the house for an entire day, shadowing her, learning everything she needed to know, everything she did, timing her, watching but never helping or interfering. That was an astonishing day by itself—the sheer volume of information she had about the few people in residence seemed amazing, and the way she immediately prioritized and moved forward on things was just... neat. He couldn't imagine being able to look at the big picture so quickly and know when it was time to set aside the financial paperwork to pick up a package at the post office and then return in time to help prepare and serve lunch, finish the paperwork, stopping only for a basic review of some of the rules of pool—which her owner apparently enjoyed—and then managing to finish the work schedule by the end of the day without a towel misplaced, a scrap of envelope on the floor, or a clatter of dishes.

The more contact he had with her, the more liberty he was given to touch her. He always made damn sure he knew explicitly what he could do, and stayed well within his limits, no matter how much his cock ached. Sure, a little teasing here, a spanking there, maybe a little hair pulling and nipple twisting—but he never took his dick out or did more than press it against her.

Then, one morning, Anderson was very clear. "From now on, think of Tara as a general-purpose slave," she instructed. Tara, her face composed, took this as calmly as a direction to use her as an assistant in a law library. But Michael felt both a shiver of delight at the more-than-welcome permission to act on these so vigorously controlled feelings. He nodded, trying not to appear too eager.

"I want to know exactly how she responds—and I want to see what her trainer would write, not what a young, healthy sex partner would write. It's up to you what you do—Tara will tell you if you request something that her owner has forbidden. Interviewing time must be taken into account, though, so don't be piggy, bucko. I'm going to cut down just a little bit on her chore time in order to make her more available to you, and Joan will be working more with Vicente in the kitchen and on the books. You do not have to do anything more sexual than what you have already done; I am more than willing to hear about how you might explore any possible use within reason. But you do not need to ask my permission anymore." Anderson, dressed that morning in a long black broomstick skirt, checked her watch as she made the appropriate notations on the daily schedules and gave the top sheet to Michael. "Any questions?" she asked after he had a moment to scan it.

"Nope—all clear," he replied cheerfully.

"Good. Then let's make ourselves useful." She left as usual, with no particular warnings or encouragement.

He turned to Tara and grinned. "Where are the condoms?" was his first question.

"Upstairs, sir," she answered softly. "May I get one for you?"

"No—but you can get me—oh—six. Lubricated and unlubed, okay?" It was such an effort to keep his tone even, his body posture relaxed. Finally! He was singing inside. Finally, we're going to have a normal slave household here. He did pump one fist into the air after she'd gone. He went out into the hallway to watch her ascend the stairs, the curve of her butt, the flash of her legs under the plain black dress. Maybe I'll fuck her from behind, he thought. Don't even undress her, just slide the dress up onto her hips and thrust directly into her, not even looking at her. Oh, that was always a good way, to not even let them see you, to not utter a word, just fuck, flip the dress back, and walk away.

Wouldn't that be a hell of a way to interview her? he thought deliriously. He'd read of interviews conducted while a slave was tied up, or when the trainer held a riding crop to encourage quick or complete answers; why not one where he would drive her crazy keeping her turned on and make her answer questions while he was fucking her?

Or maybe make a bigger production of it? Take her upstairs and give her a good spanking first, tie her up—there's got to be some rope around here. Give the occasion something to remember it by. After all, she must be expecting something new—or wait! Maybe the cold treatment would be better—

Mulling over his options, he heard Joan in the next room and crossed the hallway to see what she was doing. She was not alone.

Chris was with her, moving with her, and for a moment Michael thought they were dancing. Chris was standing behind her, his hands covering hers, and he was leading her in a movement that soon became a turn, and then a glide into a composed posture, suitable for waiting for instructions. He let her go, and then walked around her to adjust the posture, pushing her shoulders a little back, inching her chin down just a bit more.

"That's it," he said, stepping back to look at her. "Now, bring your head up, just high enough to make eye contact—slowly, slowly—no, leave your hands at your sides." Joan did as he instructed, her fingers twitching slightly, and then settling.

"Good," Chris said. "Now, on your own. Turn to leave... " He twirled a finger to direct her and she started to walk toward the door to the dining room. When he clapped, she made that turn,

quickly, but without a hint of surprise, coming to rest in a waiting mode in perfect obedience. Michael pursed his lips in grudg-
ing admiration. But apparently, Chris was not satisfied.

"Too Japanese," he complained, coming forward to push her
into an even more perfect posture. "Don't dip your head so low, it
looks exaggerated. Use those moves only when serving Japanese
people, and then only if you're sure they're Marketplace. We'll do
it again."

"Yes, Chris," she said softly, shaking out and preparing to start
the moves. Chris shot a glance toward the door, and Michael knew
that he had always known that they were being watched.

"Is there something I can do for you, Mike?" he asked. Joan
didn't even peek at Michael out of the corner of her eye, but stood
calmly at attention, waiting for Chris to return to the exercise.

"No," Michael said. "Sorry to bother you." He ducked back
into the hallway, and frowned, his stomach churning again.

She was supposed to be my slave, he thought. And here I am,
playing entry level master games with the graduate, learning next
to nothing while he's doing the actual training I'm supposed to be
doing!

Tara came down the stairs and waited for his acknowledgment.
There did seem to be a touch of new tension in her—something
that was neither fear nor pleasurable anticipation, and Michael held
out his hand and studied her when she passed the condoms to
him. Their plastic wrappers crinkled in his palm, and he saw the
slight shake in her own hand, the wavering in the too-quick breath
that she took.

The moment was gone. He couldn't screw her now, not with
the image of the training going on across the hall so fresh in his
brain. Maybe later.

"That took long enough," he bitched, pocketing the safes. "In
fact, it took too long, didn't it?"

"Yes, sir, please forgive me."

"Let's retrace the steps. I'll follow you, and you'll crawl, and
we'll still get back in shorter time than you did. Won't we?"

"Yes, sir." Glumly, she got down onto her hands and knees,

and he reminded himself to punish her for that, too. As she mounted the stairs, he nudged her to go faster, aching to get away from the sound of coaching, that careful dance going on in the front room.

He took her to bed the following day, literally threw her onto his bed, slapping her body until she brought herself up on all fours again, pushing himself into her with a release that felt almost cosmic—his entire body tingling with need. Tara whimpered like a puppy when he sank his cock deep into her pussy, and pushed back at him with just the proper amount of eagerness, willing, happy, but not slutty. He barely managed to last ten minutes—and it was an uphill struggle all the way. She was so pretty under him, red-cheeked, little pink marks where his hands had struck, her hair in disarray, her body trembling with the force of every thrust!

And when he finished with fucking her, he tumbled her over onto her back and played with her body, one hand on her pussy, while he leaned on his elbow. "You needed to get fucked," he said with a grin. "Hell, you need this every day."

"As you say, sir," she breathed, her hips moving up slightly. His fingers parted her wet lips and slid between them—she had seemed tight, a little dry. Well, she is older, Michael reflected. He resolved to have her bring some lube next time, since the slick surface of the condom wasn't sufficient. He'd had wonderful experiences with a cinnamon-flavored one that left a tingly sensation on sensitive tissues. The idea of making her buck a little more under him left him intrigued. He stabbed his fingers into her, where his cock had so recently plundered, and she did moan and spread her legs wider.

Now, that was a slave reaction, he thought smugly. A sudden guilty flash hit him—he really should have interviewed her before fucking. Yesterday's little condom fetching exercise had been devoid of any formal questioning. And by the time he had her in here with one of those condoms unrolling over his cock, he had forgotten about his great idea to conduct an interview while fucking her. He sighed, and her eyes turned to him immediately.

"Please let me tend to you, sir," she whispered, her light hand resting gently on his chest. He nodded, interested in what that could mean, and watched her roll herself gracefully up and off the bed. She found the used condom and threw it away, and ran a hand towel under warm water and brought it back to wipe him down. He grinned and allowed her—there had been times at Geoff's when a pleasure slave had done this, and it was always nice. It was clear that Tara was no pleasure slave, though—her movements were neat and sure, but they lacked a certain edge of sensuality. She didn't show him with every move that she wanted him, needed him.

"Touch me more when you do that," he instructed. "Show me how much you liked it, you little slut. You are a slut for your master, aren't you?"

Tara colored, but obeyed him, and trailed her fingers on his body as she finished her task. "I am whatever he wishes me to be, sir," she said evasively, dipping her head with the slightest of smiles.

Michael leaned back and laughed. "Oh, yeah, you're a slut for him," he said confidently. "Does he just fuck you the normal way? Or does he like blowjobs, anal sex, kinky stuff? Does he tie you up and beat you sometimes?"

"He is a man of many... tastes," Tara said as she put the towel aside and cuddled up next to Michael in the spot he indicated for her.

"I'm a man of many tastes, too," Michael said, taking one of her breasts in one hand and pressing. "Let's see how many new ones I can show you. Are you going to suck my cock like a good girl? Open wide for me like the little slave slut you are deep inside? I can see right past this professional attitude you have. You need someone to take you, don't you? Just push you down and make you a real slave girl."

"As you—"

"No, no, I don't want to hear that. Just say yes. Say, yes, I need to be taken. Make me believe it! Or else—" He pinched her nipple sharply. "There may not be too many sex toys around here, but I know where there are some clothespins. So, say it and mean it."

"Yes, sir!" she said, with the slightest of gasps. "Yes, please, I need someone to take me, sir, I do!"

"Good!" Michael declared, letting her go. "Well, until you go back to your master, I'm that man. So, I want to hear more sounds from you, and lots more begging. Disappoint me, and you'll be punished. Harshly!" He pondered how to appropriately structure punishments without his training kit, and decided he'd need to assemble a makeshift one of household items. He could just keep it in his room. If Parker could have his damn strap, surely a handful of clothespins, some rope, and maybe a cheap riding crop wouldn't be out of the question. He waved one hand, dismissing Tara, and she backed away from him gently.

What could he say about this little session with her? It was perfect. Lacking somewhat in true passion, but she wasn't in love with him, now was she? No slave could love everyone who used them, many never even love their masters. You could only expect that they loved the service—that they loved being useful, and being used. And Tara showed every sign of being devoted to her task, down to the way she brushed her hair over his toes before she quietly gathered up her dress and shoes and tiptoed out the door. He wiggled his toes after she left, enjoying the memory of that silken softness tangling itself up in him. Nice touch. He'd have to remember to write that down.

He had returned to writing after putting absolutely nothing on paper the previous day. Fortunately for him, Anderson had not asked to see his notes last night or this morning—she probably assumed that he was keeping them up. Still naked, he reached for the notebook he had begun to use, and plucked a pen out of the bed stand drawer. Lying on his belly, he began to describe what he'd just done with Tara, and what her observable reactions were. He tried to be specific—to describe what happened instead of how he felt. Then he transcribed his comments and her answers as best as he could recall them, thinking that he would have to bring the tape recorder in if he was doing his interviews before or after sex.

He wondered briefly how Tara was taking care of her next task, helping Joan in the kitchen, teaching her how to work with

Vicente. Would she still have that sweet after-sex flush? Would she have to excuse herself, splash some water on her face, and compose herself first? Did the two girls share whispered secrets about the trainers, and about what happened in these private sessions?

He tried to imagine it—Tara and Joan whispering, giggling, sharing confidences. It was difficult. Joan, for all her time in training and the years spent growing up in expectation for the Marketplace, was all natural moves, shy smiles, high-pitched giggles, and expectant glances. Tara was reserved, controlled, her every facial expression planned. It was the mark of someone who was experienced and talented—they overcompensated, trying to be perfect, and hated themselves when they failed. Geoff always said it was a mark of low self-esteem.

Michael thought that was a bunch of crap. It was just slaves doing the best they could. Some started out confident, others grew into it. It really didn't matter as long as they did their jobs correctly and weren't annoying.

Tara did hate it when she messed up—wincing before even a hint of a reprimand, tending slightly toward sulkiness when she had to wait to be punished. Joan looked embarrassed or ashamed and submitted to her disciplines with a good attitude, always promising to be better in the future. Tara couldn't understand why she had fucked up in the past.

That was a good observation, he thought, starting a new paragraph. I better write it down. He did so, adding that Tara could probably use a few more pep talks about pleasing one's owner, and then rolled onto his back. It was pleasantly warm in the room. Of course, the house had to be kept warm, for the comfort of the occasionally naked slaves. If he wanted to, he could wear shorts and a T-shirt—but he didn't. Nope—a dress shirt every day, although he was already tired of ties. Leashes made of silk, as far as he was concerned.

But Parker wore one every day. Jackets, too, most of the time. Neatly pressed pants, rarely jeans, and when he did wear them, they were black Levi's 501s, never pressed, but neat and crisp-looking on him. Boots, always—lace up, or engineer style, or a short boot that looked correct with the suits yet just a little bit more butch than your average men's dress boot. Whichever he wore, they were always shined to a mirror-like surface. Michael wondered who did them. Boot polishing didn't seem like something either girl would be trained to do—although it certainly wasn't difficult to teach. Good make-work, too.

Parker, Parker. Michael still hadn't figured out what he was doing in Anderson's house. He had done a little catch-up reading in the binders that Anderson had so neatly cataloged and to his chagrin realized that Chris Parker had been around for quite some time. He was mentioned several times in Anderson's yearly reports, mostly about techniques he had designed for training novices. And he was even referenced here and there, although Michael didn't have the heart to look up the articles which were referenced. He didn't want to read what Chris Parker thought about patience, or motor memory, or... anything else for that matter!

But he had been working at the entry level house on Long Island for at least three or four years, maybe longer. So why was he here, with the Trainer of Trainers? Surely, he was already as trained as he could be! Was he some special student of hers? She didn't treat him like a partner or a student, although he treated her like a goddess. If they were lovers, they sure didn't show it. No, it seemed that he was part guest, part assistant, part acolyte, and all business. His focus was on the house, and what Anderson told him to do, and whatever he was writing when he shut himself away with his computer and sheaves of papers.

Not that I'm living such a thrilling life myself, Michael reminded himself. But it would be so much easier of he wasn't here! I wouldn't have his goddamn example to work against every fucking day. Whatever I'm allowed to do, whatever I get to see, he's always there, he always lets me know that he's been around longer, he did all this first. He's the star pupil, and I'm shit.

It was frustrating. But at least he was doing something. And if the Trainer of Trainers wanted him to play roles and write notes, dammit, that was exactly what he was going to do, until she told him otherwise. At least now he was getting laid! No more mistakes for him. If anything like what happened with Karen ever happened here, he'd be out of the Marketplace for the rest of his life.

Suddenly chilly, he got up to get dressed.

CHAPTER TEN

One early afternoon, Chris took Tara with him out of the house on some (as usual) unexplained errand. Much to Michael's surprise and joy, he got to work with Anderson and Joan for a little while. The Trainer gave him a sheet of questions with their proper answers, and had him drill Joan while Anderson herself watched. Every once in a while, Anderson would change Joan's posture, covering about twenty different positions in all. She used a combination of voice commands and hand signals, and Michael frantically took notes as often as he could.

The questions were about housekeeping and wardrobe maintenance and jewelry and... oh, they went on and on. Yet, Joan never missed a single one. Whether kneeling or standing or even crouched in a penitent bow, she could rattle off the way to clean linen of wine stains, set an informal breakfast table, care for opals, or tell mink from fox.

Again, it was totally devoid of erotic interest. But Michael found himself moved nonetheless. As he asked the questions and read the answers to them, he realized he barely knew one tenth of the things she did, at least about housekeeping and things like that. He had clothing made of silk in his wardrobe—two ties and one shirt and a pair of boxer shorts given to him as a gift. And he knew, generally, that silk should be dry-cleaned. But he didn't know that there were many kinds of silk, or what their names were. Joan did. And so did Anderson, who did not hold an answer sheet herself, but nodded at every correct point Joan made and then moved her again without waiting for confirmation from Michael.

Was it necessary to know all these details to be a good slave? Maybe not for most of them. But Joan's mistress was going to get quite a knowledgeable little maid for her money—one who could be trusted with almost any piece of property before she even entered the door. She might start out dusting and sweeping, but Michael knew that no one in their right mind would keep her there for long.

Even if she wasn't meant to sleep with. At the end of the exercise, he returned the quiz sheets to Anderson and went back to his room to write in his journal. He missed Tara's presence—it would have been nice to get in a quick blowjob. But on the other hand... he sat back in his chair and gazed at the wall for a moment. Was he really horny right now?

The truth was... not very. He was a little tense, the way he always was when he was allowed to work with Anderson, in any role at all. And he had gotten used to having Tara around for a quick bit of tension release. He turned pages back in the book and re-read the scant comments he made about her, and the descriptions of what position he had fucked her in, and which orifice he had used and whether or not he kept her long enough for two orgasms. The words annoyed him suddenly, and he couldn't figure out why! Sure, he still wasn't conducting in-depth interviews with her, but Anderson rarely commented on these notes and when she did, she didn't scold him or tell him to change tactics. And Tara herself was always willing and capable, and once he started to keep a bottle of lube nearby at all times, she was much more comfortable and receptive.

So, what was it?

He lost the desire to continue writing his impressions of the exercise with Joan. He put the book away and slipped into a sweater and headed back downstairs to see if he could find something else to do for a while. He was trying to get into a book about military etiquette when the front bell rang. Joan came out of the kitchen to get it, and he watched her as she moved quickly but without any panicked movements toward the door. Anderson came out of her office and looked down the front hall, and at the sight of her, Michael got up, barely suppressing a sigh. He was finally getting used to standing when she entered a room—and finding out when he should and shouldn't.

"Emil!" she said with a warm smile, stepping fully into the hall. "What a pleasure to see you!"

The man who came forward to take her hand was easily as old as she was, small and vaguely European in appearance. His neat, double-breasted suit was revealed as Joan lifted what looked like a cashmere coat from his shoulders. He had thick, wavy hair, all white, and Anderson had to lean down to kiss his cheek.

"The pleasure is all mine, all mine," he insisted, his voice melodious and slightly old fashioned in its intonations. "You were kind to see us on such short notice."

Us? Michael started to move forward, even as Anderson was leading Emil into the front living room, and then Michael saw Emil's companion.

Michael had gotten used to Tara being the image of feminine beauty in this house, and for one second, he thought the woman in the hallway was her, somehow magically transformed. He saw the pale skin and blonde hair and had to blink to clear his vision again. But it wasn't Tara at all, but a taller, more shapely and much more classically beautiful woman who entered after Joan took her wrap away. She had a stronger face than Tara, too—with high, arched cheekbones and deep-set ice-blue eyes. Her hair was trimmed very short, with a wave over her forehead. Michael regretted that; he liked long hair on women, and thought that Anderson's mane of straight black hair shot through with silver was her best feature.

But with short hair or not, Emil's companion was quite something! Michael smiled as Anderson made introductory movements.

"Michael LaGuardia, please meet Doctors Emil Kaufmann and Greta Mueller. Emil, Michael is studying here."

"How splendid for you!" the doctor exclaimed, shaking Michael's hand. His grip was dry and firm, just a little longer than a business handshake. "It is a pleasure, young man."

"Thank you," Michael responded, his eyes flickering to the other doctor. "But like you said, the pleasure is all mine."

Dr. Greta Mueller smiled back at him, and Michael felt the first honest surge of arousal he had in days. She was dressed richly, too, in a mid-length turquoise dress with a long jacket over it, and some nice gold jewelry, including a herringbone necklace that should have set someone back a few bucks. He wondered if this power couple was in the market for a slave.

Dr. Kaufmann glanced from his companion and then back to Michael, but his smile remained genial, not threatened at all. Michael was grateful for that. He'd been the target of far too many territorial snarls from men and their trophy wives—or girlfriends, as the case might be here. It was difficult to tell, with different last names.

"Tell you what, Emil," Anderson was saying. "I'll take my favorite doctor into my office, and Michael can stay with you for a while. Keep Joan useful, Michael."

Michael couldn't keep his eyes from opening wide in shock. Was he seriously being told to entertain one of the Trainer's high-powered friends?

"I cannot think of anything better," the doctor responded with a nod. "Please take as long as you like, we have no pressing business to tend to today."

Anderson gave a short nod to Michael and then opened her arm for Dr. Mueller to slide under. The two women entered the office and Joan closed the door behind them and then looked at Michael for direction.

Michael gaped for a second, and then grasped hold of himself. "Right—um—Dr. Kaufmann. Would you like some—coffee? Tea?"

"Tea sounds lovely," the older man said, his hands behind his back. Michael waved Joan off, and she curtsied before she left. Then, he turned back to the doctor and waved nervously at the chairs. "Would you like to sit out here?"

"Splendid!" The man chose the seat Anderson usually sat in, and Michael wondered whether he had actually been waiting to be invited to make himself comfortable. He took the other chair and studied the guest intently, trying to read something from him the way Anderson and Chris kept telling him he should be able to do. Well, all right. Nice, well-cut suit, good shoes, gold watch, gold cufflinks—the man knew how to dress and didn't spare the expense. He had an old-world style but spoke without a real foreign accent. He looked comfortable with himself, too, and was unthreatened by other men admiring his woman.

"How long have you been in training, Mr. LaGuardia?" Emil asked, settling into the chair comfortably.

"Well—I've only been here for a few weeks," Michael said. "But I trained for two years before this."

"My! What dedication to the craft!"

Michael stopped himself from frowning in confusion. That was the last thing he expected to hear! But he had been dedicated, hadn't he? Before he got here, lots of people were impressed with the fact that he spent years being taught how to do this. He smiled, and leaned back himself. "I guess," he said modestly. "But some people train even longer than that."

"Indeed they do," Emil agreed. "But most do not complete even two years. You are to be commended."

"Really? Most?"

"Training to become a trainer is very rigorous, no matter where it is done. And the rewards are few. Many trainers will not be able to become independent even if they complete their training. And so, they become handlers for owners, or assistants for senior trainers, or they simply move into other fields. Some, of course, enter service themselves."

"Really?" Michael cursed himself for beginning to sound like a parrot. "I didn't know that."

"Oh, yes. The finding and making of slaves is not an easy or rewarding profession, unless one has a personal calling to the task. And for some, that calling can be... hmm... mistaken."

"Oh, I knew this was for me the minute I heard about it," Michael said.

"Did you? How wonderful! And after only two years, you find yourself with our Trainer of Trainers! It must be very exciting for you."

Michael remembered the list of detailed housekeeping questions he asked of Joan and his many frustrations and the hours of trying to drag himself through one dry report after another, but he nodded anyway. "Sure," he said. "Very exciting."

Emil laughed warmly and leaned forward to tap Michael gently on one knee. "I think I would have to be deaf to not hear the resignation in your voice, young man. Don't think I don't know how tedious the early days of training can be, especially here. I know more about training than you might think."

"Are you a trainer?" Michael asked.

"Oh, no," Emil said, settling back again. "But I have many friends and associates who are. Tell me; with whom did you train for two years before being chosen to come here?"

Well, here it comes, Michael thought with genuine resignation. The careful nod and the look of amusement or pity. "Geoff Negel," he said, and then added defensively, "He's the biggest trainer on the West Coast."

"Oh, yes, I have read some of his papers," was what Dr. Emil Kaufmann said in response. Michael blinked, and Joan appeared at the doorway with her tray. Michael could barely keep his voice steady as he gazed at Emil and asked, "You have?"

"Certainly," Emil said, with a glance in Michael's direction. He accepted a cup and added honey to it, stirring thoughtfully. "I have long thought his opinion on discussion groups for clients is quite meritorious. And one cannot ignore the influence he has had on our world. Two years with him! That must have been interesting."

"It was," Michael said, still amazed at this turn of events. But how wonderful it was to talk to someone who recognized the work he had done, who even respected his former teacher! "It was totally different than it is here."

"I should imagine so," Emil said with a nod. "Did you enjoy the training in California?"

"God, yes," Michael said with a laugh. "I had the time of my life! Not that it was all fun," he added quickly. "I—we all—studied a lot. And we worked with slaves every day of the week; you never had time off unless you left the premises, you know?" He took his own tea from Joan and felt more than thought there was something else to be done. He looked at Emil, who seemed to glance for a moment across the hall, and Michael drew in a sharp breath and looked up into Joan's expectant eyes. "Er—you should bring some to the Trainer as well," he said quickly. "And some of those pecan cookies she liked from last night."

"Yes, sir," Joan said, with a slight dip of a curtsey.

Of course, he said to himself as she left. By turning her over to me, Anderson made me responsible for using her. If Joan took it upon her own initiative to also serve refreshments to the Trainer and her guest, she would be right in action—but wrong in that she was under different authority now. It had been Michael's responsibility to direct her, to make sure that she knew what the new—however temporary—chain of command was.

How convoluted could you get? What on earth was wrong with just letting them do what they were supposed to do, and punishing them when they failed? Why set it up so I look bad?

Dr. Kaufmann drank some of his tea in the silence, and then Michael felt himself snap back to the present, with a faint blush. "I'm sorry," he said at once. "Not enough sleep, I guess."

"Do you suffer from insomnia, or does the Trainer keep you up to all hours?" the doctor asked with a gentle smile.

"Actually, I sleep fine—usually," Michael admitted. "But I guess everyone has a little trouble sleeping every once in a while."

"Oh, indeed, yes. If you find it a continued inconvenience, I or Greta will be honored to provide you with any guidance you wish. So—you trained with Mr. Negel and then came here to cold New York City! From the land of young, tanned beauties to this shaded little enclave in Brooklyn, with only—what was it, two slaves in attendance? And I know Anderson does not entertain much, or take her juniors out to parties and events. It must be quite challenging for you, to accept such changes."

Michael blinked again, uncertain of what to say. But what the older man said was true, and there was no harm in admitting it. "Yes," he said cautiously. "It is challenging. But worth it."

"Is it? Why do you say so?"

"Well—she is the Trainer of Trainers. And everyone respects her. Everyone—all over the world! And, they study her—her reports and stuff. So, who would give up the chance to study with her in person, you know?"

"Many do," laughed Emil, his eyes twinkling over his tea cup. "I would say that for everyone who writes to her and begs to enter training here, there are ten who are thankful they never have to submit to such an old-fashioned training style as hers. But aside from what you have heard why others come here, why did you?"

"To learn from the best," Michael answered smoothly. "I want to be a master trainer."

"Do you? Another rarity! And why undertake that particular goal?"

Michael hesitated. Why not? was his first instinctive response. Why not be the best of the best?

"Training other trainers is a very time consuming and often frustrating profession," Emil said thoughtfully. "It is rare to see it as a goal set above the training of slaves."

Suddenly, Michael understood what the doctor meant, and he started to blush. Emil nodded slightly and smiled. "Ah—perhaps the term master trainer means something else in the house you first trained in?"

"I didn't know," Michael admitted honestly. "I mean, we never used the term. I just thought it meant—I don't know. A better trainer. The best kind of trainer or something."

"So it does, in terms of the demands of the training regimen. But you hadn't told Anderson of this ambition, because she would have corrected you. Why hide it?"

Because I seem like a major fuck-up around here, Michael thought ruefully. "I guess I thought it would be better to tackle things one step at a time."

"Yes, that's always a good idea," Emil agreed. "And now, you are spared a minor correction, aren't you? So, it worked out for the best."

Michael brightened. "Yeah, I guess it did. You know, sometimes, it seems that learning by mistakes is a big way to teach around here. It wasn't like that at Geoff's."

"And yet Mr. Negel's avant garde style was not the best for you?"

"Oh, it was fine. But... I don't know. Sometimes, I would just wonder if there was more than what we were doing."

"There is always more, Michael," Emil said. "May I call you Michael? Thank you; please call me Emil. But as I was saying... more is not necessarily better. Also, what is best for one man might not suit another, in any endeavor." He put his cup down and crossed his legs comfortably. "I find slave trainers to be fascinating people, especially those who, like you, knew that this was the best profession for them. I do hope you forgive my curiosity, but to find an intelligent young man poised at the start of the most rigorous instruction offered here in North America, someone with experience in a vastly different style—this is a wonderful opportunity for me."

"Oh, it's okay," Michael assured the older man. He liked this doctor. He had a warm, engaging voice and... and... he was just the nicest person Michael had run into since he had left California. The first one who seemed genuinely interested in him, the first one who acknowledged how much damn work it took to get here, and how hard it was to try to follow along this bizarre teaching style.

But could he trust him? Maybe if he actually said anything bad about training, this guy would turn right around and tell Anderson. As Michael was pondering this, Emil cocked his head to one side, and asked, "Tell me, Michael, if you don't mind—how did you find the Marketplace?"

That was certainly a safe story. Michael told him about his Uncle and the beach house and the two slaves there, and how he met Geoff, and gradually, their conversation warmed and deepened along with the afternoon shadows. Michael barely noticed how easily Joan kept them supplied with tea and then cleared it all away; he was too engaged in this fascinating and kind man who seemed to be so flatteringly interested in his life and opinions. He even got to explain some of his own theories after a while, and the doctor nodded and encouraged him to elaborate and didn't look scornful or doubting, just thoughtful.

"See, I think when you show them too much attention in a positive way, they get to expect it all the time," he said at one point.

"Punishment should be the main attention they get, to remind them that their place is to serve you, and that the minute they screw up, they can get flipped and whacked. And that way, they'll be grateful when you praise them or do something they like, instead of expect it."

"But if punishment—which is merely negative attention, after all—becomes more frequent than rewards, don't you think this will only serve to encourage bad behavior, since it will guarantee attention of some degree?" Emil leaned forward slightly when he asked questions, his whole body seemingly involved in hearing the answers.

"But that's what they're there for," Michael insisted. "If they wanted to clean house and get fu—I mean, have sex, then they can do that in any normal marriage. The women, I mean. I think they're slaves because they want to be punished."

"How interesting," Emil mused. "And do you find punishing slaves to be enjoyable, or merely a training task? Do you ever feel regretful for it?"

"What's there to regret?" Michael asked. "Punishing someone is hot! That's why I love being a trainer. Back in Santa Cruz, we spent all our time either teaching the slaves how to do stuff, punishing them when they did it wrong, and—well—using them for our pleasure. It couldn't get better than that!"

"No, I suppose not," Emil genially agreed.

"I don't know whether it would be as exciting to do it over and over again with the same person, though. So, for me, it's best that I see a slave for a short period of time. I get my fun while I'm teaching them what to do, and I never get bored or frustrated with a slave that won't shape up." Michael leaned back, crossing one leg over his knee. "I'm the kind of guy who likes a little variety in his life."

"I understand that, certainly. I have to admit that in my old age, I am more appreciative of stability and predictability than I was when I was a younger man."

"Oh, I understand that too," said Michael, who didn't. "So... how long have you and Dr. Mueller been together?"

"Not terribly long," the man admitted. "Perhaps four years. But she suits me perfectly."

"Oh, yeah? That's great! Are you in the market for a new slave or something?"

For a second, the older man looked surprised, almost affronted, and Michael wondered what he had said wrong. But then, he just smiled slightly and shook his head. "I'm quite content with the one I have," he said gently. "Although, I will admit that if I were, this would be the house I would come to."

"So... is the slave you own an Anderson slave?"

Emil nodded. Michael wondered why they were there, if they didn't need a new one, but didn't probe further. Instead, he allowed Emil to return to questioning him for a while.

The door across the hallway opened and Anderson stepped out, and Michael found that Emil apparently thought it was correct to rise when she entered as well. She smiled at both of them and said, "Well, we're done in here, Emil. Will you stay for dinner?"

"It would be an honor and a pleasure," the gentleman said smoothly. "But unless you have further business with me, I think I should like to go home this evening."

"Five minutes, then." She moved aside to allow Greta to pass her, and Emil turned to Michael and nodded his head.

"Please excuse me, Michael. It has been a pleasure having this discussion with you." And with that, he vanished into the Trainer's study, leaving Dr. Greta Mueller with Michael, who instantly felt a strange surge of excitement as he looked at her. But just as he was about to open his mouth to invite her in to sit, he heard the key in the front door, and the heavy latches turning.

Joan passed him like a ghost—only able to do it because he was standing there like a deer caught in headlights—and made it into the front hallway in time to remove Chris's leather jacket. Michael cursed his luck as he belatedly motioned for Greta to enter the front sitting room, which she did with a slight smile and a nod much reminiscent of her... husband's?

"Greta! What a surprise," said Chris as he came in. Tara was following him, with a new hairstyle, and a slightly flushed look on her face. Michael frowned when he saw her, comparing her to the more composed and elegant Greta and wondering how he could have ever confused them.

"Hello, Chris," Greta said. And to Michael's shock, she curtsied, like a slave.

He felt a little off balance, as his ears continued to hear the two of them speak, but for some reason, their words made no sense. Tara and Joan vanished into the back of the house toward the kitchen as Chris came into the front room and continued speaking with Greta.

Greta the slave?

"—Master is in the study with the Trainer right now," she was saying. "He will be glad to see you before we leave."

"It's always a pleasure to see the both of you," Chris answered. He looked over at Michael, who was still standing awkwardly between the chairs. "I see you've met the new student here, Mr. Michael LaGuardia."

"Yes, we were introduced before," Greta said with a smile.

But you didn't curtsey to me, Michael thought in a sudden flash of annoyance. And why was he still standing, anyway? He nodded curtly and said, "I have some stuff to do upstairs. Excuse me." He felt Chris's eyes on him as he passed them, and heard Chris inviting Greta to come in and sit down for a minute, and he almost stumbled on the steps in his haste to get out of there.

He felt furious, but didn't quite know why. So, he didn't realize that she was a slave. That was possible! Hell, Geoff trained slaves to be able to act like girlfriends and lovers or spouses, or house guests, or whatever their owner might want them to behave like in public! And it wasn't required for owners to identify their slaves to anyone else—even to Marketplace people. And it wasn't as though they gave him any clues—she had her coat taken just like her master's, and he never called her anything but Greta, and the Trainer even put an arm around her shoulders like an old friend.

And she didn't act like a slave! She didn't hang in the background, keeping quiet...

Or, did she?

Michael sat down on the edge of his bed and tried to think about it. She did hang back, only moving when she was acknowledged. But—he'd barely had a minute to see that and then she was gone. Yet he still felt that somehow, he had been fooled—or made a fool of. His journal was laying on the nightstand, but he felt no desire to write about this afternoon, and was suddenly glad that these guests weren't staying for dinner, even though that might have been a remarkable oddity and a potential diversion from the same-old, same-old.

They left while he sulked in his room. He would have gone downstairs to get Tara for some abuse and maybe some interview time, but he didn't want to run into them, so he stayed until he heard the front door closing again, and then went down for dinner. No one commented upon his absence.

But when the meal was over, Anderson looked across the table at him and asked, "What did you think of Dr. Kaufmann?"

"Great guy," he said. "I liked him a lot. He seems very interesting."

"What about him do you find interesting?"

Michael stared for a moment and gathered his thoughts. What an odd question! "Well—he's very nice," he said quickly. "Old-fashioned and polite. Smart. He's a good guy to talk with, easygoing, friendly." Unlike my current company, he thought, as he caught Chris looking at him. But he continued, "I just found him really easy to talk to."

"You should. He's been getting people to talk to him for many years now," Anderson said with a slight smile.

Michael cocked his head in confusion. "What do you mean?"

"Tell me," she said, instead of answering him, "what you learned about Emil today."

"He's rich," Michael stated firmly. There was no doubt about that. She shrugged in response.

"That depends on how you define rich, I suppose," she said. "Emil won't ever go hungry, that's for sure. What else?"

"Well... he's an owner. Of one slave. And he's not in the market for another one. That he and Greta—Dr. Mueller—have been together for four years." Think, Mike, think, he coached himself. What else did he tell me?

"What kind of a doctor is he?" Anderson asked.

"I—I never asked," he said.

Chris lowered his head for a moment, and Michael didn't hear a sigh, but knew that one was being held back anyway.

"You didn't ask me to interview him," Michael said instantly, looking at Anderson. "I mean, it would have been rude to just start asking questions of one of your friends, wouldn't it?"

"Did you think it was rude when he did that to you?" she asked.

"What?"

"You were interviewed," Anderson said. Chris lifted his head to look at her, but she kept her gaze on Michael. "Emil is a psychologist, specializing in Marketplace personnel, especially clients."

Michael felt his anger build, coupled with embarrassment. He glanced at Chris, but the other man had turned his attention toward the kitchen, and Michael could see the door swing shut.

Oh, no, wouldn't want the slaves to see this, he thought bitterly. He had to force himself to sit still, try to keep his face neutral, even though he wanted to snap, and slam his hand against the table. "Why?" he asked.

"Excellent!" Anderson said. "Good control, Michael. I want to see more of that, although your frustration is as clear as a window to anyone looking at you. As for your question—I didn't answer it before, and I won't answer it now. I suggest you come up with some theories yourself, and we can discuss them later. In the meantime," she rose and the two men rose with her, "I want Tara in the study, and Joan is to have a little free time for being such a good girl today. Send Tara to me with some dessert."

"Yes, Trainer," Chris said. They both watched her leave, and Michael sat back down with a string of forbidden words all balled up in his throat. He knew his face was red, and he didn't care.

Chris vanished into the kitchen for a moment, and when he came back, Michael looked up at him and said, "That wasn't fair."

Chris nodded, his lips compressed. "You're right," he said simply. "Please excuse me, Michael, I have some work of my own to do."

Michael sat there in silence for a moment, stricken with the shock those two words impressed upon him. Not, "you're right, and tough shit," not "you're right, but who cares?" Just "you're right."

But he got up quickly and left before Tara came through with her dessert tray for the Trainer. Whether the door was opened or not, he knew they had heard everything. And he had had quite enough of acting dumb in front of slaves for one day.

How was this supposed to make a trainer out of him anyway? He looked at his journal again and in one motion, scooped it up and pitched it across the room. It made a satisfying thump as it hit the wall, and made him feel even more foolish than before.

CHAPTER ELEVEN

It was very late, but the light was still on under her door. Years of experience taught him that she generally slept no more than he did. He knocked gently.

"Come in, Chris."

Her room was in the back of the house, the windows shrouded with the heavy branches of the trees she loved so much in the spring. Right now, between their bare branches, you could barely make out the dim lights of the buildings which shared the long yards behind them. He put the latest pages down on her dresser and drew her curtains for her.

She was in a long, soft dressing gown, decorated with gray pussy willow branches, gently faded with age. She had been at her delicate rosewood writing desk when he came in, but as he busied himself, she crossed the room to examine his papers.

"You could have left this in my office," she said, putting them down. "I won't review them tonight anyway."

"Yes," he said. He turned to her and put his hands behind his back, and she smiled. Silently, she walked toward him, and he stood still until it became clear that she intended to pass him, and he stepped neatly out of her way.

She sat down at the vanity mirror and looked at herself thoughtfully. "You didn't even ask what Greta wanted to talk about," she said, running her hands through her hair and pushing it back over her shoulders.

"It's not my business," he said. He had turned to stand to one side of her, so he wouldn't be addressing her back. "I know you'll tell me if I need to know, or if you want my opinion on anything. It was just surprising to find that they had come here when I was... occupied."

"I couldn't very well have Emil interview Mike with you hovering about," she said. "And besides, Tara needed a good day outside the house. But go ahead. Let me hear it."

"Trainer... with all my respect... engaging Emil to conduct an interview without Michael's consent was... not ethical." The effort it took him to say this was considerable. She could feel the tension in his body as he forced the words out, and hear his carefully modulated tone as he kept the strong emotions away from what he was saying.

"Emil thought so, too," she said. She picked up her hairbrush and held it out. "Come on, make yourself useful."

"Thank you," he said softly. She closed her eyes as he began to brush her hair in long, measured strokes, lifting it gently to avoid tugging on a knot here or wave there.

"But, Emil trusts me," she said as she felt the confidence in his hands increase. "And so should you."

"I do," he said. "But my trust in you and my respect for you didn't outweigh the need for me to say it."

"Good," she said. The brush strokes never paused as he spoke—he was perfectly able to do one thing with his hands while having a discussion, or answering questions. Even under duress, she thought, a fond memory flitting by. After a little more of the comforting silence, she continued, "I explained to Emil that I needed some new perspective on the boy, and that to the best of my knowledge he wouldn't even recognize an interview when it was conducted, and that was the point of this exercise. And, as long as I didn't ask that Emil reveal anything he learned beyond a very basic profile, he agreed to do it. And," she said, opening her eyes, "he told me nothing I didn't already know."

"I beg your pardon," Chris said gently, "but what you learned is not the point. I believe that Michael's consent should have been sought before subjecting him to a professional examination."

"What about teaching him a lesson on interviewing?" she asked.

"He needs to start from the beginning on interviewing skills," Chris said firmly. "In my opinion, he should not be allowed to continue these farcical interviews with Tara. They have been far more useful to her than to him, and frankly, she doesn't need that much time spent practicing something she already knows how to do. He, on the other hand, should study more technique. From the beginning, with question construction and multi-layer styles. And frankly, Trainer—I must ask why you have not been interviewing him yourself."

Anderson closed her eyes again—was that the slightest bit of hesitation before he asked? No—only a shift as he let some of her hair fall and picked up another bundle in his hand.

"He's not ready for me," she said. "Perhaps I should have you start him."

"If that is what you wish," he said. "But I do not think I'm the best person to get honest and complete answers from him. And if you do give me this task, I would have to ask that I be permitted to take him in hand."

Anderson chuckled. "Well, that does seem to work for you," she admitted. "But you're right, it wouldn't be very helpful for him right now. I will probably have you set up an interview or two eventually. In the meantime, he stays on Tara. And I don't want to hear anything more about Emil's little charade after tonight. It's done, and I did it, and you've had your say."

He sighed, just a little bit, and nodded. "Yes, Trainer," he said. "Thank you for hearing me."

"I'll be ready for you to stop that in another fifty or so strokes," she said, leaning back. In silence, he kept working on her hair, lifting it in one hand to brush out the tangles at the ends, gently bringing it from where it fell around her face and ears. He never pulled against her scalp, but saved firmness for the ends, his hand braced to hold the hair free of her body while he worked it into luxurious softness. The gentle movements of the brush against her head were as hypnotic and pleasurable as massage. Then, in about fifty strokes, give or take a few, he braided it for her, and she gave his hand a firm squeeze when he was through. Still silent, he left her to her thoughts, and the new pages he had delivered. The silence was delicious, relaxing, and comfortable. With a sigh of her own, she picked the new pages up and started to read. She always meant to leave them for daylight, but curiosity always got the better of her, too.

Chris went back downstairs instead of to his room. He smiled when he saw the figure rising from the chair by the fireplace in the front room.

"You should get some more sleep," he said, jerking his head toward the hooks by the front door. Tara smiled back as she got his jacket for him and held it. She slipped into her own coat and the two of them went out to the front of the building together. Chris slipped a red box out of the breast pocket of his jacket and allowed Tara to light a cigarette for him, and they stood together on the stoop.

"I'll miss you," Tara said softly. Down the street from them a truck rumbled by, and Chris waited until it passed to pat her on the shoulder.

"You'll be too busy to think of us here," he said. "You have an excellent contract to fulfill, and the Judge is a demanding man."

"Even so," she insisted. "I didn't want to leave without telling you... " she blushed, and laughed, and looked down. "You know, I thought I knew what I was going to say."

"Don't say it, then," Chris said. "Just go and be a good slave." He smiled at her. "As I know you will be."

Tara wrapped her arms around her body and sighed. "Thank you," she said. "That means a lot to me. But I'm still worried. Will it be enough? Do you think he'll be able to tell... "She paused and looked at Chris sideways. "Do you think I might not be perfect for him?"

"You have exceeded any reasonable expectation in your training," Chris said. "Perfection can only be striven for, never attained. But you are an Anderson slave. He will enjoy and appreciate your service and your... newfound enthusiasm?" They both smiled through the smoke and he waved it away. "Your enthusiasm," he repeated. "I'm sure of that."

She sighed a little and nodded. "Thank you. I needed to hear that. I'm so nervous about going back, even though life there is much easier than it is here."

"You'll be fine."

"I hope so!"

Chris took her chin in his hand and repeated, "You will be just fine. And, you will enjoy this contract, knowing that your master has the best trained, most responsive and intuitive slave he could ever hope for."

Tara turned her head and dropped a kiss into Chris's palm, and he laughed as he withdrew the hand. "Save it for your master," he said.

"May I call you?" Tara asked, suddenly shy again. "If—when I get a chance?"

"If I'm here I will be pleased to catch up with you. And if, for some reason, Anderson is not available, I will always be happy to be a contact for you. But you know it's best not to contact me for social reasons." He said this gently, and his eyes were direct with hers, and she dipped her head in assent. "Don't worry," he said firmly. "You have everything you need to make this contract a stupendous success. Both the Trainer and I believe in you. Now, go inside and go to bed, Tara. Don't lead Joan into thinking she can get away with this sort of thing as well."

She laughed, and bowed her head in gentle submission, leaving him there to finish his smoke. She heard him come in a short while later, just as she heard him walk through the house one last time, checking doors and turning off lights.

CHAPTER TWELVE

Michael debated confronting Anderson over his ambush interview for several days. Every time he got up enough anger to feel the rush of excitement, that drive that told him, "Yes, now! Make her tell you why she did that! Make her understand what a shitty thing that was to do!" —he'd stop himself with the simple question, "What then?"

What if she didn't answer? What was he supposed to do then, just pack and leave? And really, what kind of threat was that, when she could have a dozen people out here the next day aching to take this on?

Or, what if she did answer? Did he expect her to say that he was right and she was wrong, and ask for his forgiveness?

At first, he tried to even imagine that—and after trying for a few minutes, realized that no, that wasn't going to happen on this planet.

The next step was to try to figure out the "why" all by himself. Interviewing a slave was one thing—they were set up for it, told they had to tell the truth, and they had a reason to be interviewed. Their answers might form parts of their contracts, or establish their suitability for service, let alone for a sale.

Geoff had interviewed him, before he went to live in Santa Cruz. It had been informal, more like a media interview than a job interview, with Geoff sitting on the terrace outside his Los Angeles hotel room, with a pitcher of iced tea which he insisted on pouring for them both. It had been a beautiful day, powder-blue skies fairly clear all the way to the ocean. Michael had approved of both the setting and the man. He'd been eager to impress, relaxed and excited all at the same time. And the more questions Geoff asked him, the more he wanted to be a part of this whole mythical world, somehow.

Michael ended up telling Geoff more about his life and his feelings than he had ever told anyone. About men and women, and what he did with them, and what he wanted to do, dreamed of doing. About how he saw his future in the Marketplace. He told long stories about his experiences in school and with his friends, growing up, and Geoff never looked impatient or bored. They only paused to break for lunch, and even then, Geoff let Michael talk and talk and talk. But then, Geoff did have a background in...

Psychology. Of course.

I'm so stupid! Michael thought as he realized how easily he had been manipulated. I fell for it. It did feel strange, at one point almost like a job interview, but I was so eager to have this guy like me!

But let's be honest, he immediately reconsidered. I was desperate for someone to listen to me, and I wasn't paying attention to how weird it was. Anderson never left me alone with anyone before—and no one ever seemed interested in me the way he was. Something should have clicked, something should have made me wonder what was going on.

But I told him so much! Hell, another hour, and I would have told him about Karen!

Emil was good, Michael thought. He never showed the slightest boredom, or shifted the conversation to himself—hell, that alone should be a clue, he thought with a wry smile. I must have talked at least eighty percent of the time, but I never even felt like I was being grilled or anything. Is that a good way to interview a slave, too? Or was it a special interview for trainers?

Would it work on a slave? A lot of them were very talkative, that was for sure! Hours and hours of dreams and fantasies, days worth of stories of experiences—he had watched the tapes, scanned through many transcripts. Some slaves, you just couldn't shut up, once they got started.

And then there were slaves like Tara. She was a hard nut to crack, although she didn't seem to try to hide anything. It was just that she answered questions quickly, to the point, and often in as few words as possible. Was that something her master liked, or something Anderson taught?

How can I get her to talk more, he wondered. Is that what this was all about? To show me how to seduce answers from someone? But why should I have to? I'm her trainer! She should know that she has to tell me everything! How can I be expected to know what to even ask, if she doesn't lead me with her answers? He tried to reconstruct exactly what Emil did, what he said, but there were no secrets he could find there.

The next time he had time with Tara, he kept his cock tucked away and started her on a more relaxed interview style. He didn't even have her strip, although that had become standard behavior. Nope, he sat her down in a chair opposite him and crossed one ankle over his knee and asked, "Tell me about how you found the Marketplace."

Tara nodded as she gathered her thoughts, her soft, "Yes, sir," pleasant. "I was in college," she said. "My junior year. I knew that I was a slave in my soul, but I had some... not bad experiences, but sad ones, with lovers who didn't support my fantasies, or approve of them, really. I had decided to make my life a form of service. I was going to work for some struggling legal aid society or maybe be a fundraiser for a group that helped battered women or runaway teenagers or homebound elderly. Somewhere, where what I did could make a difference, and where the workload would be too much to support much of a social life.

"One afternoon, while doing volunteer work at a meals on wheels place, I met the woman who spotted me, Corazon. She did occasional work there as well, not regularly, but everyone seemed to know her. We became friends. She seemed wild and exciting, but was fun to be with and just a joy. No matter how hard my day was, she could say a word and I would want to go and do what she had planned. I trusted her, too, enough to finally tell her one day why my old relationships never seemed to work. And that was the day she told me that she was a sadomasochist, and that she understood both my need to serve and my desire to be owned."

She blushed a little as she said this, and suddenly, Michael realized that Corazon must have seduced her as well. That was to be expected—the Marketplace valued slaves who were bisexual, but he had somehow never actually asked Tara if she had women in her past as well as men.

He looked at her, sitting up correctly, but not too stiff, her pretty breasts neat under the simple dress she wore while serving, her shapely legs demurely together. It was easy to imagine her in the embrace of another woman—a darker-skinned woman, tan to her fair, with dark curly hair, and deep, dark eyes, maybe with curvy hips and a sensuous smile. Just enough to melt that slight chill that Michael occasionally felt from Tara. Long, pecan-colored fingers stroking those pert, pale breasts while Tara moaned and gasped and begged for more, the way he had taught her.

He couldn't keep himself from just lightly touching his crotch. His cock was already hard, eager at the image his mind had conjured up. "Very nice," he said, not quite sure whether he was remarking on her answer or the fantasy image. "What did she do with you?"

"Sir, I am unsure what information you wish from me, I apologize. Do in what way, sir?"

"Well, did she play with you? Have sex with you?"

A soft smile, a softening of her eyes. Tara nodded and said, "Oh, yes, sir. Although I had some experience before, she took me to places I had never been. She was the first who made me cry while beating me. She enjoyed severe bondage and often made me beg for mercy just from that, even before there was any other kind of torture."

"Oh, yeah?" Michael shifted in his seat, aching to touch the slave. So odd, to see this older woman as the target of a Marketplace spotter—but if she had been spotted back in college... in her twenties? He would have to dig out her file and look at it again. How long had she been a slave? Was there even some sort of SM scene back then?

Tara nodded again, and continued. "She introduced me to many things, sir. Every day with her was discovering something new about her tastes or myself—and as we grew to know each other, I knew more and more about what I needed. I craved guidance. I wanted to feel needed and used and appreciated, with fewer choices and more direction. Most of all, she made me realize that I wanted to be owned. And when I told her that, she began to tell me about the Marketplace."

"So... you told her you wanted an owner first," Michael repeated.

"Oh, yes," Tara said. "In fact, I told her I would give up everything to be owned and used properly. But she insisted that I stay in school, and little by little, she told me that she knew places where that sort of thing could happen—that she knew people who did this in an organized and ethical way. I began to dream of it."

"And then she brought you in, huh?"

"She left me alone for the last part of my senior year. After I finished my degree, I went straight back to her," Tara said. "All I could think of was our time together and what she told me about the Marketplace—and how I could be valued if I stayed in school and had a marketable skill. In my last year, I took accounting courses and as many pre-law courses as I could handle. I sharpened my typing skills, and learned word processing and database software. And when I went back to her with my resume, she took me at once into formal training. She was like a dream come true for me, my way into a fantastic world I'd only dreamed of. I will never forget her, or the trust she had in me."

"Wow," Michael said. But the story made him annoyed. So, she was spotted and trained by the same person, huh? Someone who actually sent her away and then trusted her to come back, like it was that easy! He knew it wasn't that simple, it wasn't that clear cut. Tara could have walked away from the whole thing, gotten engaged, or married. Or just forgotten it, and gone into the soft world, to...

"Enough about that," he said, snapping his fingers. "Time to remember what a slut you are. Here's a dream come true for you, slave girl, one hard cock."

She went instantly to her knees, her fingers undoing the buttons on her dress. As gracefully as possible while down there, she stripped off her dress and her bra, and shimmied her panties down her thighs, lifting one knee at a time to free them from her legs.

"Thank you, sir," she said when she was naked at last, and he had her crawl to him while he got his own cock out. He kept the condoms close at hand these days, and he slipped one onto himself, not trusting his control. At this point, he didn't care that the reservoir tip made her gag.

Making her gag was part of his intention.

He came while his cock was buried deep into her throat, while her face was bright red and tear-streaked. He held onto her head with both hands, wishing he could really mark her, and wishing he knew why he was suddenly so angry. But she thanked him again, kissing the tops of his shoes, before gathering her clothing and leaving the room in silence.

He panted out deep breaths, looking down at his spent cock, lying limp across his fly, and his hands balled into fists. Damn all of them, he thought wildly. Damn them all for thinking it's all so easy, for just knowing when it's the right time, and who the right person is. I can see! I can ask questions! I've got a brain!

Then why did it all happen the way it did?

He stripped his own clothing off, suddenly hot, and threw a robe on to walk down the hall and take a long, hot shower. It was too painful to think of the one time he had to show off what he could do.

After her initial errors in negotiating, Karen eagerly allowed him to do pretty much anything he wanted to. She shivered when he told her he wanted to see her whipped by a woman, but she nodded and took it, every stroke making her yelp in pain. The leatherdyke in chaps and vest really put her through her paces, and left marks—it was a fabulous beating. Her skill with a single tail was what had attracted Michael's attention from the start, and he was very pleased. Not only did his chosen surrogate top work out, but Karen was deliciously and properly grateful, cowering on the stone floor of the party space to drop licks and kisses on the boots of her tormentor and her weekend master.

"Would you like to fuck her?" he asked the sweating woman, pitching his voice so that Karen could hear him clearly.

"Hell yeah, sure—but I don't do guys. Even when they're cute like you!" They laughed together, and Michael liked her even more. He nudged Karen with his foot and said, "Get up and collect my toys, slut. You need to get fucked."

And sweet Karen, bold Karen, with the dancing eyes and the charming smile, had leapt up, done exactly what he told her, and never uttered a single word of discouragement to the three-way that became the centerpiece of the party. With a dildo, his cock, and their four hands, Michael and his new and temporary friend worked her over, invading every orifice, trying out every combination possible, literally using Karen until she begged for mercy. And she did beg—desperately, her words disjointed and jumbled. But she never used the magic word which would end the scene. Instead, she tried to plead with them, making promises, crying, and finally screaming herself hoarse.

When the party ended, Michael had to half-carry her back to his room, where finally, she would spend the night on the floor, cradled in a tangle of blankets and sheets. He knew that she didn't fall asleep for a long time, because he wasn't sleepy himself. But he enjoyed the feel of the room, her heavy, harsh breathing, and the thought that he had spent a thoroughly enjoyable weekend among the mundanes. And never did he reveal a single thing about his business or the Marketplace—he felt justifiably proud of that. Karen was obviously prime Marketplace material—a few more sessions like this weekend, and he would be able to bring her in himself.

He would have to convince Geoff to let him manage her training. And why not? Geoff would see that she had the potential, and permission would certainly be granted. Then, he could train her, write her contract, and be both her spotter and trainer of record. Geoff would give him a cut of the proper training house fee. And what's more, he would be fully established as a trainer, and one who could spot. The bright young star of the Californian Marketplace. He could write it up, describe the weekend and his thoughts about Karen, and become one of the subjects that other trainers read about when they aspired to that level of mastery. Soon, he'd have his own training facility, with his own special customers, just like Geoff. With assistant trainers to do all the shit work, and an endless stream of young, hot slavemeat of both genders to use, abuse, and fix up for some lucky owner. He'd never be bored, and never want for anything.

The only problem would be to make sure that Karen didn't fall in love with him. It happened all the time—transference, identification, you name it. Slaves fell for their trainers like teenage girls go for hairless girl-looking boys, naturally, and deeply. So you had to establish a distance, early on, and keep them off guard. Be just unpleasant enough to make them doubt that they truly loved you. Oh yeah, that would be a piece of cake.

Other than that, he would have to do just a little training, to make sure she was really Marketplace material and not just into this stuff for the weekend. It didn't take all that much to be a good slave for two days. He would have to test her—try her out in any number of things, sexual acts and personal service. Push her, take her to her limits and bring her back again.

But he could do this! He had already started, hadn't he? It was only natural to take things to the next step. And once he did—if she was as good as she seemed—he could be the perfect Marketplace professional, a spotter and trainer all in one! Even Geoff didn't spot!

Karen took to his subtle steering in predictable stages. She was more than eager to continue seeing him beyond the weekend, and had in fact been agonizing over not being able to keep in touch as they both lay awake far into the night. Over a breakfast of waffles and strawberries in the hotel coffee shop, Michael assured her that he would love to continue seeing her—but that he had no intention of being her boyfriend.

"I'm not the settle down and marry kind of guy," he explained. "I'm the master, and you're the slave-to-be, and that's the only relationship I'm interested in pursuing. But if you're into it, if you really want it—need it, even—I can make you into a perfect slave. I can teach you everything you'd ever need to know about service. But you have to understand that I'll never be a guy to take home to meet the parents."

"I understand," Karen had responded. Her waffles were barely nibbled at. Her eyes were ringed darkly, partly because of the lack of sleep and partly because of an errant cuff or two the previous night. Her whole body seemed achey and marked, and she was as tense over breakfast as she had been kneeling on the dungeon floor. "It's all I've ever wanted, master."

Perfect, perfect! Michael nodded looked at her with a cool, distant expression on his face. "Then get down on the floor," he said softly.

She panicked for a moment, and he stared at her. The coffee shop was full of other people from the conference some in collars and harnesses, but no one was actually on the floor. Waitresses bustled by, pouring coffee. Silver clanked in bins, and the sizzle of bacon frying seemed louder than ever. Karen stirred, but still didn't leave her seat. She bit her lip.

"Or don't," Michael said with a shrug. "It does matter to me, because if you don't, I'm paying the bill and leaving. If you do, we can discuss when we can meet again. Unless you make me wait too long."

He had gotten the idea from a mainstream book about two people having a doomed SM love affair. As he saw the fear and shame register in her eyes, he knew it was a terrific test. When he saw her rise and then hunker down onto her knees beside him, taking care to pull her legs from the aisle so that no one would trip over her, he smiled. He cut a piece of her waffle off, dipped it in a pool of syrup from his plate, and fed it to her by hand. When she ate it and licked his fingers, he could barely keep himself from taking her back up to the room to reward her with some more personal attention. It was just like what Geoff had shown him that night at dinner, with the arching male slave! Wouldn't Geoff be pleased to see how well Mike had taken to his teachings?

But instead, he fed her three more pieces, enjoying the envious looks from both men and women, and then told her to take her seat back and finish her breakfast. A few people rolled their eyes. A tourist or two stared in shocked silence. The waitress looked a little tired of all this leather silliness as she refilled his coffee.

But Karen looked as though she had discovered paradise. He

knew that look, having seen it in his own mirror. There was no longer any shred of doubt that she would be his first soft-world-to-Marketplace slave, and that she would bring him the start of fame and fortune. He smiled at her with all the patience and fondness he could feel, imagining Geoff's paternal pride. Oh yes. His future was assured, sitting right here at breakfast.

It took him three months to teach her the very basics. He knew the timing on that was far from ideal. Technically, you were supposed to be able to train a total novice to the level of a first public sale in about three months. Only special-use slaves, trained as cooks, or guards. or teachers. or large household managers. and other, more complicated services, were supposed to take longer. And that was only because they needed the time to work in their fields.

For a general purpose slave, all they needed to know were a few positions, a few dozen rules of behavior, and how to cultivate and maintain the correct attitude toward their service, their owners, and themselves. Attitude was Karen's weakest point, followed by her faulty memory between training periods. But that wasn't her fault, not entirely. Partly at fault was that Michael didn't have access to her full time—even weekends would be problematic, since he was never guaranteed every weekend off from his work at Geoff's place. But partly it was that Michael had never trained someone so out of context before. It took him a week just to get past the first minor roadblock in their relationship.

Wanting to ease her into the world of the Marketplace, he had decided not to tell her about it before she was fully ready to present to Geoff. Making her ready meant setting up a false kind of relationship with her. She lived a good 80 miles away, so it was easy to explain that he wasn't going to be spending a lot of leisure time with her. But neither could she stay with him, or contact him when he was at work. He tried to establish these conditions as ones created by his right as her master, but she was no Marketplace slave yet. All she knew was that she had found herself a lover who was hiding his life from her.

"Are you married?" she asked, lowering her eyes. "If you are, that's okay, but I'd really like to know."

"Listen, I told you I'm not the marrying kind. These are just the rules of the relationship—take them or leave them."

She leveled her eyes up to meet his and sighed. "Then—I have to think about it," she said carefully. "I want what you offer, I really do. But how do I know if I can really trust you? Playing for a weekend is one thing—committing myself to a new lifestyle takes real trust."

At first, he had been furious. "You trusted me enough to do whatever I wanted with you!" he yelled. "I could have tied you up and had you gang-raped, and you would have gone along with it!"

"This is my life you're talking about, Mike," she insisted, tears coming to her eyes. "I'd be stupid if I just signed it all away based on nothing!"

He had left her crying that night, shouting that she could have her world of fakes if she wanted, but he needed total and absolute trust or nothing. But on the long drive back to Geoff's place, his heart sank, and he knew she was perfectly right. No one was brought into the Marketplace unknowing; they had to want to be there. And the only way to want it was to know it existed. She would in fact have to be a fool to trust him when he had given her nothing but good sex with attitude.

But how to manage it all? She still had potential—hell, her insistence on knowing what she was getting into was even stronger proof of that. But how could he train her without being in full training mode? Could he really act like her boyfriend/lover and still manage to instill in her the basic requirements of a Marketplace slave?

And what would he tell Geoff? That he had a girlfriend? It would seem odd to say the least. He had all the sex he could possibly want, and it was very rare for someone working in the Marketplace to date outside of it—there were too many things you had to keep secret. Hell, just coming up with reasons why he was leaving the house for his time off would be something new. There weren't a lot of times when he felt that a weekend away would be any better than what he had there, even if he did end up working a little.

Damn—one lie could lead to dozens. But he had to have her, had to fashion his own client from scratch. It would be just the thing to elevate him from the status of Geoff's trainee to an independent man. Surely, that would get the attention he wanted, establish him. Once that was done, he could call this Anderson and get himself apprenticed to her for just long enough to be a high level trainer like those people he had met in England. Or hell, maybe she'd be looking for him.

He sent roses to Karen the following week, and took out a voice mail account, giving her a telephone number to call. He told her that he worked for a reclusive millionaire as a personal assistant. He figured it wasn't too far away from the truth. And he told Geoff that he had found a new girlfriend, which led to jokes made about his age and the energy of youth, and, unexpectedly, a grant of even more time off.

You won't regret that, Michael thought, as he started marking out days to spend training Karen. And you won't be angry at this little white lie when I tell you what I've done.

He repeated those sentiments over and over again, as if to reassure himself that they were true.

CHAPTER THIRTEEN

"Good morning, Vicente," Michael said, breaking a yawn. "God, you're up early."

"Oh yeah," the big man said. "Early to bed, early to rise, so they say." He was pristine, as he always was in the morning, black and white checkered pants and shiny black shoes, white chef's coat—the perfect chef. Later on, as the day wore on, he would change clothing, become dusty with flour or dotted with tomato sauce, or even grimy with newsprint and ink. But every morning, he looked like he stepped out of a movie set. "You're up early too," he noted, glancing at the clock. "Bad sleep?"

Michael nodded and dropped his butt on the stool. He looked at the cabinet where the coffee cups were, but before he could open it, Vicente pulled a cup out of the drain basket and filled it. "Here you are," he said, sliding it across the counter. Michael smiled weary thanks and breathed in the aroma.

"Mmmm." It smelled strong. "Colombian?"

"Brazilian," Vicente said. "Like me!"

"Oh, that's where you're from. I couldn't figure out the accent."

"Accent? I don't have one!" He laughed and poured some coffee for himself. "You do. You all do."

"Well, I guess you have a point." Michael breathed in more coffee and took a sip. God, what a night. His sleeping problems had started during his third week—he would stay up for hours just waiting to get drowsy, and then wake up every hour or so until dawn. Since Emil had asked him about his sleeping patterns, he had examined them more carefully, and was a little shocked at how many times he'd not gotten a good night's sleep. He couldn't figure out what was happening—he always slept well before. He cut out the coffee after dinner, asking for decaf, but that didn't seem to change anything.

"You worry too much," the cook counseled. He checked the wall clock and pulled up another stool. Raising one finger, he wagged it earnestly in Michael's direction. "Always, you are frowning, looking here, looking there, always looking for—what? Someone to jump out at you?"

"It's tough being a student of the Trainer of Trainers," Michael said. He forced a grin, trying to make it seem like a joke.

"Oh, yes. But it is better than being a carpenter, yes? Better than working at the Waldbaums store." He jerked his head in the general direction of the local supermarket and made a face. Michael laughed—Vicente's hatred for the huge, brightly lit shopping center was now quite well known. Helping out with the shopping had become almost automatic now that Michael knew where it was and had proven adept at fulfilling an order. Sometimes, he took Tara with him, but to her, this was old hat. She could probably make the list for Vicente without even taking a kitchen inventory. But she did come in handy to carry the bags.

"Sure, this is the life," Michael agreed, sipping the hot coffee cautiously. "I bet the fringe benefits of this job were kind of a surprise to you, huh?"

Vicente frowned himself, digesting the question. Before Michael thought to define "fringe benefits," the man brightened and nodded, and then shook his head. "No, Mr. Michael, I take no fringe benefits. Ms. Anders', she used to offer, but I don't need all these women. I have my girlfriend, yes? She is enough for me."

"No kidding? Well, that's, um, great. I hope she appreciates you."

"I think so, I think that she do. She is good for me, too, and that is as it should be. All this playing with many girls—or boys, yes?—that is for the young." He pointed at Michael and laughed. "Like you—young and ready for everyone, all the time. And look what happens—you don't get good sleep! Not like Mr. Chris, no, he sleeps damn good. Isn't that right, Miss Joan?"

Joan stood in the doorway, smiling at the sally. "Good morning, Vicente, good morning, sir."

Michael grunted. "What, does everyone get up earlier than me?"

"Oh no, Anders', she sleeps when she likes. It's Mr. Chris who gets up real early, like a farmer. Don't he, Miss Joan?"

"After sleeping very well, Vicente." She looked expectantly toward the back door that led to the postage stamp porch and the narrow, fenced in backyard. Michael found himself looking too, and saw the shadow of someone coming up the steps. Hell, he probably was the only one who usually slept past eight, the great Trainer notwithstanding.

Joan poured a fresh cup of coffee, added a dollop of milk to it and opened the door. Chris came in, breathing heavily and shaking droplets of icy cold moisture from his shoulders. The weather had taken one final nasty turn, even as the trees outside showed tiny green tips. He was dressed for cold weather jogging, in heavy sweats and an insulated vest, all gray, with a pair of heavy black gloves. A scarf was twisted around his neck. His hair was wet, curled up on the sides and in the back. There was a rolled up newspaper under one arm.

He looked surprised at Michael's presence, but nodded to him before handing the newspaper and his gloves to Joan. She took them neatly in one hand and passed him the hot coffee. It had all the look of a regular ritual—certainly they had had time to establish it. Michael wondered whether Tara had done similar duties for him, earlier.

"Lay out some clothing for me and get on with your duties," Chris finally said. Joan dipped her head and body slightly in acknowledgment and left. The three men watched her exit, and then Chris turned to Michael. "Good morning."

"Same to you. How does she know what you want to wear?"

"From observation, hopefully. If she ever expects to rise from housemaid to chambermaid, and then on to personal maid, she'd better learn to judge a person's habits and tastes within a relatively short period of time. Ten years can actually see her rise to housekeeper if she's attentive enough, or, she may be the companion and personal maid for one of the ladies of her household."

It had all the sound of a lecture, and Michael compressed his lips as he nodded. He always wanted to know why things were being done, and how the training went on, and it was just dandy that Chris was the one who spent more time answering the questions. Just dandy. Also dandy that Joan was learning about Chris's habits and not Michael's.

Fact was, it was galling that he had to ask these things of Chris. And Chris made things worse by always being so carefully patient, quick with an answer, never acting like it was a bother. Yet under all that patience and good temper was a veneer of contempt, just a hint of condescension. It was almost like Michael was beneath him, a kid who needed remedial education and soft words. Someone from whom you could expect very little.

Like right now, even as Chris was stretching out a little, Michael could see the twisted edge of that sardonic little smile that always meant a controlled amusement. Michael began to regret coming down early. It would have been better if he had just stayed the hell in bed.

"Don't worry," Chris said, in that annoying way he had of reading silences. "You're doing things as properly as can be expected." And with that, he nodded to Vicente, who grinned and nodded back, and the Chris left the kitchen.

"Jesus Christ," Michael muttered. "Just rub it in, why don't you?"

"Now, now, Mr. Chris don't mean any harm," Vicente said with a laugh.

"Doesn't he? He hates my guts."

"Oh, no he don't. If he hates you, he don't talk to you at all." He began to lay out breakfast ingredients, and poured the remainder of the first pot of coffee into a carafe. "You got to lighten up, Mr. Michael, eh?"

"I don't see how. I don't know what I'm doing, I have no idea whether I'm doing it right—and Parker makes me feel like I'm an idiot." Michael found the words coming out without any real volition, and bit his lip angrily. Griping to the cook, oh that's real professional.

"Listen to me," Vicente said, leaning over to top off Michael's coffee. "I been with Anders' now, oh, many years. Every time she gets a new student, there is something different. One time this way, one time that way. If I don't know how you supposed to be a student, how do you know?"

"Really?"

"Very truly. And Mr. Chris, oh, I know him for maybe... six years." He paused to think. "No! Seven years now. More, maybe. And do you know, when he come here, years ago, Anders', she don't talk to him for weeks—months, maybe! Every day, he do the work, he go do shopping, he take out the trash, he clean the rooms, right along with the slaves. And he types, always types. Never once does he ask her, why you treat me like this—not out loud. Then, one day, he give her this big damn stick."

Michael laughed out loud. "No, really?"

"I swear before God, this is true. He come in with this stick, so long." He measured a distance of about four feet off the floor. "He give it to her, she laughs too, just like you, and then, then she talks to him."

"Months?"

"It was a very long time," Vicente said.

"I don't know if I have that patience."

"Then you must learn it, Mr. Michael." He sighed and smiled when Joan came back in. "This morning, we make omelets. Mr. Michael, out of my kitchen!"

"Yes, sir," Michael said, hopping off the stool. He nodded curtly to Joan when he passed her, but wasn't wondering when he would be able to get a piece of her. He was wondering how long he would have to chop the damn wood and carry the water. He felt the usual renewal of strength—this trip was proving to be a regular roller coaster of confidence and self condemnation. But if Mr. Perfect Parker could do it, so could Michael LaGuardia. Any day.

The initial awkwardness of being among strangers gave way to a familiarization with the habits of his housemates and the various jobs expected of him. Pages began to fill in his notebook, observations of how Tara responded to everything, notations about movement and language, attitude and emotional display. In fact, the scope of behaviors he got to witness was fairly mind-boggling. It had all seemed simple before—train them to be obedient, and to not show emotions like boredom, displeasure, or annoyance. Get them to be expressive in bed, honest during formal interviews, and suitably submissive in everything else.

But there were so many variables here, so much to take into consideration! Anderson's bizarre requests seemed jarring at first, and then mysterious, giving way, finally, to the realization that they were deliberately strange in order to cover every possible situation a slave such as Tara might be expected to respond to. There was no way of preparing someone for everything, so the alternative was to prepare them for anything.

Anderson liked that. It was the first line in his book that she circled and checked. "That's one of my oldest rules," she said happily. "That one goes all the way back. Now, you're paying attention." She referred him back to her library, to a series of monographs on the topic, and he felt like a star pupil sent to the head of the class. But she didn't alter his duties in any way.

It was still a relief to have the use of Tara as a sex partner, though. Having that outlet took away the heaviest distraction of his first few weeks. But there was something attached to that freedom. Anderson never gave him the slightest hint that she disapproved of his getting his rocks off—hell, she was the one who gave him permission to do it! But Parker—Michael got the distinct impression that Parker didn't like it.

As usual. Parker didn't seem to like anything about Michael or what he was doing. But this was more obvious. Michael would appear slightly disheveled from a bout with Tara and Parker would be the first to see him. He would scan Michael's body, taking in the rumpled shirt, the wrinkled pants leg, the mussed hair. And he would hit Michael with this look—disgust, mixed with a little contempt and a dose of amusement. He usually wouldn't say anything, but later on, some sharp comment, some pissy little jibe would hit Michael and it was too clear where it was coming from.

It was a total mystery why the man would act that way. Trainers weren't supposed to be jealous over the damn slaves—slaves come and go, and either you get 'em or you don't. And besides, Parker was gay, he said so himself—sort of. Why would he care if Michael was getting a little from the slave he was helping to train? Tara was certainly not complaining! Hell, she had a great time with him, and was probably thanking her stars that she had a trainer who didn't just treat her like some corporate assistant. True, they never did get around to some really in-depth interviews, using some of the techniques and detailed questions that he found in one of the more basic Anderson training guides. But Tara had already been interviewed to death, hadn't she? Between the Trainer herself and Chris, and her years of experience? So, obviously it was better for her to be able to be judged on her performances, and not on whether or not she answered a question quickly enough.

He wrote these opinions down in his journal, making them less antagonistic and more rational-sounding, and continued to write detailed descriptions of what he did to her and how she responded and whether he rewarded her with an orgasm or punished her with a spanking, and he tried to ignore Chris's occasional hostility. It just made no sense. Instead, he concentrated on doing everything he could to make himself useful to the Trainer, and focused on that alone.

One night, Michael found himself alone on the first floor. Vicente was off, and away for the evening, probably visiting that girlfriend of his. She was Jamaican, Michael had found out, and the two of them liked to go dancing. It seemed amazing to have such a mundane life outside the Anderson house—he couldn't imagine doing the same thing.

Chris was also out, having taken the car God-knows-where. Another little mystery trip that no one spoke about. Maybe he had a boyfriend.

Joan was with her Japanese tutor, upstairs. Tara had been given some free time, and the Trainer herself was catching up on weeks of newspapers and magazines, tucked away in her room with a plate of brownies and some chamomile tea. She sure had a sweet tooth—it was amazing how she managed to stay so thin. It was probably genetic. From time to time, Michael could look at her high-cheekboned profile and see the faces of the Native American women who still lived on the reservations. His curiosity about her origins had replaced the curiosity about Vicente's. He wondered if maybe she had a touch of South America in her.

A quiet night in a quiet house. He had been unsure about how exactly to start a fire, so he didn't. On nights like this, he missed both the friendly crowdedness of Geoff's place and the presence of a TV. It would be great to lean back and channel surf for a while, just clear his head and enjoy some mindless entertainment. He had looked through the CD rack and found a few albums that he liked, but listening to music by himself didn't feel right. Music was background for socializing. He would go out himself, but he had no idea where to go.

That reminded him sharply of his intention to seek out the local SM scene. He went to the office and pulled out some of the local papers Chris had mentioned to him during the first week, and began to scan. He had jotted down two likely organizations and two public SM/sex clubs when the unfamiliar sound of the doorbell made him jump.

He got up to answer it, knowing that Tara wouldn't make it downstairs in time. Standing on the stoop was an older man, as tall as Michael, with black hair and a salt-and-pepper beard. He was wearing a blue winter jacket with the hood flipped back. He looked familiar.

"Hi, what can I do for you?" Michael asked.

"I'm Grendel Elliot," the man said. "I'm here to see Anderson."

"Sure, come in." Michael held the door open, and closed it firmly behind the man. It was frigging cold outside, and the chilled air swept around their ankles. Anderson hadn't said a word about expecting anyone, but then she never did. "Um—can I take your coat?"

Grendel shrugged the jacket off and rubbed his hands together. Michael hung it up in the hallway and indicated the front room. "If you want to take a seat, I'll go tell Anderson you're here."

"No need," Grendel said. "I think the lady on the stairs will take care of that."

Michael turned to see Tara halting in mid-step. "At once, sir," she murmured, turning gracefully.

"Good eyes," Michael commented. "Want something hot to drink? Or a drink-drink? I think I can handle that."

"No, I'll wait for the client. Anderson will no doubt have someone to show off." He extended his hand. "You're Michael LaGuardia. I saw you in San Francisco last year, when you were with Negel."

"Great memory, too," Michael said, shaking. Of course, it was the last Marketplace event he had gone to before leaving California. "Glad to meet you. I've heard good things about your house."

"Thank you." No corresponding compliment about Michael's former house—well, that was to be expected. New Yorkers were always in a disdainful competition with California; there was no reason why this wouldn't extend to Marketplace people.

The creaks of the stairway announced Anderson's arrival. She looked genuinely happy to see Grendel, and swept into the room to take his hand. "It's good to see you," she said.

"And you. You should come out to the Island every once in a while. Ride the horses, take some time off." He smiled at her and let her hand go. "Alex says hi. So does Rachel."

"You be sure to take my 'hi' right back. Have you met Michael?"

"Yes, we just got through the standard greetings."

"Then let's get down to business. Come into my office, and we'll talk."

Grendel nodded and headed over, and the two of them left Michael alone in the front room. He saw Tara vanish into the kitchen and counted off exactly one minute until she reappeared with a tray and headed toward the office. He wondered if Anderson had told her, or if she knew what Elliot liked. Whether she was always supposed to serve something to guests, or whether she needed directions or relied on instincts.

He waited for her to come out, in order to ask her. No sense in just sitting around doing nothing. It was a pity that she wouldn't gossip with him—he would love to know what business was being discussed behind that closed door. And why Grendel Elliot—Chris Parker's former employer—had just happened to arrive on a night when Parker was out.

⁂

Grendel paid the proper admiration to Tara when she left, and Anderson was properly modest. They sat back in their chairs, her fresh tea steaming on the desk, his coffee cradled in his hands.

"So, what are we going to do about him?" she asked, playing with a bracelet on her left wrist. One tap of her finger sent it spinning.

"I was hoping you could tell me," Grendel said. "I—we thought it was for the best initially, but now—why is he waiting so long? What is he waiting for?"

"I think he's waiting to be told what to do."

"Great! Tell him to come on back home."

She laughed, and after a second or two, Grendel shrugged. She sighed and looked down briefly. "You know I can't do that. It's against my best interests."

"What about his best interests?" Grendel put the coffee cup down on the desk and leaned forward in the chair. "I don't suppose you've gotten any closer to figuring out what he really wants, have you?" His sharp eyes asked the real question.

It's not wants at all, Anderson thought, as they stared at each other. It's what he needs.

"There's a hunger so strong in him that it makes a Green Beret look unmotivated," she said. "Do I know what he wants? He's a damn tease—one minute, he's offering everything, the next minute he's the proper, reserved companion who has no personal agenda."

Grendel shook his head. "You know he wants to be a slave."

Anderson pursed her lips and gave the bracelet another turn. "Yes. And no."

"That's helpful!"

"Sorry, Grendel, but that's all there is. Believe it or not, he doesn't say much about it."

He hit her with a sarcastic look, just the edge of an eyebrow raised in exasperation. "Now pull the other, Trainer."

She snorted derisively. "Oh, sure, he's got all the right symptoms. Despite what you and Alex played with, he's still prime material."

"Well, I suppose I asked for that." Grendel lowered his head and ran fingers through his hair. "I... it seemed like the best way to handle him. His responses were... amazing. God, what a player!" He became more animated, pushing himself up in the chair. "I never had so much fun doing that level of emotional torment. It was almost vampiric, but I can honestly say we probably fed from each other more or less equally."

Anderson smiled slightly. "That's the way it works best, isn't it?"

"For some things, sure," Grendel said. "The trouble comes when we confuse the pleasure with utility. And believe me, Anderson—there isn't a more downright useful boy to have around. I thought we were prepared to continue without him when he was ready to move back here, but I swear, a week doesn't go by without me wondering how the hell we ever kept up before." He sighed. "But it was too much. We used him, all right, used him like a slave. In so many ways. Except for the obvious. He's caught in this state of... liminality. And you're right. We put him there. It was wrong to drag it out this long."

"Don't throw that pity party yet, Grendel, I think what you did was exactly right," Anderson said. "Don't you think I do the same thing?"

Grendel forced a slight smile. "Here's where I get to say that he never told me much about you."

Anderson laughed. "Well, I hope you didn't expect otherwise, my friend. But you know, I don't need a five-dollar sociological term for the boy, he's been betwixt and between all of his life. He was happy with you, and useful, he was doing what he was born to do, and that was fine—for as long as it lasted. But we're all grown-ups here. Nothing is forever. It was time for him to finish up this paper and move on."

"But how has he moved on?" Grendel insisted. "He's beyond your student, Imala, he doesn't belong here doing apprentice work. He's a Master Trainer—he surpassed our house ages ago, and we've been holding him back.

"The paper is just an excuse, and a lame one at that. So, if he doesn't move on, then why the hell wait for some bolt out of the blue to change the way things are? You know what he wants. We know what he wants. And so does he, however much... ah... " He paused to consider a word. "However much nonsense he feeds us all about wanting only to do the right thing."

She smiled at his neat avoidance of even a mild profanity. "And if I told him when he came back to pack his bags and go back to you, what would that solve?" she asked. "Would you take him on as what you're so sure he wants to be?"

Grendel looked down into his lap and nodded. He stretched out a leg to reach into his pocket, and pulled out a silver chain with two small rings set into the ends. A lock dangled from one end, with a key inserted into the bottom. He dropped it into a glittering pile on the desk and retrieved his coffee.

Anderson eyed it but didn't pick it up. "This is a new development."

"Alex and I discussed it last night. We do miss him, and not just as a trainer, although he certainly is priceless there. He brought a sense of balance and security to the house. And, he kept us on our toes, which is a good thing!"

"He does do that," Anderson admitted with a nod.

"If he's not going to go on to be an independent trainer, then the only other path for him is to the auctions. There's no way around it. Who else would he work with, other than you? And I've been imagining him on the block—and every time, I start to think about how we couldn't afford to buy him. And I think of how many people would love to get their hands on him—and how deeply he—" He paused, and took a breath. "He was happy with us."

"That's charmingly—submissive of y'all," Anderson said, settling back in her chair.

"Well, what else can I do? Don't you think I've been wondering if I drove him away? If I denied myself and him something that could have worked just because it would have been difficult to manage?"

"I notice your pronouns have changed a bit."

"You're a riot, Anderson. Now stop analyzing me, and give me the real story here."

"All right, I'm sorry about that. It's habit; I have to learn not to do it with my friends." She stopped playing with her bracelet and leaned forward herself, putting her elbows on the desk. "Here's my most basic analysis of our boy. He's still figuring out what he wants, because there's nothing perfect for him to go after. He's owned, he's served, and he's trained, and nothing has worked out perfectly, has it? Call it a mid-life crisis, call it a damn heavy case of depression, call it irresponsible—but he's waiting for someone to up and tell him which way to go. I won't—I can't. And you've just become someone who might. Now, he has to consider that offer, and make up his damn fool mind."

Grendel grinned as her accent became stronger. "You wouldn't like it if he took me up on this."

"Oh hell, if it makes him happy, he should do it. And if anyone will go out of their way to make him happy, it'd be you and Alex. However inappropriate I may think that is." He laughed, and she waved one hand limply at him. "It's true," she protested. "The next thing you're going to tell me is that everyone should do this kind of soul searching to make their slaves happy. And believe me, if that's what's gonna come out of your mouth, there's a house in Santa Cruz that recently lost a trainer... Maybe they'll take you in."

"But you made your best point, Trainer. He's been there, done that. Paid the dues. Maybe it's time he got what he needs to make him happy."

"Happy again? Now, since when does everyone have the right to be happy? We have our jobs to do, Grendel, and sometimes they're not going to be richly, personally fulfilling. No matter how much we pay in dues. You have to weigh the plusses and minuses here—where do you think he should be? Off playing, or doing what he has to do?"

Grendel laid a hand down over the collar. "This shows I am not playing any more."

"Oh? And what will you use for leverage in these mental games he adores so much, these emotional torments you feed from—when he has what you've only teased him with for these few years? Hmm?"

Grendel's eyes narrowed, and he folded his hands. "Will you act as his trainer and make the offer?" he asked, his voice tense.

Anderson stared at him and started to say something, but she bit back the words. Then, she smiled gently. "Of course. Why, Ah'd be honored, suh." She raised her shoulders and bent her head in an exaggerated bow. "But I'll also answer his questions honestly when he asks them. As his trainer."

"That's fair," Grendel admitted, relaxing again. "A damn shame, since he'll listen to you, but fair." He ran his fingers through his hair again, sweeping it back. "But if he's smart, he'll take the chance on a collar. I shudder at the thought of being in your debt, Trainer of Trainers, but I'm glad I came."

"I'm glad you did, too, and believe me, there are few things worse than owing me anything, Mr. Elliot. But we'll see what Parker says, and more importantly, what he does. How is Rachel working out, by the way?"

"Wonderfully. Excellently. But she was well trained, as you know. Well prepared, at least. We always feel a little short staffed—the trainees have to learn household chores earlier than usual. But it all works in the end."

"That's what we hope for, Grendel. That it all works out in the end."

Chapter Fourteen

Chris came in at 12:30. The early-to-rise household seemed asleep as he let himself in the front door. He was preparing to hang up his coat when he heard the discreet cough beside him. It was Tara.

She said softly, "I'll take that, Chris. Trainer is waiting for you in the kitchen." She took his coat and bag, and he patted her fondly as he passed her heading toward the rear of the house. It took skill to come up behind him so quietly. He rubbed his chest through the shirt before he stepped into the harsh white light of the kitchen.

"An early night for you," Anderson said as he came in. She was seated by the counter, idly flipping through Vicente's index file. There were a few cards on the counter beside her.

"And a late one for you. Is there something wrong?"

"No, I wouldn't say that. But come on in and set a while. It's time for another chat about you."

He sighed, but took a stool. "What happened?"

"I saw Grendel tonight."

He stiffened, and looked a little surprised, and a flash of pain showed just for a second. He recovered his composure and nodded for her to continue.

"Well, there's no reason to mince words. He brought this." She nudged the collar across the counter toward him, from where it had been hidden by her sleeve. "If you're willing to serve, they're willing to own."

That one got him. He took a deep breath, and his right hand came up to cover his mouth, index finger tucked across his upper lip. Anderson didn't smile, but she knew that gesture, as she knew dozens of others in him, some of which he probably wasn't aware himself. This one was a cry for security. And a sign that he was very, very tired. She looked at his eyes under the steel rims of the glasses, and then focused her attention on the chain. She generously gave him the time he needed to gather himself, and when he started stroking his mustache and let his hand drop a little, she nudged it again.

"Nice quality. Not their usual style, is it?"

"No, it isn't." Chris sighed and picked it up. "No, they usually use steel, larger links. This is a formal style." He let it slide from one hand to the other. "So. This would be... acceptable... to you?"

"If it were not, I would have said so to Grendel. No, I think this is something important enough for you to make the final decision on." She didn't have to stress the word "final"—she could see he caught it anyway. He ran his fingers along the chain thoughtfully, looking down for a moment, away from her eyes.

"What do you think?" he finally asked.

"It's about time you asked me that." Anderson stepped off the stool and stretched. "What do I think? I think it would make you very happy—for a while. And then you'd realize that it's all too easy for you, and you'll start thinking of new ways to make your life harder, and I'll hear from you in, oh, a year? Maybe two."

"It's a kindness that you're so gentle with me," he said wryly, rising along with her.

"You don't respond to gentleness, my boy. You like a boot in your butt to get you going. Now, I'm giving it to you. You think it'll be different because you'll wear a collar? Hell, Grendel and Alex will give you anything you want to come back and make things better."

He closed his fist around the collar. "I'm sure you didn't mean any disrespect by that, Trainer."

She waggled her finger at him. "Don't go all formal on me, buster. You know I like them both. They're my friends, and you love them, and that's great. But it's not enough for you. You can't keep running away from these decisions, Chris Parker. One of these days, it's gonna be one way or the other. You play, or you serve. Or give it all up and join a monastery."

"We don't have monasteries," Chris said softly.

"Well, whatever y'all have. Be a rabbi, whatever. Don't change the subject. If you take this offer and go back, what will you be?"

"Their majordomo, I suppose. I would be best suited for the job."

"Right. And Rachel will go back to being housekeeper then?"

He sighed. "Which would not be fair to her."

"Forget her, we're talking about you. So there you'd be, in the exact same place you were last year. And what will have changed for you? You'll still need the attention, won't you? Or will you wean yourself off of all that, and be happy just training?"

"I could be."

"Oh, give me credit for having half a brain, Chris Parker."

"It could be different. If I were truly theirs, I could—"

"Parker."

"But I could be useful, Imala—"

"Training novices? For how much longer? How many times are you gonna break them in and let them go? How long can you go on without the credit, without the freedom to establish your own school?"

"Maybe I don't want my own school," he snapped. "And it's not about my own school, is it? It's about yours!"

Anderson gave a little hoot of surprise and smiled. She leaned slowly against the counter and said, "Ohhh. My first name, and a raised voice."

He looked a bit shocked himself. He immediately stepped back and drew himself up before her. "Trainer, I'm very sorry for losing my temper. And for the tone of voice. Please excuse me—I'll not do it again."

She softened her smile just a little and reached out to touch his shoulder. "And if I called you to formal manners, you wouldn't hesitate, would you? You'd hit the tiles so fast, you'd smash your kneecaps. And it would be a relief, wouldn't it?"

He closed his eyes and turned his face away from her. "Try me, Trainer."

"Oh, no, I don't think so. Let's go up front and pretend that we're equals, all right?"

He followed her mutely, and sat stiffly in the arm chair by the fireplace.

"Would you rather go formally into the Marketplace?" Anderson asked. "In two months, you could be at the Amsterdam auction."

"Don't you think I've considered that? It's been on my mind for years."

"Yes, I know. But you haven't asked me to prepare you in quite a while. I just thought you'd decided not to leave your life up to chance. It's a valid decision, especially for you."

"No, it's not!" Chris banged the arm of the chair, hard. "I've spent years teaching other people how to bear it, and dammit, I should be able to do it! But I can't! I'm not—I'm not good enough for the block."

Anderson stared at him for a moment, and then laughed out loud. "Excuse me? Mister, I trained you! I watched you change—in more ways than one! Chris, I could have put you on the block years ago, and not as a novice, either. If I put you up today, I could easily say you were my crowning achievement. Perfect control, perfect obedience, and pretty hot in the sack to boot.

"With these new muscles of yours, you'd look beautiful up there—and fetch a very respectable price, too. More than enough for your purposes, certainly. You're not common, no. You'd be pretty unique, and that would gain some attention that I know you'd rather not have. But your old fears don't apply any more. You've added to your basic value in a way that Grendel frankly called priceless. So, if that's what you want, let's not chase the colt around the field; let's just do it."

"And then what? Who do you think will bid for me, Trainer? And for what purpose?" He rubbed his chest and looked frustrated; he jerked his hand down and held onto the chair arm again. "You tell me. What would any potential owner want from me?"

Anderson nodded. "Okay. Now we're talking about it like adults."

"All I can be now is a trainer! There's just no way around it. I'm not priceless because of my obedience or my responses or my attitude..." He paused and looked down at himself, running one hand down his torso. "Or my body," he added bitterly. "Hell, I'm not even valuable in the one service skill I was trained in. I only have value because of what I offer professionally as a trainer. Or, as a... curiosity. A trophy. If I go back to Alex and Grendel, at least I can pretend—" He broke off, and hit the chair again.

"Oh, and that will solve everything, won't it, Chris?"

"I hate you, Imala. Have I ever told you that?" He looked up at her, challenging.

Anderson laid a finger on her chin, thinking. "Why, as a matter of fact, I do recall your muttering something like that way back when you were doing something involving a kitchen floor and a toothbrush."

They gazed at each other. Tension began to shift, and slowly, he relaxed, throwing his arms over the edges of the chair and sinking back into the pillows. "Now, how the hell did you hear that?" he asked, amusement in his voice. "I thought you were asleep."

"Seeing through walls, reading minds—nothing, compared to my parabolic hearing. What was it you said? 'I hate this fucking place, I hate that fucking bitch,' I think it was."

"You know, little Golden Butt could benefit from some of your super powers. You should hear what he's muttering."

"We're not talking about him, Parker, we're talking about you."

He looked back at her, seriously. "Tell me what to do, Trainer. Please."

"I won't. You don't want to hear what I want you to do. And you know I need you to make the correct choice yourself, or stay right where you are until you do. At least here, you're doing what I want."

"Then—I can't decide. Not yet."

"Okay. I'll call Grendel tomorrow and tell him that his offer is being considered."

"Fine."

"Fine. And if you're ready to stop beating up on that poor chair, why don't you show me the finished project?"

Chris touched his chest thoughtfully. "It was a little messy tonight. The bandages will be on for a few days. I'll show you as soon as they come off."

"All right, I'll wait. But I do want to see it. For now, come on over here and work off some of that excess energy on my shoulders. Tara and Joan are just not strong enough to do it right."

He got up at once and started rubbing his hands together. "Why don't you ask Mikey? I'm sure he does a divine massage."

"Why don't you keep your mouth shut and your hands moving, wise ass?"

He came up behind her and placed his hands on her shoulders. But before he began, he bent down and kissed her lightly on the cheek. "I'm very sorry I'm such a pain, Trainer. You are better to me than I deserve."

She smiled and turned slightly to give him one back. "Damn, this beard is scratchy. What would you do if I told you I didn't like it?"

"The razor is upstairs."

"Ah, you're a good boy."

"I try, Trainer, I try."

CHAPTER FIFTEEN

It seemed barely possible, but the time had come to say goodbye to Tara. Michael felt strange about it—for four weeks, he had participated in her training, but he didn't feel he knew her at all. Anderson never invited him to her private interview sessions with her, and Michael was always bad at extracting deep information out of a file. He did manage to get some details about her life out of her, but not the in-depth level of knowledge that a trainer of Anderson's caliber habitually sought with their client. He went back over his notes from the few interviews he did manage to remember to schedule, but realized that there was little he could say about her life before the Marketplace, or what her true personality was like, or even how many owners she had. The book on interviewing techniques had offered dozens of questions, but he had actually asked her only a few. And when he looked back at her file, he found that the sketchy information made available to him didn't seem to enlighten him as much as just hammer home how much he didn't know. Why hadn't he questioned her with the file in his hands, at least once? He regretted not paying closer attention.

Toward the end, Tara worked almost exclusively with Anderson, reviewing, being tested, and being polished. It left Michael with a lot more time on his hands, and that kept him constantly running into Chris and Joan. The tension escalated, and nothing seemed to be able to stop the rise.

It would seem innocuous on the surface. A moment in the corridor, an exchange of glances. Michael would always try to keep himself neutral, but as Joan began to actually improve before his very eyes, his resentment grew.

His journal had begun to bulge with pages and pages of scrawled notes. From time to time, Anderson would ask to see it, or would ask him what page he was up to, but still she gave him little formal instruction. He found himself re-reading some of her works and memorizing passages. He wanted to sound prepared if she should question him—but she rarely did. And as he saw more changes in Joan, he began to actually practice some moves when he was alone in his room.

It had started with that first sight of Chris doing that movement dance with Joan. It had seemed like the obvious way to teach, but that would require that a trainer be as graceful as a potential slave, and as skilled in all of the arts. It went against Michael's previous training. But something in it seemed so right that he researched the topic on his own. It was right there in front of him, in Anderson's writings and in the notes and essays by the trainers she admired.

The best trainers, they insisted, were slaves and former slaves.

It was hardly a new concept. Hell, it was almost common; it had even been part of what the leatherpeople called the "Old Guard" style of SM. One had to work their way up the ranks, as it were, by starting as a junior bottom, working up to senior bottom, and then to junior top and so on. Conventional wisdom usually held that the best tops were bottoms first.

Michael had run into that attitude first with Geoff. Geoff, who had never been a slave, obviously disagreed.

"It's a common fallacy," he had explained. "The fact is, there are natural tops and natural bottoms. There's no reason to explore something that's not a part of your nature just to make someone else happy. I expect that my trainers will be open-minded about new experiences, but I don't insist that they act in ways that are contrary to their nature."

And that made sense. But Michael had tried bottoming anyway, just to see if he could figure out why the slaves liked it so much. He picked up a hot-looking guy at a leather bar and went home with him for some bondage, a little spanking, and some minor cock and ball torture. It was all devoid of intercourse—Michael made it clear he wanted SM only, no cocksucking or buttfucking. And that was okay—tops in the leather world were well used to bottoms setting limits, and this one went along with it.

The spanking was downright fun. The man's hands were slightly rough and large, and the way they felt when he massaged Michael's buttocks was simply pleasurable. Michael relaxed and purred when the spanking began. Each warm slap pleasantly shook his lower body and sent thrumming signals through to his balls. He knew his ass looked good, and he liked the way the man admired it, stopping frequently to squeeze and cup the cheeks. Michael was bent over the back of a big leather chair, his body well supported, the scent and feel of the leather gently arousing. And when the top growled at him, telling him to admit he liked it, Mike grinned and cheerfully did—and tried not to laugh. There hadn't been the slightest feeling of surrender in what he was feeling—only an erotic sort of relaxation. The verbal exchange killed that, though.

The genitorture started with a rough hand job to get him tumescent. That was accomplished rather quickly, and Michael watched as the older man pinched and pulled at the loose skin around his balls, playing with sliding the skin on his cockshaft back and forth. It was weird—but not especially painful. Clamps were painful, though, and he was astonished to find that his erection didn't vanish when they were applied. The top was pleased though, and his excitement was plain. He twisted and tweaked them, changing where they would go on and off, tapping them, pulling at them—until Michael finally felt the whole thing had become annoying and casually called his safeword.

And was promptly released and congratulated on how far he'd come in his "first session." They had beers in the kitchen afterward, and the man asked if he could watch Mike piss before he left. Michael thought it would have probably been closer to the man's true desires to pissed on—but he obliged him with what he asked for and went home.

He tried it again with a professional dominatrix, and took his only flogging from her. That was a little better, but when the session was over, he didn't feel very, well, submissive. His back was warm, and tender in some spots, and it did feel great when she ran her long nails down his body. He liked her wardrobe—she had worn high stiletto boots and stockings and a wonderful PVC corset all in red and black. She was also into some verbal attitude, and that didn't seem as jarring as it had been with the gay top. Maybe it was just more theatrical with her—but Michael got into it. It was sexy.

But he couldn't see wanting this regularly, or being thankful enough to want to lick her boots or even bring her a cup of tea. It was just okay. Pleasant sensations were nice. But the minute they became more than exactly what he liked, they just became frustrating or annoying. So, he decided that he wasn't made to be a bottom, and stopped exploring.

But this was something different somehow. Michael had put his body in the hands of sensual tormentors, but had never tried to be submissive. Had never actually done the tasks which made up so much of the actual training. Now that he thought of it, he realized that whenever Geoff wanted to show a movement or demonstrate a response, he called in a more experienced slave. It was only natural to use them that way—yet it wasn't thought of as using the slave as a teacher.

That started him thinking about Parker. The guy had to have been a slave once, that was how he knew all that stuff. Michael wondered how long ago that would have been, and who trained him initially. Anderson, probably—except that she didn't do novices. So, who trained him first? And how long ago was it? Could it have been Elliot and Selador?

There was one way to find out.

Anderson's computer had a modem and a connection to the Marketplace records office—she was entitled to that. Geoff had had a connection too, but mainly used it to write long letters back and forth with other trainers and his network of spotters. You couldn't just dial in and get any information you wanted; there were levels of safeguards with codes to allow someone access to certain information. By himself, Michael had no standing. He could log on, put in his ID code, and get what were essentially email privileges. But Anderson had full access, and he had her code.

Technically, he wasn't supposed to use it for this kind of research. But there was so much available in the online archives that

she had given him a code in order to download files only available
to fully recognized trainers. He was only supposed to do it when
she gave him a specific assignment—which had been twice, so far.
But he was familiar with the software enough to do a quick search.
No one would ever need to know.

He made the call and listened as the atonal sounds of the
modem echoed from under the desk. The archives asked for a name
and two codes, and he filled in the blanks using Anderson's information. Soon, he was presented with a full menu of options. He
went immediately to sale records and set a search for Parker, Chris
or Christopher. To narrow the search, he entered his nationality,
gender, and kept the search to dates after 1970. Parker didn't seem
much older than thirty-three, but you could never tell.

A green dot blinked slowly as the search began.

Michael kept eyeing the door, expecting Parker or Anderson to
march in at any minute and demand to know what he was doing.
But Chris was busy with Joan and Anderson with Tara—there was
no one in the house who cared what Michael was doing. He tapped
the desk nervously. And bit back a curse when the search turned up
a 49-year-old Christopher Parker who was black and currently living with an owner in Nova Scotia.

The system asked if he wanted a detailed record of that Christopher Parker. He hit the function key for no, and it asked if Anderson
wanted any other files today.

Search: Anderson, first initial unknown, female, American. His
finger almost slipped as he hit the key to launch the search. Two
minutes later, six files popped up. He examined them one at a time,
until he hit one that made him shiver.

Anderson, Imala. New York, NY. Master Trainer...

That was her! He hit the key for the full file, flushed with the
excitement of finding her origin. A basic identity file popped up,
the screen filling in information which confirmed that this was
her file. Her first name was... Imala? He'd never heard that name
before. Birthplace—Augusta, Georgia. When the first page of the
file was complete, he hit the return key to request the next section,
the Marketplace timeline that would reveal all of her standings,

whether she had been a slave or an owner, who had trained her...

File unavailable. Damn! And you just couldn't ask the damn machine why. He left the individual records area and tried asking for it as an archived file.

PERSONNEL FILE ANDERSON, I. IS SEALED. THERE ARE 312 FILES IN THIS ARCHIVE UTILIZING ANDERSON AS A SEARCH PARAMETER. SELECT. MORE. SEARCH. DOWNLOAD. EXIT. RETURN TO MAIN MENU.

He hit exit and logged off, feeling a little wasted. What a disappointment!

But maybe not. He turned the machine off and thought about it some more. Who would have the ability to seal off an individual file like that, and why? If he could search slave records, and other trainers, why not Anderson? Was it her decision to block such access? And if so, at what level?

And stranger yet was Parker—he knew the moves, he walked the walk—but he had never put his butt on the block. In fact, despite his having published works for other trainers, why wasn't he listed as a trainer? His record wasn't even sealed—it was just plain missing! How very interesting.

But ultimately, not very helpful. There wasn't any way he could use this information—he certainly couldn't let Anderson know he was snooping in the personnel files. He wondered what would happen if he punched in his own name. Had Geoff made a formal report about what happened? If it was in his file, did that mean that every full trainer, all over the world, could read about that one dreadful mistake he had made?

He switched the computer back on, and with a twinge of fear started searching for himself.

Karen had bought the lie about his life, or at least made peace with herself about it. And she took to the training very well for a complete amateur raised in the wrong environment. Oh, it took him a long time to make her unlearn what she had learned—despite her claim that she was self-taught, she had picked up these habits from somewhere. A lot of it came from fictional books, some classic and some pretty laughable. Michael borrowed them from her and enjoyed them for their erotic content, if not for the light they shed on slavery. He returned them with notes attached— "Never do that," or "Works only in novels." And whenever he caught her imitating her fictional role models, he would paddle her until she cried, and burn the book in front of her. It happened twice—and replacement books never showed up on her shelves. Not bad.

It was almost terrifyingly exciting. Just being alone with her, without Geoff's plastic-covered charts and neat files, without the endless videotaping and question-and-answer sessions, was so thrilling it was difficult to keep it a secret. He was her god—he would arrive at her door and she would be ready for him: collared, naked, and shivering with anticipation. Eagerly, she would serve his every whim, and suffer for every infraction. He would sprawl out in her bed, while she lay on the floor with only a light blanket and her chains for comfort.

She was allowed no privacy, no secrecy. She had to ask for permission even to relieve herself, and he would often watch her, just to let her know that no door could be closed to him. Many of these things went beyond what Geoff taught—bathroom habits were assumed to be the province of individual owners and slaves were warned of that potential, but that was it. Really having the power, Michael decided, was much better.

He would put her in bondage and photograph her, and toss the photos under her face while he fucked her later on. He drilled her relentlessly in how to move, how to talk, and even took some of Geoff's basic training manual out of context to give her pages to study. He took credit for them, and warned her never to reveal them to another person, and she swore that she wouldn't.

She rarely wavered in her dedication to his training; in fact, she thrived upon it. She told him more than once that he was the most dominant lover she ever had—that he always knew exactly what to do to make her feel properly submissive, and never once let her slip. He was proud of her admiration, and eager to show off his skill every time they met. Sometimes, he would drive back to Geoff's place, half falling asleep at the wheel, exhausted from the expense of energy one weekend with her took from him. But it was worth it, every minute. She responded to him like a dream, and punishing her for her errors made him feel like he could take on the world and beat it into submission.

Once, when he arrived and she had her period, she was cranky and didn't want to be touched.

"I'm sorry, master," she said to him, wearing panties and a robe. Her hair was tangled, and she looked like she had just come from bed. A far cry from the freshly washed, primed, and already aroused woman who was supposed to greet him at the door. She grimaced and forced a smile, one arm bent over her lower abdomen, and kept talking. "When I'm like this, I just can't do anything right. I'm bloated, I have these awful cramps—I should have known it was coming—"

He slapped her, hard, across the face, and she reeled back in shock. Geoff rarely—if ever—used that much force against a slave's face. He gave swift, light taps with his fingers only, or held onto their chins with one hand, scaring them as he calmly delivered his discipline. But Michael had itched to just lay a hand across someone's mouth like they did in the movies or on TV—and the effect was pure adrenaline on him. Karen's eyes snapped open wide as one hand flew to her cheek. Blood drained from her face and then rushed back as she blinked and gasped.

"You're disobeying me," he said coldly. "Get those clothes off, and get down on your knees, you're going to be punished."

"But—listen, I don't feel well—"

He grabbed her by the hair and jerked her down to her knees. "You're a slave," he hissed, pulling his gear bag over to her. "You feel what I want you to feel. You're not sick, you're only on the rag. That doesn't count for an incapacitating illness."

"Mike, please—"

He pulled out his brand new gag and pressed it into her mouth. The ball spread her lips and forced her mouth open and she coughed against it as he settled it in place. She was crying as he buckled it on, but didn't fight him as he stripped her robe off and then cuffed her wrists behind her back.

"If you're not in the mood to serve me, you won't have to," he said, pulling some rope out. Expertly, he bound her ankles together, bent her knees, and lashed the ankle rope to her wrists, leaving about two feet of slack. It wasn't a hogtie, it didn't bend her backwards, but it did keep her from going anywhere. And she would hurt like hell when he let her out.

He knew about the dangers in what he was doing—the handcuffs alone were considered by most Marketplace people to be barbaric items, suitable only for law enforcement or punishment, and then only used sparingly. The gag and the bondage were strictly because he liked the look—bondage at Geoff's or at his uncle's was a more elaborate affair, designed to create access, rather than deny movement. But she was crying—he had to stay close, to make sure she didn't get her nose all clogged and lose the ability to breathe. He also had to make sure that her hands didn't lose feeling. So, he took a seat behind her and read her own magazines, flipping through mail order catalogs and listening to her muffled whimpers and moans, watched her wiggle her fingers and shiver.

He undid the bondage when he was bored.

"I don't believe you did this," she said to him, spitting out the trails of saliva that had gathered in her cheeks. He grinned to see the puddle of drool where her chin had rested on the floor. "Safeword, fucking safeword!"

"I told you I don't play that way," he replied, helping her up. "Let's get you washed off."

She pulled away from him and reached for her robe, tossed on the floor beside where she had been bound. "Don't touch me," she cried. "I think you should leave!"

"Yeah? And if I leave, how will you let me know how sorry you are for having these temper tantrums? Because if I do leave now, I'm not coming back. You don't control me, Karen, you surrender control to me. And if you can't do that, I'll leave, sure." He hid the panic he was feeling, desperately hoping that she would see it his way. Angry at her return to the mundane way of handling things, he grabbed the robe out of her hands and used one corner of it to wipe off the mouthpiece of the gag. She stood there, shaking, and watched him as he tossed it back on the floor.

"I'm going to take a shower," she finally said.

"Yes, that's what I suggested. Don't close the bathroom door."
He turned away from her so she wouldn't see his relief, and went
into her kitchen. That wasn't the way she should have reacted! She
should have cried, and begged his forgiveness! She should have
kissed his hands, his feet, begged him to hold her and tell her it
was all right! He did everything right. He enforced his dominance,
and his rules. That was what she had learned to expect. That was
what she wanted, what she loved! What went wrong? He grabbed
a soda from the refrigerator and gulped it down, and checked his
face in the mirror hanging in the hallway. Okay, he looked cool.

He went to the bathroom, where he could hear the shower running. Good girl, she left the door open, like she was supposed to.
Inside, he checked her medicine cabinet and pulled out two tablets
of ibuprofen and put some water in the cup by her toothbrush. He
had to rescue this situation, make her understand. He couldn't let
her just throw this all away because she fucked up once!

The water stopped, and she pulled the shower door open and
reached for her towel. But he was holding it open for her.

She stared at him for a moment and then stepped into the
towel, letting him wrap it around her body. He handed her the
tablets and the cup, and she took them without comment. He put
the cup back on the rack and turned her around to face him.

"If you want to be a slave, you can't have cranky days and show
them to your master," he said, trying to sound as strong, yet as
patient and caring as Geoff. "I know things are going to go wrong
sometimes. Cramps, or a headache, or just one of those days when
you want to snap at everyone and take a few heads off. But you
have to rise above that. It's part of being a good slave."

"But I don't control those things! If I could just turn them off,
don't you think I would?" Her curls bounced as he ran the edge
of the towel over them. Her eyes were still red and puffy—she
looked like a kid.

"Listen—soldiers have to turn them off and they do. Doctors
and actors have to turn them off, and they do. Everyone who has

a responsibility to something bigger has to be able to control those minor annoyances—and they do. If you want it badly enough, you will, too."

"I don't know if I can," she said, falling toward him, leaning against his chest. He hugged her warmly—thank God she wasn't talking about forgetting it all. Finally, she was responding correctly! She was just having a minor set-back, that's all.

"You will," he promised generously. "You'll learn while doing."

It was all he could say, really. This part of the training was his alone.

Geoff encouraged his clients to tell him or the undertrainers when they were having bad days. Every non-intentional discomfort was tended to in some way, especially if some kind of therapy could alleviate future symptoms. Chiropractors and massage therapists were called for lower back pain and headaches. Migraines were treated by physicians, allergies by specialists.

"You have to help them overcome what are actually mood-altering situations not of their owner's control," he had advised. "This will allow them to devote their time and emotional attention to their duties, and not their problems."

Michael thought that was coddling them. Hell, he went to work when he had a headache! Never missed a day. And they were supposed to be slaves, for crying out loud! How could a master expect to be spending more money in order to get his slave to a chiropractor? Not to mention how many doctors were available for slaves to just go to without having to explain the marks, the chains, the piercings or whatever. As far as he was concerned, slaves should go to doctors when they were seriously sick or injured, and the rest of the time just deal with it like every other working stiff did.

So Karen survived her period and cried in his arms a little bit, angry at herself for not even trying to live up to her agreement with him. After a very stern lecture and a spanking, he forgave her magnanimously and even allowed her to sleep with him that night. He didn't insist on fucking her, mostly because the idea always struck him as a little gross. But he did enjoy a very long time having his entire body licked, kissed and sucked on, culminating in a nice, long session of cocksucking. He felt that such an evening more than proved his point that she could still be entertaining when she was bleeding.

It was almost time to bring her to Geoff. Just a few more weeks, and then he would explain everything to her. The Marketplace was perfect for her—she had no heavy ties to the community, wasn't overly involved with her family, and she had broken up with her last boyfriend. Her job was okay, but she admitted that she only took it because it was close to home. Her house was rented. It would be easy for her to give it all up—and when Geoff saw her, he would fall in love. Perfect, perfect, perfect. Michael was already composing his introductory letter to Anderson.

Dear Ms. Anderson—I am 24 years old, a one year trainee of Geoff Negel. Having recently put my first slave on the block, I feel I am ready for the advanced training you offer. The enclosed files and Mr. Negel's letter of recommendation will attest to my having spotted, initially trained, introduced and market-prepped the slave Karen...

"Excuse me, sir?" Karen said, raising her head.

"You heard what I said. I'm a trainer for a real-life slave market. I saw you, and decided that you would be perfect for us, and in the past five months, I've been training you by our methods. Well, some of the... our methods, but mostly mine. And now, it's time to bring you in. You're ready. You've made me very, very proud." Michael was sitting on her couch, and the sun was setting beyond her living room windows. He decided that the drama of the glowing disk settling beyond the hills would be perfect for the closing of one life and the opening of another. Karen was on her knees facing him, naked, her hands on her spread thighs. It was a position he had decided to make standard—it looked very pretty and relaxed. So much of what we do is drama, he thought happily.

"Do you mean you want me to be your slave? Full time?"

"No. I mean, I'll take you to our training house, you spend a week there, meeting people and getting checked out, and when my boss accepts you, you get to join us."

"A week? That would be all my vacation time, sir." She looked a little excited, but a little shocked, too. That was easy to understand. Michael forced himself to remain gentle and easy with her, remembering how Uncle Niall had spent hours explaining it all.

"Well, see, once you joined, you wouldn't have to worry about vacation time, Karen. You'd quit your job, and come and be a real, full time slave. My boss would support you while you were in training—you'd get full room and board, medical care, the works. And, you'd finish your training. I'd say it could be done in less than a month. Maybe two, tops, if we decide you could be a pleasure slave." He didn't think she could really qualify for that—although sweet and pretty, she wasn't as fully bisexual as the people Geoff called pleasure slaves. But maybe she just needed more practice.

"And then?"

"And then you'd be sold," Michael said, knowing that this could be the difficult part. "My boss would do a lot of research, and find a good owner for you. They'd pay a lot of money for you—and some of it will actually be yours, once the term of slavery was up. Most of it, in fact. We never leave you without some kind of support. It's a great system, really. Our owners are checked out—they're not freaks and weirdoes. They're good masters, who know how to keep slaves."

"I'm sorry sir, but I don't understand." It was a stock phrase that he taught her to use before questioning anything—especially if she was questioning his judgment. "There can't be any such thing. Slavery is illegal in the United States."

"Well, yeah, slavery by force. But people can enter into personal service contracts."

"With all due respect sir, people don't get sold in personal service contracts."

Michael pondered that. Niall had explained it, a long time ago, but it had all seemed largely theoretical and tangled up in a lot of dull legalese. Geoff merely admitted that in a US court of law,

Marketplace contracts would probably be considered null and void, which was why there was no real way of enforcing them. Which was why they had to be so careful in choosing the people who would feel themselves bound by them. Damn, damn, he shouldn't have even brought that part up, it only got confusing. Let an expert explain that part, he thought. Backtrack, get back to the point.

"Look, it's not your problem. The Mar—this, um, society, has people who know what they're doing in respects to contracts and stuff. And besides, I know you really want to be a slave. You were made to be a slave! Well, this is the only way to do it for real. To have no control over your life, to be sold to the highest bidder, trained, worked, used—all the things you've been talking about for the past five months. Forget what's legal—this is what's real."

"But—I don't want to belong to anyone else," she said. The softness had gone out her eyes, and Michael experienced a moment of doubt. Something was going wrong.

"I realize that it's a scary prospect, but I assure you, it's all safe. And you'll love it in training, everyone does—"

"And I love being trained, sir. By you. Why do you want to do this? Aren't I good enough for you? Or did you always have selling me to someone else in mind?" Her voice was rising, and he could see her shifting in her kneeling position.

"Now wait a minute," Michael said sternly. "Watch your tone of voice with me, slave. Just because we're having a discussion doesn't mean you can misbehave."

"Why not? You don't want to be my master, anyway!" Karen leaned forward for a minute, looking down at the floor, and then suddenly got to her feet.

"What the fuck are you doing?" Michael yelled, springing up.

"I need a drink!" she snapped back. "And unless you want to become an abusive boyfriend and beat me with your fists, I'm going to get one. Would you like one?"

Michael's mouth dropped open. As a matter of fact, his right hand had closed into a fist, although he hadn't realized it. He opened his fingers slowly and took a deep breath. "You get back where you were, Karen, or I'm out of here."

"That's your answer to everything," she said, never veering from her liquor cabinet. She opened it and pulled a glass and a bottle out, and poured. "You've always been free to leave."

"Karen—" Michael made an inarticulate sound, like a muffled scream, and slammed his open hand against the coffee table. "Dammit, you don't know what you're throwing away!"

"Well, you're not actually telling me, are you?" She said, turning. She took a drink, and wiped her mouth with the back of her hand. "You promised you'd make me a slave, but it was always your slave, Mike. I bottomed to that girl because you were there, because you wanted to watch, because you were sharing me. It made me feel obedient to you. But you never said anything about selling me to anyone else! You never said shit about some secret society where you'd just trade me away like a used car! You weren't honest with me, Mike. That was a really shitty thing to do." She looked like she was ready to cry, but she was holding it back. Or maybe her anger was holding it back.

"It's not like that, Karen. It's much, much better. You don't understand—people spend years just trying to find us. All the stuff you're used to, it's nothing compared to what we do. The conference was just one weekend—think about living that way full-time! But it's not forever—it's just for a year or two. And if you like it, you can negotiate for longer times. Or you can take your share of the money and start a new life. It's a great deal!"

"Oh yeah? And how much money will you get for me, Mike? How much have I been worth to you?"

"Karen—baby—you're priceless. You've been a joy to train, you're really very talented!" Michael paced toward her, and then backed away a little when he saw the anger on her face. This wasn't going well at all!

"You didn't answer the question," she said.

"Well, I don't know! You never do—I mean, probably nothing. I don't get paid a percentage, I get a straight salary. Really, more of a stipend. I was doing this for you, Karen. To give you the life you could only fantasize about."

"And what if I fantasized about you? Can't we forget all this secret society stuff and just be master and slave?" Her voice was shaking—it was getting harder for her to maintain control.

"I—I just can't do that right now," Michael said. "You see, owners have to register with the, um, organization, and provide living space and prove that they can support a slave, and I—I can't. And, well, I'm probably going to New York soon—"

Or maybe not, he thought miserably.

"Then there's nothing left to say," she said, after draining her glass. "You don't love me—you don't even want me. And I'm not some airhead piece of property ready to hop into any kind of slavery without even having the control to pick my own fucking master. Get out."

"Karen!"

"Get the fuck out before I call 911!" she screamed.

Michael backed off, cursing. He picked up his gear bag and went into the bedroom to throw his things in it. "I don't believe you're doing this, Karen! This was your only opportunity to really make something out of your fantasies!" He shouted over his shoulder, knowing that his words would reach her clearly. Damn, he had brought a lot of stuff here! When he got back to the room, she was wrapped in her damn robe, and had poured herself another drink. Her hands were shaking.

"If you strip and get back into position right now, I'll explain everything very clearly," Michael said, standing by the door. "You'll see what a mistake you almost made."

"Thank you for everything, Mike. You were a great dominant," she said. Her lip quivered and she turned away. "Take care."

He slammed the door so hard he cracked the glass in one of the inset panels.

And it had only gotten worse from there.

LaGuardia, Michael, Los Angeles, California...

He asked for his own file, and scanned it. Two years with Geoff were listed as his training. He was ranked as an apprentice trainer, no authorization to release slaves for sale. There was a list of names and numbers of the slaves whose training he had participated in, and under references, where Geoff's name used to be, there was

nothing. Two years of work, and not even a reference to show for
it. There was also no indication that there had been an incident,
except that he had two years of training and then... nothing.

Yet Anderson knew. How? Who told her? And why the fuck had
she shared it with Parker? And why wasn't it updated to list him as
her apprentice now, anyway?

He logged off again and watched the blue-green lines of the
monitor collapse into black when he shut the machine off.

CHAPTER SIXTEEN

The two weeks after Tara returned to her master went by with excruciating slowness. There was just so much to do in such a small household—and despite losing one slave, Joan filled in the minor tasks so neatly that there was barely a blip in Michael's schedule.

Anderson still made no move to shift Joan into Michael's hands. But she did start inviting Michael to watch some of the training sessions, especially the ones where Anderson was teaching her style of seeing through walls.

"It's a matter of knowing how long things take, and how a particular person behaves," she began. "It's knowing that people do form habits, and that once you learn the habits, there isn't anything left to anticipate there. You don't even have to think about it—one action triggers another, seamlessly. It's the basis for all anticipatory behavior."

"But what if you don't have a habit to work from? What if someone arrives home unexpectedly? How do you know what they'll want?"

"That's part two, reading emotions. We're all empathic to some degree—my clients hone their empathy until it's as sharp as it can get, and keep it keen with constant polishing. But we begin at the beginning, Mike, with habits. Joan already knows Chris's—now, she must apply herself to yours. For three days, I want you to live your life as naturally as possible, and pretend that she isn't there. On the fourth, we will start seeing how well she's made a study of you."

So once again, he was being used as an exercise. Plus, having lost the easy sexual companionship of Tara, he was once again horny upon rising and feeling deprived. It would almost have been better for Anderson not to allow him to screw Tara while she was there. Because now Joan was in Parker's hands—and no way was Parker going to let Mike get any tail.

It was interesting to watch Joan at work, though. Tara already had her skills when Michael arrived—Joan was still learning them. And just as it was fascinating to see her improve during the first weeks in all the movements and speech patterns, it was equally interesting to watch her try to keep one step ahead of him.

Her major fault was in misjudging time. She tended to come in too early, stand ready for too long. It was a common beginner's habit, Anderson told him. They'd rather be early than late, because lateness was almost universally thought of as rude. But being too early had its disadvantages as well.

"An early chauffeur makes his master feel pressured to leave. Early meals get cold, or wither. Early erotic attention is inappropriate; early personal attention is intrusive. The client has to be like an actor and make their entrance at the right time, and hit their mark."

At least Michael always had something new to write about in his journal. He would need a new book soon; probably should have started one as soon as Tara left. But no one told him about these things—he had to figure them all out by himself. It was a pain.

But still, he kept silent. He refused to complain to Anderson, and even kept discussions with Vicente, whom he now was allowed to call Vic, to neutral topics, like music and movies and sports. He was totin' that water and choppin' that wood—and sooner or later, the Trainer would whack him with some sort of metaphorical stick, and the real training would begin.

In the privacy of his own room, he timed himself doing small tasks, and began to anticipate Joan's arrival. He enjoyed having her as a valet—someone helping him dress always made him feel positively decadent. But she rarely made the right choices in clothes, and he felt bad for her when she was scolded for it. It didn't seem fair—he didn't have any regular schedule of what he wore. He just opened the closet door and picked out what felt right that morning. How was she expected to know? Chris was really easy—pick out any dress shirt, a tie that went with it, and boom, instant outfit. He probably didn't really care anyway.

It struck him as odd the first time he realized that he had taken Joan's choice in clothing, despite not liking it. It didn't exactly work, because Anderson pointed out that the shirt and tie had never been paired before in her sight, and quizzed him about whether or not he had ever expressed a desire to wear then together. He hadn't realized that she had paid so much attention to how he dressed—yet she knew better than he did! Joan ended up getting a talking to about how to judge Michael's tastes better. She even had to apologize to him!

But he had taken her choice because he was afraid to correct her himself. No, not afraid—he actually didn't want to. It didn't seem like a big deal to him to wear a more conventional outfit, or a more conservative one, if that was what she thought was best, even though he would have chosen differently. He wanted to praise her, wanted to see her make that tiny nod she did when he accepted something and she knew she had chosen correctly. And, lately, he was actually trying to save her from punishment. He had never done anything like that before.

As spring began, the house gained a new client. Michael hadn't even known that he was coming—he just appeared at the door, suitcase in hand, a broad grin on his face. Anderson greeted him with a big hug—apparently, he had been there before.

"Michael, this is Lorens. He's from God-knows-how-to-pronounce-it, in Denmark."

"I am very honored to make your acquaintance, sir," Lorens said in excellent English. Michael shook his hand, and marveled. Now, here was a classic slave. Lorens stood about a hand taller than Michael, and had broad, straight shoulders and a narrow waist. His hair was a bleached, almost white-blonde, cut in a military crew that didn't really suit him. His eyes were a clear, light blue. He was a type, the Viking conqueror, the muscular ski instructor. His big hands would gave a hell of a massage, and those sweet little-boy eyes probably charmed more than one society matron into behaving scandalously. He was the cover of a romance novel come to life.

"I told him over the phone that he was in luck," Anderson said, patting the big man fondly. "I seem to have an abundance of

trainers and I'm down to only one client. A perfect time to polish
him up."

"What is he here for?" Michael asked.

"Lorens has hit the jackpot. His lady is ready to take him on
for the rest of her life. He's doing one final session with me as a
gift to her. You're so sweet you give me cavities, Lorens, but you've
got it where it counts." She punched him on the bicep and
twitched her head toward the back of the house. "You know where
to go, big boy. Come back when you're unpacked and properly
dressed. We'll do the interview as soon as you're ready."

"At once, Trainer!"

Watching him stride down the hallway, Michael whistled. "Jeez.
Arnold, watch your back."

"Yes, he is a big fellow, isn't he? Always was. The first owner to
send him to me exhibited him—bodybuilding, you know, the
tours and the contests. He's won several. I think he was Mr.
Scandinavia or something like that one year."

"I believe it. He belongs to someone else now? Why? Did he
start losing?"

"Yes—interest. Lorens is a slave—he's never wanted to be anything but in service. The demands of his tours, the endless com-
petitions, the celebrity status—they just weren't what he wanted.
He was sent to me mostly at his request for more traditional slave
training—his original owner actually wanted very little from him
in terms of service." She shook her head, seemingly amazed at
the foolishness of such a man. "When his contract ran out, he
didn't choose to renew. Came to the United States to try the market here, and found that he couldn't be guaranteed a buyer who
wouldn't do the exact same thing with him. That was when he
came back to me."

She smiled and shook her head again, this time in amusement.
"My, that was a challenge. Here was a man made to be shown off—
and all he wanted was the quiet security of personal service."

"But you're never in control when you get on the block,"
Michael said. "He could get any training he likes, but it's up to the
buyers to choose him. I mean, Geoff used to try to match buyers

and slaves, but it doesn't always work out that way."

"No, it doesn't, although I occasionally do that sort of specialty work myself. For special clients. So, I kept him for, oh, eight months, I think."

"Jesus Christ!"

"Yep. Made him the best darn personal servant a body could ask for. And then, I had him registered through a small sales house, and listed him as a domestic. His first sale netted him so little, he had to sign on for two more years just to pay me back."

"I thought you took a percentage."

"No. I generally charge fees. I know what I'm worth, and I don't leave it up to the market to determine my value. I also take a percentage on resales. The number of sales or years depends on the time someone spends with me. It all works out in the end."

"Oh." Michael wondered how much the Trainer made—it couldn't be much, if she lived with only one servant in this relatively common house in Brooklyn. She's cheating herself, he thought. If she got a good percentage on every slave she trained, she'd be filthy rich by now. But then, to have to serve for four years to pay your trainer back? How much was that worth? He blinked and looked at her as she continued.

"When he left that contract, he decided to go back on the block and try again. Apparently, three times is the charm. He was purchased by a woman who lives in Seattle and writes novels. She wanted someone to take care of her, give her back rubs and make her soup. Originally, she thought she was going to buy a woman— instead, she bought Lorens. He had the skills, he had the temperament—and he types."

Michael laughed. "How long ago was that?"

"Six years. They had a two-year contract, and then a four-year one. This year, on his anniversary, he told me that they wanted to make the arrangement permanent. That's—pretty rare." Anderson nodded again, looking pleased with herself.

"You'd think that after six years, he wouldn't need any more training."

"He probably doesn't." That was Chris, who was standing in

the doorway. He must have seen Lorens in the back. Michael wasn't sure how long he'd been there, listening. "I'm sure she has him trained to everything she needs. But this gives him a way to make the separation between the Marketplace and the rest of his life. He'll be in formal training one more time, making sure that he needs nothing else, and he'll have this time to reflect on the commitment he's about to make. When he gets back to her, he will be her slave in truth—committed by honor and integrity to serve her until her death—or until she sends him away."

"Oh, everyone could use a little bit of training, no matter where they are in their abilities," Anderson said.

Chris smiled and bowed. "As you say, Trainer."

She laughed. "Okay, let's start changing things around here. Chris, you're assigned to Mr. Scandinavia, but you're still overseeing Joan. Mike, you start drilling Joan tomorrow, using Chris's schedule—and his methods. Am I understood, gentlemen?"

They chorused, "Yes, Trainer!" and she grinned.

"Now, that's what I like to hear. Dismissed!" She turned on her heel and went into her office, closing the door behind her. Michael looked at Chris with that sinking feeling settling into his stomach. It was justified. The look in Chris's eyes clearly said, "Your ass is mine."

The woman had to be a sadist, Michael decided. A genuine, extremely pathological, I-want-to-make-people-cry sadist. Sending him away would have been kinder than turning him officially over to Mr. Perfection. And to have them work together on the woman who was supposed to be Michael's project?

But working together wasn't quite the idea, was it? No, it was training Michael in the Chris Parker school of perfection, where trainers who didn't know how to demonstrate things were a little less thought of than, say, your garden variety slug. Where the trainer had to be the very essence of control, touching harshly only to teach or correct, tenderly and briefly to praise. A trainer does not take advantage of their position of authority, oh, no. At least a junior trainer doesn't. Which was what Michael was.

It was pretty annoying having to actually take notes on that stuff. But Michael never knew when Anderson was going to swoop down and ask for the journal, so he wrote and wrote, dutifully recording whatever Chris told him during the day. He consoled himself with the fact that he was finally in some kind of formal training. He also decided that his time with Chris was a test of sorts—Anderson was most likely making sure that he was committed to the job. He'd probably pretty well established that he'd keep doing the little household tasks and helping with the role playing exercises as long as she wanted him to—this was probably step two.

It was hitting him with a big motherfucking stick.

And despite his basic disagreements with Chris on some methods, it was fun to get back into proper training. It was similar to Geoff's style only on the surface—Joan was far more experienced than most of the slaves who ended up with Geoff. She was already a competent slave—now, they were making her into an exemplary one.

It was also good to be able to get back into the interview portion of training. Michael had never realized how truly vital those regular interviews were until he had participated in Tara's training without ever being allowed to attend her interviews with Anderson. Watching and listening to Chris and Joan, he now realized how bad his own interviews were, and how shallow. From time to time, he felt a deep sense of chagrin. Why had he spent so much time fucking and playing and so little time actually asking questions and listening to the answers?

Even Geoff interviewed every day—he called it part of the communication process. Michael called it excess. Anderson recommended alternate day interviews for two weeks, and then once a week thereafter for the remainder of the training, wrapping up in daily brush up and review sessions the week before a slave left. And of course, at any time there might be a quick question-and-answer period, or a closer examination of something triggered by the flash of resentment or resignation in a slave's eyes, or a second of hesitation or a word said in the wrong inflection.

For the first interview with Joan, Michael remembered his first week and his disastrous first session with her, but Chris merely invited him to sit and take notes if he wanted to. Michael did, and relaxed as the process began.

Interviews were always different—you could ask a prearranged series of questions, administer an IQ test, or simply sit back and chat about topics of interest. The idea was to use the time to get to know everything possible about the client, not only their history of experiences, but their thoughts and feelings, likes and dislikes, their deepest fears and grandest hopes and fantasies. Knowing all these things allowed a trainer to not only design the proper program for a client, but to decide what could be used as a marketing angle. Or, in a case like Joan's, what could be reported to the owner as a potential resource or weakness.

Chris's first displayed style was direct and military. He would ask a question and want it answered right away, phrased properly, and with the proper inflection and emphasis. It was a little unnerving. But Joan took it well—she was poised, most of the time, and displayed very little fear when Chris raised his voice or slammed the desk for emphasis. Michael found out why.

"My trainer in Japan was a very... loud individual," she explained. "He used to shout at me quite a bit—every day, as a matter of fact. He would lean over me, and scream at the top of his lungs, and expect me to scream my answer back until we were both quite red in the face. Any time I would flinch, he would hit me. Soon, I learned not to flinch. Soon after that, I learned how not to feel like I should be flinching, which was much more difficult."

"Good instinct," Chris commented. "It's one thing to steel yourself against discomfort or fear. It's another thing entirely to create a place where you just don't feel them."

"How do you do that?" Michael asked, writing furiously. "Create a place? You mean, like in self-hypnosis?"

"Very good, Mike." Chris nodded encouragingly and Michael concentrated on writing. Every time Chris did that, his tone of voice would carry such an air of condescension it was infuriating!

"One of the most important things a client learns when confronted by aggression is how to remain calm when it is called for, and how to maintain personal discipline in protocol," Chris explained. "It will not do to snap back at the mistress or whine at your housekeeper."

Joan shook her head vigorously. "Oh, no, Chris, I shall never do that!"

Chris seemed to start nodding, his head moving down as if to glance at his own notes, and suddenly he leaned over, his face within inches of Joan's, so fast that Michael jumped in his chair. The senior trainer barked, "Then what will you do when confronted with your sloppy manners by someone who knows much better than you, missy?"

While Mike's heart pounded, Joan only dipped her own head in a gesture of humility and submission and said, softly, "It is entirely my fault, Chris, and I will strive to better myself; thank you for your correction."

Chris leaned back and shrugged. "Not bad. But you must watch the habit of automatically apologizing all the time. It can become cloying. And, there will be times when you are not at fault and it will be important to make that clear. But that should be rare—your owners are fairly well used to managing their staff, and your housekeeper, Mrs. Harrison, is a very reasonable woman."

"How do you know that?" Michael asked without thinking.

Chris looked over to him and cocked his head. "I made enquiries," he said rationally. "I interviewed Mrs. Harrison before Joan got here."

Of course he did, Michael thought morosely. Interviewing the staff where a client was going to work, well, of course he did that. As Chris directed his attention back to Joan, Michael lost himself in his bitter thoughts. It just wasn't fair, no matter what Anderson thought about fairness. Not only was Michael learning from the man who did everything right and never screwed up, but Chris was always just on that edge of patient humor—when he wasn't being sarcastic and cutting.

But it didn't stop him. He kept asking questions, and kept taking the damn notes. It was hardly the first time he felt so humiliated. After all, the resolution of the Karen affair was just about as painful, and dragged on for much longer than one would have thought.

Michael had returned to Geoff's place with only one goal in

mind—to forget that Karen ever existed. He had told Geoff and the other trainers there that he had a girlfriend he was visiting, thus explaining his weekend absences. But he never made mention of the kinds of things he was doing with her. It wasn't common to have what the other trainers often maliciously called a "vanilla" lover on the side—in fact, it was almost unheard of, unless some sort of parental subterfuge was going on. It was conventional wisdom that said Marketplace people should date each other—better to not have this secret looming over a potentially intimate relationship.

Michael had finally realized why this was conventional wisdom. He was in a rotten mood, nervous and snappy, and was called to Geoff's large, airy office to explain why.

"I—I broke up with my girlfriend," he stammered, twisting his hands together and finding the colors of Geoff's pseudo-Impressionist paintings utterly fascinating, much better to look at than Geoff's fatherly eyes. "It was a rough weekend. It was—real bad."

"I'm so sorry to hear that," Geoff said immediately, wrapping one arm around Michael's shoulder. "It's always tough to lose a lover. Why don't you take a day or two off? You're much too tense to manage the clients. Breakups can leave a person with a lot of negative energy, and you might fall into some bad reactive behaviors without even knowing it. Go over to my beach house, or to your uncle's for a few days, until you cool down. If you feel like it, maybe you can call her and get back together. If not, maybe a few days of rest and quiet meditation will help stabilize you. We need you here, Mike. We care about you. Help yourself; take some time to heal."

Michael tried at first to fight it, but in the end he took Geoff's advice. He couldn't actually go to the man's own beach house—that would have been pushing it. He did go back to Uncle Niall's, and abused Ethan for about two days, much to Niall's amusement and titillation. "When you live this way," he said to Michael one night down by the beach, "you sometimes forget to get, well, elaborate with the boys. It's good to see Ethan get a workout like that. Geoff must be teaching you right, boyo!"

But Michael remained in a hard, gloomy funk for both days. Finally, on Sunday afternoon, he took Ethan up to the guest room and had him suck his toes, a guaranteed way to get him off. It was something he had never even thought to teach Karen to do—it was firmly associated with men, and Ethan had been the first one to do it to him. It took him a long time to get fully erect, and a long time to shoot, but he kept himself on the edge of orgasm for as long as possible, wanting that temporary agony, that stretch of timeless thoughtlessness. Finally, he shot off, adorning Ethan's hairless chest with his ejaculate, and collapsed back on a pile of pillows. Ethan was never allowed on the bed. He squirmed on the floor like a good boy, his cock hard and his body tense. His hands were tied behind his back.

Maybe I should have taught her this, Michael thought. The moment of orgasm had not even taken Karen off the forefront of his mind. He sighed, and when his breathing was back to normal, sat up. He pressed his foot over Ethan's cock and balls, and listened to the answering groan.

"How did you find out about the Marketplace, Eth'?"

"Sir—ah!" It was fun to torture a slave while they had to answer questions. Michael twisted his foot a little and smiled when Ethan's face scrunched up in pain. Then he stopped, and rested his heel on Ethan's thigh. He wanted some real answers here—it was no time for fun and games.

"Thank you, sir," Ethan gasped. "I heard about it from my spotter, Claudio. He told me after about four months of testing me."

Four months! Michael had worked on Karen for five! But then, he had only seen her on weekends, and not every weekend at that. But—maybe it wasn't a matter of timing. Maybe it was the way he broke it her? "What did you think when he told you? Did you believe him? Did you think he was nuts?"

"Oh, no sir!" Ethan raised his head, his eyes wide at the thought. "I thought he was bringing me the word of God, sir! You wouldn't believe how happy I was. I was ready to leave that minute."

"You were?" Michael jabbed Ethan's balls with his toe, making the slave wince. "Come on, tell the truth. You had to be skeptical at first."

"Sir—I would have been, I guess. But Claudio—he prepared me for it. It was like I always knew he had this secret, that he was somehow different than the guys I usually hung with, you know?" Ethan bit his lip and closed his eyes in humiliation. "Please sir, forgive me for speaking without thinking, I'll try to control my words—"

"No, no, get up, I want to hear this." Michael kicked Ethan's thigh and pushed himself back on the bed, pulling one leg up. He watched Ethan roll onto his side and up onto his knees—it was sometimes a hard move to do gracefully. But there were more important things than criticizing the boy on his movements. "Tell me in your own words what happened. I'll forgive lapses in formality."

"Thank you, sir." Ethan shook his head to get some wisps of hair out of his eyes. "Claudio picked me up in a gay bar in San Antonio," he began. "I was at the University there, and just coming out into leather. But I always had the fantasy, you know? Even back in Oklahoma, I always used to dream about the man who would one day come and take me away to be his slave. I left home because I realized that he wasn't ever coming to Mill Creek. I'd done some leather stuff, played around with some SM—wore a black hanky in my back pocket, looked for Daddies and truck drivers—it was okay. But never more than okay. It just seemed that everything was just sex—not that it was bad! Just—limited. Then, I met Claudio."

His eyes shone with the memory, and Michael fought back a scowl.

"He was a real topman, an old fashioned kind of guy—and a loner, too. I have to admit, I was scared of him at first. I heard he played heavy. But he never brought any of his boys to the bars. He wasn't a member of any of the clubs. He would just come around, you know? Then one night, when I was looking for a new Daddy, he was sitting at the end of the bar and I decided to make the first move. I figured the worst that could happen was that I'd take a hell of a beating. But I could have been into it—sometimes, that was enough. But instead, he bought me a drink and let me talk to him. I mean—all night. I must have told him my whole life story that night."

Like I got Karen to tell me hers, Michael thought.

"It was very slow, sir. He didn't take me home and tie me up, not at first. But he would come and visit me, have a few beers, and we'd talk some more. Every once in a while, he would ask me for something—not tell me to do it, but ask me—to run a little errand, or to help him with some chore. And it just seemed natural to help—and then one day I realized that he'd stopped asking. He was just telling me to do things, and I was doing them just as naturally as if he was asking me politely, as a pal. One night, I asked him what he was doing. He told me he was seeing if I had what it took to be a slave."

Michael began to feel warm, despite his nakedness. He nodded impatiently. "Yeah? And then what?"

"I told him that all my life I wanted to be a slave—and if he wanted to test me further, I would do my best to prove it to him."

"And he wasn't screwing you?"

"No sir, not yet. He made me earn it."

"How? More errands and chores?"

Ethan shook his head. "No sir, not exactly. I was expected to serve him in those ways regardless of whether or not he was using me. That was my function. He would make me earn sex—and release—by taking beatings, or doing embarrassing things, like takin' a piss outside instead of using the bathroom, or wearing skimpy little outfits." Ethan actually blushed, and Michael wondered what those outfits must have been like; the boy was mostly naked here at Niall's place.

"One month, he didn't let me come at all," Ethan continued. "It was horrible. I thought my nuts were going to explode. Then, for one week straight, he had me jerking off almost every hour. I'd have to stop what I was doing and wank my rod until I shot, or he'd whup me good. I don't know what was worse."

"But how did he know you were ready for the Marketplace?

Did he ask you questions? I mean—what was it that made him stop at four months and tell you about it?" Michael's questions tumbled out, and he was shocked at the bitterness in his voice. It was highly inappropriate to show such anxiety in front of a slave. But he needed to know—and there was no one else to ask.

"He gambled me away in a poker game, sir," Ethan said with a little smile. "I think that was the final test."

"How did that work?"

"He had a few friends who he played poker with on Monday nights—they usually watched football at the same time. I was at his place one Monday, cleaning the kitchen, and when he got home, he called me to the door. I ran over to see what he wanted, and he said for me to get some clothes on, he'd bet my services in a poker game and lost, and I belonged to a friend of his for a few days. And I better not fuck up."

Michael snorted. "So what? People do that all the time. It's no big deal, you go do the guy, it's a change of pace. What—was the guy really ugly or something?"

"No, sir. The guy was a lady."

"Oh."

"I'd never been with a girl before, sir. I mean, I never even dated in high school or anything. I've known I was gay since I was a kid. I didn't know what to do, for a second. And then I thought, Claudio wouldn't have me do anything that wasn't okay. And I promised Claudio I'd do what he told me if it would make me a good slave—and even if I personally didn't like girls, I mean, women, it wasn't anything that was against my morals or anything. And it was his rep on the line, too—he'd done this, believing that I'd do what he said. I couldn't let him down."

"So you went."

"Yes sir, I dressed and hopped in her pick-up, and she took me home and ran me 'til I near about fainted. Women," Ethan said, a look of serious amazement crossing his face, "can come a lot of times."

"Yeah, they can. Did you enjoy it?"

Ethan squirmed a little. "Well—I enjoyed being useful to Clau-

dio. And I knew that she was enjoying me, and that made me
happy. Sir, in truth, I like men, I love their bodies, and women just
don't do it for me. But I did the best I could, and I tried not to let
her know how weird I felt. And about a week later, Claudio told me
about the Marketplace."

"Okay, Ethan get up, you can go now." Michael untied the
slave's hands and nodded when Ethan bowed himself out of the
room. He laid himself back on the bed and sighed. He had done
everything wrong! Not that this Claudio had the only way to spot
and pre-train a slave, but it sounded much better than what
Michael had done. Maybe I should have read up on it more, he
thought miserably.

Oh well. There was nothing to be done now. He would have to
find some new way to gain the attention of the trainer in New
York. Nothing had changed his goal—but it looked like he needed
to head in another direction to get there.

He was glad that he hadn't told anyone about what he was really doing with Karen. With her gone from his life, he could just
start again. Next time, he'd be better at this. It was clear that he had
just chosen the wrong first candidate, and she just magnified the
perfectly understandable minor mistakes that he had made himself.
When he got back to Geoff's place, he'd do some more research
on spotting and entry-level training. There had to be some videos
somewhere.

So, somewhat sheepishly, he returned to Santa Cruz, and Geoff
hugged him warmly and sent the newest client to his room for
the night. The shame of his failure vanished in an evening of ac-
robatic sexual romps that made Michael feel much, much better.

CHAPTER SEVENTEEN

The phone rang at one o'clock in the afternoon, just as Vicente had finished laying out a luncheon salad and a stack of roast beef sandwiches. Lorens, in white shorts and a tank top, was carrying plates from the kitchen, and Joan, looking very round and dark next to him, was directing the action as part of her training in management techniques. Anderson, watching from the dining room door, raised one finger to stop Joan from picking up the call and got it herself. Michael kept watching the workers as they neatly laid the table and vanished. It was hard not to knock into each other in the small space of the formal dining room, but somehow, they managed it.

"Yes, he's here. Hold for a moment, please." Anderson laid the receiver down and tapped Michael on the shoulder. "Would you go get Chris? This is for him."

"Sure, Trainer." He jogged upstairs and down the hall, to where Chris's room was, and knocked on the door. "Chris! Phone call."

Chris came to the door with a frown on his face. Michael could see a laptop computer open and running on the desk by the window—sometimes Chris worked for hours on whatever he was writing. "Do you know who it is?" he asked.

"No. Anderson picked it up."

"Thank you." Chris followed him back downstairs immediately, and Michael knew that it was in reaction to that magical name. At the slightest hint that Anderson wanted something or had decided or judged something, Chris moved. If Anderson called him to the phone, it had to be important. Chris looked more tightly wound than usual that day—something that happened every once in a while—but still, he stopped his work and went to take care of business.

Slaves should be so automatically trusting. Michael sighed and walked past Chris to get to lunch. Anderson was already seated, feeding a kneeling Lorens a cherry tomato. She did things with him that she hadn't done with either of the female clients, with more touches and more personal attention. It was always interesting to see what she had planned. She really did alter her methods and style for each individual slave.

They could hear Chris quite clearly from the front room.

"Excuse me, Mr. Parese?... That's impossible... Mr. Parese, you must be mistaken!"

At the sound of Chris's rare higher pitch, the tone he used only when he was genuinely angry, Michael put his sandwich down on the plate. Joan, pouring a glass of soda for him, seemed under control but he could tell she was listening too. Anderson clucked her tongue and Joan quickly finished and fled back to the kitchen.

"You did what?... No, don't do a damn thing, Mr. Parese. I'll be out tomorrow, to straighten this out... Mr. Parese, you listen to me. If Robin is not conscious and available to me, I will certainly make sure you're investigated. I will be there tomorrow to pick her up." The phone made a loud ringing noise as it was slammed into the cradle.

"Joan! Get out here!"

Michael hadn't even taken a bite. His mouth was open in amazement at the abusive sound of Chris's sharp command. Joan looked composed, however, as she ran out of the kitchen, neatly avoiding the backs of chairs, to the front room.

"Here—call a travel agent, and get me on a flight to Los Angeles tomorrow, as early as possible. Find me a hotel to the north of the city, and book me a suite, two bedrooms. And find out who's the medical contact for that area, call them, and tell them I will probably need a visit tomorrow, oh, hell—late afternoon, I suppose. And a car—I need a car. Go, take care of this now."

"Chris?" Anderson said, leaning back to look into the front room. "What's up?"

He came in, flushed and scowling. "Those damn idiots—

Robin's owners have decided that she's stolen some earrings or something from a guest! They found them in her room—decided that she was guilty, just like that!" He snapped his fingers dramatically. "After all, why bother to investigate? She's a girl, girls wear earrings, so naturally it had to have been her!"

"Chris?" Anderson pointed to a chair.

Amazingly, he ignored her. Michael closed his mouth and took a long drink from his glass. This was better than a movie.

"They beat the shit out of her, Anderson! He said she was unconscious! What kind of barbaric, misogynist assholes—"

"Parker!" Anderson slapped one hand on the table top. "Control yourself."

Chris looked at her and then blinked, as though he was as surprised as she by his behavior. He dropped down into the previously indicated seat and ran one hand through his hair, pushing it back. "Yes, yes. Please—forgive my outburst. That was ill-mannered."

"Forgiven. Now why on Earth are you going out there? Just call the local investigative representative and have the girl removed. She can be cared for and sent back here, and the whole thing can be taken care of properly. There's no need for you to charge off like John Wayne."

Michael smothered a snicker, and concentrated on spreading mayonnaise on his sandwich.

"I—I have to go. I'm her trainer. She needs me."

Oh boy! Disagreeing with the Trainer, too! This was turning out to be a real historic occasion, Michael thought viciously.

"I agree. She needs you to advocate for her. But she doesn't need your personal attention on-site. If you did that for all your clients, you'd always be on the road. Now call Joan back, and handle this the proper way."

There was silence. Anderson had turned to her plate, but then slowly looked back at Chris, who was sitting very still, and definitely not calling Joan.

"Parker?" she said gently.

"Are you ordering me not to go?" he asked.

Michael thought he could die right then. Mr. Perfect, questioning an order from the Goddess of Trainers. Now you're on the hot seat buster, he thought. How does it feel to squirm for a change? And I get to see it all.

Anderson picked up another tomato and fed it to the blushing Lorens. "No," she said finally. "I am advising you, as your senior trainer, not to go."

"Thank you for your advice. I regret that I can't take it at this time. Please excuse me, I have to go into the city before I leave." He stood, and actually waited for Anderson's slow nod of permission to be excused! Oh, it was too much! Michael couldn't hold it in any more.

"So, one of the perfect slaves has sticky fingers, huh Chris? Wonder what went wrong there?"

Chris had already turned. Michael saw his shoulders stiffen, and his hands curl up into fists. Anderson started to rise, and Michael just caught the look of alarm on her face, but Chris's tightly controlled voice cut through the tension. "I'll thank you, Mr. LaGuardia, to keep your ignorant mouth shut."

"Oh, and I'll thank you—" Michael began, but Anderson, now on her feet, shut him up.

"That will be enough, Michael! Chris, I believe you have some work to do."

He left without looking back. Anderson turned to Michael and said sharply, "That was entirely uncalled for!"

"Trainer, I'm just giving back some of what he shovels at me every day! If he can't take it, he shouldn't do it." Michael was stung, but feeling brave. It was worth a lecture just to have made Chris that angry!

"Try not to revert to style, Mike, it makes me wonder what drugs I was on the day I chose your file. I seem to have lost my appetite. Lorens, clear this away, and come upstairs. I need a back rub."

"Yes, Trainer!" He bowed his head almost to the floor when she left, throwing her napkin onto the table. And within minutes, Michael was alone with his salad, sandwich, and an empty glass of soda. He went to the kitchen to fill it and hid a chuckle from Vicente, who had a very serious look on his face.

Oh yes. Altogether a very amusing luncheon.

CHAPTER EIGHTEEN

Chris landed in sunny California early in the day, and picked up the car reserved for him at the rental counter. It was hot in the City of the Angels. It was always hot in California, he thought. He hadn't worn the sunglasses since the last time he'd been there, but they still worked. They couldn't take the edge off the blinding headache, though.

It took about twenty minutes of map-reading plus one stop at a gas station to figure out the way to the Parese and Appleton home, up in the hills. It took another two hours to get there, dealing with traffic and unfamiliar roads. "Just outside of the city" meant different things in different parts of the world.

Robin. Sweet, desperately searching Robin, the sprite of slavery. With her natural patience, and her constant inner struggles to do the right thing, to not fail—oh, she had been a joy to teach. Totally unaware of the impossibility of his plan, she had gone along with everything, offering only the meekest of complaints, enduring what would have terribly confused and probably broken a more gradually trained novice.

It had been so irresponsible of him to take her on. He had been due back at the house in three weeks, and was slumming, spending time with Ron, drinking when he shouldn't be, picking up hustlers and making them cry. Anything to get his mind off training, and the endless stream of eager novitiates. Trying not to think of the drills, and their faces and bodies. Their hatred. Fear. Contempt. Worship. Love. The eternal confusion of it all.

And then, next to the narrow, teasing eyes of Ken Mandarin, this girl—this small, elfin girl, so bashful and so needy, you could feel it from her. Even standing in a leather bar, the smoke and beer and piss a mask of atmosphere that kept you from thinking of anything but sex, she was like a lure. He couldn't turn her away.

Being intercepted on the night of her sale had been—interesting. It had provided some new twists to his relationship with Grendel and Alex. Some new aspect of his life to use as a springboard, a way to make things, as Anderson correctly pointed out, more difficult. But even the new teasing wasn't as difficult for him to endure as the temptation to take Robin to bed had been. Watching Rachel take her pleasure of her, and then watching Gordon Reynolds do her—and knowing that while he was doing Gordon in the master bedroom, Gordon's slave Leon was fucking Robin in the other room—it had been a personal torment of surprising proportions.

Most... intriguing.

As time passed and his—situation—changed, there were a series of such incidents. The meeting of eyes, and the instantaneous knowing—followed by the hunger and the drive, and ultimately, the separation. But Robin had been the first to belong to him alone.

It was irrational to think that she still did. But there was a distinct lack of rationality in what he had felt when he heard the sputtering voice of her angry owner. It was terrible to lose control like that. But there was never any question about his coming out to get her.

If Anderson had—

But she hadn't.

He wanted a smoke, very badly. But he kept driving, and didn't stop for cigarettes.

The houseman was a lithe, feral-looking Hispanic with a soft voice and properly deferential coldness. It would have been more impressive to dress him in elegant whites, razo- pleated soft pants and a billowy shirt, open to show his beautiful chest. But in typical Californian fashion, he was wearing what looked like a bathing suit, in a purple neon.

"I'm Parker. Here to pick up Robin. Where is she?" The anger swelled again, and Chris took a deep breath as the man led him through the house. He barely noticed the place—wide, tall, plenty of light, plenty of air—he barely registered the fireplace, the gleaming, narrow kitchen, the pool glittering out one of the sliding glass doors. He just followed the slave, trying to keep control, and then realized that they were heading out of the house again.

"Where are we going?"

"To the—rear, sir. She's—outside." A flash of shame crossed the man's face, and Chris nodded. The anger had settled high. It wasn't hot any more. It was cold.

"Take me to her," he said softly.

There was a shed made of beautifully weathered pine back beyond the pool and the outdoor shower. It did have a poured concrete floor. Chris followed the man and let him open the door, letting light flood over a body striped with welts. For a moment, Chris almost lost it—it couldn't be Robin, left all alone in a goddamn shed, like a beast. It had to be a mistake—it had to be a nightmare. He stepped forward and looked down. She stirred groggily, and he realized that he had left the bag in the car.

"Well, I can see your masters have afforded her every humane effort," he said leaning down to examine her. The wounds visible seemed fairly clean. "Has she been here since?" he asked abruptly.

"Yes, sir."

"There's a brown leather bag in my car. Fetch it and bring me a wet towel and a comb."

The man left immediately, without even a "yes, sir," and Chris sighed. He stepped into the shed, right up next to Robin and squatted down. She turned, groaning, and shifted onto one side. It took her a moment to focus, especially since she had one hell of a shiner, and one eye was swollen shut. Chris heard a sound behind him, and looked out the door of the shed. There was a man standing out there, some distance away, with long brown hair pulled back in a pony tail. It was Jimmy, one of the owners. They stared at each other for a long minute, and then Chris deliberately turned away and put a slight smile on his face for Robin. Even as he softly said "Hello," he was fighting the sudden urge to get a tire iron and kill the two men who purchased her and the houseman who was ashamed to reveal what they had done. It passed when Robin tried to get up, her fingers touching his boot as though making sure that he was really there. A glance over his shoulder revealed that the owner was gone. In a minute, the houseman returned with the bag, towel, and comb, and Chris indicated a spot to put them down. He sent him away sharply, and heard the footsteps retreating, but paid no attention to them.

He cradled her in his arms and soothed her. And took her away from there without even attempting to see the owners, who were obviously and wisely hiding from him.

When he arrived back at the house in the early evening, having left Robin drowsy and bandaged, he was ready to meet the men who did this. He had of course, met them once before, on the night of Robin's sale. He had been slightly disappointed for her—what a shame for such a delightfully sexy young woman to be sold into an all gay male household. It had not escaped Chris that although Robin was happily bisexual, there was a core part of her which reacted most strongly to a woman's touch, a woman's voice. But it was a prime opportunity for her—it would give her the chance to develop stronger erotic control. And it would not be a difficult existence—she would get to do the work she loved, and enjoy the life of a full-time slave. Certainly, she had not complained to him in their three telephone conversations. He had taken that as an indication that things had worked out for her.

Apparently not as well as could be expected. Although she had seemed to enjoy a good relationship with her owners and with the three other slaves in the household, someone had quite obviously set her up for this fall.

It was so difficult to really know someone—to see into their heart of hearts and know what tempted them and what made them afraid. Any number of interview sessions would reveal everything but the single secret that would only come out after a tragedy. There were always slaves who got past the psychological testing and the interviews with the potential to defraud or harm their trainers or owners. So it was always possible that Robin had become a thief. But when her first words to him were "I didn't do it," and he could look into those uncomplicated, amber-colored eyes, he believed her without reservation.

He checked his image in the rear view mirror and slicked back one errant curl. His hair was beginning to thin, and that bothered him less than he thought it should. Yes; he was calm, he was cool—and the urge to kill someone was much lighter than it had been earlier.

Eric Parese was a fashion model. It wasn't difficult to look at him and be instantly distracted. But he was the one whose anger had exploded into the wreck that was Robin, and all Chris saw was a suspicious, hostile boy, angry at something and feeling threatened at the same time. His lover Jimmy seemed more casual about it all. As usual, Chris was the shortest man present. The Hispanic slave was introduced as Raul, and Chris nodded brusquely.

"Get me some coffee," he said. "Do you have someplace private where we can talk?" he asked the owners.

Raul shot a glance at his two masters and headed for the kitchen. Jimmy forced a civil smile and pointed down a hallway, to his office. Eric was surly, but he came along, and the three men sat in silence until Raul served the coffee and beat a hasty retreat.

"I'm ready to hear the story," Chris said.

"It's very simple," Eric said immediately. "We had a guest here, a friend of ours, Eve Panski. Tom, her husband, had given her a pair of earrings, emerald earrings—and while she was here, they went missing. We searched the house for days—and then, in the office your slavegirl uses, we found them in a bud vase. A little extra bonus for when she left, I guess."

"That's absurd. Haven't you ever heard the phrase circumstantial evidence?"

Jimmy broke in. "We know that our boys aren't thieves. Besides, they don't wear earrings." He grinned, and then lost it when he realized that neither his lover nor the stranger from New York were amused.

"Robin is no thief, gentlemen. She did not take the earrings, and she did not hide them in her office."

"How can you prove that?" Eric asked. "All we know is that she's the newest slave here, and the one with the shortest contract. The earrings were found in her room, cleverly hidden. What are we supposed to think?"

"Apparently, you've thought precisely what you were supposed to think. It hasn't occurred to you that the damn earrings were planted there for exactly this purpose?" Keep the control, keep the voice steady, Chris reminded himself.

"By who?" Eric demanded.

"That's what I'm here to find out."

"Oh? And who the fuck are you, Miss Marple?"

"I don't think you should care if I'm Lord Peter Wimsey—if I don't find out what happened, then I'll have to file a formal complaint with the Marketplace concerning your treatment of slaves. There will be an investigation. All your slaves will be interviewed, and the doctor who took care of Robin's infections and cuts today will have to make a statement. You will be interviewed as well. And all of this becomes part of the record of your house, gentlemen." Chris rose. "If that is what you prefer, I'll take my leave of you."

"Are you threatening me, you greasy little punk?" Eric shot up too, and shook one fist. "I'll make sure you never train another slave again! I'll have you investigated! I'll—"

"Yo, Eric, Eric—calm down, man!" Jimmy stood up, too, and the three of them faced each other, close enough to touch. Jimmy did grab hold of his partner and pulled him closer, holding one arm. "Listen, there's no need for any of that. If he thinks one of the boys did it, let him question them. There's no harm in that."

"Our boys didn't do anything!"

"And he'll find that out. You'll see, Mr. Parker. Carl has been with me for ages. Raul, he's the best. And Jeff's a good kid. It had to have been your girl. Look, it's her first sale, you never know what you're going to get with newbies."

"As a matter of fact, the first slave of yours I'd like to speak to," Chris said, "happens to be your other 'newbie,' Jeff. The good kid. If you could arrange for me to have a place away from general traffic, please?" He was so close to trembling—the tension was really getting to him. And the headache had never gone away. The aggression coming from Eric made him want to haul back and smash those beautiful teeth, hit that under-worked stomach until he felt the lower rib crack—

But it was time to put the kid away. He forced another tight smile as Jimmy pointed the way upstairs. A moment later, he was joined by Jeff.

Jeff was a handsome young man, dark-haired and -eyed, with a slender body and the slightly nervous twitch of someone used to being on the receiving end of a lot of casual abuse. Chris smiled genuinely for the first time. There would be nothing casual about what he was about to do. He indicated the staircase and started to shrug off his suit jacket.

"Jeff, I'm Chris. Get your sorry ass upstairs."

He followed the youth, tossing the jacket over one shoulder and whistling.

When his left fist cut up and sank into Jeff's middle, it felt almost like an orgasm. The right fist completed the feeling, and Chris paced back, allowing Jeff space to collapse and giving himself a moment to come off the balls of his feet and stretch out. It was beyond question unfair and cruel to use a sucker combination like that on someone called to attention.

It was satisfying as hell. Feelings crashed and mingled—the desire to kick the kid, the need for a cigarette, a fantasy image of doing the same thing to Eric, a touch of old pain at the thought of Robin, hanging by her wrists, having fucking garden stakes used on her—(because I told them she feared canes)—and here was the piece of excrement that caused it all.

Jeff coughed and gasped, and then gagged. He clutched his stomach and cried out, "Why'd you do that?"

Chris bent down and grasped the slave by his chain collar and dragged him to his feet. He stood taller than Chris by about five inches. "That should have been, 'Sir, why did you do that, sir?'" Chris said softly. On the final 'sir,' he clipped Jeff on the upper chest, right under the collarbone, where it would hurt. And then stepped back again as Jeff raised his arms to protect himself.

"I still haven't heard you say it," Chris said.

"Sir!" Jeff croaked, his hands in front of him, slightly bent over. "Please—sir, why did you do that sir?"

"That's better. Much improved. Now get down on your knees;

we're going to have a little chat." There was a chair, but Chris remained standing. He had risen to the balls of his feet again, and the nervous energy would probably need to be worked off a little more before he could sit quietly. It was so hard to pull punches when he was like this.

"You're one of Lu's boys, aren't you, Jeff?" he asked. "I looked up your file before I left New York. This is your first house; these are your first real masters. Are you happy here?"

"Yes, sir." He looked incredulous at the gentle tone Chris was using. Still clutching his stomach, he knelt, spreading his legs as far as seemed comfortable—apparently this was a house position.

Chris was not impressed. But he kept his voice even. "Do you know who I am?"

"No, sir."

"I'm Robin's trainer. I'm here because Robin's done a terrible thing. Apparently, she's stolen something from one of your masters' guests. I'm here to find out how and when she did it—and that's assuming that she did steal the item. Do you know anything about this?"

Jeff lowered his eyes. "No, sir."

Chris nodded solemnly. "I see. Get up, please."

Jeff rose, and the minute he pulled his shoulders back, Chris landed a shot right against his upper right cheekbone, firmly snapping his fist into the underside of his eye, the force slamming Jeff's head to one side and throwing him backward. Jeff brought his arms up to defend himself again, sheltering his head this time, skipping backward, a strangled cry of pain mingling with a bitten off curse.

"That was for telling me a lie. The next lie you tell will get you one just like it on the other side. Then I start with your chest and work my way down to your nuts. Kindly give yourself a moment to reflect on what something like that will feel like on your balls."

Jeff kept retreating, almost tripping over the edge of a rug, stopping only when his back was up against a wall. He felt the spot under his eye and gasped in amazement and shock, and held his arms up again as Chris followed him.

"You can't do this!" he shouted, holding up one hand as if to warn Chris away. "You're not allowed to d-damage me!"

"Yes," Chris agreed. "That's correct." He walked calmly over to him and grasped the collar again and pushed Jeff's head back against the wall, his left fist up under his chin. "Except for one thing." He drew back his right fist and slammed it forward, and Jeff gave a strangled scream. But the fist impacted with a dull crunching sound on the wall next to his ear instead of hitting his face. The young man jerked with surprise and terror, and looked back at Chris's face, at the gentle smile.

"You didn't say 'sir,'" Chris said. "Try again."

While the slave stammered out approximations of his line with "sirs" at the beginning and end of the statements, Chris looked at his hand. No surprise, he had abraded the skin over his knuckles. Someone was going to be pissed about that. He let Jeff go again, and walked back to the bed, where he'd thrown his jacket. He pulled a handkerchief out of the inside pocket and waved it at Jeff.

"Come and get this," he said.

Jeff crouched by the wall for a second, and then took cautious steps over to the bed. He reached out and took the square of cotton.

"Now go and get this damp. Wring it out, I don't want it to drip."

Chris watched the boy go, and flexed his hand. Oh, he was going to make this last a good long time. He hoped that Jeff was going to be very stubborn.

About an hour later, he invited Jimmy into the room.

Jeff was sitting in a wooden chair, his arms wrapped around the back. They weren't tied. Nor were his ankles, which were tucked behind the front legs of the chair. His body showed rising bruises on his chest and two gradually darkening black eyes. There was a cut over one eye, which had been covered by a Band-Aid. He had been sweating profusely—the scent of him was heavy and sour, like bile. His face was streaked with tears.

"If you wanted to torture him, we could have loaned you some toys," Jimmy said, after looking at his property. "I didn't know that you got your jollies this way, Mr. Parker. Weren't you the one who threatened us with an investigation?"

"Oh, I'm full of surprises, Mr. Appleton." Chris pulled Jeff's head back. "But not as many surprises as this one has in store for us. Tell your master the first story you told me, Jeff."

"Please—" Jeff's Adam's apple bobbed up and down nervously, and he gave a choking sound. "I didn't know anything! Sir!"

"Good, now story number two." He let the slave go, and walked around to his front, where Jimmy was standing.

"I—I heard—sir! I heard that sh-she took the earrings, sir!"

"Very good. Now the third story, the most recent."

Jeff licked his lips and turned his head so he wasn't looking at his tormentor. He gazed beseechingly into his master's eyes. "I saw her take them. Sir! I saw it! It was her."

Jimmy looked at Chris, frowned and started to say something. And then he drew in a deep breath. "I think Eric needs to hear this," he said. Chris shrugged, and stayed there, flexing the hand until the two men came back together. He heard them out in the hallway, Jimmy saying something soft and urgent to his lover. A brief argument. And then they came in.

"Why didn't you say anything when we questioned you the first time?" Eric demanded immediately. He stopped and stared at Jeff's physical condition, and almost started to say something else, but Jimmy laid a hand on his shoulder and he turned his attention back to Jeff. "Well? We asked you the first day, when they were just missing, and you didn't say anything then! Why not?"

Jeff licked his lips again, and shot a glance at Chris. He looked back at his handsome owner and said, "I—I was afraid. I didn't know what to do. You seemed to like her so much—and she could get me in trouble—"

"Get you in trouble! Jesus Christ, what the hell did you think we were in? I asked you, Jimmy asked you—and again, when Eve called back, we asked you again! Why on Earth did you lie to us?"

"I thought—I was scared! I didn't know what to do—I didn't want to get her in trouble—I thought she'd just return them! I don't know!" Jeff looked like he was about to cry again. He kept looking at Chris, who was ignoring him, and then back at his masters. "But I didn't do it! No matter what she says, I didn't do it!"

"Did Robin accuse him?" Jimmy asked.

"No, actually," Chris answered. "I had to prod her for a few minutes, and then she still had trouble imagining it. I will tell you one thing—I certainly didn't tell him that she accused him."

"Supposition," Jimmy said.

"Fine talk from a man who didn't recognize circumstantial evidence."

"I think I need to think," Eric said suddenly, turning away from Jeff. "I think we've waited on dinner long enough. I don't like this—it doesn't sound right. Let's eat, and figure this out afterwards, okay?"

"Fine. You'll stay, Parker?" Jimmy saw Chris's nod and turned to Jeff. "And you'll stay right here, boy. I don't want to hear the creak of a floor board from downstairs. Understand?"

"Yes, sir," he whispered.

It was always awkward having dinner with strangers, being an unwanted guest. Everyone was nervous. Discussion topics were slim, and friendly comments forced. But Chris felt much better.

The boy would break because he was guilty. There had been a moment at the beginning, when there was that shred of doubt— just the off chance that instincts can lead you wrong. And it was also tricky interviewing under duress. Hurt them too much, and they'll tell you anything. It was a fact of life—hell, spies and soldiers knew it. And they had far greater motives to hide what they knew.

The desire to hurt lingered, as it always did when this mood was upon him. But it wouldn't take much to finish the job. Chris looked up, focused on Jimmy, and realized that Jimmy had asked him something.

"Please forgive me, my mind was wandering," he said. "Jet lag, I suppose."

"No problem. I was asking if you'd like a different wine. I noticed you haven't tried the one we poured."

"Actually, this is a fine vintage—an excellent choice," Chris said. "But I've had to cut down on drinking, and I think my fatigue wouldn't go well with a glass. Please don't take offense."

Very civil. Actually, he wanted a drink almost as much as he wanted a cigarette. A single malt scotch, straight up, would be lovely. He drank some mineral water and waited for the return upstairs. It had been a long day.

It took exactly two hours after they finished lingering over dinner. One hour was wasted as the two owners argued over who, if anyone, should be hitting their boy.

"Gentlemen—please. Let's try to solve this without any more direct compulsion," Chris said.

"Now's a fine time to come up with that suggestion," complained Jimmy.

"There is something to be said for using a two-by-four to get a mule's attention. Now that we have it, there's only one thing left." He turned to Jeff, whose condition had not exactly improved in their absence. "Jeff, we all now know that you're lying. We know that if you had seen Robin—or anyone else—take those earrings, you would have answered your masters truthfully on the day they asked you about it, isn't that true?"

"Yes! I mean, I would have." He looked at his masters with a desperate plea. "I told you, sirs, I didn't know what to do!"

"Why not?" Chris asked. He raised his voice. "What took priority over telling your masters the truth?"

"I didn't wanna get her in trouble!"

"What?" Jimmy asked incredulously. "You hated her guts!"

"Oh," Chris said, rubbing his wounded knuckles. "That was another lie, wasn't it?"

"No!" Jeff scrambled up, kicking the chair back, his hands covering his genitals. "You keep away from me! Master, don't let him—he's fucking crazy!"

"All right, Jeff, I won't let him," Eric said, his voice tight. He strode over to Jeff and raised one hand high and hit the side of his face with a resounding slap that sent the slave reeling. "You did it, didn't you, you little fuck? After everything we've done for you— you coulda had a great life—but you had to take care of the girl, didn't you?"

"He's very excitable," Chris said, *sotto voce* to Jimmy. The man with the pony tail had the decency to look deeply ashamed. He blushed and coughed.

"I didn't do it! I didn't mean it! Master, please!" Jeff was crying now. Jimmy pulled Eric off of him before Eric's hands had settled around Jeff's throat, and Eric calmed himself enough to face Chris.

"I guess we owe you an apology," he said, his beautiful lips pressed together tightly. He hated every word.

"Oh, I guess so," Chris agreed. "Not to mention suitable reparations toward the property you almost ruined, plus some suitable fate for your 'good kid' here."

Jeff was blubbering, pressed against the wall, insisting on his innocence.

"You might also work on getting a full confession for the record," Chris added.

"I don't care," Jimmy said. "I think we've got some bigger decisions to make. We have to call Mr. Lu, first of all—and what about Robin?"

"I care," Eric snapped. "If Robin doesn't want to come back, that's only natural. We'll give her a good recommendation, and won't file any complaints. We'll say it was an amicable mutual separation. And yes, I think I'd like to hear the whole story from this prick. Parker, you seem to enjoy this—why don't you stick around and help?"

"I'd like to, Mr. Parese, but I have a client who is waiting for me. But if I may, I do have one parting gesture I'd like to make to little Jeffy here."

"I don't think I want to watch," Jimmy muttered as he excused himself.

It was enormously unsportsmanlike to take advantage of an opponent when he was down for the count. But he was never my opponent, Chris thought, lifting a squirming and fighting Jeff up to a standing position. Only my target. Unfair. Cruel. Definitely not the mark of a gentleman.

"I told you Robin was my client, didn't I, Jeff?" he asked softly.

"Yes," he sniffled, his right arm roaming between his lower chest and his genitals. "Please don't—"

"I left one thing out. I also love her deeply." Chris feinted with a right, and Jeff dodged directly into the knee that slammed up between his legs, sending him crashing against the wall. He instantly rebounded with a cry of agony, and on the way down, Chris clipped him sharply on the back of the head. He hit the floor, limp.

"Jesus, what was that?" Eric asked, coming forward to bend down next to the boy.

"Knock-out," Chris answered. "I didn't want him to suffer for too long."

Eric looked at him with a mixture of disgust and admiration. Chris sighed. It was a familiar look. "Most people use whips and things in this life, you know," the owner said. "You play with knocking people's heads around, you're asking for trouble."

Jeff started to stir already, coming to with an awful groan.

"Yes," Chris said, nodding. "That's true. Especially if you pull the punches so much they're not very effective. Oh well. Now he'll have to dig his balls out of his liver and he'll have a splitting headache. Tender my sincerest apologies."

He was almost out the door when Eric spoke again. "You're a sick bastard, Parker."

"Yes," Chris said, agreeing with him one more time. "I've come to see that."

CHAPTER NINETEEN

"Mike, you'll run Joan today and tomorrow, and then until Chris gets back," Anderson had instructed. And Michael leapt at the chance. At last he was alone with his intended slave. He felt as giddy as a bridegroom, and studied her schedule late into the night in order to be able to supervise her perfectly.

I think I've been watching long enough to know how, he thought before he went to sleep. Now, all I need is a few days for Anderson to notice how well I do, and boom, Joan will be mine, and the training will have begun in earnest.

But it really wasn't very different once he got down to the actual work. Joan attended him in the morning, as she was doing already; he followed her work with Vic, and checked off tasks completed. Her exercises that day were not very intensive—she was working on multiple task management, the same thing that Tara had been doing toward the end of her training.

He did get to interview her alone, though.

"So, tell me how exactly how you're going to be used when you get home," he asked to start off.

"Sir, I will be an upstairs maid. My duties will be to service the rooms assigned to me, see that they are clean and dusted, serviced with fresh linens and flowers, aired and stocked with suitable supplies. I will answer to the housekeeper directly, but will also be below the lady's maids. During times when Japanese or American guests are present, my services will be required to make their stay more comfortable."

"Is that it?"

"That was all I was told, sir." She smiled enthusiastically. "I'm quite looking forward to it."

"So, you really don't expect to be used sexually?" Michael still had a hard time believing that.

"Sir—please forgive me—but my owner can have any number of beautiful women at his service. He may purchase one, or he may... make other arrangements. Why would he want plain old me?"

Michael raised his eyebrows. "But you're not plain! I mean, you're kind of chubby, but on you, it's cute. And you are attractive, especially when you smile."

She blushed and made herself attractive. "Thank you, sir. But in truth, I will be a maid, probably for several years, if not all of my contract."

"Well—what about guests? Sometimes in America, a host will make their slaves available to the guests."

"I suppose that is possible, sir. But I'm sure His Lordship will have proper arrangements for honored guests as well. It might seem rather insulting to guests to be offered a maid, after all."

"I never thought of it that way," Michael mused. "And you want to do this for ten years. Why?"

"For the experience, sir. It's rare to find these large manors anymore, and few families can afford to keep them staffed like this one is. It's like living in a novel sometimes." Her eyes glowed with excitement and Michael found himself smiling. "And so many in my family have done it—it will be a grand tradition I'm carrying on. His Lordship is a good man, and a good employer. I know I'll be well cared for, and when my service is done, I'll be free to marry, or leave, or do whatever I want."

"What if you want to marry while you're in service?"

"Well, sir—it's against the policy of the house for maids to be married," she said. She gave a little shrug. "So if I did find someone wonderful, I would probably have to wait until I had become a housekeeper's assistant or perhaps moved into another area of service—or he would have to simply wait for me."

"And... you won't miss not having sex?" he asked gingerly.

She lowered her eyes with a slight smile, and when she raised them again, Michael felt a strange thrill he didn't at once identify. It actually took a moment for him to realize that she had instantly aroused him—and it didn't come through his cock for a change.

It was the way she moved, and the way she drew her breath—and the sure knowledge that what she had to say to him was something entirely new.

"I beg your pardon, sir," she said, with just the slightest of blushes. "But I shall almost certainly not be celibate. As a member of a large household staff, I may be fortunate enough to find a special friend or two with whom I may be permitted to become intimate."

"Other slaves?" Michael asked.

"Perhaps, sir. Or, free household members who are not too above me in station."

Michael blinked as he thought of that. Slaves permitted to form relationships—sexual relationships!—under their owner's noses? Unheard of!

"Er—who would do the permitting?" he asked.

"At first, the housekeeper," Joan replied. "If I advance in station to become a lady's maid, I might become directly answerable to the Lady of the house. Otherwise, I shall be unworthy of her notice, especially over some minor matter."

"It's so different here," Michael said. "Who a slave has sex with is no minor matter in any house I've ever seen."

"I understand, sir. And indeed, in a smaller household, it might be a different matter all together. But I have the great fortune of being given the rare opportunity to perform service of a pure nature. If my owners wish me to remain chaste, I shall do as they request. But if it does not interfere in my duties and I have not been remiss in any way which might cause me to be punished, then it should not trouble them if I seek pleasure among the other staff members. And of course, senior staff might wish to use their status to order me into sexual service. But frankly, sir, I think it's unlikely I shall form a regular relationship in that fashion."

Michael shook his head. "It's another world," he said. "And you really want this?"

"With all my heart, sir! Ever since I was a girl, I was drawn to service, even before my parents told me about just how powerful it could be. I have dreamed of this for many years, and I look forward to my term. I can't imagine anything better!" Her face was bright, open, and eager, and he could hear the breathless quality to her voice that exceeded even her warm pleasure at imagining her sensual options among her future workmates.

"Amazing. You know, I can't imagine making a plan that would cover the next ten years."

"And I can't imagine a life without this security, sir."

He nodded. "I guess that's what makes you a slave and me a trainer, sweetie. Interview ended, let's get back to work."

Even if the day didn't seem different than any other, it was great to feel like he was in charge. It got even better when Anderson invited him to sit in on one of her catch-up interviews with Lorens. Although he didn't get any deep insights on how the Trainer did her own interviews, he did feel like he was truly her apprentice. He hung on her every word, took copious notes, and learned more about a bodybuilding regimen than he ever really needed to know.

"You've lost inches, Lorens," Anderson commented. "Chest, arms, legs—everywhere. How are you cutting down?"

"Very slowly, Trainer," the big Dane said. "Now, I am down to a one hour workout every day, plus a little running and a little bicycle for stamina and good health. Not so much protein any more. My lady does not like too many muscles!" He laughed, and it was difficult not to laugh with him.

"One hour a day sounds like a lot," Michael commented.

"When I met him, he was working out four hours a day," Anderson said. "It's not an exercise, it's a religion. When do you work out, Lorens?"

"In the morning, very early. I come back home before she is awake to make breakfast. I run in the afternoon, while she is working. Sometimes, I take the dogs. And we have a great cycle, for two riders, which my lady enjoys riding—but she never pushes the pedals!" He smiled and breathed in deeply. "I am very happy, Trainer. It is all I wanted."

"It's good when it works out that way," Anderson said. "I'm glad it did for you, Lorens. And your mistress. Now, let's get back to the program—I see she likes some pretty fancy manners around the house. You never turn your back on her, you never sleep when she's awake—nice touches. How does she punish you?"

He never lost his smile. "Oh, she is very clever, Trainer. When I fail her in any way, she sends me away. I am forbidden to serve. Sometimes, for her pleasure, she has a gentleman friend who is also very strong, and there is a whip which I have felt many times. It is an honor then, to take pain for her." He rounded his shoulders and demonstrated how he braced for it. "But when she is not pleased, I am alone. She invites another slave to come and serve her."

"And the last time that happened?"

Proudly, he answered, "Fourteen months ago, Trainer."

"I don't know what you're doing here," she said wryly. "But I'm glad you came. You set a good example."

And he did. He was a classic Anderson slave—attentive, subtle, and surrounded by a kind of attitude that was almost palpable. Other trainers had mentioned an aura that followed exceptional slaves—and Lorens had it. If he had any obvious fault, it was that he was exceptionally cheerful, but that was the demeanor his owner preferred, and you couldn't argue with that.

Michael was alone in his room that night when he began to reflect on what he had really learned so far. There was no order to it, nothing that he could write down as an outline: This is how to train slaves. Yet there was a feeling he had, a sense that there was something here that was eluding him, something larger than a mere lesson plan.

He stood in front of the mirror at attention, studying his posture and correcting it until it was the standard expected by Anderson—and by Chris. He laced his fingers behind his neck to throw out his chest, another common posture, and straightened his head a little. Damn! There was so much they had to remember—and still maintain a calm and serious demeanor, or be cheerful in the face of bad days and the unfair twists and turns of life. What was inside of them that Anderson could see but he couldn't? What made Chris so damn sure that his slave Robin was innocent—and what bound him to her? She was just one of what— dozens? A hundred?

He let his arms down and felt the gentle twinge of holding the
position too stiffly. Damned if he could figure out how to hold it
softly!

He wondered if not being able to figure that out had anything
to do with not being able to figure out what exactly he was learning other than patience.

CHAPTER TWENTY

Chris could see Anderson's silhouette as she parted the drapes and watched him settle with the cab driver. He wondered if Lorens was nearby, waiting for her to sleep so that he could or whether he was tossing and turning in his bed, feeling awkward and wakeful.

He opened the front doors with his key and felt the emptiness of the hall. No one was waiting to take his coat, so he hung it up himself. It smelled like smoke. Anderson wasn't going to like that.

"Hail the conquering hero. Wasn't that a line from something?" Her voice was hard, and Chris paused before walking into the front room.

"I'm sure it was, Trainer."

She was dressed tonight in red—a wool vest embroidered with zig-zagged tribal patterns, layered over one of her worn white cotton shirts. Her long skirt was a deeper red than the vest. No silver jewelry tonight—only a dark stone dangling from a chain around her throat. There was a fire lit, although the weather didn't really warrant it. It looked like it had been burning for some time—there were no pieces of wood left in the metal stacking frame.

"But you wouldn't presume to correct your Trainer, would you?"

"That would depend on the circumstance," he said wearily. "As does everything else." She didn't invite him to sit, so he remained standing.

"I'm still finding it hard to believe you went out there."

"It was the right thing to do. An investigation would have—"

"Would have ended in the same result," she interrupted.

"With all due respect, Trainer, I don't think so."

"Obviously. So off you run to California, where you proceed to—what? Brutalize some former street kid? For what? To avenge the harm done to your client?"

Chris smiled and stopped hiding the hand with the bandaged knuckles. "Someone's been telling tales out of school."

"Chris—what on Earth got into you?"

"That's a telling question, Imala. What I did may in fact have a great deal to do with what's gotten into me." He paused for her sigh of exasperation and shrugged. "I cannot in good faith offer an excuse other than this: my responsibility to Robin demanded that I be there for her. My current—condition—made me less able to handle my anger, which is regretful. You were correct, it would be impossible for me to do that for everyone whose training I've participated in. This was a special case. And I'm satisfied with all but one aspect of it."

She angled her head suspiciously. "I can't wait to hear what that is."

"I should not have hit the wall quite as hard as I did."

She shook her head. "I'm a sucker for a straight line, Chris, and you know it. I'm still disappointed."

He spread his hands in front of him. "I await your discipline."

She smiled. "Is that why you did it?"

"Certainly not!" he replied indignantly. "Besides, if I had—you wouldn't do a thing." His mouth jerked up on one side as he struggled to keep serious.

"True 'nuff," Anderson said. "Well, I suppose everyone has to come to this crossroads eventually. I'm glad it finally happened."

"And is that why you forced it?"

"Certainly not, to coin a phrase." Hers was strong, but lacked the same indignation. "If I wanted to get rid of you, I'd throw you out."

"That's a comfort. But there is no crossroads, Trainer. You didn't order me to stay, and I didn't defy you by going."

"Impasse?"

"No. Just a disagreement. Nothing to be overly concerned with. May I be excused?"

"Sure. After you make good on a promise to me. You still haven't shown off this thing you've been building for so long. Let's take a gander now."

He looked slightly surprised, but shrugged again and nodded. He unknotted his tie and slid it from around his throat, and started to unbutton the shirt he was wearing. It was wrinkled from the hours on the flight. "I'm sorry," he said somewhat belatedly.

"It's all right, Parker. I know you're shy."

He pulled the shirt out of his trousers and took it carefully off, draping it across the back of a chair. He was wearing a sleeveless undershirt, which he pulled up over his head in one smooth motion. Then, he stepped closer to allow her to examine the creation that was his upper body.

"Oh my," she said softly, rising. "You have been a good boy." She ran a finger lightly across the top of one shoulder, outlining the muscular structure that had just begun to form two years ago. The firelight danced and made rippled patterns down his chest, which was perfect, considering the subject matter of the tattoo. She examined it, bending down to see more of it. Her fingers lightly traced under the pectoral muscles, and she moved them away when he shivered. "Sorry about that. But there's something about so much work that demands a respectful and admiring attitude."

He blushed, and she laughed out loud. "Thank God I can still do that, Parker! Sometimes, you do have me worried."

"Do you like it?" he asked, ignoring the tease. "The colors? You don't think it's—excessive?"

"No, dear, I don't. I think it's perfect. Now, I think I'll go to bed. And—you may, too." She tapped him lightly on the shoulder when she went by. "There's a lot of work still to be done, Parker, crossroads or not. Let's try not to have any more emergencies, shall we?"

He picked up the shirts and his tie with a sigh and nodded at her back. "Of course, Trainer. Good night. Oh—Trainer?"

She turned to him. "Yes?"

"'See, the conquering hero comes! Sound the trumpet—beat the drums.' I believe that's Thomas Morell."

"Parker, whatever you are—you are always a wiseass."

"Undoubtedly."

She laughed again, and he followed her upstairs after banking the fire and checking the doors.

CHAPTER TWENTY-ONE

"Now, observe. Watch her very carefully as she goes down."

I wish, Michael thought bitterly. But he obediently looked at Joan as she dipped into a kneeling posture which was not one of Anderson's standards. The British woman was kneeling with her knees drawn up tightly together, her back straight and shoulders back. Her palms were resting on the sides of her thighs, fingertips straight down. Her chin was lowered. It was not the most attractive of postures, but it looked good with the maid's uniform—very formal.

"Correct the position," Chris said. It was the order Michael dreaded.

It was one thing to know how something was done, another thing to do it. Michael had also discovered that seeing something done and knowing how it should be done was also quite different than correcting minor errors when it had been done! All the necessary points were there—toes pointed, back straight, head down, fingers down—what else was there?

Several times, he had tried to do something, anything. He would push her shoulders back a little more, and then see that he had pushed her out of line. Or, in another move, he would walk around her, studying her for a long time until she actually moved out of position. That's when he would criticize. Both tactics failed. He also tried just saying that he thought she had executed a task or movement perfectly—and then watched as Chris made some correction or another. It seemed that whatever he did—or didn't do—was wrong. If Anderson had been an indirect instructor who rarely made a point of saying "this is how it's done," Chris Parker was the teacher from hell, knowing every possible answer and making sure that Michael was aware of every mistake he made.

Chris also maintained that slightly snide attitude about it all—he never called Michael stupid, but Michael heard it anyway.

He looked Joan over with a sigh, checking items off a mental list. They were all there this time—or maybe her head was a little too tucked? Her chin shouldn't be touching her chest—was it? No, it wasn't. He was tired; a steady thumping pain right behind one eyeball was making him feel more impatient than usual. In one week, Parker had upset Michael's latest resolve and brought back all the anxiety and the feeling that nothing was happening. He shook his head. "I have no idea, Chris. I have absolutely no idea."

Chris started to say something, but then switched his attention to Joan. "Bring your chin up just a bit, girl, right there. Yes. The remainder was satisfactory. Go and see if Vicente needs any help."

"Yes, Chris," she said rising. She was a little stiff—the position wasn't made for lengthy periods of time. But like the good slave she was, she waited until she was out of sight to stretch out properly. When her footsteps receded, Chris turned to Michael.

"The knowledge of ignorance is a person's first step toward education, Mike. Isn't it about time you got off that first step?"

"What's that supposed to mean?"

"It's too late in your training for you to keep relying on not knowing what to do. A slave gets to ask twice—a trainer should be able to ask once and then be able to do it. If there's a special problem here, I would appreciate knowing it."

Michael fumed. "First of all, I am not a slave, and I can ask however many time I need to, until you explain it right. I don't understand why everything has to be so absolutely perfect! The position was plain—all the elements were there, she had the right attitude—any owner would be thrilled to have a slave that could pull that off every time!"

"Not the owners who patronize Anderson," Chris answered evenly. "She holds her clients to a higher standard because the sloppy, haphazard training cultivated by gentlemen like your former employer have ruined the market."

"What?"

"You're getting tiresome, Mike. I think that's enough for today.

We'll work together tomorrow morning. She's going to be practicing some basic flower arrangements, and I don't think you have any experience there." Chris nodded a dismissal and waited for Michael to leave.

Michael had no such intention. "Not until you explain that last crack, Parker. Geoff wasn't Anderson, but he turned out great slaves. To happy owners! His methods were different, that's all. I didn't much approve of some of his stuff, but he's a good man, and a good trainer. No one's ever complained about one of his slaves!"

"That's not true, Mike, and I'm surprised that you believe it. If you like, I will be glad to pull up the files and show them to you. It's trainers like him who have flooded the Marketplace with inferior, rapidly trained novices whose dedication to the craft of service—to the lifestyle, if you like—is at best questionable." Chris folded his arms casually, but his voice was sharp. "Year after year, I see more stories of contracts broken, leaks of information to the press, discussions among the dabblers—the word is getting out, Mike, and it's because of trainers like Negel and the flotsam he gathers and shapes into slaves. Not to mention the dilettantes he selects as his junior trainers."

"You shut your mouth," Michael growled. "I don't need to hear this shit from you."

"Yes, you do. You need to hear it from someone, before you end up right back where you came from."

Michael gritted his teeth and folded his arms. "Okay, go ahead. Tell me what a waste of time I am. It'll be nothing new."

"I don't suppose it will be," Chris snapped. "Here's truth, Michael Xavier. You were trained in a 'tradition' not even a decade old. A philosophy that takes the entire drive for honorable service and turns it into kinky sex. I would hazard a bet right now that when I pulled up the files on slaves sold through Geoff Negel, 100% of them would be beautiful. Muscular men, shapely women. Would I be correct?"

Michael nodded. "Owners want their slaves to look good. It doesn't take a genius to figure that out."

"Would he have taken Tara?"

"Sure, she was okay."

"Even at the age of forty-six?"

Michael set his jaw and felt a deep twinge of shame. No, Geoff wouldn't have taken her at forty-six. There was a belief that the younger a person was trained, the better they'd behave. Also, owners preferred younger slaves—

Unless they were bookkeepers and researchers, maybe. He felt that familiar old sinking sensation, and tried not to think of the thousands of tasks and skills which age and experience would lend value to.

Chris nodded, as though following Michael's train of thought. "All right, let's assume that he would take Tara. We know he'd take Lorens."

Michael dropped his arms and began to nod.

"Yeah, I know," he said. "But no way would he take Joan. I mean, not the way she is. He'd want her to lose the weight. Take up aerobics, go on some diet."

"And why?"

"Because people like skinny people! Come on, it's not unrealistic! There are lots of houses that only take beautiful slaves! You go with what gets bought."

"The owners will buy quality, Mike. Years ago, Marketplace slaves were not always assumed to be sexually available, let alone skilled. In some areas, it is still considered tacky and uncouth to take your slave to bed—one does not make love with a social inferior." His tone changed to slightly mocking. "Now, thanks to the trainers who serve up the idea that a slave is nothing more than a kinkier than average plaything, there is this sudden proliferation of slaves who are quite agreeable to look at but hardly talented or dedicated to their service. Slaves who expect to be matched with similarly attractive owners who will require nothing more than sexual availability and willingness. Slaves who think nothing of jeopardizing their master's reputation, or the safety of another slave. Slaves who are actually in it for the money, Michael. Or because they were failures at everything else."

Michael took a step back; there was a lot more here than just a lecture. "Hey, chill out, Chris. This seems to be getting out of hand."

"I'll tell you what's getting out of hand, Michael LaGuardia. Trainers like yours, who believe that you can take a selfish little failure off the streets and Pygmalion him into being an acceptable slave!"

Shit—this was about whatever happened in California. Michael held one hand up. "Listen, I don't even know what went on there, Chris—but I sure as hell know that Geoff wasn't involved."

"No? Think again. The man who supposedly spotted and trained the slave who caused this entire situation was certified as a trainer by your own teacher, Mr. Geoff Negel. And who knows what tragedy would have followed you if your scheme to turn a weekend 'sub' into a slave had actually gone beyond the spotting stage?" Chris grinned in his nasty way and cocked his head to one side. "Perhaps I'd have to go clean that up, too."

"You son of a bitch!"

"Watch your language, Mike. I'll see you in the morning. You may leave."

Michael trembled with anger, but there was nothing else to do. The only other option would be to hit the short, taunting man, and that would surely ruin everything once and for all. He nodded and turned stiffly, feeling the heat of the controlled rage. He didn't even know where he was going, and was surprised when he found himself back in his room. He locked the door, feeling slightly foolish, but knowing that the slightest interruption would set him off. The bed creaked as he sat down and buried his face in his hands.

He had gone back to Geoff's with a heavy heart but with some measure of confidence. He would just have to pay more attention to the techniques of spotters. There was a whole library of slave narratives describing their experiences in entering the Marketplace—he would have to read them or watch the tapes and take some notes. Maybe he just approached it the wrong way. It was obviously Karen's fault—she had misled him into believing that she had real potential.

At first, there was no clue that anything terrible had happened. Work continued, and Geoff was encouraging and sympathetic about the "breakup" that Michael haltingly described for him. Michael was very careful to leave out any hint that he and Karen had been doing anything more than sleeping together and doing pretty standard "date things" like going to movies and to the beach. He fell back into the ongoing training with ease, marveling at the difference between the obedient, docile slaves at the ranch as opposed to the curious and demanding Karen. He began to wonder how he had ever been hoodwinked. Weeks went by without incident, and he believed that Karen was all behind him.

One evening, he was called to Geoff's office, where he met someone he had never been introduced to before. The house lawyer.

Geoff looked more sad than anything else. He was sitting at his desk, framed by the twinkling lights of the patio shining through the huge window behind him. His shoulders were pressed back—he was not relaxing in his chair the way he usually did. The desk lamp was shining on a pile of what looked like reports of some kind. His kind eyes were just a little sharper than usual; there was something terribly wrong.

"Mike, this is Nani Okawa, our lawyer. I've asked her to sit in on this meeting because of some disturbing things we've found out about the woman you say was your girlfriend."

Michael paled and felt his knees buckle. He found a chair and sat on the edge. His mind was blank.

"She wasn't really your girlfriend, was she, Mike?" Geoff asked. His manner was still calm, his voice reassuring.

"No," Michael managed to say. The shame mingled with relief as he got that out. "She—I thought—she told me she... " His voice trailed off as he tried to organize his thoughts. He looked at the lawyer, so prim in her designer silk suit, her legs demurely crossed at the ankle.

She raised one eyebrow and picked up a piece of paper from the desk. "This woman has been attempting to have you investigated and charged, Mr. LaGuardia."

"Charged? With what?" Michael shouted, shocked and panicked. "I never did a thing to her that she didn't want!"

"She claims, in her report to the police, that you offered to make her a prostitute. That you had identified a large organization which handled these matters, and tried to harm her when she resisted." Her voice was matter-of-fact, but he could hear a faint trace of disapproval.

"That's a lie! Goddamn lies, all of that!" Michael turned to Geoff, his eyes wide. "I never told her anything about the Marketplace—nothing that could be traced! I never said anything about prostitution, I was always very clear—I mean, there was only one time, and when she didn't go for it, I dropped it and left! I never laid a fucking hand on the bitch!"

"Now, Mike, there's no need to fly off the handle. Let's listen to the whole story and get it straightened out," Geoff said. "As it turns out, there isn't a real case. The police will come to interview you, but we don't believe it will go further than that."

"Thank God," Michael said weakly. "How did you do that?"

"It wasn't Mr. Negel," Okawa said. "Lucky for you, your friend doesn't have any evidence. The police who took her report noted quite clearly that she owned almost every object she claimed you used on her, and that she freely admitted to being, as she put it, a 'sexual submissive.' They have to come and interview you, but thanks to your keeping that one secret, they've had trouble finding you."

"How did they find me?"

"Oh, we told them."

"What?!"

"Mr. LaGuardia, despite the non-standard ways our organization does business, we do recognize that we operate within the United States of America, and we must cooperate with authorities in any way we can." She pulled another paper out of the pile and scanned it. "Also, your doings had already exposed us to potential annoyances. I suggest you look at this."

Michael took the orange sheet of paper and read. It was a flyer for a Los Angeles SM group called Gates of Pleasure. They were apparently promoting a line-up of guest speakers and special events for the year. The list was esoteric—a seminar on basic bondage, a speaker discussing age-regression play, a piercing workshop—pretty standard stuff. His eyes scanned the list once, trying to see what the lawyer was pointing out to him, and then he caught it.

It was called "Secret Societies," and the featured speakers included "Slave Karen."

"Oh my God," he whispered. "But she knew nothing."

"We sent someone to tape the event," Okawa said. "The transcript is here. Apparently, after she told her story, audience members encouraged her to press charges, which is what she has done."

"But I never did anything to her!"

"Mr. LaGuardia—I suggest you look at this." She pulled a multipage document out of the pile and opened it to a folded over page. "Start at line six."

It read:

> MOD: Have any of you heard anything about a hidden slave market active right now?
> SK: Hell, I was recruited for it.
> MOD: When did that happen?
> SK: Just a few months ago, at Leather Forever.
> (AUD: Much amazement.)
> SK: No, it's true. He looked just like anyone else— showed me a good time. But he figured he could make me his slave and then sell me off to this organization he kept talking about. He was a great master—handsome, skilled, brutal, creative— everything a beginner could want. He seemed more real than anyone I knew—and I loved him. But I could tell early on that there was something dangerous about him. Any time I got nervous, he'd get violent. I wasn't allowed a safeword; he said that real slaves didn't need one. Every time I asked a question, he'd threaten to leave me forever.

   (AUD: Disapproval, boos, hisses.)

   MOD:Those guys are really slick like that—they iso-
      late you from your community, and then convince
      you that you're worthless without them.

   SK: That was it, right on the head. I felt worthless,
      like I couldn't live without him. And when he told
      me he was planning to sell me, I nearly lost it. He
      got violent—brutal.Threatened to leave me again,
      and swore that I'd never be a real slave. When he
      left, I was crying, hysterical. Almost suicidal.

"It wasn't like that," Michael said, dropping the transcript into his lap and feeling nauseated. "She—she didn't want to do it. I left. I never touched her... she wasn't crying when I left!"

"Well, she did a lot of crying at this meeting. And I can't even imagine what the repercussions of this will be." Okawa took the transcript back and placed it with the other papers. "Thanks to you, she'll be blabbing something about us in every SM club she gets invited to."

"But what about—I mean, her charge—what should I do?"

"When you meet with the police, you will tell them the truth—that you were engaged in a sexual relationship with her which included bondage and discipline games.That you had a disagreement, and then you broke up.

You haven't heard from her since. They have no physical evidence—no semen, no photos of bruises, no testimony from witnesses. In fact, we found several people who remembered you two as a couple from that Leather Forever conference where you first picked her up."

"Oh God, I just don't believe it," Michael moaned. "Wait! What about the house? Are they coming here?"

"It's about time you thought of more than yourself," Geoff said, shaking his head. "Michael, Michael—I gave you my complete trust. And you betrayed it.Went against my instructions—no wait. I won't jump to conclusions. Nani, why don't you take a break? I'll see you later."

"Sure thing, Geoff." She stood and left, and Michael slumped into his seat.

"Go ahead and tell me, Mike. But the truth this time."

"I thought she would make a great slave," Michael said glumly. There was no point in hiding anything now. "She responded perfectly! She was hot, and willing—and smart! And she learned real fast—she had the basic positions down in less than a month!"

"You taught her our methods, Mike?"

"Well, all spotters do! But only the basic ones, you know? Attention, show, present, at rest—and I made up a few I liked, too. So she doesn't know which ones are real." Mike grimaced. He was really grasping at straws.

"Okay, Michael. And then what?"

"I didn't tell her a word about the Marketplace. Even that last day, I never called it by its name. I never told her about you, or told her where the house was or how we do anything. I just told her I could make her dream of being a slave come true. But she lied to me, Geoff!" He leaned forward again, suddenly strong in his convictions. "Just like she's lying now!

"Like you lied to me?"

"I'm sorry," Michael said. "God, Geoff, I'm really sorry."

"And I accept your apology, Mike. But now, we have to do some damage control." He stood up and stretched a little, and Michael nodded eagerly, waiting to find out what had to be done. "First, there's the police interview. Nani has agreed to act as your attorney and make sure you don't get confused by the questions. She doesn't believe the investigation will be very in-depth. We expect that Karen will be advised that she waited too long and has instigated nothing but a he-said/she-said complaint. She will also be reminded that her history and reputation will become central aspects of the case, since she is not charging rape and therefore will not be protected by law. It's a pity, but the law and the justice system favor us strongly in this case."

"I don't think it's a pity—I didn't do anything wrong!"

"Yes you did, Mike. You exposed the Marketplace to danger, and you showed a young woman something she shouldn't have seen. Because of your inexperience, we'll never know whether she had true potential. Plus, I'm beginning to question yours." He fixed Michael with a stern, fatherly stare, grave and sad, and Michael squirmed a little under it. "After the interview, we'll hear whether the police intend to investigate further. You will go live somewhere else, and be considered on suspension until everything is cleared up."

Michael nodded. "Geoff—I just thought of something. What if we paid her off? To shut her up, and make her drop the charges. I bet that would work!"

"Okay," Geoff said, sitting down again. "How much can you afford?"

"Me? I can't afford anything! I meant the Marketplace! You know, to protect their interests?" Michael was close to panic. He shifted in his seat and gripped the edge of the chair. "You said that they do that sometimes!"

"Yes, Mike—to protect their valued members. Not to cover the asses of junior staff members who act on their own, breaking the rules." Geoff shook his head sadly. "If you had asked for specific spotter training, if you had come back and mentioned to me that you needed a spotter, and could you reserve the option to train the client should she come to our house—something could have been worked out, Mike. Or maybe not—maybe the time just wasn't right for this young lady, or for you. And you would have waited another six months, or a year, or three years! What would it matter, Mike? You'd have a place to live, food, and vacations, health benefits and training—and access to the best trained slaves in the country. But you put that all on the line when you went out-side to get your own, Mike. The Marketplace will not expend any substantial money or effort to keep you out of trouble. Their in-terest is in keeping the name and details of our organization out of the media."

Michael's jaw set, and his eyes narrowed. His fingertips were white with the pressure of keeping them locked onto his chair. "Well, what about what I could say about the Marketplace, Geoff? How come no one cares what I could do?"

"That's simple, Mike. Because if you say a word, you'll be shunned. What's more, so will your Uncle Niall. We'll cancel all current contracts he holds and remove the slaves from his house until you make restitution for any harm you might cause. And even if you do, you will never be able to visit him again, not while he owns slaves. You will be barred from any contact with us. You'll never train, and never own a real slave, Mike. Think very carefully about this—would it be worth it?" Geoff's voice had turned very hard, but he softened and leaned across the desktop. "Mike, listen to me. You made a bad mistake—and people do make mistakes. Don't compound it. I'll pretend I never heard what you just said, and we'll keep going on the damage control. You do as we say, and maybe you can be back here soon, and life will go on. Trust me, son. We'll help as much as we can if you just cooperate."

What else could he do? He could never really go to the media and start blabbing about the organization that had made his life so pleasurable—especially considering the consequences. He had never thought that they'd punish Niall for what he did. The thought of his beloved uncle losing his assistant and his boy-toy lover made Michael's gut ache. To be forever cast out of all contact with these people—to never be able to own those two slaves he was always fantasizing about—no, the price was just too high.

So, he waited for the police, and did his interview. He was a little nervous, but the two men who questioned him didn't seem to be very adversarial. He was as honest as possible, admitting to a sort of SM-based relationship with Karen. He described the various kinds of roleplaying they had done, and referred to the seminars at Leather Forever as examples of where he might have learned those things. He agreed to make himself available for further interviews. When they left, they shook his hand and apologized for the bother.

In a way, it did seem a little unfair to Karen. But she had prejudiced her own investigators, the lawyer explained, by being a bad witness. She had not reported the event after it happened, but after she had received some small notice for discussing it. She was not the virgin-pure victim that the media and the courts loved—she was the exact opposite. There were witnesses, including the leatherdyke invited to play with them back at Leather Forever, who could say that Karen had consented to the relationship with Mike. Michael himself had no criminal record. He was cooperative, and clean-cut.

The case was never pursued. After a few months, Karen stopped talking about it at SM gatherings, although she did publish a written account of her relationship and distributed it via the growing "Information Superhighway." She had changed Mike's name to Jon. After that, no one paid any attention to the tale. There were other things to care about, other items of interest.

But not for Michael. Every day he was kept away from Geoff's place, tucked into a small studio apartment and forbidden to go to LA or San Francisco and take part in the soft world activities there, was a purgatory of boredom. He watched TV, mindlessly channel surfing for hours. They didn't even give him Marketplace books and reports to read, let alone training tapes to watch. He was in temporary exile.

By the time he was called back, he was tearfully grateful for the reprieve. He agreed at once to enter Geoff's staff again at the lowest level, doing paperwork and assisting other junior trainers. Geoff made him write out a full report on his failed attempt at spotting and pre-training, an exercise, he said, in reviewing the past mistake so it would never happen again. It was excruciating, especially the part where Geoff had Michael read the thing to him, and Michael had to watch Geoff react to every time Michael reported having used Marketplace techniques on a soft-world novice.

But even working the scut jobs was better than being outcast. In short time, he was able to make his way back up to where he had been when he left—no matter what had happened, the slaves still responded to him, and he did get good results.

But he was tainted, and everyone knew it. Geoff was careful to coach the other staff members not to mention the incident to Michael's face, but he knew they talked about it behind his back. He knew that his reputation had suffered a terrible blow.

It became absolutely necessary to leave Geoff's house as soon as possible. It was clear that there could be no future for him there.

Even if Geoff did certify him as a full trainer, there would be nowhere to go. He had to find a new house to work his way through, to erase the whole Karen incident from his past.

He had found out that one didn't apply directly to Anderson, that the process of being selected for her apprentice involved sending a request to the management office which represented the North American Marketplace interests. He did include a letter to the legendary trainer in his application. It wasn't quite as personally lauding as he would have preferred. But he included copies of his rating sheets before Karen, and mentioned that he realized that he needed training in a different style if he was to ever become a proper trainer.

It took another six months for the answer to come. Geoff seemed confused but pleased for him, and wished him luck. His going-away present was a Movado watch, which Michael reluctantly sold before leaving the city. His entire savings was less than what it would take to secure and rent a New York apartment for three months. There would be no stipend while he was with Anderson—only room and board. This was because Geoff hadn't sponsored him for the special training. There would be no way to know how long he was going to be there; but he wasn't afraid. He was a quick learner. The Trainer of Trainers would see that, and before long, he would get her approval. There would be no mistakes like the Karen incident.

But it seemed that Karen and Geoff would be with him forever! He could never just put that behind him and go on.

It just wasn't fucking fair.

CHAPTER TWENTY-TWO

Finally, someone got tied up at Anderson's house.

Lorens looked very good in bondage, too. A rope harness wrapped around his body, crossing one hard, defined muscle and gently curving around another. He looked like a poster for some Italian Hercules movie, bound between the columns of a temple. That was it—Samson! If Samson had been a Viking.

But this particular temple was only the doorway to the room where the slaves slept. Michael had seen the bolts sunk into the corners, but had never asked about them. After all these weeks, it seemed like whatever purpose they had served was long over.

Apparently, he was wrong. Chris did the actual bondage, under Anderson's direction and Michael's careful observation. The short trainer was an expert with the rope—lines slid through his hands without tangling, and the actual patterns he made were symmetrical and pleasing to the eye as well as secure and useful. Lorens was patient, cheerful and even stoic when thinner strands of rope were used to make his cock and balls look like a macramé project. Joan was watching as well—earlier that morning, Chris had mentioned to Michael that despite her probable non-sexual role in her master's household, she would be surrounded by the evidence of slaves used for more sexual and erotic purposes. She might even have the responsibility to care for them should they not be able to care for themselves.

Thus—Lorens in bondage. A study in body art of another kind. It would be Joan's responsibility to check on him, to notify Chris of any problems and to be able to report on the slave's condition at any time. For Lorens, the exercise was simpler.

"Look pretty," Anderson instructed as she left the hallway.

Chris finished the job and trimmed the last bit of extra rope off with his pocket knife. He pinched one of Lorens's nipples fondly and Lorens grinned even as he closed his eyes and threw his head back with the sharp pain.

"That's nice," Michael said. "Can I—?"

Chris nodded, and said, "You may." His emphasis on the correct word almost made Michael sigh in exasperation, but Michael controlled himself and nodded an acceptance of the rebuke. Eagerly, he stepped forward. It had been a long time since he had played with a man, and Lorens was one strapping example of manhood. His nipples were somewhat large, probably due to some special attention. Michael asked about them before he took them between his fingers.

"Yes, sir," Lorens answered quickly. "My Lady, she likes for them to be sensitive. Every day, there are cups put on them to make them larger, suction cups, and sometimes clamps."

"That's nice," Michael said, giving them a twist. They felt like they were rooted in steel—they twisted nicely, but Michael could feel the tension of the muscles beneath them. Lorens grimaced slightly, but prettily. "I always thought that slaves should have sensitive nipples. It's so easy to control them that way."

"One would hope that control didn't depend on an owner having to create a physical sensation," Chris said. "You may play with Lorens as far as his bondage allows whenever you have free time, Mike."

"Yeah?" Michael let go of his toy and turned around. "Please, let's be clear, okay? Play how?"

"Use him, if that's more direct. Sexually, if you like."

Michael looked at the behemoth before him and tried to imagine fucking him. It seemed a bizarre image. His buttocks were probably as firm as his chest—slipping a dick between the cheeks would feel incredibly tight. He dropped his hands to caress Lorens's cheeks, testing them—hell yes, they were firm. Michael felt the beginnings of an erection and grinned. "Whatever you say, bossman," he said lightly.

"Not now," Chris said. "First, we have to go over the ways to structure a hierarchy of responsibilities. We'll work downstairs and let Joan get on with her task."

Michael sighed and let Lorens go. To his credit, Lorens looked a little sad to lose the contact, but not so much that he looked sulky. Michael followed Chris, not quite ready for another long, dull session of theory. He would not get to fuck Lorens that day, because after spending so much time dealing with minutiae, even a Greek god in rope bondage seemed too much of an effort. Never had dealing with slaves and masters been so unerotic.

Most of training had always seemed to be physical, with a little bit of psychology thrown in. You taught people what positions to use, what things to say, and how to accept pain and give pleasure. That was mostly why it was so much fun to be a trainer. You got to do the heavy SM work, the physical disciplining, the sexual testing—and then, before it got too boring, you got to work on a new client. You had to know a basic amount of what made people tick—some motivational theory was helpful.

But with Chris, there was a philosophy to choke down, too—and endless hours of discussion about possible circumstances. It wasn't enough to make up role-playing exercises for the slaves—you had to figure out what the slaves might encounter and discover the best responses so that you could drill them and create tests for them.

It was chafing more and more with each passing day. Michael tried his best to keep his frustration hidden. He was going to get no sympathy from the Trainer, and showing anger or impatience only worsened Chris's acerbic responses and gave him a new excuse to belittle Michael until there was nothing left to do but smolder for the rest of the afternoon, or evening, or throughout the next day.

It wouldn't be so bad if so much of it wasn't as dull as watching paint dry. Who cared what a slave should do if a guest towel was found to be frayed and the housekeeper was not available? Jesus, just do whatever seems right and collect the punishment later if it's wrong, that's what Michael thought. No need to make it into an issue! But to Chris, it was all part of teaching a client how to think—how to prioritize, to negotiate, to make do. It wasn't enough to take a guess and take the consequences—a client

of his had to be able to do the right thing as often as humanly possible. No, check that. A client of his had to be inhuman, like he was.

Oh, it was a cheap shot. But there was no end in sight to this
new torment. Joan continued to be chiefly under Chris's direction,
and Michael continued to be low man on the totem pole. Anderson
worked with Lorens privately, or occasionally with Joan, and refused to discuss changing Michael's lesson plans. "Either you get
along and learn," she cautioned one evening, "or you get yourself
a plane ticket home. Do you understand? This is where I find out
whether you're my kind of material, Mike. Don't embarrass me."

It had been embarrassing enough to go to her again with his
complaints of Chris's treatment and attitude. Now, she had made
it very clear. The line had been drawn, and there was nowhere to
go but on this track or back where he came from—which was not
possible. But the balance between his temper and the will to stay
and endure what he had to in order to get that approval from the
Trainer seemed increasingly less stable.

Michael finally got his hands on Lorens and his cock inside of
him about three days after Chris gave him permission to do so. He
had been cautious, making sure that it was okay with the Trainer,
too. Then, one evening after all the formal teaching was over, he
pulled the big man into his bedroom and treated himself to not
one, but two blow jobs, one after the other. It was like being freed
after a long imprisonment. When Lorens dived for his crotch the
second time, taking him in and expertly working him back to full
erection, Michael couldn't contain the sighs and groans of relief.
Now here was some dedicated sword swallowing! Here was a slave
who knew how to get down there and work that cock, swirling his
tongue, sucking on the tender flesh on the underside, taking both
balls into his mouth—things Michael used to take for granted.

He sent the slave away when he was totally spent, nodding at
the backwards exit Lorens made, never turning his back on his
user. It was a nice touch, but kind of creepy sometimes. Idly
scratching his chest, Michael wondered why it hadn't felt this good
when he had Tara doing it. Tara wasn't bad—in fact, she was damn
good for an older woman. But there had always been something

lacking, something that Lorens seemed to have. A joy, perhaps, in what was happening. Tara always behaved like a good slave—she did what she was told, as well as she could. But Lorens was happy sucking dick, and showed it, while Tara—well, Michael never really asked how Tara felt about it. In fact, he basically told her what to say about it, and she said it often. He loved hearing her cultured, reserved voice behind phrases like "Please let this slave suck your cock, sir."

But had she really, really felt the call to service him properly? Had she had much experience doing it before him, and maybe he was just more demanding than her Judge or her previous owners? What made Lorens's approach so much different from hers? He decided to ask Chris the next day. A discussion about good cocksucking would definitely be more interesting than one about how to discover the habits of a weekend guest in the first day.

"Lorens is eager to be sexually used by you because he's gay," Chris said offhandedly. Michael had taken a long time—almost five minutes—to try to explain the differences between the slaves before pitching his question.

"He is?"

"So he tells us. I don't believe he has any reason to lie."

"Wow!" Michael folded his arms and shook his head. "But he's in love with his mistress, isn't he? I mean, that's what I would have guessed. His eyes light up whenever he thinks about her."

"Yes. But that's more because she's a proper owner for him than because she is the appropriate gender for his masturbatory fantasies." Chris had been working with Vicente on the paperwork for the house, and they had just finished sealing a stack of checks for utilities. Michael had passed the cook at the door and slid into his recently vacated seat.

"I just can't imagine a gay man being happy with a woman as his owner," Michael admitted. He thought of Ethan, squirming at the memory of being sexually used by a woman. "Most of the ones I knew would hate it."

"Then they're not Marketplace material," Chris said. "Our clients are slaves, not lovers. They are not expected to be in love with their owners, nor are their owners expecting to love them."

"It's not a question of love—it's a question about what gets your dick hard." Michael laughed, and leaned back. "Lorens says that his owner likes for him to fuck her every once in a while. What does he do, close his eyes and think of a guy?"

Chris looked shocked. "That would be rude," he said. "I'm sure he does what she orders to the best of his ability with the sole purpose of pleasing her. Tell me—have you devoted any time to wondering how heterosexual men or women cope with same gender owners? Or, for that matter, how lesbian clients deal with heterosexual male owners?"

"Well... it's just that it's harder for a guy to, you know—get hard—if he's with the wrong partner. A woman can at least deal with it and she doesn't have to show that she's hot. But it's harder for a guy." Michael snickered. "No pun intended."

"You think so? You're wrong, Mike—as usual. Every slave goes through the terror that they will be required to be sexual with people they do not find attractive, or are of a gender they do not respond to erotically. It's part of the fear of being sold, of losing control over your life." Chris's voice had sharpened again, and Michael knew that this was going to become another intense "discussion." He began to wish he had never brought it up.

"Did you devote any time to wondering how the client might feel just about being sold to someone physically repulsive to them? It happens all the time—yet somehow, they cope. Then, they learn to cope with performing whatever service is requested of them, to the best of their ability, and showing the proper attitude, despite what might be genuine revulsion toward their owner. That's because they are called to something higher, Mike. Service, not romance. The best a trainer can do is cultivate that love of service and hope that the trials their clients have to go through won't push them away from the Marketplace."

"Okay, okay, I get it," Michael said quickly, raising his hands.

"No you don't." Chris stood up and put the paid bills into the "out" basket, clearing the worktable off. "All you see are slaves, each having a number of holes which you can put your cock into.

Each having a set of skills at pleasing you, regardless of their inner orientation or preferences, regardless of their ultimate destination or degree of training."

"That's not true!" Michael retorted.

"Oh?" Chris stared at Michael directly. "What is Tara's sexual orientation?"

Michael started to say "heterosexual," but then stopped. Chris wouldn't have asked him a question like that if the answer was so obvious. He remembered her story about the spotter named Corazon.

"Bi," he said finally. "She had to be bi."

"As is happens, she was not," Chris said. "In behavior, yes. But before she joined us, she considered herself a lesbian—and still does, despite her sexual behavior with her owner."

"Yeah, she's a dyke. Tell me another one," Michael sneered. "She had a great time with me!"

"That's not what she reported," Chris said, a tight smile forming. "She said that you were quite an average lover, who did not spend any time in foreplay, who climaxed quite within standard time limits, and was of average size."

"You son of a bitch! She did not!"

"Listen to the tapes of the interviews, Mike. I could find them in the log."

Michael felt the heat of embarrassment flood his collar. "She told me she came!"

"She lied," Chris said. "As she was instructed to. As she was trained to do! Just as she was being trained to be pleasing and seem willing for her Master. All the while you were thrusting away into her, she was doing nothing more than her duty, while you were doing your damnedest to make her unhappy. Blind to the fact that she was performing. Unable—perhaps even unwilling—to see the truth."

"Anderson told me to! I had permission! Besides, she had to learn anyway, right? It's like you said, she has to learn to do it for the service of it." Michael could barely get the words out. A vague feeling of guilt began to form, mingled with his growing anger and the bizarre sense of betrayal; the woman said she had a good time! How dare she say—how could she tell them?

"Oh, Michael, grow the hell up! If you had taken the time to question her about anything but what kind of sex she was going to be having, you would have found out that her owner was going to be the only man to use her sexually. You might have found out that she did not intend to continue in the Marketplace beyond this position, after which she had plans to retire and find an appropriate lover and settle down. With even a few minutes of serious thought, you might have surmised," Chris continued, now ticking items off on his fingers, "that since this was her final service, it would be appropriate for you to give her what she deserved—an honorable rest from pleasing rutting men who don't know the difference between a real orgasm and a faked one."

"I wasn't in charge of her," Michael sputtered. He got up, tired of being lectured to, tired of that accusing finger. "She could have told me any of this stuff—"

"She was ordered not to volunteer it, in order to give you plenty of chances to find out for yourself, through the proper interview process. But naturally, you didn't bother to ask. Simple questions, Michael! Not 'what kind of sex do you have?' but 'what kind of sex do you prefer?' Or, how about asking something devastatingly obvious, such as 'what are your plans for the future?' But every chance you had, you were either clutching at her body, asking her lewd questions, or plotting about the next time you would have the chance to do either. You're not a trainer, Mike, you're a user. An opportunist looking for the easy life and the easy lay."

"That's not true! You're—going back on what you already said! She was a slave—she had to do what she was told! And if you told her to lie—what do you mean I had to ask? I asked her plenty of stuff! And how am I supposed to both get her used to being used and be nice to her at the same time anyway, huh? This is just some sort of set-up!"

"Yes, it is," Chris said. "You were set up with perfect opportunities to actually do the task you were set to do—and you wasted them all by thinking with your dick instead of what's between your ears. If there is something worthwhile up there." He put the pen he'd been using back into the cup, and worked his way around the desk, seemingly ignoring Michael.

"Fuck you!" Michael said, the profanity exploding out of him. "You're doing this on purpose, you little bastard! What about you, huh? You don't ever screw a slave, right? Keep that little prick in your pants, don't you? At least I get a chance to find out if they're good—you just prattle on and on and on until they get sick of you!" Michael's voice was much louder than he intended it to be, but he couldn't even think any more. Goddammit, it was too much to take! "Well, I'm sick of you, you scrawny fuck, and your whole service bullshit. You don't like kinky sex, fine! But don't condemn what everyone else does just because you can't get it up!"

Chris took two deep breaths, letting them out slowly. He shook his head in mocking sympathy. "You can find records of that particular situation in the same files, Mikey," he said, his eyes dancing with pleasure. "I advise you to read them, they'll be most educational. But for now, why don't you just calm yourself down; keep in mind that you can get over these doubts and inadequacies with training and patience."

He headed for the door, casually dismissing him. Michael trembled with captive rage, and then the barrier broke. It was like feeling waves crash through a wall of sandbags, sweeping everything else out of the way. He snarled, "You fucking asshole!" and took a swing.

His fist connected against the side of Chris's head, cracking the frame of his glasses and smacking into the corner of his eye. Chris reeled back suddenly, his head snapping away, and his glasses flew off, one lens popping out to roll away. A blood spot turned into a trickle, and Michael moved in closer to connect with his left fist. But his aim was off—in school brawls he had never fought with an opponent a head shorter than he was. Instead of hitting low and on the side, he smacked into Chris's upper arm. It was a righteous shot, though—he could feel the impact shoot up his arm and into his shoulder. It should have pushed Chris back, made him reach for the wounded part in agony.

Chris grinned, his dark eyes clearer than ever without the shielding of the glasses. Michael cursed that taunting grin and swung again, right to the jaw.

But Chris wasn't there any more. His fist sailed through empty space, and he felt an awful explosion on his left side that forced the air out of his lungs. The little bastard had caught him with a lucky one to the ribs. But it didn't have that much strength behind it! Michael turned to follow his opponent and threw out another punch, and lost his new breath when Chris snapped a jab into his right side.

There was something wrong. Michael moved in, crowding Chris with his taller frame. He elbowed to one side, trying to duplicate that first shot, and then he felt what seemed like a land mine imploding on his left upper arm. It was a sickening pain, and as he desperately tried to pummel the shorter man with his right arm, he realized that his left one wasn't going anywhere. He connected again, his closed and aching fist smashing against Chris's upper arm again, and was astounded to hear the senior trainer laugh out loud. He reeled back, putting his arms up in defense, and Chris shook his head, wiping the blood trail away from his eye.

"You idiot," he said genially, dropping his hands.

"You asshole!" Michael screamed. He released his right arm in a wild swing, and felt it neatly blocked, and once again, Chris was not where he should have been. Crowding in, he tried for a lower punch, a quick rabbit to the midsection, and the forward motion of the punch almost threw him right by where Chris had been standing. Chris was not only moving out of the way, he was almost dancing, bouncing on the balls of his feet, and still that damn smile was frozen on his face. Michael saw the blur of movement away from his fist again, and for one second something was triggered in his mind. But his anger was too hot, too overwhelming. He gave up trying to punch the smaller man, who infuriatingly wouldn't hold still. Instead, he shifted back to give himself aiming room, and then lunged, ready to drop Chris with the classic schoolyard *coup de grace*, a knee to the groin. But he never made it.

The fluorescent lights of the office seemed like the blazing sun beating down on one of those ragged guys in a cartoon, the ones always shown crawling around in the desert looking for water. Michael heard the steady ringing of a clock he distantly knew wasn't there. There was also someone talking to him, but he couldn't make out the words over the constant buzzing sounds. He tried to smile, tell them everything would be fine, and then he realized that he was going to be very sick.

Someone came closer to him as he gagged, and lifted his shoulders. He turned his head politely away and lost the contents of his stomach very carefully onto the carpet, and then finished his smile. His head was pounding, in about four or five places. He looked up and saw Lorens, looking very concerned.

"You're cute," Michael said.

"He is Opey," Lorens seemed to be saying. Michael nodded, and felt a new site of pain, and closed his eyes.

"Oh, shit," Michael said, stretching out parts of his body. He was in his bed, and although he wished he had been unconscious when they brought him here, he remembered every step of the journey. No one had ever explained just how much it hurt to be hit repeatedly on the head! I mean, he thought bitterly, you watch boxing, and they take it all the time. In the movies, the guys take turns swinging at each other's jaws until one of them trips over something or falls out a window.

They never get hit in the jaw in a viciously planned knockout, fall backward and hit their heads against a table and a chair on the way down. No, check that. Sometimes they do, but then they get up and kick the other guy's butt.

"That's what you get for throwing a punch at a boxer," Anderson said, as she industriously bandaged his forehead.

"A boxer?" Michael felt sick again, but there was nothing left to bring up. "Oh, man."

"Well, not a professional one, of course. Too old; started training too late. But he's not bad. On some days, he's a regular killer. There, that'll do it. You wanna go to the hospital now? You were dead set against it before. Do you remember?"

"Yeah," he said. "I think I'm—okay."

"Then just stay awake for the next twelve hours. We'll keep an eye on you for the next two days; I've had minor concussions myself a few times." She beckoned to Joan, who came forward with a glass of water and a straw.

"Concussions? I have a concussion?" Michael repeated, panicking. His head pounded, and he pushed the drink away.

"Well, of course, kiddo! What do you think boxers do? They hit each other over the head until one of 'em gets a concussion and passes out. Very civilized sport, huh?" She smiled and patted his shoulder. "We'll have the serious chat after I'm sure you won't take a left turn into coma-land. Sure you don't want those X-rays?"

"Maybe I'd better," Michael said weakly.

"Good boy. Let's get to work on Parker's guilt trip right away." She stood up and left the room, and Michael carefully sipped the water. And cursed his stupidity until he ran out of creative words.

CHAPTER TWENTY-THREE

Michael looked into the mirror in horror. There were bruises on his sides, right up against the curve of his rib cage. There was a really ugly one on his left upper arm—now turning a nauseating shade of greenish yellow. But his face! His lips were split—a doctor put in a stitch below his lower lip, just as a precaution. He had taken a lot of damage because, unlike a professional boxer, Michael hadn't been wearing a mouth guard. His own teeth tore up the inside of his mouth, and one of them was loosened.

There were also three stitches where his head had bounced off the side of the table. There were two huge lumps on the back of his head, and another smaller one below his mouth. He looked exactly like someone had held him for someone else to take shots at. He sighed and stretched. It would all heal, he had been reassured. There was no permanent damage; most of it was bruising. His concussion was very minor—his reactions were up to speed within six hours of the incident.

He could only smile at the memory of the emergency room nurse who carefully asked him if his lover had done this.

"He's not even my friend," he had mumbled. "Besides, you should see him!"

She had given him a long suffering glance and gone away. But indeed, she should have seen Parker. Not a damn mark on him. Well, except for that little cut next to his eye, which was probably caused by the edge of the broken metal frames. He didn't even have a black eye, for crying out loud!

Twice, twice Michael had felt the density of those biceps on Chris, but never had he suspected that they were anything, well, dangerous. There were a lot of musclemen in the gay community, for example, but that didn't mean shit when it came to fighting.

Chris probably could have taken shots to his arms all night long before he started to feel inconvenienced.

He pulled a robe over his marked body and sat down in the
chair by his window. It had been two days; the concussion watch
was officially over. It was time to hear the verdict, figure out what
to pack, and where to go. When the knock sounded, he forced
himself to look relaxed before calling out, "Come on in!"

It wasn't Anderson.

Chris walked in and closed the door behind him. Michael tried
to set his jaw, but the effort made his mouth hurt. He watched as
the other man walked past the bed to stop about six feet in front
of Michael's chair. He was dressed today in a full suit, dark gray and
single breasted. His tie was muted colors, dark and touched with
an appropriate burgundy color that reminded Michael of old
blood. The new glasses were shiny—the frames hadn't acquired
the patina of the old ones yet. He wasn't even wearing a Band-Aid
on his cut—apparently it had healed enough.

"I would like to offer my apology to you, Michael," he said. It
sounded a little stiff, but at the same time, sincere. "It was wrong
of me to take advantage of you like that. You had no way of knowing I was trained to fight, and I could have defused the situation instead of inflaming it. I am prepared to make amends in any way
appropriate, and I assure you that this will never happen again."

Michael nodded, amazed at how completely sane it all sounded.
How—right—it sounded. He blushed and lowered his head.
"Yeah, it's okay. Um—I accept. You know, I was going to hit you
the first night I came here," he remembered. "Jesus, we could have
gotten this done way back then!"

"I don't think so," Chris said. "I never would have hit you that
night. However, I would have certainly held a grudge had you
managed to hit me."

"Oh man, I should have been paying attention. You blocked me
that night so easily—if I'd just thought about it, I would have
known you were a fighter!" Michael shook his head. "I think
sometimes that everything started to go wrong that night and it's
just never let up."

"Perhaps. Thank you for accepting my apology—I will be at your service should you think of some way I can atone for my bad judgment." He executed that neat little bow that Michael almost had nailed (or so it looked in the mirror), and turned to leave.

"Wait—there is something," Michael said.

Chris wheeled back. "Yes?"

"Teach me." Michael blushed again, and felt a renewed pounding in his head. "Really teach me. Make me understand this stuff—I'm not getting something, and I don't know what I'm doing wrong!" He was close to tears, and ground his teeth, substituting physical pain for the much more threatening emotional one. "I can't screw this up any more! But you know what's wrong—you can make me understand, I know it!"

Chris folded his arms and nodded. "Of course," he said, "this depends upon what Anderson chooses to do. If she releases you and sends you away, I will have to wait until I finish my project here in order to find you and do this. It might be a time-consuming occupation. Are you sure this is what you want? I assure you—it will not make you like me any better."

"I don't care," Michael said stubbornly. "Maybe not liking you was a part of it. Always having you here meant that I couldn't get everything I wanted. Hell, it was like having an older brother on the football team, you know? You got all the attention, and I was just a fu—screw-up. I don't know. But if I leave this, I have nothing. I'll be a bum, hanging out at my uncle's—if he'll still have me—and hoping that I win the lottery."

"You always had more options than that," Anderson said, pushing the door open. Michael rose even before she crossed the threshold. She waved one hand, and he collapsed back. "You could have applied to any auction house, any other school, any large slave holding family—you could have gone to Europe, or to Asia, or any corner of the world. You could have stayed with New Age Negel, and become the Swami of Slavery in about ten or twenty years, or even started your own breakaway training program. But you're impatient, Mike. You want everything now, or at least within the year. You want the best, but you have no idea what it costs to acquire it. And you feel personally slighted when you don't get it."

Michael nodded bitterly.

"And now—what? You want to stay, don't you?"

"Yes, ma'am, I do."

Anderson looked at Chris who shrugged. She looked back at Michael and pursed her lips. "This is officially your last chance, buckaroo. You listen up, because if you 'fuck-up' this one, I'm skipping your butt across every body of water between here and the Pacific, with three bounces on the Mississippi."

Michael cringed a little at the obscenity, but nodded again. "I understand, Trainer."

"Well, I sure hope you do." She turned on Parker and jabbed a finger at his chest. "He's all yours, Muhammed Ali. Start him the way I start my classics, and ride him hard. I want to see how you work, and I want daily reports. I'll finish with Lorens in another two weeks, and Joan will be here for another two or three months. Before Joan is ready to leave, I want Mike to be where he should have been when he first got here. Got that?"

Two voices answered, "Yes, Trainer."

When she left, Chris turned to Michael and shrugged. "That settles it, then. I will see you at five o'clock Friday morning in suitable jogging clothes. You'll also start dressing more formally—you sometimes make the attempt, but often miss."

Michael was about to say that Joan didn't always coordinate his clothing the way he preferred, but he kept his mouth shut and nodded.

"I'll rearrange your schedule today, and we'll begin officially on Friday morning. And Mike—you will learn how to do everything we've been teaching the clients. I hope you are prepared to act— as you've put it—like a slave. Because in my school—those who teach must be able to do."

"You got it, boss."

"You've got it, Chris," Chris corrected. "I will see you on Friday. If you feel you cannot run because of your physical condition, I suggest you bring a doctor's note."

Michael stared at the closed door after Chris left and realized that the pounding in his head had subsided a little. But that did nothing to relieve the butterflies doing sorties through his stomach. What had he thought after his first big gaffe here? That it was imperative that he not screw up any more? And how many times had he made that promise to himself since coming here? Twice more? Four times? A dozen?

He stood up and went back to the mirror. Carefully, he inclined his shoulders, bowing his head a fraction, cocking it to one side. It looked right but his back was too rounded. Again—should he briefly close his eyes? Yes, it added a touch of humility. Again, this time with the robe off, so he could see the angle of his shoulders better. Again...

No promises this time.

Anderson pushed the back door open, allowing the light from the kitchen to spill out over the steps and the rich scent of the budding garden to come wafting toward her in exchange. It was mingled with a more acrid scent, and she sneezed.

"*Gesundheit*, Trainer," Chris said. She looked down—he was seated on the top step, his legs kicked out in front of him. Smoke trailed out of his mouth as he spoke. He was in his jeans, thank goodness—the back steps had to be damp and a little grimy. She made a mental note to have Lorens clean them tomorrow. If he was going to insist on sneaking a smoke, there was no reason to get dirty doing so.

"I wondered where you were," she said, stepping outside.

He took a drag on the cigarette and politely expelled the smoke away from her. "And here I am," he said. "You know, Trainer— eavesdropping is not generally regarded as the height of good manners."

She chuckled. "Are you lecturing me?"

"Oh, no, of course not."

"The Trainer hears everything, my dear—as you well know. So do the slaves. The only one who deals in ignorance is the master.

My, that's an old one." She looked down, and then sighed. Tucking her skirt under her, she took a seat beside him.

"He had already put me in a difficult position—now, you've committed me. And I wonder who put that idea into his head to begin with?" More smoke shot out, followed by a short, harsh cough.

"Not I," Anderson insisted. "And that's the truth, Parker. You know he's been dancing around the solution for weeks now. All he needed was a push."

"Or a concussion."

"You seem to be prone to handing those out this year. Is the strap out of order?"

"Not a lecture from you too, please. Dr. Quigley has already scolded me quite harshly. I have promised to go to the gym more often and consider adjusting my meds again." He flicked some ash off his knee. "Yes, the strap still works—but I think my own warranty may be running out."

"Since you've already gotten the lecture, perhaps I should do something more... direct."

He blinked slowly, and then one eyebrow raised in a come-hither look that Anderson couldn't help but laugh at. Chris snorted in amusement himself and sighed.

"This further limits your options, you know."

"Of course I know." He ground out the cigarette and pulled another from the pack. He used a kitchen match to light it, and flipped the match into the garden still lit. They followed the descent, and the sputtering death of the light.

"I detest that habit," Anderson said.

"Tell me to stop!"

They stared at each other as he took another drag. The end of the cigarette glowed, and he turned his head away, breaking the intensity of their contact to add more white smoke to the air.

"Give it to me."

He immediately plucked it out of his mouth and passed it to her. She examined it for a moment, and turned it around in her fingers. "It's a disgusting thing to do," she said, tapping ashes off.

"Unhealthy. And it's inconsiderate to do it in front of non-smokers. Give me your hand."

Chris extended his right hand, his arm crossing in front of his body. Deliberately, he turned it palm up.

Anderson raised the cigarette to her own lips and drew smoke into her mouth. The tip glowed, and she let the smoke billow out, as she tapped ashes away one more time. She turned the glow downward, and aimed it at the center of Chris's palm. He remained still, his eyes on hers, and there was only the slightest stiffening of his body as the heat from the tip came closer to his skin.

Anderson lifted the cigarette away and ground it out on the step. "You didn't make your obeisance," she said softly.

"No, I suppose I didn't." Chris brought his hand away slowly, curling his fingers into his palm. "Was that a decision?"

"There is no drive more compelling than the drive to serve, my friend. My dear friend. If you are everything you've struggled for, there was never any decision to make." She stood up, stretched, and brushed her skirt off. "I'll see you in the morning."

"Good night," he said as she walked back in the house. He stayed where he was, gazing out onto the garden, for a long time. The night grew a little more chilly, but he didn't move; somewhere in the matted grass, a match lay, a twist of burnt ash.

He lit another one, and pulled a cigarette out of the pack. The tip glowed amber and copper, and smoke billowed up again. The second match joined the first, and he pushed his back up against the house, drawing his knees up to his body. He stayed there until the pack was finished.

Chapter Twenty-Four

It took another week to get the nuances of that one acknowledg-ment bow down exactly. Michael worked alongside Joan now, and she acted as a teacher more often than not. It was humiliating at first. Michael burned with fantasies about what she thought of him now—the cocky trainer apprentice now reduced to following her around and doing the very same exercises she did, only clumsily. And while Chris wasn't quite as snippy as he had been before, there was a strong, underlying feeling to it all, as though this was what should have been.

It wasn't exactly starting from the beginning. Knowing the feel of the house came in handy, and so did knowing what tasks were routinely assigned to the clients and which ones Chris and Vicente took care of. And oddly, after all the reading and note-taking he had done, only now did some of it begin to sink in. How training and skill led to confidence, which led to pride, for example. It was all very good on paper. But it was also contradictory—slaves weren't supposed to show pride, except in the smallest of ways, and too much confidence was often interpreted as arrogance. How was a client supposed to strike a proper balance? It was impossi-ble to describe before, and didn't get much easier as he learned. But each time he repeated a task or movement, or figured out the correct way to say something, another gram of understanding seemed to click into place.

It didn't always happen like that. Far from it. And there were parts of Chris's methods which were still maddening, especially his insistence on full formality when they were at "work." There were times when it all seemed silly, exercises in role-playing for someone long used to acting. And there were times when he was alone with the mirror, mouthing words and making moves, and wondering how someone could behave like this all the time. What could he say to someone to inspire them to this level of service?

He asked Anderson over dinner.

"I don't know," she said thoughtfully. "I never had to inspire anyone—they all came to me. I always figured that some people just had it in them—not only the potential, but the need. Like a person who grows up always knowing they have to be a soldier. You don't need a war to get them, just an army that takes recruits. And they may never want out—they'll be in uniform until they are forced out, and then they'll hang out with old soldiers until they die. No one goes out and gets those people—they just show up to the recruiting station with their kit bags and never look back. That's what the best slaves do, too. They keep showing up, until someone takes them in."

"But what if it's not that obvious?" Mike asked. "What if it's buried inside? Do you think someone can really not know it's there? And if they don't, do you?"

"Sometimes," she admitted. "Sure, it can be latent, waiting to be popped out. Chris sees it more often than me, I guess. He's got a good record in spotting."

"Really? You've been a spotter?" Mike's eyes widened.

Chris nodded. "I've been everything," he said.

"Then you can tell me!" Mike struggled to keep the insistent sound out of his voice. "I've been wondering since—since Karen—" He paused, swallowed, and continued. "When do you tell them? You see it in them, you draw them out, do the preliminary interviews, and play with them a little—but when do you let them know about the Marketplace?"

"You don't have to let them know," Chris said. "Most of them believed in it long before they met you. And if they didn't believe it existed, they will the minute you tell them."

Mike's face fell. "Then I was really wrong about her."

"She would have made a very nice girlfriend-slave," Anderson said strongly. "Probably a lot of fun. You would have been the envy of all your friends in the Leather Forever world, and I've no doubt you'd pierce her nipples as a wedding gift." She seemed to be making fun, but her voice was gentle. "You spotted the wrong level, that's all. What interested me was that after you, she seems to have made a career out of complaining about the lack of real masters in that community. It will be intriguing to see if she comes to us later on."

"You—you've followed up on her?" Michael exclaimed.

"I'm not as isolated as I look," Anderson said. "And when it affects one of my students, I learn anything I can."

Michael didn't know what to say. He had never looked into what Karen was doing! Should he have? He looked up into Anderson's eyes again and asked, "And do you think she really will come back to us one day? Actually get into the Marketplace?"

"No," Anderson and Chris said at the same time. They both smiled, and Anderson coughed politely. "No, I think she's also proven that she can't be trusted. If she had made a stronger effort to find you before airing her complaints in public, perhaps. But no decent trainer would take her on, knowing that she tried to air our doings in public."

"Perhaps an indecent one will," Chris noted.

Michael, for once, kept his mouth shut.

The change in training style also meant a new dry period sexually. Lorens was declared off limits again, and Michael found himself dreaming of pumping his cock between those powerful thighs, grasping the man's heavy dick and twisting it in order to hear the cries of pain and feel the tensing of the anal muscles. He also dreamed of Karen, her sweet mouth working in his crotch while her hands were tied behind her back and a vibrator buzzed away between her legs. The surprise came when he dreamed of being on the bottom.

He dreamed of that dominatrix from ages ago, whipping his back and running her long fingernails down his flanks. Only this time, they continued around to his balls, and the pinching tightness as they drew his nuts up and together made him moan out loud even as something sharp started to slide between his own asscheeks—

And then he woke up. Sweating under the blanket, his cock

erect and his heart beating so hard he thought he was having an attack of some kind. He kicked the covers off and lay there naked, allowing the sweat to evaporate off his body as he stroked his cock, back and forth, pulling at the skin. It was hard to concentrate on his usual images, so he went back to the dream, to the woman in leather, the scratch of her nails, the probing of his ass, the cool rush of air against his exposed anus, and then the touch, the pressure...

He shot his orgasm up almost without thinking, and groaned. Warmth splattered his hand and belly, and then turned rapidly cool. He shivered and pulled the blanket on top of him again, not caring about the damp spots he was going to leave. He was more concerned with that dream, and the force of his pleasure. He fell asleep again, the scent of his semen surrounding him, and didn't remember any more dreams when he woke up.

※

"Chris, what's a classic?" Michael asked.

"A classic what?"

They were taking a breather by the park Chris ran through every morning. Michael had a much longer stride and covered ground quicker, but he lacked the stamina that the smaller man had. He needed to rest more often.

"Anderson said that you should start me like a classic. What does that mean?"

"Ah." Chris patted sweat off his forehead. "That's old guard. Classic training, as in the way she was taught, the way I was. The way no one is taught any more."

"Really? Why not?"

"Because it's too time-consuming. Too demanding. It lacks the all-important element of immediate gratification." He stretched a little. "But don't worry—you won't be expected to undergo the whole training process."

"Why not?"

"Because you wouldn't accept it."

Michael frowned. "How do you know that? I've been accepting so far, haven't I?"

"Yes—but can you do it for seven years?" Chris turned and started up again, and Michael fell into stride beside him. There was no talking while running, so Michael didn't get the answers to his burning questions until after breakfast.

"One year introductory training," Chris ticked off his fingers, "two years in service, two years managing other slaves while remaining in service, one year in formal apprenticeship to a master trainer, and one year as a journeyman trainer."

"Jesus Christ! Four years as a slave, just to be a trainer?"

"Five years, depending on the temperament of the master trainer. Anderson's master trainer was that kind of a man—his apprenticeships varied very little from a slave contract." Chris nodded admiringly. "Some trainers used to include a two-year experience of owning a slave as well. You can see why hardly anyone does it any more."

"Is that what you did?"

"Yes, and no. I have never managed to do things properly. But I have done everything, in one way or another. Just—in the wrong order." Chris looked a little uncomfortable admitting this, but he seemed direct and truthful, and Mike was more than a little bit flattered by it.

"When were you a slave?" he asked, pushing a little.

"After I was an owner," Chris said with a grin. "Ages ago, eons. And don't bother to ask where I was sold—the Marketplace does accept non-traditional service arrangements as part of their experience records, and I was in one."

"Oh." Damn, another dead end. No wonder he wasn't in the computer. "How come she didn't start me as a classic when I got here?"

"Because you didn't show that you had any potential. Not that you have much now, mind you. But re-starting you like a classic means that you have the opportunity to take a better look at what you're doing. It gives you more time to figure out where to go— it gives her more time to measure your dedication."

"I am dedicated!" Michael protested.

"You might be," Chris admitted. "Let's see how much. You're far too relaxed in posture and attitude. Get up and present."

Chris didn't hit him—but every time Michael got into a vulnerable position and braced himself, he could imagine the sensation of each blow. He could feel Chris's eyes sweeping his form. That day, as he carefully arranged his body and thrust out his ass in that humiliating posture designed to give an owner or trainer a proper target to chastise, he could swear that he felt a hand caress him. It sent shivers through his body, especially since he could see Chris clearly out of the corner of his eye, too far away to touch him.

The weather was warm the night Michael decided to take advantage of his time off and finally go to the local men's leather group. He had stayed away from the local ISMAO Chapter, mostly because of the scary idea that somehow Karen had spread the word about him through that organization. The Equivocal Coalition had provided an evening or two of mild amusement, but when he caught some attitude from the threatened male "doms," he decided it wasn't worth the hassle. New York did have a few SM clubs, like dance clubs, and he investigated them as well. But he found them universally uncomfortable, either too large or too small, hot and smoky or cold and noisy. He preferred to go dancing instead, wearing his leather jeans and making out in the darkened corners with boys or girls as the mood struck him.

But he missed the companionship of a room full of people who understood the lure of leathersex, the passion of power. Dealing with the new and complex realities at the Anderson house had not dampened his excitement at all—in fact, it seemed to have heightened it. The dreams and waking fantasies were symptoms, he had decided, of a need to go out and have some fun. This time, he would know when to stop. This time, he was in control. He had picked up a calendar of events at the local Gay Communal

Association, and found a listing for the Gay Men's Leather Association. They had weeknight seminars and discussion groups, plus an
occasional play event at one of the public clubs. It seemed worth
checking out. At the very least, he could get some information
about where the best pick-up places were.

He dressed carefully, knowing how important image was in a
group of men. The leather jeans and boots, of course. A chain
wrapped around the left boot provided an eye-catcher and a possible collar for some temporary companion. Black shirt, leather
vest with run pins, and a black hanky tucked into his left rear
pocket. He hung his keys left also, after he worked the wide belt
through the loops in the pants. He threw his cover into a bag along
with some rope, a few condoms, and some lube. No sense wearing the thing on the subway. New Yorkers didn't look twice at
someone dressed in black. But the cap with the chrome brim was
a bit much for Brooklyn. He'd put it on when he got downtown.

He had already told Anderson and Chris that he was off to the
city that night. Anderson didn't need him—she was doing a private session with Joan. Chris was upstairs doing something by
himself while Lorens and Vic were laughing in the kitchen. The
sense of freedom that swept him as he walked to the subway was
overwhelming. Maybe I have been working a little too hard, he
thought. Well, not too hard, but more intensely than I'm used to.
That's where all these bottoming dreams are coming in; I'm feeling like I'm being stepped on. I need a little vacation.

The evening at the men's organization was pretty typical. There
were about forty men there, some in full leather dress, most in
jeans or work clothes. Michael was heavily cruised, and he returned
the compliments, eyeing possible candidates left and right and
swapping meaningful glances and firm handshakes accompanied
by lingering gazes at crotch level. God, it was fun to play with the
boys. Much easier than courting women, that was for sure.

The topic was something about playing with fire, and a demonstration involved swiping someone with alcohol, setting the alcohol on fire and manipulating flames on their skin. It was
fun—Michael had done it a few times in the past. Very impressive,

especially for people who didn't realize that the speed in which the flames are moved and smothered prevented anything more than first degree burns, and then only after repeated dousings. Michael had never heard of any Marketplace owner doing that with their slaves. Maybe it was considered too esoteric. He decided to ask Anderson if she had. Maybe she would let him try it on Lorens. That would be a sight.

After the demonstration and the obligatory question and answer period, Michael stayed a while and flirted and introduced himself as a visitor from California. He could sense a little attitude coming from the older men; he wrote it off as jealousy. He knew he looked sharp and the admiring glances of the other men confirmed his knowledge. He also knew that older tops tended to resent the younger ones. It was that old guard stuff again. And he also knew that strangers were always threatening—you never knew where they came from, how they played, whether they were going to take you home and commit atrocities on your corpse, becoming the headline in the next day's tabloid. Or at least get you so drunk that you get tattooed with a bull's head surrounded by a wreath of roses.

As the evening drew to a close, Michael shuffled through the come-ons and offers to find the genuine ones. He was left with two possibilities—going home with one guy about his age, who looked like he would be a good lay, or heading off to a bar with a couple who looked much more than merely interesting. He'd never been with two guys before. That might be fun. And Dave, the topman in the couple, seemed like a hot guy himself—maybe they could both do the bottom, whose name also happened to be Mike, and then kinda get into each other.

The bar they took him to was called The Shaft, and it was buried in the recesses of the meat-packing district, not far from one of the clubs Michael had investigated earlier. There was no cover charge, and the music was techno/dance, and beers were cold and served up by bare-chested men in leather shorts. The place was not quite as crowded as it would be on Saturday night, but it was a hell of a serious crowd for a weeknight. Michael bought the first round and hoped they wouldn't stay too long. Not only was he going to run out of money soon, but he was seriously horny.

They showed him around, taking him on a quick tour of the bar, introducing him to a few of the regulars, and then settling at one back wall with their beers. Mike the bottom knelt next to Dave, and drank from Dave's bottle. Michael enjoyed it, flirting with Dave while his slave was alone on the hard floor, seemingly ignored. It was part of the game—part of the fun. Michael imagined their interaction later in. Would he get to fuck Mike's mouth, or ass, or both? Would the two tops take him at the same time, fucking both ends at once, forcing sounds of lust and pain from him?

"Hey, look over there—that's the guy who brought us out," Dave said suddenly. "That's Ron."

Michael turned to see a tall, well built man in jeans, chaps, a black T-shirt and vest. There was an understated simplicity about him—no chest harness, no chains, no gauntlets or whips—even his cover was plain, lacking the chrome brim that Michael's sported. He looked to be in his forties or so, although it was kind of hard to tell. His hair was black—he looked every inch an old-time leatherman.

Their eyes followed him as he walked through the crowd and threw his arms around a shorter man standing by the pool table. Michael felt a little weak in the knees for a moment. It couldn't be! But another look and a shift in position gave him a better view. The shorter man, the one with the cute butt framed by his own pair of chaps, was Chris Parker.

Dave was asking him a question. It was drowned out by the thumping of the music or the pounding of his heart.

"Are you all right?" Dave asked again.

"Uh—yeah. It's just—I know Ron's boyfriend!"

"Well, what do you know? I tell you, the community gets smaller every year. Why don't you go over and say hello? I'll send my boy to get us more drinks."

"Uh—" Michael caught himself quickly. Should he have

admitted to recognizing Chris? Damn, that wasn't proper! But Dave caught his hesitation and laid a hand on his shoulder.

"Listen—you go over if you want. The boy's going for drinks. If you want to socialize, we can come over after you say hello. Okay?"

Michael blessed the man for his tact and thanked him verbally. And then he started to make his way through the crowd. His curiosity was too much to bear—what on earth was Chris doing with a soft world topman? And just look at how Chris was dressed! Michael took in the chaps and jeans, T-shirt and vest, and realized that Ron and Chris were dressed pretty much identically. He also realized that this was the first time he had ever seen Chris in short sleeves, let alone in leather. It was a strange mixture of emotions and thoughts brewing inside of him as he approached them. It was definitely amusing to have caught Chris slumming.

Chris caught sight of him as soon as he was in view and damn near did a double take. Then, he laughed, one hand crossing his abdomen, and said something to Ron, who glanced over his shoulder. It must be okay to approach then, Michael thought. He came forward and half waved. "Hey, boss," he said.

"That is Michael," Chris was saying.

Ron had been smiling as he turned, but as soon as he saw Michael, his eyes narrowed. Michael was about to extend his hand for a shake and an introduction, when he saw a blur of darkness cross in front of his face. Not again, he thought, ready to retreat. But the hand never hit him. He felt his cap take the impact, and heard it hit the floor a few paces away. Conversation dipped a little in their vicinity, and a few men raised questioning eyes over long necked bottles.

Michael looked into the eyes of the man he had never met before and asked, hotly, "Why the hell did you do that?"

"Bad enough you come out in unearned leather, boy," Ron growled. "But you don't wear a cover in front of your teacher!"

Two men standing off to the side made "ooo" sounds and turned away with soft laughs. Most of the younger men ignored the scene entirely.

Michael tensed, and started to prepare a retort, but stopped himself and took a deep breath. He glanced at Chris, who had leaned one hip against an old fifty-five gallon drum, and was eyeing him with interest. Michael looked back at Ron and nodded. "I didn't know," he said. "I'm sorry. Uh—do you mind if I go get it?"

"No, it's okay. But don't put it on in here until you earn it." Ron turned back to Chris and Michael fought off the growing blush that crept up his collar as he chased after the hat. He bent down to pick it up, and someone said, "Better tuck those keys too, boy!" He looked around to see who had spoke, and a gray-bearded man in an ancient motorcycle jacket met his eyes. Michael picked up the cap and unhooked the keys from his belt loop. He shoved them in his pocket and rammed the hanky further down into the back pocket as well. He got a nod of approval and returned to Ron and Chris. He was shaking.

What the fuck am I doing, he asked himself, trying to control the trembling. I am not a bottom! But he stopped at the correct distance away from the pair and waited for Chris to acknowledge him before he stepped closer. For a moment, he thought he was seeing things—what were those lines on Chris's arms? He focused his gaze and realized that Chris had tattoos—damn, tattoos, on his forearms! They looked like swirls of some kind—snakes maybe, or vines. What do you know—under that corporate exterior, the guy had tats. He wished suddenly that he had decided to wear a T-shirt, too. It was goddamn hot in the bar—so hot that he was already dripping with sweat.

"Now I'll introduce you," Chris said. "Michael, this is Ron. Ron, meet my student, Michael."

This time, Ron did stick out his hand. "Sorry to be so hard on you, kid," he said, shaking Michael's hand firmly. "Chris here's told me you haven't been brought up on formal manners. That's part his fault, but then he hardly knew you were coming out here, did he?"

Michael shook his head. "I didn't even think of telling you where I was going—and I got dressed and left without seeing anyone." He snuck a peek at the tattoos, and figured them to be flames.

Nice work, too. He looked back up to avoid being distracted.

Chris shrugged. "It was only a matter of time before I brought you here. But I would have instructed you on what to wear, first."

"I just came from a meeting. Um—Gay Men's Leather Association." Where they discussed flames. Michael wondered if it would be appropriate to bring that up.

"Ah. Well, you're here now. Were you planning to go home with the two who keep glancing over?"

Michael looked over at Dave, and Ron looked with him and laughed. "Well, what do you know?" the older man asked. "They're old buddies of mine. Trained them both. You remember, I told you about them."

Chris nodded. "Yes—you thought the bottom had potential."

"Still does. But they're in love—why ruin a perfectly good relationship?"

Michael looked at the two of them, and then at Chris. He didn't dare to ask the question out loud. Chris laughed and nodded. "Yes, he's in," he said, punching Ron on the arm. "Or rather, he knows that we are."

"Hey, watch it, squirt, I'll have to hurt you!" Ron threw a feint and Chris weaved and caught Ron's fist. It looked playful, yet Michael still had a fading bruise on his upper arm. He winced and swallowed hard.

"Anyway—" Ron said, backing off and leaving Chris alone, "those two are all right. Kinda twink, but not bad. Very eager. You could go home with worse. Or much better." Ron took one long gaze over Michael's body and nodded. "Yeah, I think you could do better."

Michael had never been so frankly appraised in his life. The earlier cruising at the meeting or even in the bar had all been sport, in fun. But Ron swept him up and down like he was a piece of meat—or a piece of merchandise, period. Like a client. He wished that he could just break away and go back to Dave and his slave boyfriend and have another beer and maybe go to their place and get his cock sucked. But it would be rude to initiate his exit. He had to be dismissed. He looked at Chris, and knew instantly that

Chris wasn't going to let him go. He felt disappointed, ashamed, confused—

And he felt an erection.

Oh shit, he thought. "Please," he said. The word caught in his throat, and he had to cough to get it out and continue. "I need to take a piss."

Chris gave a brief nod and said, "Bring back two beers." Michael shifted nervously, and Chris smiled as he tucked a bill into one of the pockets on his shirt.

Michael didn't remember where the bathroom was, but he just hugged the wall until he found it. Inside, he fumbled for his zipper and forced piss through the hard-on. Dry ice sizzled and shot white smoke up into the air. Next to him, a man with long blonde hair and a bushy mustache gave his own cock a shake and licked his lips. Michael looked at him—big, beefy, tattooed—nothing like what he usually liked.

"Where?" he croaked.

One of the two stalls had an "Out of Order" sign on it. Of course, the classic. It smelled of piss that men had poured into it anyway—the walls were dank and covered with graffiti. But Michael didn't care. He stepped up onto the rim of the toilet and braced himself against the walls. The blond bear liked that. He grinned and pulled a condom out of his vest pocket, and hurriedly slid it over Michael's dick. Then, he headed for Michael's crotch like a dog for dinner.

Michael almost cried out as the warm suction began. He threw his head back and gasped, and thrust his hips forward. The guy took his whole cock in, an enthusiastic—no, starving—cocksucker, just eating Michael alive from the crown on down.

It didn't take long. Michael's body was tense with holding the precarious position over the toilet. The bushy guy had plenty of room to maneuver, so he used it, pulling his head all the way back and slurping his way all the way down to the base again. There were no fancy moves, only honest sucking and swallowing, and Michael felt the orgasm build like an approaching subway car, rumbling and tearing its way through his body. He shot into the rubber with such force he almost lost his balance, but the guy kept sucking until it was all out, and the cock had begun to shrink again.

"Thanks, man," the stranger said, backing out. "Anytime, for you."

Michael nodded weakly and stripped the condom off. He dropped it into the toilet and zipped up before he got down. Taking a deep breath, he exited and washed his hands. Realizing that his eighty dollar cap was missing, he ran back to the stall—it wasn't there. But it was on the floor in the next stall, and the men in that one obligingly handed it out to him.

It would all be very funny if it wasn't so—intense. Michael wiped the hat off and went to the bar and ordered the two beers.

"Someone's been a bad boy," Ron said when Michael came back. Michael stared at him in horror. "Yeah, you can't hide anything from me in my bar," the leatherman added. "I could see eyes following you all the way back here. Must have been quite a show."

Chris took his beer and sighed. "You keep going out for fast food, Michael. What do I have to do to get you into a four star establishment?"

"Jeez, what does a guy have to do to get a little privacy?" Michael asked, blushing again.

"Don't suck cock in a leather bar!" Ron said.

"Or get it sucked," Chris added. "I don't believe Mike has ever sucked cock."

"That can be remedied," Ron leered.

"I sucked cock," Michael found himself saying. "Back at school. Before SM. I had a buddy, this jock named Charlie. Charlie Campbell." He couldn't stop talking, but the two men were listening to him. "He—he was on the soccer team. Nice body—but we were buddies. One night, we got drunk—and we were watching these videos—"

"Great!" Ron shouted. "And you did him?"

"Yeah." Michael wished he had a drink, and suddenly, there was a cold bottle being pressed into his hand. He looked at Chris and thanked him with a look and took a long drink. "I sucked him

off, and then he did me. And for the rest of our time there, we
kept—doing that. We never really talked about it. Never really
planned it. But the videos would come out, we'd have a few beers,
and then I'd do him. And he'd do me."

"But always you first," Ron said.

Michael nodded.

"And after a while, you really didn't need a few beers," Chris
added.

Michael handed the beer back and didn't answer.

"Fuckin' classic, man," Ron said with a laugh.

"I think I should take Michael home," Chris announced. "I
think that's enough fun for the night. Ron—it's great to see you."

"You too, kid. Say hello to Brian if you ever talk to him. Good
luck with the training, Michael. You'll need it!" Ron raised his beer
in a farewell, and then turned into the crowd and went stalking.
Chris shifted his head in the direction of the door, and Michael
followed wordlessly. They walked over to the main avenue to hail
a cab.

"I'm sorry if I ruined your date," Michael said finally. "I know
I shouldn't have come over."

"No, technically you shouldn't have, but it's all right. And you
certainly didn't ruin a date, Michael. Ron's not my lover." Chris
seemed amused at the possibility.

"Oh."

"He's my brother," Chris said. "My big brother."

"That's the truth," came out before Michael knew what he was
saying. He blushed and felt like he should duck, but amazingly,
Chris threw back his head and laughed out loud.

"Mike, let's get you home before I have to spank you."

And if there was anything left for Michael to say, it vanished
from his mind and he rode home in a pure and amazed stupor. He
never did get to ask about the tattoos.

He slept on his belly and moaned in the early morning hours.
He awoke in the dark, pushing his ass up, his dick as hard as a rail,
his hands clutching the pillow. He gasped and lay shaking under
the covers until the sun rose.

CHAPTER TWENTY-FIVE

The evening at the bar seemed to be a turning point. Oh, it wasn't that Chris became a buddy and lightened up, or even that he was more forthcoming with those little personal details like having a brother nearby who was older and into this SM stuff. But it did seem that Michael felt more and more like a person when Chris talked to him and less like a vaguely stubborn object that needed a kick before it would work properly.

It was also a turning point for how Michael saw Joan. The memory of standing on the side, waiting to be recognized, the sensation of sweat trickling down the back of his shirt, the humiliation of being spoken about to his face—all these things were the most simple and obvious parts of a slave's existence, yet they filled him with such complex emotions! God, how could he have ever really known how it felt?

There were times when he wanted to kick the walls and throw furniture around, partly because goddammit, they had been right, and he was wrong, and he hated being wrong—and partly because of the self pity that sometimes threatened to make him give up.

Years, he thought, skimming through his old notes. I spent years learning the wrong way. And then, I waste months here, holding onto it. It was embarrassing. It was also frustrating.

But every morning, he got up at dawn and ran with Chris, and then applied himself to everything he was told to do, whether it was doing the movement dances with Joan, listening in on the wrap-up interviews with Lorens, or folding laundry and discussing sports with Vicente. In evening sessions, he would ask Chris questions, and take even more notes, and then review them before going to sleep. Most of the time, he barely had energy to masturbate before sleeping—and the wet dreams took over for him when he didn't. It was like being a teenager again.

One morning, he was sitting in the dining room, lingering over breakfast. He heard Chris's footsteps approaching—he had long since learned how to tell the difference between Chris and Anderson—and without thinking, he pushed back his chair and rose.

Chris looked a little surprised. Michael's mind seized up—he wanted to laugh it off, to say that he thought it was the Trainer approaching. But he couldn't say anything. Chris nodded and began to inform him about what the agenda was for the day, and they went to work without mentioning it.

❧

"Did you have someone special when you left England?" Michael rolled over onto his stomach.

"Do you mean a boyfriend? Oh, no, there was never enough time for that." Joan giggled, and her body shook. They were together in the slaves' room. It was at the end of the hallway on the first floor, near the kitchen, and consisted of two single beds with two footlockers, with one shared closet. Michael had been sent there, to sleep, in order to experience the Spartan quality of the experience. But being with Joan made it seem more like summer camp. He did away with her need to be on formal terms with him, and found that to be far more interesting than sleeping in a single bed, which seemed narrow and kind of juvenile.

"Not enough time? Why not? You weren't a slave then."

"No, but there was always quite a bit of work to be done—the family was always occupied. If it wasn't school, it was music lessons, or helping at my aunt's candy shop—and I did a bit of rugby too, when I was younger. Also, I had decided quite early that I wanted very much to do the service."

"Wait—the aunt in the candy shop—that's Edith?"

She was pleased that he remembered. "Yes, that's right. And when I go home, her husband, Henry, will retire from service and

run the shop with her, after they take a tour of the world. Wouldn't
that be wonderful? A tour of the world!"

"You've already had one. Japan, America... I haven't been anywhere." Michael pulled at the ever-stray lock of hair in front of
his eyes.

"Well, with all honesty, I would have rather not gone to Japan.
It's a lovely country with some perfectly lovely people—but it always seemed too crowded. And it was very hard at first—I couldn't
bear the food, and the tea wasn't exactly what we were used to at
home." She smiled nervously and sighed. "I did get used to it,
though."

"What made you get used to it, Joan? Was it that you knew you
might not be acceptable for service without it? Did it make you unhappy?" He sat up and folded his legs under him. "I don't know
if I could do that—go to a foreign country and live with strangers
and learn a whole new way of life, just so I could possibly be useful sometime in the next ten years."

"I'm very sure that His Lordship knows I'll be useful, or else
he wouldn't have sent me," Joan said confidently. "And better
someone in the family get the experience overseas than some hired
stranger, right?"

"But you didn't like it," Michael insisted.

"Well, no," she admitted. "But I knew it would only be for a
year. And if I had failed—oh, that would have been a shame. Mum
and Dad would be very disappointed, I think."

"So—you're doing it for them?"

"No, not exactly. Not any more in the sense that a boy follows
his father into the same university or the same branch of the services. It was something they did—I saw them, and it made them
happy. They were so proud—and the service made them..." She
paused, turning over words in her head, and then shrugged. "I
don't know. Special in some way. Apart from the rest of the world.
Now, I get to be special, too."

"And in ten years? Or eleven, maybe?"

"I'll come out of the service, and His Lordship will give me
enough money to purchase the inn I've had my eye on since I was

a little girl," she sighed. "I always wanted to run a small country inn, to have visitors from all over the world, and be the mistress of my own house. With my experience in service, I'll have the finest inn for miles around. My sister is a cook—when she leaves the service, she'll come and work with me."

"Sounds nice," Michael commented.

"I wouldn't have the chance if I didn't do the service," Joan said. "You see? In just ten years, I can have everything I've always dreamed of. Where else can you have such a thing?"

"Nowhere," he admitted.

That night, Michael had the energy but not the inclination. He lay awake, listening to the rhythmic breathing coming from Joan and the gentle, rumbling snores from Lorens, who had camped out on the floor. It seemed so impossible that people lived this way, ready to be sent away, traded, used, and dismissed. Yet here were two slaves who had found stability in their service—one who was in love, and the other who knew that for the next ten years, her life was going to be secure.

And Tara, gone back to her master, who would use her and enjoy her near-perfection, and then lose her when the contract ran out. Michael wondered if she had decided to leave the service because she could not be guaranteed a woman owner. What was it like, thinking of spending the next four years of your life knowing that any pleasure you got had to come from serving someone, or from jerking off? That your primary lover could never know that you didn't think they were hot? He also wondered if she would ever tell her future lovers about the years she spent in a collar.

What did you do for those years? someone would ask.

"I was a slave," Michael whispered out loud.

❧

"It's here," Anderson announced over breakfast. "Lorens's Prince Albert. We'll put it in tonight."

Lorens, who was fully dressed for a change, beamed in silent pride as he poured coffee and orange juice.

"Great!" Mike said. "I've never seen one put in. Who's gonna do it?"

"I will," Anderson said. "This will be my—twentieth, I think. I'll have to check. For the more esoteric ones, I call in Greta. But this one I like to do. It's a very popular piercing, although I must admit that I'm getting a little annoyed at how damn popular piercing has become. It used to be a solemn ritual symbolizing the deepest kind of commitment. Now, there are people piercing their eyebrows, for heaven's sake." She shook her head. "Sometimes, I think I'm too old. But that's nothing new. We'll put the ring in Lorens's cock, and he will treat the experience with the proper reverence."

"I most certainly shall, Trainer," he said warmly. And he positively glowed when she swatted him across the rear on his way out of the room.

"How do you know what to do, Trainer?" Michael asked. "You said that you treat every client differently, and you do! But how do you know what to do with each one?"

"The interview is the key," Anderson said. She had started answering his questions too, and he had filled another entire notebook. "Not only do I spend more interview time with the client than any other trainer, but before a client arrives here I've logged about twenty hours of interviews with their owner, or their past owners. I know exactly how they've been worked, what's planned for them in the future, and what they hope will happen regardless of what's planned. Remember—the interview is the most vital part of a training regimen. And it is never over."

"Oh, wow," Michael said without thinking. He blushed and flipped open his book. "That one's going with the everything/anything quote."

"Great," Anderson said with a snort. "He's putting together a best-of collection."

"Soundbites from The Trainer?" Chris said softly.

She stared at him, hard, and he stirred his coffee thoughtfully. She turned back to Michael and pointed a long finger at him. "Just you remember, boy, that there's more to this than slogans."

"Yes, Trainer. I understand."

"Good. I'll see you later, for the piercing. Don't bother to take notes on the technique, it will not be on the exam."

Lorens was unbound, as his owner had specified. He was naked except for his collar, fresh out of the shower, glowing with health and smelling of soap. He was bright eyed with anticipation, but oddly dignified as well.

The worktable had been covered with plastic with a paper overlay, and a lamp had been brought in to spotlight his crotch. Anderson laid out the needle, ring, antiseptics, and other tools, all of which came out of sealed wrappers. She was gloved, and Lorens's cock was probably more at attention than it should have been, if it had a brain and knew what was about to be done to it.

Michael felt a shrinking between his legs—no doubt his cock had a brain, and was in full sympathy with the brainless one on the table. But he was fascinated, and kept his eyes on Lorens's face. The man showed no fear at all, only a kind of intense desire. Chris was in attendance, but it was obvious it was Anderson's show. When she picked up the needle, Michael was able to watch the initial positioning, and then turned quickly to Lorens's eyes, because it was just too intense to watch a dick being skewered.

Lorens's lips curled back, and sweat sprang up on his face. The eternal cheerfulness gave way to agony, and Michael barely realized that he had stopped breathing. The powerful man's muscles tensed as he gripped the sides of the table, and a terrible groan came from between his teeth, followed by a quick exhalation and a series of panting breaths. His eyes remained open all the time. Michael felt dizzy, and realized that he needed air in his lungs. When he drew some in, he looked back down between Lorens's legs, and there it was.

A gold ring ran through the pee-hole, and then through his dick. Anderson dropped the curved needle into a can and dabbed at the piercing area with a piece of sterile gauze. "A nice job if I do say so myself," she said, reaching for the antibiotic. "This should heal nicely if you take care of it, Lorens."

Lorens was in tears now—the agony was gone from his face,

replaced by a kind of pain that was multilevel. His dick was going
to be sore for a while, Chris had told Michael earlier. It might even
get infected, as some piercings did. But the man seemed much
more grateful than in pain. He whispered his thanks prettily, and
Anderson patted him on the inner thigh before she snapped the
gloves off.

Michael was amazed to find that once again, he had a hard-on.

⁂

"What were you thinking of, when the needle went in?" Michael
asked. Lorens, his arms under his head, thought about it for a moment. They were whispering in the dark—it was after lights out,
and Joan was already asleep.

"I was thinking of Her," Lorens said, and he said it just like
that, with the capitalization. "That she wanted me to endure this,
to take this—that she will be pleased with me when I return. And
then, I thought that the Trainer had stabbed my penis through the
head!"

Michael smothered a laugh. "Was it really that bad?"

"Perhaps not," Lorens relented. "But I have never felt anything
like that before."

"What would you say if she wanted to put a bigger one in? Or
a different one, somewhere else?"

"I would say to her, 'yes, Mistress,'" Lorens said confidently.
"Pain is momentary. Even this will cease to hurt one day. But I want
to serve her forever. I will endure whatever she asks."

"But—what if one day she gets tired of you—not that she will!
But—what if she did?"

"What is the use of wondering about that, Michael? She may
tire of me, yes—but she has said that she desires me forever. I trust
her with my body—with my life. I trust that she will take care of
me, and I pray that she trusts me to care for her." He smiled, and
his teeth glowed in the moonlight coming through the window.
"I hurt now, Michael, very much. But I will sleep deeply, because
I trust my Lady, and I know everything will be all right."

"So why isn't piercing on the exam?" Michael asked Chris the next day.

"What do you mean?"

"Anderson said that I could watch the piercing, but not to learn the technique. She said it wouldn't be on the exam. But why not? Shouldn't I learn how to pierce?"

They had been reviewing Michael's first training schedule, and Chris had finished his critique and left Michael time to revise. Michael put his pen down and cracked his knuckles as he asked the question.

"It's too early for that," Chris answered. "Piercing is taught at the final stages, along with other marking skills like tattooing and branding—if they are taught at all."

"But isn't it something a trainer should know?"

"Not any more," Chris sighed. "In earlier days, yes—the trainer would be responsible for the marks of slavery. In fact, some trainers would place a certain mark on all their slaves, or a series of marks to show the kind of training they had gone through. I have seen some heirloom piercing jewelry from times when medical doctors were called in to supervise. But these days, you can get a nipple piercing at a mall. Clean, professional shops are all over the country, and experts are available at weekend conferences and for private consultations. Many clients come to us already pierced or otherwise marked. So, very few trainers bother to put the skill on their agenda."

Michael mulled that over. It seemed to make sense, yet...

"That's a shame," he said suddenly. Chris looked up at him and cocked his head expectantly. "I mean, that piercing was special," Michael said. "It wouldn't have been the same for Lorens if some stranger did it. It came from his trainer, you know? That's... romantic?"

Chris nodded, slowly. "It is indeed," he agreed. "Write about it, if you please."

And for the first time, Michael went back to his room to write and didn't feel the slightest twinge of annoyance over the chore. He wrote until his head started to drop, and slept deeply.

🦎

"Okay, Chris, here's the situation—you have a client who just can't be improved beyond a certain point. Maybe they're just naturally clumsy, or not so bright. What do you do with them?"

"That depends on where they are. Are they owned? Novices? Have they been in service before, and what is their record like? Do they have unrealistic goals, or do their owners?" Chris pushed up the sleeves of his sweatshirt, revealing those tattoos again. Michael admired them even more in the daylight—they weren't cartoony at all, but actually kind of stylized and understated. Now that Michael had seen his arms, Chris was casual about occasionally baring them. He had other marks as well—high on his left arm were three V-shaped scars that didn't look like cuts. Michael thought they might be burns, brands. But he never had the courage to ask.

"Um, let me think—figure that they're novices. They're being trained for first sale."

"The first thing to remember is that no one is guaranteed a spot on the auction block," Chris said. He scanned the park for a moment when they heard the sound of approaching feet, and he waited until the other jogger ran by. "If they're not good quality, that's too bad."

"Well, assume that they're good—but they just can't seem to get much better in some areas."

"Then you could try specialization—find out where they are good and focus on that. But you still send the clumsy one to dance school and get a tutor in for the under-educated one, because you never know what their owners are going to want. Some slaves can be sold on one good point alone. If Lorens didn't have a brain in his head, still he'd get a buyer, because he's pretty. People will buy the most astonishingly bad piece of goods because it's pretty." He looked distracted again, and then pointed to a bench. Michael sat down, and Chris sat next to him.

"Let me tell you about my greatest failure," Chris said quite casually. Michael closed his open mouth and nodded, not willing to make a sound and spoil this unique moment.

"A client came to my former house to be trained, entirely on her own initiative. She found out about the Marketplace through eavesdropping, located a spotter who was less than reliable, and got herself a ticket in. She was unsuitable from the beginning—except that she was breathtakingly beautiful."

Michael nodded.

"I trained her, with the others, or at least I tried to. And she did improve, dramatically. Within one month, we had changed her speaking habits, gotten her to control her temper, and tried every trick available to get her to question her presence. Quite amazingly, she persevered. Stayed with the program. Toward the end, she was actually presentable material, although not voice trained. For many reasons, including the fact that the house could use the money, she was presented for sale. Bids were highly competitive, and she fetched a high price. She was deemed a very narrow success."

Michael remained silent while Chris gathered his thoughts.

"She—turned out to be unsuitable," he said, looking down the path. "During the third month of her service, her owner contacted the house and requested that she be removed from service, and that he be refunded her purchase price."

"Shit." That slipped out all by itself. Michael wanted to clamp a hand over his mouth. But Chris nodded solemnly.

"Very deep shit indeed," he said with the slightest trace of mirth. "It had never happened before. Not to me, not to my house. We were using methods I had adapted, a style taken from my training and expanded upon—and my methods had failed. And not only that—methods can be altered, after all—but I personally had failed my house. I should have known that the training would not hold when she realized that her fantasy about service was not about to materialize. I should have dismissed her before she got to the block, or certainly I should have warned my employers. Instead, I remained silent. I—we—the house needed the money. The proliferation of new trainers has hurt the older houses, deeply." Chris sighed.

"But it wasn't just you," Michael ventured. "I've heard of Elliot and Selador—they're not exactly new at this."

"No. But they trusted me, and I let them down. I had veto power over any slave there, Michael. It was my job to keep them if they had talent, or send them away if they didn't. I chose to be hopeful when I should have been efficient." That was said firmly, and Michael knew it would be pointless to argue. "The moral of this story is simple, Mike. There was a client with one strong characteristic—and through some intensive training, she was rendered capable of hiding her worst flaws. But no amount of covering up could change her essential character, or her lack of dedication to the life. What do you do with someone who just can't be improved, Michael? You find out if that weak point will undermine everything else they can learn, and if it can, you send them away."

"Thank you," Michael said. "I appreciate your telling me the story."

"You would have heard it eventually anyway," Chris said, getting up. "Hell, if you keep going to these Leather Forever conferences, you might run into my former client."

"She'll probably be Karen's new girlfriend," Michael muttered.

Chris looked surprised, and then laughed. "Yes," he said, nodding. "She might very well indeed."

CHAPTER TWENTY-SIX

Lorens left as suddenly as he had arrived. The ring through his cock seemed to be healing just fine, and as Anderson had repeated during his stay, there was only so much she could do with him besides making sure that he was emotionally prepared for the commitment he was about to make. There was no doubt in Michael's mind that he was. Michael had never seen a more contented slave.

And maybe that was the key—being content seemed to make all the difference. Lorens had an owner whose gender didn't jibe with his orientation—yet he was content with his service to her, enough to devote his life to her. Tara was not in love with her owner either—in fact, it was the same situation. Yet she was willing to deal with it, and take on extra training because something in the service satisfied her. Not enough to stay in it for life—but enough to see through a contract she had entered of her own will.

And Joan, who had no problems with the sexual needs or orientation of her owner, was perfectly happy with the exchange of her service for a stable lifestyle. They were not all happy with their lot—but they all seemed content.

Michael tried to think about any time he had felt content. It didn't take him long to realize that he never had been. He looked through the early pages of his journal and tried to remember why he had wanted this. To get a better job? Was that all?

No, it wasn't. It was Anderson herself, from the beginning. The illusion of her, that respect from other trainers, the reams of material from her which had pretty much been the basis for the modern American Marketplace. The Trainer of Trainers—she was the zenith of the profession. Solitary and strange, the lifeblood of the lifestyle who didn't bother to even show up to present her own papers. Whose very word could make or break a person's entire career. What had he thought of her? That she was the master of masters—the top of all tops...

Michael sprang up in bed—his bed again, thank God he was alone. His heartbeat sped up, and his mouth went dry. He pulled his knees up and sat with his back braced against the headboard. He reached for the early journal again and flipped the pages. There were his questions, all lined up, page after page of them.

What makes a person a slave? What do they feel that makes them want to give up a normal life, and surrender it all to someone else's control? What does it feel like to really submit, not just for an hour or a day, but for years?

"What was I thinking?" he whispered out loud. "Oh Jesus, what am I doing?"

I came to the Trainer of Trainers, he thought, with chilling certainty, to have her teach me what it was to be a slave. Of course, you bastard, who else could make you feel it? Of all the fucking arrogant, bull-headed, asinine things!

But what was really happening, he wondered, trying to get a grip. Nothing! The Trainer does not own slaves. She doesn't even make them—she only improves them. And—well, there was nothing there. He had deep respect for her still—deeper, if that was possible. But there was no internal drive to submit to her, no emotional charge. She had shown nothing to him that he could interpret as her wanting to teach him anything but her most basic training techniques. She treated him with honesty and directness, and never attempted to control him the way she controlled the clients.

Then, there was Chris.

I am not gay! was his first thought. But look at what was happening whenever he was with Chris—that moment when Michael's cock signaled that being denied a pleasure by Chris's direction was a good thing—the sensations of flushed pride when Chris popped out a rare compliment—his increasingly automatic respectful responses—standing when Chris entered a room. Damn, what was going on here?

Whatever it is, I have to remain in control, Michael thought furiously. This is not good. It's—transference. Or whatever the shrinks call it. I'm all alone here, and there just aren't too many people to fixate on. It's natural for a student to get crushed out on a teacher. It's no big deal—it will pass. Besides, I had to learn what it felt like to be a slave anyway. Now, I know.

He gathered up the notebooks and threw them into the nightstand drawer. Sleep didn't come easily for him that night, and before it did, he promised himself that he would do nothing to let Chris know about these self-realized truths. It would be best if he could just finish out his training somehow, and go his own way. He fell asleep trying desperately not to think of where he planned to go.

CHAPTER TWENTY-SEVEN

"It's time to start wrapping Joan up," Anderson said after one of her interviews with her. Michael felt surprised.

"Already?"

"It's been long enough, Mike, and I think she's covered the ground her owner specified. She's conversant about American culture, well trained for the household tasks she'll be expected to perform, and her Japanese has improved. I'd like you to write a report on her, describing her improvements in every area you can identify, please."

"You got it, Trainer."

"We'll finish her off in two weeks then." Anderson shook back her hair, which was caught in one long pony tail that day.

"Trainer—is there a new client coming?" Michael asked.

Anderson shook her head. "I haven't picked one yet. I may take a few weeks off. Let's play it by ear for a while."

"Sure thing." Michael tried not to wonder what would happen to him if Anderson took a little vacation. He was out of money. He called his parents and got them to "loan" him a few hundred dollars, and he still had a voucher good for one-way airfare back to California. But there wasn't enough time to complete his training before Joan left. Hell, it seemed like he had barely started! And the thought of staying in the house alone—or with only Chris for company...

Better to not think about it. He focused on helping Anderson and Chris finalize Joan's training. He sat in on interviews and worked into the night composing questions and making comparisons of Joan's progress reports. It was amazing to note how much she had improved, especially considering how impressed he had been with her that first night. In these months, she had become an

Anderson slave. And kept up her Japanese lessons, too. It was kind of weird, because he had actually had sex with Tara, and should have felt close to her—but Michael knew that he would miss Joan a lot, and think of her often. He liked to think that eleven years from now, he could go to a little village somewhere in England and find her running an inn, with a husband and a huge family of people with a secret that they passed on from generation to generation. He imagined her plumper than ever, wearing an apron, and directing a maid who might never know exactly how her employer learned all these skills.

He had no idea where he expected to be in eleven years.

It was hard to keep control sometimes, especially when he stopped thinking about the secret desires and concentrated on his work. What would happen was a slip—a shifting of focus that left him unprepared for sudden rushes of emotion or hunger. It was like keeping a lid on a boiling pot. Every once in a while, the rolling of the water seemed calm enough to stop watching. That was when the steam started to escape.

It happened when he was watching Chris bent over the book-keeping with Vicente. The two of them were consumed by their task, and didn't notice Michael watching them from the front room, through the open office door. In fact, Michael didn't realize that he was watching them until he felt a trickle of awareness—how the folded sleeves of Chris's shirt accentuated his powerful forearm, and how the slender colored flames caressed the musculature...

He managed to get upstairs without attracting attention, and stayed there until he was back in control.

Sometimes, it came on him naturally, and he felt it coming. He knew, for example, that watching Chris do a final drill with Joan, covering the advanced positions they had worked so hard on, would be distracting. He hadn't counted on the intense urge to do them with her, though, especially the sudden desire to drop to his knees in the profound posture which most often led to kissing a boot, or the floor between an owner's legs.

It seemed a much warmer year than usual.

Late one evening, Michael was working in the office. His writing improved when he wasn't near his comfortable and inviting bed. And the later it was, the quieter it was, with few or no interruptions. He jumped a little when he heard a knock on the door and it swung open. It was Chris. His tie was askew, the top button of his shirt open. It was as disheveled as he got. "You should get some sleep," he said. "Early day tomorrow."

"Yeah, I know," Michael said. "But I want to finish up this report before Joan leaves. I don't sleep much anyway. What are you doing up so late?"

"Same thing. Writing." He leaned against the door jamb.

"I was meaning to ask you about that," Michael said, seizing the opening. "Do you make out reports too? Or are you working on something else?"

"Both. Primarily, I'm preparing my first major presentation to the Academy."

"No kidding! That's great!" Michael leaned back. "Are you going to present it in person?"

"Probably," Chris shrugged. "I've never been to Okinawa, and I'd like to see the house where Joan trained."

"I never realized that so much of my time was going to be spent writing," Michael noted. "I hated taking notes in college. Writing papers was always a pain. If I'd known what I was going to be doing in a few years, I would have been an English major."

"It would have been better if you majored in psychology," Chris said. "They make you write quite a bit for that one."

"Geoff was a psych major. Was that yours, too?"

Chris nodded. "Part of my presentation is my re-worked Master's thesis."

"Masters? Wow, that's cool. Your parents must have been proud, huh?"

He smiled tightly. "I suppose so. They had their hopes on Ron at first, but his coming out of the closet was quite a set-back for them to handle."

Michael shook his head. "That's a shame. He seems like a nice guy. How did they take it when you came out?"

The smile broadened a little. "Oh, not much better. A great deal worse, in a way. I was a great disappointment to them."

"Jeez." Michael swallowed and looked away. This was so personal—so unexpected! He looked back at Chris, who didn't look at all upset, and shrugged. "It's too bad when people are like that. But I guess two gay brothers can be a bit of a shock."

"Yes, gay brothers—you could say the concept was very shocking. They've slowly started to come around. I recommended a good therapist for them." There was something far more humorous going on under Chris's voice.

Michael sensed that something he said was unintentionally funny. He smiled slightly. "Chris?" he said cautiously. "Can I ask you a personal question?"

"I never guarantee an answer, but you may ask."

"What are those marks on your upper arm?"

"Brands. One for every year in true service." He touched them idly.

"Wow! They look like sergeant stripes, you know."

"Yes, I intended them to come out that way."

"You did? Not your... owner?"

"I had them done after the service was completed," he explained. "Just a personal reminder. I think it's time you went to bed, Michael. I'll give you a few hours off tomorrow afternoon if you need to finish your report. Come upstairs, I'm locking up."

Michael immediately closed his book and tucked it under his arm. He was halfway up the stairs before he realized that not only had he obeyed immediately, but he had inclined his head as Chris had left the room.

Standing before his mirror, he traced three stripes on his upper arm, and tried to imagine the sizzle of flesh burning, the sight of Chris's face contorted in pain, his head thrown back, sweat dripping over his eyes. He threw his own head back and gritted his teeth.

And came, so quickly and terribly that he fell to his knees. He hadn't even touched himself. Oh God, he thought, hugging himself on the floor and rocking back and forth. Oh God, help me hang on.

Chapter Twenty-Eight

He tried to hold it back, but couldn't. When the car pulled up and Joan picked up her coat and bag, he felt tears in his eyes.

"You be good," he said, hugging her. "I'll come visit you at that inn."

"God's blessing on you, Michael," she said, kissing him on the cheek. "You'll be a wonderful trainer. Thank you so much, Chris. And a million thanks to you, Trainer."

Anderson bent down to kiss her as well, and stroked her hair back. "You'll do me proud, girl. My best to your family."

She walked down to the car, and Michael missed her keenly. He turned back to Anderson, and asked, for the first time, "What about me?"

"I'm not finished with you yet," she said casually. "I'm going to decide what to do next. Consider the next few days a little time off, for good behavior. And Mike," she said, meeting his eyes, "you have been a good boy. I'm very pleased with how you're coming along."

The relief he felt was embarrassingly obvious. "Thanks, Trainer." He watched her happily as she walked down the hall and through the front room.

"And I'm not finished with you either, boy," Chris said from right behind his shoulder. Michael jumped—it was one of those off-guard moments.

He turned and smiled and managed to ask, "What does that mean?"

"You know what it means," Chris said. "I'll see you later."

It was a long day with that "later" hanging. About one hundred times, Michael decided to walk up to Chris and ask just what he had meant. He even practiced it in his mind. "Chris," he'd say,

"I'm sorry, but I don't understand what you meant. Please explain it to me?"

But he didn't. I'm not afraid of the answer, he thought. It's just that it might have something to do with my training, and I don't want to push it. It's just one of those "catch you off guard" things.

After a quiet dinner, Anderson broke open a box of cards and started shuffling. "Anyone care for a few rounds of bridge, poker, or gin rummy?" she asked. Vicente plopped himself down in a chair in a way he never did when the slaves were around, and Chris grinned as he pulled up to the table. It seemed that "later" was not going to be after dinner. Michael excused himself.

He was never very good at card games, and didn't want to spoil what was obviously a tradition by playing bad hands. Instead, he went upstairs and did stretching exercises in his bedroom. He thought of going out, but knew that he wouldn't.

"Later" might still be that night.

It wasn't.

The following day, Anderson took one of her rare journeys outside of the house, heading off to some local mall to do some clothes shopping. Chris went with her, and they returned with boxes and bags enough to fill the dining room table. Michael was surprised and a little embarrassed when Anderson gave him a box as a gift. It contained two really classy dress shirts and two silk ties.

"I'm gettin' mighty tired of the ones you have, bucko. This is to give my eyes a rest."

He accepted them with as much grace as he could muster and tried them on in his room. They looked wonderful on him. As he knotted one of the ties, he felt a strange thought curl up inside him—that it wasn't Anderson who chose this particular shirt, the one with the delicate pinstripes that exactly matched the light blue centers of his eyes.

He wore it to dinner. And avoided meeting Chris's eyes for the entire meal.

Again, when the dishes were cleared the cards came out. "I really am a creature of habit," Anderson said with a chuckle. "Besides, I have to win back some of my hard-earned cash from these two hustlers. Care to join us for a hand or three, Mike?"

"I'm not much of a card player," he said, excusing himself again. "I'd only lose my new shirt."

Chris sat down to play. Michael went back upstairs.

Michael jumped when his door opened. He was standing in front of his mirror again, his mind a blank, his guts tight with expectation. When he caught the scent of the leather, his blood raced.

Chris was wearing the chaps, over jeans. He was still wearing a button-down shirt, a crisp white that contrasted with the darkness below his waist. He gave a quick jerk of his head, toward his own room, and walked back out.

Oh God, Michael thought. This is it, and I don't even know what "it" is! But he followed automatically, and when he walked into Chris's bedroom, closed the door behind him. Chris came up to Michael and turned him around. His powerful arms pulled Michael down, until their lips met. Michael had never really kissed a man before—the sensation of Chris's facial hair scraping against his lips was startling and threatening at the same time. He found himself relaxing into the kiss, and moved his body up a little, feeling the hard strength of Chris against him. He moaned into Chris's mouth when he felt the hand that caressed the length of his cock, tracing it as it rose behind his fly.

Chris pulled at Michael's hair, but gently, and left stroking his dick in favor of opening his shirt to get at his nipples. Michael moaned again as Chris's fingers brushed one, and then the other.

"Is this what you want?" Chris murmured into Michael's ear. His breath was hot, and Michael wanted to melt into him—God, it was good! Another gliding brush of a nipple, and then the buttons were all open and the shirt tails were being pulled up and out. "Is this what you like?" Chris asked.

"Oh, yeah," Michael sighed. He grinned and reached out to start unbuttoning Chris's shirt.

Chris caught his hands in both of his, and held them so tightly that Michael felt himself wrenched downward. Quickly, Chris changed his grip, twisting Michael around, and throwing him down to the floor, making him land hard on his knees. Michael fell

forward onto one arm, the other one twisted up his back so hard
that he cried out in pain.

"Too bad," Chris said. "That's not what you're going to get."

Michael's dick didn't seem to care that his heart had taken a
leap from erotic excitement to terror. Michael squirmed until it
hurt more, and then hissed through clenched teeth, "What are you
doing?"

"Giving you what you came for," Chris said. Michael felt a softness slither around the captive wrist. Then, he felt a sharp pain,
and he fell forward again, this time hitting the floor. His other hand
was easily captured and bent back, to be secured in a quick wrapping that bound his hands together.

"Stop it!' he cried, fighting and knowing that he couldn't fight.
"Please—"

"'Please' belongs with the proper requests," Chris said, flipping Michael over. He laid the new shirt open and pinched
Michael's nipple sharply. "'Stop' isn't one of them. I'll stop when
you've had enough."

Michael bucked up, and regretted it instantly—it hurt his
shoulders on the way up and his wrists when he fell back on them.
"I—I don't want this!" he sputtered.

"No?" Chris opened the waistband of Michael's trousers and
pulled them open as well. Michael cursed and felt tears forming as
Chris freed his erection, jerking it out and taking it in his fist. "This
says something different."

"Stop!' Michael begged. "I didn't consent! I don't want to—I
don't—"

"You don't want to what, Mike? Be used like a slave, or be a
slave?" Chris dropped the cock and started methodically stripping
Michael, leaving the shirt on. Michael kicked out twice, and Chris
smacked him hard on the inner thigh, twice for every struggle.
Michael bit his lip, amazed at how much that hurt.

When Mike was bare from the waist down, Chris squatted
down next to him again. "I notice you're not screaming for help,"
he said. "Despite the fact that both the Trainer and Vicente are
downstairs and could probably hear you quite well."

"Fuck you!" Michael spat.

Chris raised one eyebrow and looked amused. "Bad boy," he said calmly. And with calm, deliberate movements, he drew back his arm and smacked Michael's penis so hard it slapped against his belly. At the same time, he brought one hand down to muffle the scream that Michael barely knew he was sounding.

"Come on, up with you," Chris said after he pulled his hand away. Michael gulped in a lungful of air and rolled over when a neatly placed kick caught him in the thigh. From his belly, he was dragged up to his knees. His cock waved in its erect state—the smack had done nothing but hurt it and make it hungrier.

Michael never hated his penis so much.

"Don't think that you're the first," Chris said, pushing Michael across the floor on his knees. "She gets children like you all the time."

Michael felt himself pulled to a stop, and looked up as Chris walked around him. Chris sat on the bed, and reached over to pick up something. When he came back to meet Michael's eyes, he was holding a pair of barrel-shaped adjustable nipple clamps, attached together by a chain. He twisted the barrel and opened the jaws, and then calmly compared the opening to the size of Michael's nipples.

"No," Michael whispered.

"But I'm only following your dictate, Mike. I understand that nipples should be sore, as much as possible." Chris leveled a stare at Michael and his tone shifted to something a little less light-hearted. "If you pull away, I will hurt you."

Michael stayed still as the jaws closed around each nipple. They were tight, and he gasped as Chris adjusted them.

"Now, back to the subject at hand." Chris placed one boot over Michael's cock and pressed. Michael dropped back, until his ass rested on his calves, and grimaced as the pressure became too much. Chris lightened up—a little.

"Tell me why you came here," Chris ordered.

"To learn how to train," Michael gasped out.

The boot twisted, and Michael clamped his mouth shut,

fighting against the scream that wanted to come out. "Try again."

"I swear, please!" Michael said, the pressure making him begin to shake. "I didn't realize—I didn't know!"

"That's better." The boot went away, and Michael felt a tear trickle down his face. He bobbed slightly, and then brought himself backup onto his knees. "Tell me what you know now, Mike."

"I don't really know... it's all so confused in my mind! I never wanted to bottom—I don't want to! But I keep having these dreams, and I keep thinking of things—oh, Jesus, my nuts!" The loss of the pressure had been followed by a tingling sensation, and then the rush of blood back to his groin. Michael groaned, and pulled his legs together.

Chris kicked them back apart with his boot and grabbed hold of the chain from the nipple clamps. He tugged at it and pulled Michael up higher on to his knees. "I'll pay more attention to your nuts in good time. Now, tell me about these thoughts and dreams. This is recent to you, huh? You never saw it before?"

"I don't know!" Michael insisted. He gasped, and then almost reeled backward when Chris tightened the clamps.

"Then let me guess," Chris said, twisting the chain and holding Michael in place by his tits. "You came here because no one's good enough to master you, the favored son of Hollywood. Mr. Golden Butt himself, too pretty, too smart for the West Coast. And if there ever was going to be someone who could bring you to your knees, your dick hard and your entire body aching for a kiss or a kick, it had to be the master of masters."

"No," Michael cried, "No! I didn't want to!"

"Don't lie to me, boy. You've been looking for Daddy to come and make you a man, and all you've found are models as soft and false as you are. So you run away from the easy life to find the big, bad Trainer of Trainers, knowing that she'll fall in love with your sweet ass and want nothing more than to make you her one, true slave."

"No, that's not true!"

"Isn't it? Well, your dick is hard now, and you're still not screaming for help. I think you like this."

Michael gritted his teeth and growled out the pain he felt in his nipples. "Just—sex—" he gasped. "Come on, fuck me, man!"

"Oh." Chris nodded and dropped the chain on the clamps. "Oh, thank you. Not that I wouldn't have fucked you anyway—but I am happy you've chosen to fight a little more."

Without even thinking, Michael's eyes dropped to Chris's crotch. There, framed by the chaps and straining against the silver buttons of the 501s, was the outline of a cock that put to rest any notion about height as relevant to dick size. Chris laughed as he followed Michael's eyes, and then stood up. Michael wasn't sure what was happening when Chris's hand came to a stop in front of his mouth. He was surprised when he felt the folded handkerchief being pressed between his teeth. He grunted as Chris pulled him up onto his feet and then shoved him face down across the edge of the bed. Right in his line of sight was the brown strap that Chris had infrequently used on the slaves in training.

Michael tried to control the shaking that swept his body. He heard a rustling sound, and saw the shirt Chris had been wearing fall onto the bed. One arm, the slender flames dancing, extended to pick up the strap.

"This is for not addressing me properly," Chris said. Michael felt something heavy against his lower back, and then the slamming, stinging thud of the strap, laid hard across both asscheeks. He bit into the handkerchief and it did help muffle the cry. "It's ten for each offense," Chris reminded him. "After address, there's still not answering questions directly, lying, and acting defiantly."

Michael counted every stroke, every explosion of pain. They landed in precise formation, covering him from the top of his ass to the backs of his thighs. He squirmed, he jumped, and he shifted against the bed, every movement reminding him of the tight clamps on his nipples. But every second he had to concentrate on them was disrupted by a new kind of suffering.

It was relentless, inhuman, and it was so terrible that he couldn't hold back the tears. How could the other slaves have taken this without screaming, without fighting? He counted desperately, through the twenties, and then the thirties, and when forty strokes had been given, he spat the handkerchief from his mouth and gulped in air, sobbing between breaths.

"You're a wimp," Chris said. "Tara could have taken that better than you."

Michael bit the bedspread, and felt the wave of heat that seemed to be radiating from his ass. Oh God, it hurt, it hurt!

"Now, let's get back to dreams and thoughts, shall we?"

Michael hit the floor hard, and slumped forward. The sudden upward tug on the nipple clamps made him gasp, and their removal was like needles being driven through his nipples. He reeled, and Chris caught him by the hair. Michael looked up and almost fell back in shock.

Chris had one hell of a well developed chest for such a little guy. His pecs were firm, and you could see the start of some nice cutting down his body. Or you could—if you could get past the glorious tattoo that covered him from just below his nipples down into his waistband.

It was a bird—like an eagle, Michael thought deliriously. But at the same time, he knew it wasn't an eagle that rose out of the flames, red, licking flames that surrounded the outline of the wings, claws extended into the crotch area, and a glittering pile of ashes mingling with the top-line of pubic hair.

A phoenix, that's what it was. In golds and reds and scintillating blues, the eyes malevolently, proudly centered on that muscular chest, claws stretching down a line to that big fat dick below. Michael gasped at the beauty of it, and then whimpered as Chris shook him by the hair.

"Tell me about your fantasies, Michael."

"Yes, yes," Michael choked out, tearing his eyes away from the swirling colors of the tattoo. "You're right—whatever you say!"

"But I want you to say it, Michael. And I want to believe what you say."

"Will you—will you let me go?"

"No deals, boy. Talk, or we can go on to act two." Chris dropped one hand to his crotch and fingered the erection under his jeans. "I can always beat you again after I fuck you."

"Oh, God—I swear I didn't know," Michael said, looking away. "I've always—always been a top. No one ever made me bottom— I tried, but it didn't work. Never—the right person. I don't know! And then—Geoff was so soft—and I thought—I don't know, I thought he'd punish me! After the Karen thing, I thought maybe he'd take me aside—but he was just the same. It was all the same—always the same fucking thing," Michael stammered and caught himself. He wasn't even sure what he was saying. But Chris was nodding, so he continued. "I started thinking about trying it your way—doing what the slaves were doing. And every time I did something, it started to feel right, and I didn't know why! I mean—I thought I was just learning how to do it so you would get off my case—and then I saw you at the bar—and Anderson didn't care—but you—you—" He gasped for breath again, and struggled to keep the tears from flowing.

"Okay, I can fill in those blanks. I'm believing you, Mike. So now the big question—how long have you wanted this?"

"I don't—" Michael gasped as Chris pulled his head back by the hair, stretching his throat. "Since the first time Ethan knelt by my bed!" he choked out.

And amazingly, it was true. Michael felt more tears welling up, and when Chris let him go, he fell forward, against Chris's leg, the warm, rich scent of the leather suddenly soothing instead of frightening.

God, all these years of being the topman, getting the service, getting the attention and the obedience, and it all came back to that moment when Ethan fell into what was obviously a practiced position and eagerly leaned forward to deliver a morning blowjob. Michael had taken it, gratefully, but when he closed his eyes, he saw himself, leaning over the edge of a bed, his cock hard and his eyes full of devotion.

"Why didn't you go for what you wanted then?' Chris asked.

"My uncle—how could I tell him I wanted to be a slave? He expected me to be this natural master—and by the time I met Geoff—I was—used to it." Michael sniffed, and drew in a ragged breath. "It was always so easy to be the master—I would tell them what to do, and they'd do it! And—and everyone told me I was so good, that I could be a trainer—and it was so nice, sometimes, so easy!"

"It's not so easy," Chris said. "As you've found out."

"No!" Michael agreed, dropping his chin.

"So, your little plan goes astray—you can't seduce the Trainer, because she's got her own boy already here."

Michael shook his head. "I didn't plan it."

"All right. I'll allow that it was unconscious. And then what?"

"I—I hated you," Michael burst out. Astonishingly, Chris laughed.

"That's nothing new," he said. "When did you figure out what you wanted from me?"

"Two weeks ago," Michael whispered.

"Poor baby," Chris crooned. "To wait so long for what he so desperately needs. I don't think I'm going to wait another minute." He stood, and unfastened the buckle on the chaps and the top buttons of his jeans. "Now, I get to indulge a fantasy I've had for a while. To ream you out, good and proper."

"Oh, God!" Michael swallowed and twisted backward. "I never—"

"A virgin?" Chris stopped, and grinned. He walked away from the bed and picked up something from his nightstand. A bottle of lubricant. He looked down at Michael and picked up the wet and wadded handkerchief he had spat out before. "I think you'll need this."

It was a question. Michael moaned, and closed his eyes.

And nodded.

Face down, pressed into the edge of the bed, his asscheeks spread wide as the cool lubricant slid inside of him—one finger at a time, and always Chris talking, telling him how long he'd waited to pull apart those sweet cheeks, to open up that never-fucked hole. Michael moaned deeply as one finger became two, slick, sliding back and forth, pressing into him, pressing against that area no one had ever touched before, making his nuts tighten with pleasure.

Three fingers were accompanied by regular, open hand slaps against his ass, waking up the heat already laid down. Michael panted through his nose and his muffled cry echoed in his ear as he felt the head of Chris's impossibly hard cock press against his asshole.

"This will last until I get off," Chris said. "I advise you not to shoot your load before I do. Not only will I beat you for coming without permission—but it will be excruciatingly painful for you if your ass tightens up after you splatter my bed."

And then, he thrust in.

Michael bit down, hard, and saw stars. All he could think of was, it hurts, it hurts, it hurts! It felt like he was being split in two. In that first second of pain, his mind went blank. Around the third or fourth, he felt sympathy for every asshole he had thoughtlessly invaded with his cock, thinking that it only hurt for a second, and then they got used to it. But how on earth could anyone get used to feeling like they were burning from the inside out?

Chris slowly filled him, until he could feel flesh, mingled with the open straps of the chaps, the folded-back fly of the jeans. Everything that touched him set off ripples of reaction, and he panted and bit the gag until the intense pain of the intrusion started to settle down to a dull kind of stretched feeling.

And that was when he started to get really fucked.

He wasn't being made love to—he wasn't being screwed or even being laid. He was being fucked, his body pressed down and opened, a cock shoving down into him over and over, each time threatening to pull out, or to slam back in with full fury.

The pain never really left—but it began to mingle with a terrible kind of pleasure. It was humiliating, but the very motion that made him feel so used was also awakening sensations and emotions that made his cock hard, and made him moan between gasps.

"Yes, that's it," Chris panted. "That's my boy. Come on up, and push your sweet ass back for me." He pulled against Michael's bound wrists, making him shift back. Michael felt the floor firm beneath his feet, and pushed up as he was directed. Immediately, he felt the reward of Chris's hand on his dick. He moaned.

"Don't come," Chris warned again. "Your shot belongs to me, boy. You hear me? When I'm ready to make you come, I will."

Michael whimpered and nodded, and braced his forehead against the bed. It hurt—he felt like his entire body was stretched out around his asshole. But he could hear Chris sigh with pleasure every time he pushed back, taking in more cock, and every sigh drove Michael to work harder.

"Good boy," Chris said. "Good boy. Taking it all—such a good boy. Take my load, boy. Here it comes." His hand tightened on Michael's cock, and Michael groaned heavily into his gag. Every thrust as Chris neared orgasm was a full, hard slam that drove Michael down against the bed. He couldn't stand any more, and his knees buckled, but Chris followed him down and ground his dick in between Michael's cheeks and growled like an animal.

Michael moaned as Chris finished and slowly, slowly pulled out. He lay there, breathing heavily and feeling the twitches of his oh-so-empty ass, the ache in his nuts, the stiffness of his cock, the tingling pain in his nipples. He kept cataloging his aches—from his shoulders and wrists to his asscheeks, which still felt hot and tender. He didn't know how long he lay there, but it did seem to be a long time. Like a year.

He felt something cold touch his ass, and jerked.

"Just cleaning you up a bit," Chris said matter-of-factly. Michael closed his eyes as he was tended to, and tried not to feel ashamed. But he was anyway.

He stumbled as Chris pulled him back off the bed, and fell hard onto his knees again. The handkerchief dropped out of his mouth. The rope around his wrists was removed, and he felt the shirt being pulled off his back. He shivered, and in the next instant was covered by a blanket, and shoved down onto the floor.

"You," Chris said, "will sleep there." He was wearing pajama bottoms—Michael blinked, wondering when he had changed. Chris was still talking. "Do not get up without permission. Do not leave. I'll speak to you in the morning. Do you understand?"

Michael found the strength to nod. Chris stepped over to the head of the bed and came back with a pillow, which he tossed onto the floor. Michael wrapped one arm around it, and tried to control his shaking.

"Thank you," he whispered. How had his voice gotten so hoarse?

"Go to sleep," Chris said. "And that's 'thank you, sir.'"

"Thank you, sir," Michael repeated. "Oh God, thank you."

Chris bent down and stroked him, gently on the head, and then along his body. "Good boy," he whispered. Michael trembled for another five minutes, and fell asleep from sheer exhaustion, with Chris's hand still on his body.

He woke up before dawn, earlier than the usual time to get up for a run. For a moment, he was confused—his first thought was that he had been in an accident. He was aching and in an unfamiliar and uncomfortable place. But he remembered the previous night in a sudden flood, and shivered, huddled under his blanket on the floor.

Like a dog in a bed, he thought, and shivered again.

He assessed the damage to his body. He was stiff as hell, and his shoulder was sore, probably from sleeping on it. His butt cheeks weren't hurting, but he felt a strange looseness from the inside. Or not so strange, considering the size of Chris's endowment and its preternatural erection. So, he thought, cuddling back down for a moment. This is what it's really like. To be well fucked and left at the foot of the bed.

What a rush.

What had taken him so long to get here? Why hadn't it worked before?

He knew the answer. He had been too close to home. It was true what he told Chris the previous night—there was no way he could have told Niall that he wanted to be a slave, not own one. And everyone just assumed that owning a slave was the way to go—never had anyone even asked him if he ever considered being one. It was so much easier to just go along with things.

I should see a shrink, he thought ruefully. I was in one hell of a denial.

He rolled over, muffling a few low groans, listening to Chris's steady breathing. Oh, it would be nice to be able to cuddle right now, to pull into that hot little body, all compact and full of muscles. Damn, and I thought I couldn't get into men, he thought. He had to push his face into the pillow to drown out the snort of amusement that followed. Chris had sure gotten into him!

There was just one problem—he had to take a wicked piss. He eased himself up slowly, and wrapped the blanket around himself. Chris's room had a bathroom adjoining it that was shared by the next bedroom on the floor. Michael tiptoed into it, and eased the door almost completely shut. He didn't want the light to disturb Chris, nor the sound of the door shutting. Carefully, he searched for the light switch in the dark, and flipped it on. And screamed.

He leapt back, hitting a towel bar, and yelped. Staring at the awful thing in the sink, he tore at the door until it was open, and threw himself back into Chris's room.

Chris was sitting up in bed, scratching his chest. He yawned, and said, "That's ten for disobeying me and another ten for waking me up."

Michael felt a chill on his legs and realized that he had wet himself. He dragged the blanket around his body and pointed at the bathroom.

"Oh, damn," Chris said, stretching. "I guess leaving that vital part of my anatomy in the sink didn't start your day off right, did it? Well, it's your own damn fault. If you'd obeyed me, we wouldn't have this problem. Now, I have to punish you and explain things—and all before breakfast."

Chapter Twenty-Nine

Michael made a retching sound, and covered his mouth. Chris immediately looked serious, slipping his glasses on and pointing one finger at him. "If you pull a 'Crying Game' scene on me, boy, I'll rip your dick off and you can see if it feels any better than mine."

"You're a woman?" was what finally squeaked out when Michael got some order set in his mind and managed to make sound come out of his mouth.

"Oh, don't work so hard at being dense, Michael. Do I look like a woman to you?" Chris got out of bed, and Michael shook his head, no. Except for his height, and perhaps a slightly more rounded butt than guys usually had, Chris's body looked one hundred percent male.

Down to that part lying in the bathroom sink. Chris walked past Michael and into the bathroom, carrying a pair of jeans. When he came out, he was wearing them, and the cock was presumably back where it belonged.

"I never met... anyone like you," Michael said weakly. He slumped down into the floor, sitting cross-legged under his blanket.

"That's probably an understatement," Chris admitted. He reached into his closet and pulled out a T-shirt. When he turned his back, Michael saw another tattoo, on his right shoulder. This one was not as elaborate as the one on his chest and belly. In fact, it was a mere outline, in red, of a rose on a long stem tangled with thorns and tiny leaves. As Chris pulled the T-shirt down, he turned back to look at Michael. "You're in no shape to run, and I feel like taking the morning off. You can play twenty questions with me about all sorts of private issues, or you can focus on your real problem of what you're going to do now."

The sun was coming up. Michael looked at Chris, and then toward the window, and then down at his body.

"I think," he croaked, "I would like to take a shower."

"Good idea," Chris said. "Clean my bathroom floor as well, will you? I'll see you downstairs."

Michael groaned as he got to his feet, and headed toward the bathroom. He knew intellectually that what he had seen in the sink was gone, but it was hard nonetheless. He wiped up his own piss and then left hurriedly, choosing to shower in the blue bathroom.

In the shower, he winced as the needles of hot water hit his ass. I guess it is still a little sore, he thought, soaping himself up. That was one hell of a beating—one hell of a night.

He looked down at his cock, and felt a wave of confusion. What had he seen? And what had he felt? It sure felt like a real cock in him last night—but then, what did he have to compare it to? And if it was a fake—what on earth did Chris have down there?

Michael didn't want to think about it. While he soaped himself up, though, his own cock reminded him that there had been quite a few erections last night and no finale. He slid his soapy hand over the shaft, remembering the feel of Chris's hand—and stopped.

Chris had said that Michael's orgasm belonged to him. Michael let his cock go, and stood under the water. How strange. I could never understand how they managed to keep from jerking off, he reflected, washing the other parts of his body. I always figured that the slaves cheated whenever they could. Most of Geoff's did. But I don't want to cheat. I want to be good.

He rinsed off and dressed, and concentrated on what Chris had mentioned before leaving. It was true. There was this whole new situation now. The Trainer wasn't going to want him—and he wasn't sure he wanted to be a trainer anymore. Damn, but it was all confusing! One month ago, he could have said with certainty that he was going to become a great trainer, and that Chris was a guy. Now, one night seemed to have changed that all around.

Or maybe not. He combed his hair and straightened his tie and looked at the man in the mirror. You got the shit beat out of you last night, he thought. Got yourself royally fucked, too. So—what changed?

Nothing at all.

Anderson had apparently given Vic the day off. Michael found Chris in the kitchen, sitting on the counter with his back against the back wall, eating an apple with a cup of coffee at his side. Michael looked at him and shook his head. "It's hard to believe this is you," he said.

Chris shrugged. "I often lighten up after I get laid. Especially if there aren't any clients around. Of course," he said, taking a swallow of coffee, "there is you. But we haven't decided what to do with you yet."

"I hope I have some say in it," Michael said.

"Oh, you can say whatever you like. But you won't be very successful fighting your inner nature for very long."

Michael shook off a fit of trembling and took a coffee mug out of the cabinet. "Is that the voice of experience?"

"Don't try to analyze me, boy. It's taken more professionals than you could shake your dick at, and I still leave them stumped. Let's just say that I know this—when the drive is to service, nothing will stand in its way." He took another bite of the apple and pitched the core neatly into the garbage. "Except maybe—just maybe—the Trainer of Trainers."

"Mention her name, and she appears," Anderson said with a yawn. "Will one of you not-slaves kindly fetch this old lady a coffee?" She was wearing a robe that looked like it was made from colorful trading blankets, the lapels overstitched and a little threadbare. She took a cup from Michael, who poured a new one for himself. "You two are a bit much. Thumping all night, screaming before dawn—I felt like a frat house had moved in next door."

"My apologies," Chris said seriously. "I didn't realize I was being so noisy."

"Me too," Michael added. "I'll try to scream quieter next time." He snorted.

Chris's head snapped to the side. "Down!" he barked. Michael looked at him, realized that he was serious, and dropped to his knees, groaning as he hit the floor. Judging the anger to be real, he bowed his head down, until his forehead met the tile.

Anderson whistled low through her teeth. "At least it was a productive night," she commented.

"Not really. Yesterday afternoon, you had a possible apprentice trainer. Today, we have a possible client. Just how productive is that?" Chris hopped down from the counter and nudged Michael with his foot. "Up, boy. And try not to forget what you learned about yourself again."

"Yes, Chris," Michael found himself saying. "I mean—yes, sir." He blushed as he got up, and rubbed his knees. They were sore as hell.

"Sometimes, productivity can be measured in how much time isn't wasted, dear heart. I can always bring in a new apprentice in the fall."

"But—I mean, may I speak?" Michael asked.

"Yes, sweetie, you're not on formal manners, only on basic respectful ones." Anderson leaned against the counter.

"I still want to be a trainer," Michael said. "A classic trainer."

"Oh-ho!" Anderson chuckled. "That requires a sitting position. Let's take this into the front room."

"Now—do you have any idea what it takes to be classically trained?" Anderson asked when she was comfortable in her favorite seat. She left Michael standing, and he nodded as Chris took the other chair.

"Yes, Trainer, I do. One year of basic training, two years in service, two years managing other slaves while in service, and... and..." Michael tried to remember. "One year with a master trainer—no, two."

"And you're prepared to give up seven years in order to do this?" she asked.

He nodded. "Yes, I am. Trainer, it's the perfect solution. I could do it—go into service, and actually be a slave for four years—then

I'll really know what it's like! I'll be ready for the real training when I finish that—and Chris said that no one is trained like that anymore, so I'll be unique!"

"Not quite," Chris snapped. "You're still an arrogant little snot. You can stand there and compare yourself to Anderson? To me?"

"No," Michael admitted. "But maybe in five years, I might compare myself to where you were once."

Chris waved one hand dismissively. "Get on your knees boy, you're obviously breathing in some heady fumes."

Michael went down, more carefully this time.

"It's an idea," Anderson said. "Not your best, I'm afraid. It may seem like a good idea right now, Mike, but the first time you get up on that block, it's your body that's on the line. And if you find that you love the service, what then? Someone's wasted a year of prep training on you. Or, more likely, you become a trainer in service and stay there, where you're not of much use to me or the network of free trainers. It would be better if you decided to go into the Marketplace as a slave. If it doesn't turn out the way you like, you can always go back into training later on. But don't start the classic program unless you're planning to see it all the way through."

"I will," Michael said.

"Hm. I think—I have to think about it," Anderson said. "Why don't you go take a nap or get a newspaper or something. I'll be ready for you in about three hours."

"Yes, Trainer." Michael rose gingerly and inclined his shoulders to her, and then to Chris.

Chris rolled his eyes as he left. "I've created a monster," he complained.

"It's not a bad idea," Anderson said.

"He'll never last the program. He'll either love or hate service and either way, he'll never come back to training."

"Then why did you fuck him last night?"

Chris laughed at the use of her most forbidden word. "Because he needed it! Because I couldn't stand his puppy-dog eyes following me around, and because he's so damn cute. I'm entitled to be shallow every once in a while."

"Sure thing. But face it—you took him down because you thought he was making a mistake."

"And he still is." Chris pushed his hair back and sighed. "Imala, I won't fight with you on this. If you choose him that's your decision."

"Except for one thing, my boy. Who do you think will be here when he comes back in five years?"

Chris scowled. "You're too young to retire."

"Maybe in five years I won't be."

"Oh, damn," he said softly. "Five years. Five years until I commit my life to the true service. Yes, I'll be here. If I have the full five years."

"You'll have the full five—if you supervise Michael."

"Oh, suck my dick," Chris said, still scowling.

Anderson raised her eyebrows and laughed. "If that's what it takes, kiddo, I think I still remember how."

"I'll break him," he warned.

Anderson shrugged. "If he can be broken, he isn't fit to serve."

"I don't even have my own place," Chris pointed out.

"No. But you do have a standing offer from friends in familiar surroundings. I'm sure Rachel would love to have someone new to abuse. And Grendel and Alex would love to have the extra help." Anderson smiled. "See? It all works out."

"Sure. Everyone gets what they want save for one notable exception."

"Oh, I don't think so," Anderson said soothingly. "Service demands sacrifice, my friend. And that's not from one of my papers."

"Yes, I know. Don't worry, Imala. I may bitch, but I will also do the right thing. Let's hope this kid you selected can learn that." Chris rose and stretched. "I think I'd better make a phone call or two."

"That's my boy," she said fondly. He shot his crooked smile at her before he left, and she kept her smile on her face until he was gone.

"Damn and double damn," she muttered, drawing the robe closer around her. Oh well, she reflected, pushing herself up. Omelets and eggs.

CHAPTER THIRTY

Arrangements were made quickly, all around. The Trainer wanted to take a vacation, so there was no sense in dawdling. Calls were made to prospective clients and their owners or brokers, and dates set for later on in the year. Grendel and Alexandra were only too happy to extend an invitation to the new trainer-in-training, and Rachel was delighted at the prospect of getting her old playmate back. It was almost time for the summer group of candidates, and extra help was always appreciated.

"Where will I go after the year is up?" Chris asked Anderson that night. "I won't be able to stay."

"No," she agreed. "You'll just have to establish a place of your own, I suppose. Or, you can travel a little yourself. I think that would be best. Just as long as you keep in touch with your little Golden Butt."

"I assure you—he will be always on my mind."

"So, you're dead set on this?" Anderson asked Michael. He nodded enthusiastically. They were in her office for what she called her final interview with him.

"Trainer, this is the first time I've been sure about anything. It's like I've been drifting along for years, and now I can see where I'm going!"

"I believe that you believe that," she said. "Only time will tell us if you're right. I hope for my sake that you are. We need more dedicated trainers, Michael. And no matter what anyone else says, this is the best way to make them."

"I understand that now."

"Do you? Then I'll ask the question I asked you when you first came here. What is the purpose of the Marketplace?"

He opened his mouth, and then closed it with a frown. "I'm

not sure," he admitted. "I guess it's to provide some kind of context for people into this kind of life."

"What kind of people?"

"Well—everyone. Tops and bottoms."

"Not exactly." Anderson said. "We have many outlets in modern life which are able to provide you with a context for control or lack of control. But we've lost the notion of service for service's sake—a life devoted to an ideal. Everyone needs a reason to do things which were once culturally entrenched—you do it for the money, or because you'll get a college education, or because the person you've chosen is your messiah, or your favorite rock star. But what if this drive went much deeper than that? Where do those people go? And how do they know that they'll be able to live a life based on that drive without falling prey to emotional swindlers, mass murderers, or fanatics who will throw their dedication or their lives away on a whim?"

"They don't know. How can you know?"

"Mostly, you can't. Unless—someone's created a system under which potential controllers are carefully selected and trained to manage these potential servitors." She winked.

"The Marketplace exists to provide masters for the slaves?' Michael asked.

"Think about it," Anderson advised. "It's just a theory."

He shook his head in amazement. "I'll never be able to repay you for this. You never had the slightest reason to keep me on."

"That's the truth," she admitted. "Especially after you tried to look me up in the computer files. That was pretty sneaky."

He turned white. "You really can see through walls!"

"No, dear. But I can operate a computer. And if you had paid attention to the software for the archives, you might have noticed a function which pulls up a list of the last twenty files you requested. I rarely try to call up my own, since I'm the one who had it sealed." She leaned back and rocked in the chair. "That was naughty of you."

"I'm sorry," he said sheepishly. "Especially since I didn't get a single useful thing out of there."

"Ha! Well, some secrets are made to be kept, Mike. Others are best left alone, period."

Michael remembered the morning in Chris's room, and the questions. He hadn't asked any of them. Things had happened too fast, and after the decisions were made, it seemed less important than it had at that moment. What it would be like working under Chris in another environment, Michael couldn't guess.

But he was more than willing to take it as it came.

"I'll send you regular updates," Chris said. "And I'll be back as soon as he's sold, to let you know what I've decided to do. Don't be surprised if I wind up as a towel boy in some monastery or join the circus, because I'm not going to be doing anything ordinary for the following four years."

"Fair enough," Anderson agreed. "If you need help getting wherever, you can count on it."

Chris looked out the window, and watched as Rachel supervised Michael loading the car. "It is for the best, isn't it?"

"Oh God, Parker, yes. And you know it is."

He lowered his head. "I didn't want to go back where I came from," he said softly.

"Don't think of it as going back. Think of it as using a familiar launch point." She hugged him across the shoulders, and kissed him on the forehead. "My best boy. Go play for a while. With my blessing."

He hugged her briefly and kissed her on the mouth. She smiled when he pulled away. He danced down the front steps lightly, on the balls of his feet, and sauntered to the car where a man and a woman vied for his attention. Her little fighting cockerel.

Imala Anderson closed the door and turned to Vicente. "What do you say to California?" she asked wickedly.

"Oh, you are a bad one," the man chuckled.

"Yes," she agreed, her face suddenly changing. She sighed, and linked an arm through his. "Sometimes, I have to be."

ABOUT THE AUTHOR

Laura Antoniou has become well known in the erotically alternative community as the creator of the Marketplace series (*The Marketplace, The Slave, The Trainer, The Academy,* and *The Reunion*), the first three volumes of which were originally published under the name Sara Adamson. One Marketplace character also appears in her first book, *The Catalyst*, but she leaves the reader to figure that out. The only independently written Marketplace short story, "Brian on the Farm," appears in Lawrence Schimel and Carol Queen's ground-breaking anthology, *Switch Hitters: Lesbians Write Gay Male Erotica, and Gay Men Write Lesbian Erotica* (Cleis), which has been published in English and in German. "That's Harsh," a new Marketplace story that appears as a bonus story in *The Slave* (Book Two of the Marketplace) won the 2011 John Preston Short Fiction award, presented by the National Leather Association.

Antoniou has also had great success as an editor, creating the *Leatherwomen* anthologies which highlighted new erotic work, *By Her Subdued*, a collection of stories about dominant women, and *No Other Tribute*, which features submissive women. Her nonfiction anthologies include *Some Women* and an homage to author John Preston entitled *Looking for Mr. Preston*. Antoniou's work has been published in the United States, Germany, Japan, Israel and Korea, to international acclaim.

Winner of the National Leather Association's 2011 Lifetime Achievement Award, Antoniou is a highly demanded speaker at schools, leather/SM and sexuality conferences, and has become well known for her rants, thinly disguised as keynote speeches.

Antoniou is currently finishing the sixth book in the Marketplace series, entitled *The Inheritor*. She has no intention to stop there.

THE MARKETPLACE SERIES

The Marketplace Series
Now Published by Circlet Press's Luster Editions

Circlet Press is proud to be returning the entire Marketplace series by Laura Antoniou to print, as well as launching all-new ebook editions. These books are the first in our Luster Editions line of erotic books and books of alternative sexuality that are not science fiction or fantasy.

The Marketplace
—available now as ebook or paperback
The Slave
—available now as ebook or paperback
The Trainer
—available now as ebook or paperback
The Academy, January 2012
The Reunion, Spring 2012
The Inheritor—in the works!

Stand-alone short stories also available as downloads for 99 cents each!

For Want of a Nail
That's Harsh!
California Dreamin'

For More Information
www.circlet.com

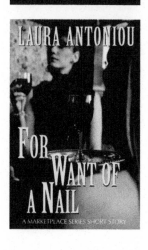

CPSIA information can be obtained at www.ICGtesting.com
Printed in the USA
BVOW08s0935020515

398684BV00001B/29/P